Also by Robert McKean

The Catalog of Crooked Thoughts

I'll Be Here for You: Diary of a Town

Mending What Is Broken

A Novel

Robert McKean

Livingston Press
The University of West Alabama

Library of Congress Control Number: 2023934043

Typesetting and page layout: Joe Taylor, Cassidy Pedram
Proofreading: Jack Estes, Scott Robinson, Brooke Barger,
Cassidy Pedram, Savannah F. Beams, Jacob Dial, Dior Wilson,
Haina Franco, Summer Chadwick, Jessica Meeks, and Cal Stephens,
Rachel Robinson, Kaitlynn Clark, Annsley Johnsey
Cover design and art: Pauline Kao Hilborn
Cover layout: Joe Taylor
Acknowledgment: portions of this manuscript previously
appeared in *Adelaide Magazine*.

Mending What Is Broken

In memory of Belle Adams,

teacher, poet, loving aunt

It was my turquoise; I had it of Leah when I was a
            bachelor:
I would not have given it for a wilderness of monkeys.
—*Shylock*

Ganaego, Pennsylvania

Breakfast with Doves

The world is heartless.

When the final disposition came down from family court, confirming what surprised no one, that he'd forfeited his shared custody rights to his daughter, Peter Sanguedolce thought his world had come to an end. And perhaps it had. It was January. Ice dams climbed the roof. Wind moused about the drafty casement windows. The front door froze shut. In the basement the ancient Lennox boiler bellowed, summoning itself for another Western Pennsylvania winter, and, as fresh steam hit the condensation in the pipes and the radiators gurgled like drowning sailors, he heard clear as a bell his mother forty-odd winters ago asking his father worriedly, "Steve, d'you think the furnace is going to blow up?"

It didn't, it probably won't.

Gloomy skies, purses of hardened snow beneath the shrubs—all of it to set the affective faculties going like the sympathetic murmur of adjoining strings when a piano key is struck. He loves music, he hates ice dams. Before breakfast, Peter empties the four plastic buckets in the attic that Mortie Siegel at Savage's Hardware and Sporting Goods sold him, red, yellow, green, blue. A dual major in college, materials science and English Lit., Peter guesses that Mortie's buckets are polypropylene, although Rubbermaid appears close-lipped on the matter. The blue one is as brilliant as the copper sulfate in his old chemistry set. His daughter Jeanette loves exploring these upper regions of the old house, but it's rare for Peter to have reason to mount the narrow staircase to the attic. Light stabs through the fissures between the browned roofing boards; a bat, off-duty in daylight hours, dangles by his toes; and around him, what three generations of Sanguedolces failed to carry with them into the afterworld: boxes of Literary Guild novels; the duffel his Uncle Nico lugged home from Korea; bags of petrified shoes; a wardrobe housing suits with five-inch lapels and slippers whose turquoise satin still retains the shape of his mother's toes. On a round-screen television rests a capsized model ship, his grandfather's, gifted to him by a coke-puller in lieu of payments for his child's piano lessons. It's as if Nonno Franco's folk art brigantine has foundered and come to grief here. The canvas sails, the size of ladies' hankies, have torn from their spars, and the ship's string-ropes become fouled with webs spun by the tiny white spiders who have taken to living in its hold.

Someday, Peter vows, eying a crucifix with a missing arm, *I need to do something about all this.*

The day before the court orders were passed down, the third week of December, he'd bought an eleven-foot Fraser fir from the St. Ursula altar boys. Their hands were chapped; their chilblained toes squeaked in their cheap sneakers. He tipped lavishly. The presents he'd

  Robert McKean

picked out for Jeanette, to be hidden beneath the skirts of that regal tree that languished, never erected, outside on the icy veranda, she opened the day after Christmas, under the critical gaze of her stepfather, Elliott Fields, who, unshaven and dyspeptic, monitored disgraced Papa and daughter's sad, quiet holiday. His fault, all his fault. Nobody to blame but himself. Before abandoning the attic, Peter ensures that his ice-dam leaks are striking Mortie's colorful pails dead center, *plop, plop,* then, nodding to the sleeping bat, he descends in search of his chief consolation: simple carbohydrates.

He's lonely, he has no work; *ergo*, he eats.

Baking whole wheat sourdough bread has become his passion. He has his cultures, his thermometer, his rattan proofing baskets and Danish whisk, his 900° F oven mitts, his wooden spoons, his organic flours. The loaves rise in the shape of parsons' hats. So much bread does Peter manufacture, so many loaves lining the counter like the hats of a gathering of country clerics, that one person cannot possibly eat it all. After dropping off extra loaves at the rescue mission in town, he's taken to fattening up the birds, too. There used to be more birds. That was before the removal of his neighbor's tall arborvitae hedge—and it was, by the way, the sale and partial demolishment last fall of Jacob Weiner's house next door that started the chain of events that led to the revocation of his custody rights—but the chattering sparrow nation hasn't gone anywhere, nor have the cardinals that also do not migrate and the robins that no longer seem to, and, especially, the mourning dove couple who appear to have taken the cue and foregone the hassle of seasonal relocation, as well. Spotting the fat man maundering into his backyard in trench coat over pajamas, the silky, long-necked doves lift in a whistle of wings from their perches on Jacob's cockeyed roof, and, burbling contentedly, join him for breakfast.

Butter, sometimes olive oil, Sundays, cream cheese and lox.

In a corner of the yard stands a crab apple tree. The crabs, no larger than peas, ripen in autumn to marigold-yellow, then dim like dying stars, withering, blackening. Birds, sometimes whole murders of crows, descend on the crooked tree to peck at the shriveled fruit and squabble with the squirrels who hang out on the limbs like trapeze artists. Beneath the tree, strewn across its snowy apron, are the leavings of this beggar's feast: gnawed and decomposing fruit, twigs, stray feathers, colonic splotches of remarkable coloration. Once he'd been a successful businessman. His father's top salesman, and, when his father died, owner himself of the Ganaego Clay Works. When someone in Ganaego pees, chances are his waters will find their passage through Sanguedolce sanitation pipes.

A sewer pipe salesman from Pennsylvania, he liked to introduce himself.

That was before the clay works went bankrupt. Peter tears his tangy peasant bread into generous chunks and contributes to the disorder under the tree. In the slanting light of a Sunday winter morning, as he kills time waiting for twelve-thirty so he can drive across the river and spend the afternoon with his daughter in a supervised setting—it's all he lives for—his shadow looks grotesquely distorted, elongated,

Robert McKean

rendering him, weirdly and splendidly, skinny again. He worries about his daughter.

Something about his ex-wife's household does not feel right.

The Teardown Party

Previous Columbus Day

You would have thought that his neighbor's daughter might have waited a decent interval to sell the house, if only to see how her father was going to adapt to the nursing home. And perhaps for most people a few months would have served as a respectful length of time. But to Peter it seemed that hardly a heartbeat separated his elderly neighbor's unwilling removal from his home and the deeding of the property over to its new owners. Yesterday, as he was leaving for work — or what to Peter passed as work — he drove by the stockade of arborvitae that walled off the retired music teacher's small colonial. In Oak Grove, Ganaego's prettiest neighborhood, the trees had become an aesthetic bone of contention. Can you really gripe about someone's hedges? Of course, you can. Peter liked the trees well enough, if he thought about them at all. But he recognized that the arborvitae — tall, shaggy, emerald plumes — had come to be regarded as old-fashioned and unfriendly, as out of step as his neighbor himself had become in a community giving over to young families. In winter storms the frail softwoods collected ominous amounts of snow, enormous Gainsborough hats beneath which they bowed like garden ladies besotted with too many sherries. Passing your snowbound windows, you'd spot the old clarinetist out there, arctic gales be damned, furiously shaking his beloved trees. Efforts that were, for the most part, ineffectual. What snow Jacob Weiner managed to bring down, he brought down on his upturned face, blotting his glasses and sending him reeling into the street like an eyeless prophet.

Well, the world is heartless.

Heaven knows, Peter conceded, if the subject be the afflictions we blithely heap upon our fellow creatures, have I been any less a sinner? Had it not been he who signed the pink severance slips that sent men who'd labored at his family's clay works, some for as long as five decades, home to their wives without a job? Last night, returning, he drove past a line of stumps severed to the ground and the aftermath everywhere—chewed branches, fringes of crushed leaves, a brown vomit of sawdust clogging the sewer grates. On the lawn, pulled up to the old man's door were a yellow dump truck, a yellow front-end loader, and a very large, very formidable yellow demolition excavator.

"Teardown," Peter explained to his daughter.

Saturday morning. Jeanette had jumped down from her stepdad's Land Rover and run into the house, breathless. "What's *that* mean?"

"Means *poof!* Blown up, gone, reduced to smithereens."

Peter watched his daughter gather into her hand one of her braids, the long brunette plaits that he mourned would probably not survive her passage through the middle school years. She pressed the tuft end of the braid against her teeth. "They're going to blow it up, they *are?"*

"Laying the dynamite as we speak."

"No, I don't believe you!"

In a life where little remained to stir him, Peter doted on his daughter. He had money to see him through, yes, probably. He had his health, notwithstanding Dr. Vossburg's censorious clucks when he mounted the doctor's scale. But though he got up in the morning and put on a suit and went to work, he had no work, no mate, few human souls to talk to beyond Baldwin Feeney, the self-ordained evangelical minister whom he paid to patrol the defunct clay works with his Kaiser-era German Luger. And so, in that void, Jeanette was all. At ten she'd become an expert in certain vital areas of domestic management: what premium dish liquid was worth the extra money; what new upholstery fabric for Peter's mauled old armchairs might go well with his threadbare rugs; what all-natural ice cream her papa should have on hand for her visitation weekends. Possessor of three parents, two bedrooms, and an education in contemporary American divorce, Jeanette was also ridiculously skinny, at least so she seemed to Peter, whose prolapsed abdomen had a habit of finding its way through doors before the rest of him followed.

He tweaked the tip of her nose. "They would if they could, kiddo, but no, they'll push it over like a house of cards. All the smaller houses in Oak Grove are doomed, I fear. But hey, they're having a teardown party. We're invited."

"Is there a special song you sing at teardown parties?"

In her voice he heard what he adored, the mischievousness they shared: She was going to get even. Bugging his eyes, Peter fed his daughter her straight line. "Well, I don't know, darling, I'm not . . ."

"London Bridge Is Falling Down, Papa!"

Oh God, how he loved her, her droll wit, her leather Sunday shoes that clattered on the stairs, her glasses, new this fall, perfectly round—*wizard glasses* she called them—that centered her doe-brown eyes. Even if she frowned on his housekeeping—the papery moth husks she blew off the pantry shelves, the spiders she swatted with lethal precision—he loved her absolutely, without reservation. But parental duty beckoned. "You've been practicing this week, right? Every day?"

Behind her wizard glasses Jeanette's eyes drifted to the side. "Hmmm . . ."

"No?"

She groaned. "Some days I get to be a kid, *too?*"

And smart, and sometimes—although he knew he was a biased judge—he'd argue borderline wise. But then again, maybe all children of divorced parents are wise, or become so? That he didn't know, but what Peter Sanguedolce did know was that this sole offspring of his two failed marriages understood how to rescue him, bring him out of his moroseness, the hours he sat at his father's old wooden desk presiding over a business he inherited and lost. Of the world's various and imaginative forms of heartlessness, the cruelest, you might posit, is its economic exactions. But no, as crummy as he felt and as deeply as he resented the bankers who stabbed him in the back and licked the blade, crueler still is the withdrawal of love. Peter, forty-five and entering that decline of life hilariously labeled as one's *prime*, capitulated. He kissed his daughter on the forehead like a fat Pope. "You sound like your mama the lawyer. But most days, darling, *most* days?"

"Most days, Papa. I'm learning a waltz, except it's called a *valse*."

"Who's it by?"

Her eyes yearned toward her room upstairs. "I don't know . . . I don't remember?"

"Two points off. You have to scrub the pots."

"I'll look, okay?"

"It's right at the top, Miss: 'This music brought to you by the blood, sweat, and tears of Hans Whirligig.' Maybe I can hear your valse later, before you go?"

She spent two weekends a month with him, a long summer vacation, and one half of all federally-recognized holidays. This month his two weekends came back-to-back, although today's visit was not an overnighter. But even so, Jeanette had brought her Jet Blue flight bag and reserved her standard time alone in her bedroom. She was, by most measures, an unusual child. She loved ransacking the closets of the old house, discovering out-sized brooches in the lilac-scented drawers of her grandmother's dressing table and gypsy-girl caps and vests in the attic that dated from the '20s and '30s. Her mother Avis, and especially her stepfather Elliott, took a dim view of these silly, incongruous

Robert McKean

costumes she assembled. But Peter, tolerant of his daughter's delight in self-expression, encouraged Jeanette to make play of her imagination. You *do* get to be a kid some days, and her costumes—to her—were not silly. One can only guess at how hard the breakup had been on the girl. Among the most painful decisions she faced was which dolls and stuffed creatures to take with her to her new home, which to forsake.

"Just so you know," she warned as she disappeared upstairs, "it's not perfect—yet."

"That's all right, darling. It's a valse in progress. Hans will be delighted."

Marriages fail for any number of reasons. They fly apart under centrifugal forces they cannot contain; they unravel a thread at a time; they even more slowly and agonizingly grind love and promises to dust between two great millstones; sometimes they simply stop working, like a stopped clock on a mantel no one knows how to fix. Two autumns ago Peter had stood at the living room windows, where he stands now, his back to the room, as Avis, Jeanette beside her, lingered in an emotionless, almost clinical, detachment.

Don't you intend, she asked, *to at least say goodbye to your daughter?*

He'd feigned a consuming interest in the sight of some yardmen across the street. The men, dark-skinned under loose shirts and floppy hats, had pulled their truck parallel to the Khederians' retaining wall and were vacuuming up the leaves they were hauling over in blankets. In the bed of the truck, on top of the mounded leaves, two men swung by their arms from a branch of the beech that overhung the wall, wildly stomping down the leaves beneath their feet. Peter had started working in the clay works the summer he was fourteen. He shoveled coal into the smoldering fires beneath the three-hundred-foot tunnel kiln. The spines of the men he worked alongside were skewed on a bias, their wrists and knuckles all sinew and knobby bones. For manual labor he entertained no romance. But the yardmen swarming the Khederians' property worked with a recklessness he appreciated. It was not a question you answered. But *daughter*—he rather liked that, the formality of it. Avis, the attorney, was the one who manipulated language. He sold sewer pipe.

Nevertheless, perhaps unwisely, he turned to her. *What I decide to do or not do at this point with Jeanette is none of your concern. And yes, I've talked with her.*

Her leaving was a special occasion: Avis, no less attuned than her daughter to the potency of costuming, wore her Armani wool. Her hair, highlighted, was exquisitely coiffed; her nails were Macbeth-red and spectacular. Removing her glasses to reveal her eyes, Avis employed her summing-up-for-the-jury voice that attorneys only get to use in the movies. *I don't like being told that anything concerning Jeanette is none of my business, but, if you want to know, Peter, you've brought this on yourself. You've been a fool—with me, with your business, with everything and everybody you've ever touched.*

Was that true? *Was* it all his fault?

Marriage One, yes. But Marriage Two? When you fall in love with someone, you love them for their differences, their exoticism. When you fall out of love, you hate them for those same differences. And yet at that moment Avis had never seemed more stunning: The girl who changed after he met her and kept right on changing. Perhaps she was right. He wouldn't contest it. His confidence like so much else had long left him at the curb.

When Jeanette came downstairs, she was in what he called her Little Orphan Annie outfit, scarlet dress, white belt, boxy shoes. Her outfits never disconcerted him, but he was experiencing difficulty with these new glasses. Kept wanting to ask her, How is Harry doing? She had a question. "Can I take my bike?"

The bike was pink. Green and white tassels fluttered from the hand grips. It also had not made the transition to the ritzy East Stanton Junction condo. "Of course."

"When did he die?"

He knew who she meant. "He didn't, his daughter put him in a nursing home."

"I was always afraid to go into his yard to chase my ball."

Peter helped her with her pink-striped helmet. Where to put the luxurious braids? Always a problem. He let them dangle. "Well, I don't remember reading about them finding skeletons of little girls in his basement, if that's what you mean?"

"Mama says you have a morbid sense of humor."

"That a new vocabulary word? I'd rather *mordant* sense of humor."

"This thing is squeezing my brains!" Jeanette clasped the helmet in her palms and jiggered it back and forth as if it were a lid cross-threaded on its jar. "Do I have to wear it?"

"You could leave your head behind?"

"*Morbid* was in my book." She pulled away from his arms, longing to get to her pink bike. "What's *mordant* mean?"

Peter smiled. "Someone who makes funnier jokes."

~ ~ ~

A plush autumn sun, warm and dusty, shone down on the party gathering within the chain-link fence erected around Jacob Weiner's property. A Dixieland band, five waxen old men in jaunty straw boaters and red vests, were deep into a smarmy "St. James Infirmary Blues"—a performance that would have appalled Weiner. Two folding tables draped in plaid cloths offered potato salad, chips, and dips; an ice chest bristled with beer and pop. Mobbing the tables were kids of assorted sizes, who periodically broke off to chase through the yard squirting each other with plastic water pistols and unnervingly realistic Uzis. Most of the new people moving into Oak Grove worked at or around the Pittsburgh airport. They griped about potholes and taxes and spent their weekends, as far as Peter could determine, crawling across their lawns on their hands and knees searching for invasive knot-weed. He'd not yet met these, his newest neighbors-to-be, the Halbrunners, but surmised the mister as the cheerful chef behind an elaborate grill serving the demolition crew, three sun-browned men in sleeveless shirts. One contractor, owner of a belly fully the equal of Peter's, wolfed down his hot dog as quickly as the chef tonged a second one into a bun. Glass smashed. Peter winced, as did the contractor, dragging the tails of his moustache through his mustard.

"Bust them, do it—go ahead!" A woman held up a glass of wine. She was shouting at two boys who were trying to conceal the rocks they clutched. "Do it," she ordered, *"do it!"* For a few minutes then the band was drowned out by the sound of the old man's windows shattering in volleys of rocks.

The new missus, Peter assumed. "I'm going to look for Mindy," Jeanette said, "all right?"

"Sure, honey."

After she pedaled off, Peter introduced himself to Mrs. Halbrunner, who splashed out for him a generous plastic tumbler of wine. Thirty possibly, a strawberry blonde with copper-painted fingernails that looked as if they'd been gnawed by termites, Fay Halbrunner wore white toreador pants and a fringy low-cut blouse dribbled with wine. She seemed excited, stirred up. At his stray inquiry about Jacob Weiner, she laughed—uproariously.

"Randy practically had to pry the keys out of the guy's fingers— not that we needed them, you know, but *still?* What gives with the Black Forest in the back? I can't believe you guys didn't bitch about that?"

Peter, who drank little anymore, sipped at the wine. He spoke over the band. "Well, that's true. The yard sort of got away from him."

"Sort of? I expect Big Foot to come wandering out of there. You know his daughter left all his stuff? She told the realtor, I don't want it, just bury it with the house."

"She didn't leave his piano—or, goodness, his clarinet?"

"How am I supposed to know?"

"But you've been inside?"

"Why would I wanna go in somebody's dirty old house?"

Weiner, his gummy pipes sending up clouds of foul smoke, used to skulk around the neighborhood in his raincoat, his dog trailing behind. His daughter Jessica—a few years older than Peter and for whom he'd once had a secret crush—took an envelope of cash and a ring from her father's desk and ran off on the back of a motorcycle with a high school shop teacher. A few years later Jacob's wife died, then the dog slipped its leash and perished beneath the wheel of a FedEx truck. The old man grieved for his daughter, their estrangement, a thirty-year breach never healed. Peter wasn't sure why he'd asked, but walking through somebody's house seemed like a thing you'd do before demolishing the structure that person had lived in for half a century. The wine was surprisingly good. He remembered when he drank white wine like water. That was wife number one.

"Got kids?"

A more agreeable topic. Mrs. Halbrunner pointed at a swarm of children surrounding the grill. "Prestone Radiator Flush tees." She topped off their glasses, running wine over their fingers. "One of the advantages of being married to a franchise owner—all the promotional shirts and mugs you'll ever need. Or want. I can't tell you how sick I am of the smell of motor oil." She laughed—shrieked—again. "Hey, I just love your old wreck of a house! I told Randy we gotta get some of those old-timey windows, the diamond jobbies? Your wife coming?"

"Ah, well, no." His wife—Peter didn't care to explain—had established a partnership in East Stanton Junction that specialized in the legalistic vexations of the rich. The partnership hit it off so well that Avis and Elliott decided to extend it to the bedroom. Avis wanted Jeanette back at four-thirty. Peter scanned the yard for his daughter, didn't see her, sipped more wine. "Split up, couple of years ago."

Mrs. Halbrunner shrugged. "Happens."

After this disclosure, she shifted closer, even occasionally brushed him: Was that intentional? Or only the wine? The wine, probably. Only eleven in the morning and his new neighbor was well on her way. But then again, Fay Halbrunner did seem unusually happy to get to know him. She fetched for them a proprietary bowl of chips, kept their glasses replenished, asked him all about his company. You'd be surprised, Peter said, fudging the truth here a mite by leaving out the part about the clay works' bankruptcy, how much pipe you can move, especially to legacy municipalities that need to keep updating their systems. His big round face reddened as he swelled with his theme. She was curious about the pipe. Oh, some of the concrete ones, he assured her, gesturing poetically at the dump truck and conveniently omitting the part about the family's never manufacturing concrete pipe, you could drive a bus through.

"Whoa man," Mrs. Halbrunner giggled, "that's a way lot of shit!"

He was lonely. Who knows, maybe she was, too? A little too

aware of a series of transparent trains of sweat traveling sinuously down the cleavage of his happily—or not—married neighbor, Peter turned as they all did to watch the excavator. The operator, the fellow with the brotherly paunch, having started his diesel, maneuvered the clumsy machine like a giant backhoe in position and slapped the bucket against the corner of Jacob's house, as if to get its attention. Timbers cracked, the frame shuddered, and, as the Dixieland octogenarians smoothly segued into "Joshua Fit the Battle of Jericho," the operator swung his bucket wide and walloped the house smartly, causing a sizable portion of the formal dining room to implode. Plaster sprayed like wedding confetti, an unbroken window shattered, two bricks dislodged from the chimney and slid down the shingles. Blunt teeth chewing at the exposed lathe, the machine chugged in closer, snuggling up like a dangerous lover to the small, weather-stained colonial. The excavator shoved the house, bullying it off its foundation, cuffed it again, then punched it square in the mouth. The portico over Jacob's stoop collapsed, the roof ruptured, a downspout toppled into the yard like a slaughtered soldier. By now, Peter's neighbor was leaning back against him, resting lightly but comfortably on the long ample slope of his long ample tummy. Having endured two years of celibacy, two dark winters, he inhaled the woman's humid scent, took note of the next train leaving for the trip south, and watched the front wall of the music teacher's house, moaning like a thing alive, slump into the basement. A fizz of black dust rose, the chef sang out, "Burgers're done!" and to *ooohs* and *aaahs* from the rapt crowd the roof swooned dramatically like the brim of Humphrey Bogart's hat.

Robert McKean

Peter glanced into the heavens and followed a jet's contrail stitching a cloudless blue sky. *Zipper sky,* his father used to call that, his Type-A father who chose at a weak moment to voluntarily exit life, and returned his eyes to the boisterous, sprawling picnic in time to see the excavator operator, swiveling his machine jerkily on its tracks, whip his bucket as far to the side as he could and clip the back wheel of a pink bicycle.

What Peter's heart denied, his mind substantiated.

During his lumbering run across the mangled lawn, he reviewed, as if it were a movie trailer on infinite loop, the inconceivable vision of a child in scarlet dress and pink helmet, dark braids flying, flying herself, finding a spot face down, arms extended, in the unkempt grass. Screams, shouts, cries, the band breaking up into bleats and snorts, and Peter was suddenly seizing some kid by the shoulder and shouting, "Don't touch her!" Tearing the boy away so that he himself might kneel, incredulous, lost, desolate, over this small composed form in the lush grass, the center of his universe.

~ ~ ~

The excavator operator—he took it the hardest. Oblivious of the furor, he carried through on his swing, gunning his diesel and smacking the house. When one of the crew started pounding on his fender, he craned around in his seat. Seeing the incoming crowd, the twisted bike, the figure of a child prone in the grass, putting it all together, he came wallowing out of his cab. He took two unsteady steps, went bone-white, and sank away in a jumble of tattooed limbs and belly flesh. It was Jeanette who seemed the calmest. When Peter lightly stroked her shoulder, terrified that her spine or neck was broken, the girl rolled to her side and awakened as gently as she would on any school day. From under her pink helmet, she looked up at him clear-eyed. "I'm sorry, Papa."

"Don't move, we'll get a stretcher."

She sat up. "I'm okay."

"You can't be."

"I wasn't looking, I'm sorry."

"Does anything hurt?"

"I'm okay, Papa."

His big belly acidulating with adrenaline, Peter carried her home in his arms. Randy Halbrunner, twirling his tongs, offered to call an ambulance, although his voice didn't carry the note of urgency one would have preferred to hear, while his wife, meanwhile, had begun arguing with the contractors. After helping their mate to some shade, where he sat gripping the grass to keep himself from retching, they announced they had had it. Tuesday they'd be back, after the holiday and absent the party — which appeared to constitute, to Fay Halbrunner at least, an actionable breach of contract.

Peter's impulse was to take Jeanette to the emergency room. She contested that plan. "I'm all right, Papa, I'm fine."

"How could you be? You just got run over by a steam shovel?"

"I didn't get run over. It was my fault. I saw Mindy and took off . . ."

He examined her helmet: unblemished, perfectly sound. He

Robert McKean

asked her to walk back and forth across the living room, to wave her arms and touch her nose as he was doing, to recite the Pledge of Allegiance. Then, after she had dutifully completed everything demanded of her, he vacillated. "It's too scary, honey. You might have a concussion. I think we should have you looked at."

"Papa," Jeanette, child of a litigator, plea-bargained, "what if I play my valse? Will that make it all right?"

"You have it memorized? Who's it by?"

"I *told* you, I don't remember who's it by."

"That was part of the test—to see if you remembered telling me that. Then I made a joke—do you remember who I said it was by?"

"You make a lot of jokes. Mama says you make too many jokes."

About his head Peter wound an imaginary turban of gauze.

"But I know the name of it!" she implored. "It's called 'Valse Melancoliqué,' and it's in *b*-minor and it has a lot of clashing notes—and those aren't my mistakes!"

"All right." Peter folded his arms. "Let's hear it then."

As she composed herself at the piano, her great-grandfather's instrument, Peter concentrated on her, this improbable aerialist of only a few minutes ago, trying to decide like any inadequate parent what to do. She sat erect, which he liked: The posture, not of a slumped, sulky child forced to practice, but of a musician in the making. Music ages you, matures you. She kept her eyes level, which he also prized, permitting her hands to find the keys on their own. It was a musical family, after all. Peter pictured his Nonno Franco—better known all his life as Fatty—playing not this piano, but a tinny upright on the mezzanine of a pungent North Ganaego cigar factory. Fatty regaled his bored cigar-rollers below with everything from Giuseppe Verdi to the Big Bopper. Peter remembered him as he lay dying, his lips rounding into a perfect *O* in search of the thick, rank *Corona Grande*s and *Presidential*s that loll majestically in a smoker's mouth, particularly when they're free. Uncle Nico commanded the organ at the Ganaego Roller Rink, the subtlety of Nico's artistry, his lovely, lilting Strauss waltzes, all-but lost on his colliding, ass-over-teakettle skaters.

But wherever they played, whatever Fatty and Nico played, they played beautifully, winsomely, *appassionato,* and for Peter, who also once possessed the gift only to squander that too, it was this unusually solitary, skinny child, braid trailing down each delicate shoulder, for whom he held out most hope. She had talent. Jeanette, as Fatty would say, had music in her. But so do a great many children. The shakeout takes place in the teen years. Shook him out. Over the piano he chose weightlifting, marijuana, girls. By the time he came back to the instrument it was too late. He was determined that his daughter play through the shoals of adolescence and therefore have that choice whether to make music her life. He kept close attention to her tempo and touch. She was right: Hans' valse had clashing seconds and sour, melancholic twangs. An intermediate piece, not especially difficult for her. When she finished, he came up behind and clasped her in his arms.

"I think you'll survive," he pronounced.

"It was too slow, wasn't it?"

About her music he never lied. "Maybe a little more waltzy? Smidgeon of rubato? But not sappy, not like the Dixieland chaps. More *melancoliqué*. I picture these particular waltzers waltzing at the end of a very long evening."

He hoped that wasn't too elliptical. Perhaps it was. She asked, "Is my bike okay?"

The bike — he'd forgotten about the bike. "We'll get it fixed, don't worry, honey."

"We need to get it fixed today — before Mama sees it."

A second or two elapsed before he caught up with her. "We're not going to start hiding things from your mother."

"Papa, they won't let me come here!"

She really was a step ahead of him. Peter, unhorsed by a ten-year-old, sat on the piano bench beside her. "It'll be okay, kitten. I mean, we both agree you weren't hurt. It's no big thing, I'll mention it in passing."

"Papa, can't we just fix it? And not tell?"

"No, Jeanette, that's wrong."

"Can't we be wrong sometimes?"

"It's not *being* wrong, darling, it's *doing* wrong."

"Papa, *please?*"

~~~

It was Peter's father who had hired Avis Longstreet, his ex-wife. Summer after her freshman year of college, temporary help, filing clerk in the Purchasing Department. A smart girl from nearby West Virginia, eccentric by clay works standards, but a quick study. In the fall she asked Steve if she might stay on, she could not afford to return to school. So it was company money then that had paid for Avis's college degree and company money that had purchased the hopelessly myopic young woman her first pair of prescription glasses. She had an unnerving practice of walking around with her hands flitting like wild birds before her face. And then, in an exceptionally generous gesture, the Ganaego Clay Works, by that time managed by Peter, covered her law school tuition. The Italian, crocodile-leather briefcase from which she some years later withdrew his restraining order had been, in fact, his graduation gift to her.

At least the crocodile, if not the marriage, had held up well.

"Have a good week, sweetheart." Peter hugged Jeanette before she hoisted herself from his old Cadillac's dumpy seats. "You'll call?"

"Wednesday night, Papa—after my lesson."

Peter watched his daughter be whisked by a liveried doorman into the brass and cherry-wood recesses of the building that had become her new neighborhood. Later then, early that evening, nursing a faint wine headache, he stood gazing through the fencing at his neighbor's property. The excavator and front-end loader still sat in the drive. Cups and plates lay scattered about, along with the water pistols and the big green and purple machine guns, as if an epic battle had played itself out. The massive grill, he assumed, had gone somewhere safe. Jeanette's pink bike leaned against a tree, back tire flattened, rim and possibly the frame bent. Could it be fixed? If not, where was he going to find an identical pink bike with green and white tassels?

Avis bought it, he had no idea where.

A more immediate challenge was fetching it out. The swing gate was padlocked. He could wait until Tuesday, but having permitted himself to be—uneasily—drawn into his daughter's conspiracy, he recognized the urgency of the situation. Peter returned to his house and carried over his aluminum stepladder. He spread the legs, climbed, then, straddling the six-foot fence, toe of right shoe wedged in a diamond loop this side, toe of left shoe in one opposite, endeavoring to snag neither pants nor ass in this dicey crossing—thank goodness the Halbrunners didn't think of razor wire—he summoned his old weightlifter's strength to lift the ladder up and over and establish it on the far side.

Oliver Hardy, he thought smugly, *couldn't have done that better.*

Once safely within the fenced yard, he was drawn to the battered house. Knocked sideways off its foundation, the little colonial exhibited a doleful unreality, a stunned tenderness. The house was like a boxer who'd been staggered, his arms dangling at his sides. *This can't be,* it seemed to be pleading, and Peter, shocked himself at the fragility of the dwellings in which we take shelter, kept expecting to see, as figments of this unreality, his neighbor absorbed in the newspaper and his skin-and-bones hound to come shambling down the exposed hall.

Nine-letter word . . . Jacob might be mumbling, eraser between his teeth.

Peter went around the back. The grill was lashed to a tree. From its abattoir-like hulk a dreary smell of charred flesh emanated. The small roof over the rear stoop appeared to be intact. He tried the doorknob. With the house cracked open like an egg, there was no reason to expect the door to be locked, nor to care if it was or wasn't. But when it yielded and he slipped into the kitchen, he experienced a weird qualm: Did this constitute breaking and entering? Well, sure. But *whose* house was he breaking into? On the table sat the old man's salt and pepper shakers, his milk-glass sugar bowl, his fouled ashtray. A cup, liquid evaporated in the heel to a rancid green slime, rested on the counter—presumably, the last cup of Lipton Jacob brewed, set down here the morning his daughter showed up with two orderlies the size of sub-zero refrigerators.

But what are you supposed to do, as guardian, in such circumstances?

Technically, legally, Weiner consented to his admission. He ceded power of attorney to his daughter and entered the nursing home voluntarily. But when Peter would visit him, Jacob was unhappy. He insisted that the nursing home was temporary, until he got back on his feet—feet, in a figurative sense, since the old music teacher had become pretty much wheelchair-bound. Behind the stove were the scorched remains of a shelf. Up the wall streaked more black scarves of soot. For a while then it became a regular sight to see the fire engines come barreling around the bend, klaxons barking as they bore down on this block in Oak Grove.

From a nail hung the collar of the long-dead dog.

Trying to recall the name of Jacob's wife, Peter put the dirty

Robert McKean

teacup in the sink, and, studiously ignoring the ominous creaking beneath his tread, padded down the hall. He surveyed the alfresco dining room, then, concerned about the piano—not a rare instrument, but not something you'd appreciate seeing hanging by a leg over the abyss—peered into the living room. And indeed, *stupidaggine,* the baby grand, as if taking cover in an air raid, sat huddled against the wall, littered with shattered lathe and plaster dust. Which pissed him off. For Chrissakes, wouldn't *one* of the Prestone Radiator Flush kids like to learn how to play the piano? He scowled at the sofa, also beneath a shawl of dust, and was reminded of a Sunday Jeanette in her Brownie uniform signed their neighbor on for two boxes of cookies. The sofa smelled of wet dog years after the poor brute had died.

Surely, Jessica salvaged the clarinet? It was worth thousands, *thousands*.

"Her valse, she handled that very nicely, very gracefully." Peter was talking to his neighbor's menorah. The candelabrum, hardened wax wiggling down its arms, sat on its special shelf. Peter brushed broken glass from the base. "I need to compliment her more. You can be *too* critical, you know, Jacob?"

He decided he dare not risk the stairs to the upstairs rooms. Back in the kitchen he tugged open the cellar door and peered into the gloom. The old man, he was cheered to learn, employed his cellar steps as a hardware filing system, something the Sanguedolces did, as well. With the staircase shaking beneath his weight, he navigated a narrow path through a forest of condiment jars into which had been sorted variously

Mending What Is Broken 37

sized nails and screws and nuts and washers. Reaching the bottom, he discovered that any further passage was blocked: When the front wall collapsed, it had KO-'ed the furnace, bringing down with it a tangle of pipes, ducts, timbers, wires. One more smooch from that fat bucket and Jacob's piano would be down here, too. Thwarted, Peter turned and started back up, only to pause at a popped-open cabinet door alongside the stairs. Storage area. Within was a box of paint cans, then further back, in deep shadow, a second box.

Papers?

He leaned in and snagged the box by a finger—it *was* papers. Sitting on a step, he positioned the box between his feet to paw through it. The age-softened cardboard reeked of mildew, everything was browned and peppered with soot. But it was all good stuff, all treasure: letters, postcards, clippings, birthday cards, even several of what must have been Jessica's report cards. Jammed in among the disorder was a yellow envelope—a distinctive yellow—from Littlewood's Drugs and Prostheses: *photographs?* Had to be. Indeed, inside were what appeared to be prints from a single roll, black and white snapshots taken on the lawn of some house some day lost to memory: the old music teacher as a younger man in an Army garrison cap, thick moist lips, powerful nose, eyes gleaming with confidence; and the wife—*Leah,* the name of Jacob's bride drifted back—as a vigorous young woman, someone clearly possessed of her own opinions, striking dark brows arched over almond-shaped eyes, pendulous breasts, some sort of knitted cap and clunky black shoes, a baby swaddled in her arms. The prints, because they were

Robert McKean

black and white, had retained their sharpness: You could almost hear Jacob and his opinionated wife. One shot Peter lingered over: Weiner holding the infant aloft, clutching it with both hands just above face level, a young father's eyes full of passion for a daughter who would grow up and sing—as a seventeen-year-old—the mezzo soprano solo in Duruflé's *Requiem* and who, some July morning three decades hence, would have him removed from his own house.

And then he realized: Not some other house—*this* house.

The very house he'd broken into. What fooled him were the absence of the wall of arborvitae, the enormous spheres of the yews blanking the windows, the maples hovering over the roof like benevolent giants: a young family, a young house. Late Forties? No, given Jessica's age, the photographs had to date from the Fifties. Peter had always taken pains to reassure his neighbor about the runaway Norway maples. Yes, they were weed trees, and Peter's father never much cared for them, but Peter liked them, the shelter they provided the birds and squirrels and rabbits that made their homes beneath them. Not exactly Big Foot, but one Sunday eight wild turkeys had strutted forth from Jacob Weiner's Black Forest. The turkeys conducted a walking tour of Peter's backyard, then, in a thunderous clatter of wings, rose into the trees like fabulous beasts. One of the shots showed an eave of Peter's house, his parents' home before he was born. *What a find, what a spectacular find!* His spirits buoyed, Peter stuffed the photographs back in their Kodak envelope and dumped the envelope in the box. Scooping the box into his arms, he stood and brought a triumphant foot down on a step that does not hold.

As his feet go out from under him, the box—contents disgorged in a papery spray—sails away into the tangled mire below, and Peter's great belly, always first to introduce itself, takes the edge of a tread hard. Air exits him in one eloquent whoosh. Sliding downward in a wide-armed sprawl amid dozens of cascading mayonnaise jars, flailing to grab something—anything, he's not fussy—he entertains a fleeting image of a tortoise skidding down a mountain.

It hurts, well, it hurts a lot.

~ ~ ~

It was, by all accounts, an agonizing slither back up the swaying steps. His daughter's bicycle Peter boosted up the cyclone fence and tipped over the edge, where it tumbled into his languid October grass in a dear pink wreckage. Then a wobbly re-assent of the ladder and another treacherous fence-straddling that did, this time, result in the rending of his pants. His right knee swelled before his eyes; his belly glowed raspberry red. Down his underarms long magenta scratches streaked.

The extra-strength ibuprofens on the kitchen counter called out, bed called out. But there was one more thing he had to do before crawling under the covers. You cannot teach your child to be a sneak. You cannot do that. Against the advice of that uncommonly perceptive child, against—to be frank—his own better judgment, he telephoned his ex-wife to tell her that their daughter had had a near-accident and that it had been his fault for not supervising her more closely.

Avis, as expected, pounced. "Where were you?"

Robert McKean

"I was talking. Next door. They were having a teardown party."

"You mean, somebody was knocking down a house?"

"The Weiners' old place."

"While you were there? They were having a party—at a *construction site?* Who were you talking to, the plumbers?"

"Our new neighbors, they bought Jacob's house."

"Your new neighbors. Why didn't Jeanette say anything about this? Why am I hearing about it only now?"

"It wasn't Jeanette's fault—please don't go there, Avis. It was my fault. I was talking, making silly chitchat. She wasn't hurt, but I thought you should know."

"Just because I'm her mother? You flatter me, Peter. She wasn't hurt? You're sure?"

"It was a kind of near-miss, but, no, she wasn't hurt."

Avis simmered audibly. "I don't know what to say. But I'm not happy, I'll tell you that much. There's a lot of things I'm not happy about these days. But I can't talk now. Elliott's away at his lodge, and I've got a deposition tomorrow."

"It won't happen again, I promise."

"I don't know whether there's going to *be* an again. When Elliott gets back, he and I will talk."

What's Elliott Fields got to do with it? he wanted to snap. "It was careless of me, it was foolish. But please don't come between Jeanette and me, please."

"Peter," his former wife was delighted to remind him, "what I decide to do at this point concerning Jeanette is none of your business."

~ ~ ~

A June morning in 1964 the new mortgage-holder of the Ganaego Clay Works lifted into his arms his four-year-old son and, deaf to the pleadings of his wife, climbed the rung ladder to the kiln tower roof to show his boy—to display before him as if it were a fantastically detailed painting in one of his storybooks—what his papa had wagered his future on. Stephano Sanguedolce, Fatty's elder son, who manifested more interest in money than music, had swiftly and adroitly worked his way up the hierarchy of the ailing clay works from salesman to sales manager to plant manager. And from there, what would it take, Steve liked to remark, but another signature to become sole proprietor, the guy wearing the apron in the fish market?

Peter, that child set down on a sloping roof, wrapped his arms around his father's leg and hid his face. Dizzily below, as if unfixed and floating, were the office and manufacturing buildings arranged about a central quadrangle, everything built of the same ruddy orange brick blackened with the soot that had for a century sifted down over this country hollow off Cabbage Creek. Into one side of the manufactory, the largest building, hopper cars mounded with powdered clay inched forward; tractors, electric motors humming, shifted pallets of salmon-colored pipe in and out of the yards; an overhead crane lowered a skid onto a trailer; a flag, its stars and stripes also dimmed by fly ash, drooped from a pole. If you can make mud pies, you can make clay pipe. People have been manufacturing clay pipe since the Babylonians.

But not everyone can make a profit at it.

The wool trousers Peter clung to reeked of coal-gas fumes; beneath his father's nails red clay dust gleamed. Steve knew every employee whose paychecks he signed, knew the names of their wives and children, knew how to pit one supplier against another, knew how to schmooze the municipal contracts officers who chose the lucky vendors to provide the pipes to carry off to some purulent septic field what Fay Halbrunner colorfully noted was a way lot of shit. Ganaego Clay Works employees worked six days a week; their boss worked seven. Steve knew more than his plant engineers, more than his chiefs of accounting, knew always what it was he wanted, knew always how to get it. While his wife, below, retrieved her hanky from inside the sleeve of her blouse and pressed it against her mouth to stifle her cries, Steve, a master merchant who was to experience but one business miscalculation in his life, lay his palms along his child's head to turn it toward the works. And oddly, more than the vertiginous scene spreading beneath him, what the child retained most vividly was the *odor* of the works, the smell of the wet clay: Pungent, mordant, the common colloidal feldspar that seeped like an earthen hymn through Peter Sanguedolce's life, dyeing his hands, perfuming his dreams.

"Biffed a couple party-crashers in the garbage," Baldwin Feeney reported.

Over the holiday weekend Baldwin, Peter's one-man security force, had shot four unfortunate rats. Two on Saturday, one after Feeney's sermon on the Lord's Day, the fourth yesterday. Peter, feeling obligated, tramped outside to inspect the kills that Baldwin like a loyal mouser brought to show him: Cabbage Creek rats, scrawny things, tiny fiendish eyes in paper-thin skulls, paws sheathed in gray skin as sheer as gentleman's dress gloves, one second scratching for lunch, the next frozen for eternity in mortal extremis.

"Wonderful," Peter said, hands in his pockets. The diminutive bodies of the creatures, struck by the 9mm cartridges, had been reduced to hardly more than coarse fur matted with gore. It was reminiscent of some weird display at Madame Tussaud's. Not sure what to say—requiem mass?—he added, no doubt unnecessarily, "You should probably get them into the garbage, Baldwin."

"Ashes to ashes," Pastor Feeney confirmed.

Peter's knee was still game, and his bruised stomach had transitioned merrily on from raspberry to rotting turnip. Trying not to breathe too deeply so as not to antagonize sore ribs, he watched Feeney disappear around the corner with the plank displaying his spoils. The man worried him. If it weren't for the Feeney clan—Baldwin's father and uncles who'd been devoted to Peter's father—he'd ease Baldwin into retirement before it passed him by altogether. One of these days he was afraid that that antique pistol of his was going to explode, take off the man's hand or bring down a low-flying aircraft.

Wait, he thought, *there isn't any garbage anymore, is there?*

Be that as it may, it was another superb October day. An Indian summer sun showered the ramshackle buildings in sugary light. Stitching everything together in the works had always been the silvery rail lines,

Robert McKean

main trunk and spurs, and their tar-soaked cross ties. Today, the rails were without luster, rough with rust and scale. Between the ties chicory bristled, delicate blooms the color of his mother's Delft china. He noted the advancing dilapidation: knot-weed springing up in sidewalk cracks and sprawling in olive-green waves across the cement; ivy creepers secreting themselves beneath window jambs, coming inside to slither up the walls like curious lizards; and especially any exposed iron—rails, pipes, tanks, hatches, doors, hinges—burning in a slow-motion combustion, marking the works with what looked like the flags of some extinct bellicose nation. He'd labored here through high school and college, his summers and vacations, then graduated from Penn State to become one of his father's traveling salesmen, to become a good salesman, a very good salesman.

And a lousy CEO?

The financial trajectories of businesses can be difficult to account for. Peter listened to a cicada buzzing under the steps. He considered the long shadows cast by the autumnal sun. After his father's sudden, shocking death, he moved into the corner office he'd grown up playing in and managed the company for eleven years. Weathering Steve's final business gamble—an imprudent foray into interstate trucking—Peter righted the works and returned the company to profitability. But that was the '90s; everybody made money in the '90s. But after the dot-com bust, after 9-11, with a president whose most stirring message to his people was *Go shopping!*, not every business, particularly those involved in infrastructure, survived into the new millennium. But that was no excuse: *Somebody* was manufacturing sanitation pipe, *somebody* was ringing up the massive orders that send purchasing clerks scurrying to their phones and faxes, *somebody* was congratulating a young warehouseman on his first born. Holed up in the moribund clay works, understanding that—flat and simple—he failed, Peter paged through the endless legal briefs and advisory documents generated by the closure. There seemed, inexplicably, more paperwork now than there had been when the business was a going concern. The works did not go through a formal bankruptcy. Before the money ran out, Peter, accepting advice of his counsel, squared himself with the world: satisfying his employees, his creditors, and his government. He wasn't rich, but never missed a child support payment nor a tuition bill from Jeanette's private school, and, with what was left over each month, lived modestly.

Mr. Modesty, he thinks, pondering the vast corporation of his belly.

And it was in his father's office—he never learned to call it his office—where he sat brooding when his attorney, both business and personal, arrived with more papers to sign. Peter told Harvey Silverstein about his weekend, specifically his betrayal of his pact with his daughter and conversation with his ex-.

Harvey sided with Jeanette. "What form of madness possessed you to call Avis?"

"I don't know, Harv. I figured it was the right thing to do."

Harvey Silverstein, banking back his practice to care for his ill wife, a much younger woman, had forsworn his three-piece suits and cordovans and opted instead for L.L. Bean flannel shirts, wrinkled chinos, Nike sneakers. But Harvey Silverstein would never give up his heavy black lawyer glasses. He removed the glasses to rub his eyes and the loose skin of his hairless skull, then pointed the blunt end of one of those black frames at Peter—like an indictment. "Even your daughter had brains enough to tell you to keep your trap shut. Did Avis say what revenge she was going to exact?"

"She said she had to talk with Elliott first. He's off at his hunting compound—whatever that means, that's what he calls it—and can't be reached. I don't know what he's gunning for this time—bears, elephants—but whatever it is, I'm sure he'll bring one home strapped to his fender. A crack shot, our boy."

Harvey, not listening, reset his large glasses on his large nose. "We need to liquidate this place, son, so you can get on with things. You're pissing away your life here."

A recurrent argument. "I'm not ready, Harv."

"Someone'll buy it, put in pastel townhouses, fake gaslights, rooster weather vanes. Jimmy Boswell—if not him, someone else."

Peter, a referee calling an illegal play, flung a sore arm out. "I already sold Jimmy Boswell a trucking firm for pennies on the dollar! He's into real estate development now?"

"Jimmy Boswell is into everything. I really wish you hadn't called Avis. You should be doing all your communicating with them through me. I don't trust Elliott."

"Well, that much we can agree on."

"He's got the political itch, he wants to run for district attorney. I don't know if he's got the backing of the party elders yet, but first thing he's gonna do is go after your kid—he'll want her pretty face on his campaign posters. But I got nothing to tell you. We need to wait until we hear from them."

"Maybe it'll blow over, Harv?"

"And maybe the Pirates'll win the pennant."

Peter skimmed a finger through the dust on the desk. A partners' desk, a handsome old thing, leather-topped, veneered in burled walnut. The drawers smelled of fountain-pen ink and spearmint, the lozenges in the little tins that Steve had developed a fondness for. "I could open up a theme park? Give guided tours: craftsmen busy at their benches, bookkeepers with garter sleeves and green visors?"

"Peter"—Harvey looked up from his papers—"you did the right thing, the ethical thing. Instead of hanging on and defaulting all over town, you brought the business to an orderly close. You tucked everybody in bed, you brought them warm milk, you acted like an adult, you did all you could."

"I bumbled it away, Harvey."

"Big fish eat the little fish—it *happens*. Even your old man saw it coming. We used to talk about it. Why d'you think he was trying to diversify? Steve wouldn't want to see you holding on like this."

Happens. Peter, scrawling his signature on the papers Harvey was laying before him, recalled Mrs. Halbrunner his neighbor leaning back against his big tummy. *What was that all about?* The property, surprising him, was quiet when he came past this morning. Where was the wrecking crew? But Tuesday after a long weekend—they were probably polishing off their doughnuts and extra large regulars, rolling the stiffness out of their shoulders. By now no doubt Jacob Weiner's house was a heap of splinters. Peter thought of Jenny, Harvey's courageous wife, a woman once a varsity lacrosse midfielder struggling with Lou Gehrig's Disease.

"How's Jenny, Harv?"

Jenny loved teasing Harvey. She called him the *Man with the Mouth*. But the mouth had little to say on this subject this afternoon. "One day at a time, Peter." Harvey jogged the bottoms of his papers on the desk and slid them into a briefcase whose leather was as parched as his face. He once occupied the singular position of representing both management and the union in a labor dispute. *The only lawyer I can't outlawyer,* he reassured both sides, *is myself.* A foot shorter than Peter, a good hundred and twenty pounds lighter when *he* stepped on Dr. Vossburg's scale, he shook Peter's hand and padded across the room in his snazzy, multicolored footwear. "Sooner or later," he stopped to add, "you're going to have to put your shoulder to something you can call your own. You got the stuffing kicked out of you, okay, but you gotta get back on your feet. We're almost at an end here." Harvey hefted his briefcase. "I'll be back next Monday. You can't sit around on your keister forever, Peter. Not healthy."

Jimmy Boswell, Jr.

The fickleness of the business gods. Jimmy also inherited a business from his father. *Jimmy's Buicks—It's Your Money, Ain't It?* Jimmy Senior sold American exclusively; Jimmy Junior added foreign makes, then a construction supply firm, and, like a lap dancer fallen into his arms, Steve Sanguedolce's over-leveraged trucking outfit. Peter had learned in business two lessons. This was the first, when his father challenged him, two years out of college, to take over the fractious, dysfunctional sales office, and he built for his father a department that delivered the goods. That was a lesson: That he had fine stuff in him. Second lesson, a lesson learned too late, when he came to understand that the sales manager he'd hired to replace himself was a thief. It wouldn't have been so bad if there had been time to train a new manager. But suddenly, without warning, the business paradigm in the industry shifted and the clay works was caught out. It was as if they found themselves standing over a trapdoor. And so this constituted the second lesson: That things can turn that fast. He put himself back in charge of the sales office and tried acting as CEO, CFO, sales manager, and chief salesman. It didn't work, one man could not perform all those roles. But steering his father's Cadillac with one hand, speed dialing one of the three phones he carried with the other, reviewing operations reports open on the seat beside him, and dictating proposals into a Sony recorder while logging thousands of miles across the continent did help him to lose ninety pounds.

And all his confidence.

~ ~ ~

Robert McKean

The pink bike, model accident victim, rode patiently in Peter's trunk until Thursday, when the young mechanic at Two Wheels and a Dream stood the poor thing up and frowned at it. The boy possessed a Norman Rockwell mop of carrot-colored hair falling to his eyes, so it was difficult to assess what he was displeased with, the crimped rim and flattened tire, the grass-stained vinyl tassels hanging limply from the handlebars, the dirt clinging to the pedals. As for him, every time Peter looked at the wrecked bike, his heart tightened: She'd been *inches* from tragedy. How could she have not seen that huge machine?

"Not good," the young mechanic muttered from beneath his hair.

Sticking up from the slender pockets that extended the length of his overalls was an impressive battery of wrenches. "I don't need to get it fixed," Peter said helpfully. "D'you have something in stock like this, I mean pretty much *exactly* like this?"

"This?" The young man flipped the lifeless tassels. "This is some sort of Chinese off-brand. I've never heard of it. Where'd you get it?"

"My wife bought it."

"Then you need to talk to her. We don't sell crapola."

Well, phooey, his daughter happened to adore it. Sometimes, Jeanette will play a passage note-perfect, as musicians, particularly child musicians, are taught to do, and he will glow with parental pride. And sometimes, she will play a passage *musically,* playing all those same notes perfectly but with the music singing through her fingers—and that will bring tears to his eyes. With her glossy helmet, her luxurious plaits, her dark wanderlust eyes, she was on her pink bicycle with its fluttering tassels an arrow to his heart. Swallowing his irritation, Peter lifted the wounded bicycle back into the capacious trunk of the Cadillac and drove to the mall.

At Sears he scrutinized their deep phalanxes of bicycles: green, red, blue, yellow, even black, but no pink. Where *had* Avis gotten it? Benny's Bikes and Plastic Gardenias? He rolled forward one of the girls' models. Fire-engine red, bigger, closer to standard-sized. Palm resting on the saddle, Peter tooled the bike around the department. Jet black tires, sharp treads—you could smell the new rubber, the fresh paint, a tang of petroleum. Coming in, he'd spotted a display of tassels. Behind the counter hung as many helmets of various cranial dimensions as proudly hung on the wall of any Viking castle. Will it do? For child *and* mother?

Red bike, red helmet, red and white tassels?

Not sure, he retreated to the food court. Eating helped him think. Or perhaps, eating helped him not think. Whatever, Peter's mid-afternoon snack was a sixteen-inch pizza with anchovies and extra cheese. *You are what you eat.* Someone said that. That fellow who sautéed the weeds in his yard and died prematurely?

Maybe it was a proverb? No matter. You are—certainly—*all* that you eat.

At the table beside him two businessmen, ties tucked in their shirts, talked of their plans for the weekend. He'd forgotten that, the sonatina of the week—*Oh, hell, it's Monday* through *Thank God, it's Friday!*—the business world's plodding structure that gives, if not purpose to life, a sense of direction to it. He still went to work, still

Robert McKean

took the time to choose a tie that married his shirt nicely. But it was a sham, all fiction. He had no Monday, no Wednesday, no Friday. Every day was Saturday, and, although to someone sixty-plus that might sound just dandy, to someone forty-five it didn't. Before Peter left the mall, he topped off his pizza with a turkey sub with lettuce and tomato and a twenty-four-ounce Pepsi. On the way home, sans new bicycle and visualizing himself withering under family court cross-examination—*Where were you? Who were you talking to? How much had you drunk? Are you completely lunatic, letting her pedal her bicycle around a construction site?*—he pulled into a Li'l Peach and bought two canisters of Pringles, a box of English muffins, an eighteen-ounce jar of Smucker's strawberry jam because Jeanette loved it, two cans of ravioli, a Baby Ruth, and, while he was at it, waiting in line, a package of beef jerky.

At home he crouched over the toilet and put his fingers down his throat.

~ ~ ~

What was up with Jacob's house?

This week's big mystery: Why was it still standing? Nothing seemed to have transpired Tuesday or Wednesday, and, when Peter came home yesterday, he noted that the heavy equipment had vanished. Today, gripping the chain link, he peered in at his neighbor's ravaged property. The gray colonial, shifted on its axis, peeked out from behind two yews the size of Volkswagens. The little house looked as if it was considering venturing out for a stroll around the neighborhood—or a visit to the

ER. From within the jagged chimney lips a bird rose, a mourning dove followed by its mate. The downy creatures, cooing to each other, settled on the ridge—gently, one prayed. A squirrel lands four paws square on Jacob's roof and the whole affair is going to come down in one sorrowful whoosh.

Like Jacob himself.

The Weiner family photos, lost to time once and now lost a second time, haunted Peter. If the house had been reduced to flaps of wood and been borne away to the landfill, then the guilt he felt for bobbling the pictures would have dissipated, too. But with the house in this peculiar state of suspended death spasm, an opportunity—an *obligation*—remained. And really, the pictures might do the old man some good. Weiner was not happy. He blamed his downfall on his feet. Gracious, he was in the nursing home for more than that—ask the Fire Department—but it was true that the man's arthritic feet had always presented a problem. The joints of his toes—he explained all this to Peter once, unscrewing his pipe to employ as a visual aid, like a model of a foot in a podiatrist's office—were determined to fuse. Big toes, especially. For years he'd made his way in the world by rocking back and forth on the outside rims of his soles. Traveling the halls of the music school, the old clarinetist looked like a boat in a heavy swell. And now those doughty toe bones had reached their goal. Jacob, who mercilessly hectored the staff—frankly, not a greatly beloved patient—had forsaken his walker and taken to rolling himself up and down the nursing home corridors, gazing morosely out the windows at either end.

Robert McKean

So, all right. Peter fetched his trusty ladder.

The good news was that his knee had begun to function again, and, in a few minutes, not nimbly but capably, he found himself inside the cyclone fencing. The ladder was probably not visible from the street, but to be safe he tucked it beneath the shrubs, then, also for reasons of prudence, he elected to forgo the first-floor route and dangerous cellar stairs. He pried up Jacob's unsecured bulkhead doors and slipped into the basement. To be honest, he was not altogether sold on this approach, either. The bulkhead steps let in across from the walloped furnace, which was good, but also led beneath a heavy piano resting above on a sagging floor.

Best not to think about it.

Inhaling the sour odor of mold, Peter picked his way through the murky light, stepping around the countless objects that had come tumbling from their shelves, crockery, paint cans, rags, buckets, a lamp, musical scores and practice books, a rotary telephone, and jars—jars, jars, jars, washed but with labels still affixed. Only a man who filed by jars could amass such a collection. There seemed little profit in restoring things to their proper places, so he wormed his way forward cautiously and located his heaved-away box to the side of the basement stairs. The box sat on its side in a glittering sea of screws and nuts and broken glass. Trapped beneath lay a report card. He was tempted to check how well Jessica Weiner scored in courtesy and respect for your elders. The photos in their sturdy Kodak envelope had safely survived their crash landing. While he worked, concentrating on refilling his box, he became vaguely aware of motor noises and then voices, voices approaching.

Surfacing to consciousness, he realized: *I'm not alone.*

The motor noises: truck engines? *Diesels?* He strained to hear.
A casual visit to the property he might wait out. No one was about to
go looking for anyone dumb enough to be down here. But one petulant
caress from that big excavator and he'll be entombed for eternity beneath
the Halbrunners. The voices—two, he determined, one of each gender—
seemed to go one way, then another, then swung around the house, and
he identified them, his new neighbors, the Mr. and Mrs. As they cruised
past the open bulkhead, their conversation like an Ibsen play in progress
drifted into the cellar.

". . . it go! For Chrissakes, I just went back to get something."

"Your jammies?"

"Why are you making such a federal case out of this? I offered
to give her a lift home, all right? I told her I had to stop and pick up some
books, and she said she wanted to come in and see the apartment. Maybe
she wants to rent it, it's no big deal."

"I don't care what you were doing."

"I wasn't doing anything."

"You're welcome to stick your dick anywhere you want, Randy,
really, it's fine. You might try a blender."

"I wasn't doing anything!"

Peter, motionless as a mannequin, studied the octopus arms of
Jacob Weiner's furnace. Stuck in an elbow was a wisp of pink paper, a
receipt. He wiggled it free: On February 8, 1957, Jacob purchased a hat

Robert McKean

from Chester's Haberdashery for thirteen dollars and fifty-nine cents. One of his dented fedoras? Peter beamed at the faded receipt: hats, a wonderful invention. He pocketed the receipt, patted it, and listened to the voices die away. A car started and withdrew. Peter bided his time, then minced back through the Weiners' archaeological history. He should, he supposed, be appalled at the shambles down here. But considering his own house, he was the last person to be pointing fingers. The clutter used to drive Avis mad. Perhaps this, all in all, was a better solution: Upon reaching eighty, simply have your house knocked down and the contents steamrollered over? Emerging from the bulkhead steps, salvaged box held high, at head level, Peter lowered it to find himself staring into the weepy, dumbfounded eyes of Fay Halbrunner.

Pop quiz: Instantly come up with something even remotely plausible. "Ah . . . Jacob asked me to look for some stuff." Peter bounced his box and added with a flourish, "In the cellar."

Fay's eyes opened wider.

Gave his box another perky bounce. "Warm today, doncha think?"

~ ~ ~

She liked to fiddle with her shoe. One thigh hooked over the other, she would run two fingers inside the heel of her loafer, slip it partway off, then pull it back on. Amused, charmed, Peter registered this nervous mannerism, along with her propensity to rest her copper fingernails between her lips and nibble on them. They were sitting in low-slung lawn chairs behind Jacob Weiner's low-slung house. Late-afternoon sun made a fringe of whatever burnt-orange leaves clung

to Jacob's maples. At their feet the cardboard box of old letters and

photographs exhaled a breath of time lost. Fay was downloading,

something for which, fellow traveler in the land of the betrayed, Peter

was in an excellent position to offer sympathy. By this time they were, as

well, deep into the dusty bottle of plum brandy that had long languished

on Jacob's kitchen shelf.

"What problem is it of mine?" Fay, hunched over her phone,

answering her nanny when the woman called. "Tell *him*—he fathered

them." When the nanny raised further objection, Fay, working her shoe,

snapped, "Tell him I'm meeting with my attorney. *No*—tell him I'm

fucking my attorney!"

She jabbed *End Call* and held out one of Jacob's teacups.

Peter splashed into it another goodly measure of the slivovitz. Randal

Halbrunner, as it turned out, hard-working entrepreneur, owner of three

oil-changing franchises, had not always been at one of the other two of

his shops, as his staff reported when his wife called, or even in transit

among them. Rather, he'd been entertaining at a squalid apartment in

Creighton he rented—shared keys with—in partnership with a guy who

trained horses.

"They have a crib?"

"An apartment," Fay explained to her dimwitted neighbor. "I

just said, *apartment.*"

"Sorry. Outdated term. Bachelor pad?"

"Pigsty. There's this scuzzy mattress on the floor. It looks like

Robert McKean

something you'd use with your dogs—or maybe the other guy's horses. It's in the living room—*the living room!* They can't even wait to get their bimbos into the bedroom."

"How did you find out?"

"Stupid shits forgot to pay the rent. The landlord called, and I was like, *What rent?* What're you talking about? So, I went over to look at it, like you would, you know, to see what your family money was buying?"

"Kind of cheesy," he commiserated. "The mattress and everything."

"So anyway"—Fay hooked and re-hooked her legs—"we had the big fight, the one that scares the kids and keeps the neighbors on the edges of their seats all night. He swore he'd never cheat again, he'd back out of the lease, promised me eternal, undying fidelity. Then Monday he gets ready to go out. His garages're open holidays—I'm surprised he doesn't make the mechanics sleep in the grease pits—but he doesn't usually work holidays. So, where're you going? I ask. I'm going over to the apartment to pick up some things I left, he says, books and stuff. *Books?* A man who doesn't have the patience to read a street sign? So I tell the kids we're going for a ride. I stuff them in the car and we head over there—and guess what? I don't see his car, and I'm thinking, Maybe he just came by like he said? But to be sure, we hid in the bushes and then . . ."

"He shows up with his library card?"

"And the librarian."

"Oh my, that is cheesy."

"Hey, no, it was great—the kids thought it was so cool to spy on Daddy."

"Where've they been getting their women."

He hoped that wasn't coming across as a request for information. "Craigslist?" Fay shrugged. "And now he's pissed at *me*. He says it's no big deal, it won't happen again, blah, blah, blah. Well, I'm sorry, but for me it *is* a big deal, for me it's a *massive* deal."

More tears, more loafer slipping on and off. These perfidies we casually visit upon one another, the tawdry larcenies of the heart so common as to constitute petty theft: Avis, the nights he thought his devoted wife was working late, the showers she started taking immediately upon getting home, an alteration in pattern he didn't note until a day he lifted from a doorknob a blouse and sniffed shaving lotion. It was supposed to be the other way around, he understood, lipstick on the traveling salesman's collars. But with the closure of the clay works it'd been he who assumed responsibility for household chores, buffing and setting out the apple Avis liked to carry to work, running the vacuum, laundering the underwear that another man was industriously rifling with his dirty hands.

"You need to decide."

"Take him back or kick him out?"

"Actually," Peter, tender in these matters, qualified his suggestion, "I'm probably not the right person to be giving advice on this subject."

Robert McKean

"I'm *starved.*" Fay pointed at Jacob's back door. "You see any food in there while you were busy burglarizing it?"

It was later then, long after shadows had claimed the weedy plot behind Jacob Weiner's mad by north-northwest house, the slivovitz become a part of Yugoslavian history, that Fay Halbrunner, crouched on Peter's king-sized bed, her naked bottom pointed toward him, bent over the Weiner photographs. She'd deployed the black and white prints across the rumpled sheets and was intent on prying from Peter everything he knew or could remember about Weiner. Which wasn't a lot. Two bottles of wine on top of the brandy, two large steaks—Fay easily out-drank him, if not out-ate him—two romps in the sheets, one pre-prandial, one post-, and Peter was wiped out. Lying amid the multitudinous pillows that Avis had seen as her homage to Martha Stewart and viewing the world over an expanse of his hairy, dimpled, and still bruised flesh, he exerted himself to stay awake and try to explain someone as peculiar as Jacob Weiner to someone as conventional as Fay Halbrunner.

"He had—*has,* for God's sake, the man's not dead yet—a furtive intensity you can only marvel at. He lost one of his big maples once. Just fell over. Like it was tired. The next summer he noticed termites swarming in the rotted wood of the stump—you know how termites do, thousands of insects crawling over themselves in a humming ball, about the size of a basketball?"

Fay gave the sphere Peter was creating with his cupped palms a sickening look.

"Well, anyway"—moving briskly on—"for most of us it

would've been a call to the exterminators. Not Jacob. Jacob doused the termites in a pail of gasoline and threw in a match. I could hear the firemen scolding him—someone had called reporting an atomic bomb exploding in Oak Grove. But I heard him play once—I mean in public, I used to hear him practicing all the time—and that makes up for everything. The music school had a faculty recital. Somehow they persuaded—begged—Jacob to play. He chose the solo version from the first movement of Mozart's famous clarinet concerto."

"They had to beg him? He was too good to play for free?"

"No, no, you have to understand: He was extraordinarily gifted. Why his career never went beyond teaching, I don't know, but when he played that Mozart piece it was exquisite—*divine*, if I may use the word. My grandfather would've put his fingertips to his lips and kissed them."

Fay turned: The darkness between her legs drew Peter's eyes. He hadn't been offended to discover that the hair down there was a different color than the hair on top. Not at all. He'd spent the afternoon envying the daubs of sunlight chasing across her shorts—and now he knew. Such were the pleasures of new intimacy. How blessed, no matter how shallow, to have a new lover. Fay held up the shot of Jacob clutching his infant daughter above his gleaming eyes. "You're right," she declared, worrying with her teeth a fingernail as iridescent as a Japanese beetle. "The old guy needs to see these pics."

~ ~ ~

"It's pretty clobbered, isn't it, Papa?"

"Pretty clobbered."

Robert McKean

"I have twenty-three dollars saved from my allowance?"

Mourning the pink bike in the garage. He'd watched her, Jet Blue bag slung over a shoulder, racing through her lobby as he waited in the car. She looked like a petite businesswoman running late for the airport. Like her mother, alas. He was still worried about his confession, but kept reassuring himself that nothing had happened, Jeanette wasn't hurt, and that Avis wouldn't want them fighting over her. As bad as relations became, they had never made a pawn of Jeanette, never attempted to turn the child against the other. Surely, Avis wasn't going to start now?

No, he was not sure of that at all.

Avis, this morning on the phone: "Elliott's been tied up in meetings all week, political stuff, so, we haven't had a chance to talk. It's not only what happened Saturday, there's a bunch of other things, too. But I told her she could stay over. She's got something from school she's to show you, and you are to talk with her about it. But listen, I'm warning you, Peter, we get wind of one thing we shouldn't and that's it— lights out, buster."

Other things?

Why Elliott was required to have any input in their Jeanette deliberations escaped him totally. Avis changed once she remarried. True, Avis had always been in constant evolution, from party girl à la Madonna when Steve hired her to grateful, serious student to up-and-coming career woman who might well run you off the road to reach a billable appointment. But that was the professional side of Avis

Longstreet: the woman in a Barneys of New York power suit who loved to toss off tough hombre cracks like *Lights out, buster!* But this new *personal* Avis, the one who exhibited an excessive deference to her new husband, who seemed to dread crossing him in the tiniest way—this Avis Longstreet Peter did not understand. In his humble opinion these two halves didn't add up to a whole. But fine, if there were deeper stresses in her new marriage, so be it. He hadn't exchanged *I do's* with Elliott Lansdowne Fields.

"You need to be thinking about something special to spend your money on, honey. We'll take care of your bike."

"But it was my fault, Papa?"

It still bothered him: visions of a miniature aerialist sailing across a yard. The excavator boom, he worked out, must have swept in from behind, curling around her like a serpent. Had her flight occurred a second or two later she would have pedaled into the path of a five-hundred-pound bucket. He brought an arm down around her shoulders. "It was an accident, sugar. Accidents happen, although"—he appended—"people do have to be careful, you know?"

She was stoic under his mild reprimand. She squatted beside her twisted bike, thick braid trailing down each shoulder. She petted the flattened tire the way you might comfort a wounded animal. "But we can get it fixed, can't we?"

It'd been a loyal friend, her pink bike. Mastering the delicate art of balance once they retired the training wheels had given Jeanette a boost in confidence, a sense of independence. He remembered how his

Robert McKean

first bicycle expanded his world. Unfortunately, the pink bike would turn out to be, as sometimes happens in life, an all-too-brief fellow traveler. Peter looked at the mangled fender splattered with grease from the cracked back axle. "I think she's a goner, honey."

"What're we going to do?"

"You know, it's amazing, but I do believe you've shot up four inches this week. Did you notice that?"

Jeanette gawked him.

Loved catching her out, but you had to be quick. "Kids," he explained, waving an arm expansively, "they shoot up like Topsy. Buy 'em a bike and before you know it, you gotta buy 'em a new one!"

"We can afford a new bike?"

Children are smart, they get scared. They have every right to. Peter knelt on a fat knee beside his daughter and smoothed between his fingers a creased green tassel. For this, ever will he condemn himself: the failure of the clay works. Heaven knows what twaddle Avis and Elliott—and it was probably Elliott—had been feeding his daughter, her papa burning his furniture for heat, darning his socks by candlelight, spooning cold beans in his mouth. Oh, well, about the beans they were right. "We can afford a new bike, honey. We're going bike shopping."

"When? *Now?*"

"Not quite yet."

Papa the pill. He insisted, "Valse Melancoliqué" and this week's new piece. Images to savor: He, settling in his armchair; she, fussing with her music at the piano, spine erect, hands poised. In his Avis negotiations he'd been adamant about staying involved in Jeanette's musical education, but agreed—more for logistical convenience—to let her leave her longstanding Oak Grove Music School teacher, a woman whom he implicitly trusted, and study with someone Elliott knew. And even though he officially passed on this new instructor, Graystone Tanner, he remained skeptical. The young man—bright, bubbly, perennially sought-after white-glove escort for East Stanton Junction debutantes—was not challenging Jeanette. Case in point: this week's new piece, one of Debussy's children's works, "The Little Shepherd." Peter skimmed the music: Although it possessed some extended triplet passages and a complex rhythmic structure, the piece seemed rather light. Better than the usual Graystone things she carried home, yes, but in her piano bag he'd appreciate seeing a little less Peter, Paul, and Mary and Walt Disney and a little more Haydn and Mozart.

He also insisted that she count aloud.

"Papa, do I have to?"

"It's a counting exercise, that's probably why Graystone chose it. He *is* having you count, isn't he?"

"Yes, Papa."

"Swell. Can't tell you how relieved I am to hear that."

Compressing her lips, making her eyes go wide—one of her Avis Longstreet faces—Jeanette centered herself over middle *C* and dutifully counted as she played. And if her counting was occasionally erratic—*one trip-let, two trip-let, a, and, dah, three; one-and-two-and; one trip-let, two—oops!—anddahthree!*—the triplets themselves were

Robert McKean

graceful, crystalline. Her hands, small because she was small, were exceedingly nimble. He recalled that lightness of touch: It's in our hands that we age most inexorably. Jacob Weiner once let his hands drop like stones to his kitchen table, as if to disown things grown this hard and this stupid.

Jeanette, when she finished, turned to check with him.

"Very nice, honey, very nicely done. Bravo."

"My Czerny's really, really hard this week. I hate him!"

"Well, it was mutual. But let's give him a whirl anyway."

And this too fetched back memories: Czerny, the man who hated children. But it had been Peter who'd insisted that Jeanette's Czerny studies continue, and he was pleased here, too. You couldn't deny it: She *had* grown. And since physical maturity is a metaphor of emotional maturity, it was inevitable—inevitable to him—that he would fret over the models with which they were presenting the child: a mother of questionable ambition, a stepfather of dubious compass, a failed, fat papa now having a ramble in the bramble with a married woman fifteen years his junior.

A thought that brought him up short: *Is* he having a ramble?

Or had he'd only had—on a droll, lost evening—a one-night stand? Morning the day after, he'd woken alone, sprawled across his bed. On the nightstand lay a dead bottle of wine, downed in battle. He heard insect life, mourning doves, garbage trucks bellowing like pigs in rut. He stood for a long time under the scalding shower, then went in search of his clothes exuberantly flung every which way the night before. They were on the dresser, his socks and trousers neatly folded and laid beside his wide drawers, also folded. Now then, people don't generally fold the underwear of their one-night stands, do they?

Well, you might if you were Fay Halbrunner.

When Jeanette finished, he came up behind her and closed her in his arms. "Lunch, sweetie? Then shopping?" He kissed her on the top of her head. "We are in desperate need of provisions. So, bike, helmet, food—*plus* a new skimmer for the old man."

"Where're we going to go to buy my new bike?"

"Isn't everything made in China now? The Chinese bicycle store, I suppose."

"There's a Chinese bicycle store? And what's a *skimmer?*"

"Don't know what a skimmer is? What kind of an education are you getting over there? I'm shocked, shocked."

Late that afternoon Peter brought a dining room chair down to the sidewalk and settled his weight in it, as Jeanette, wobbling a little to control the larger, heavier bike, pedaled up and down the street. Each time she steamed by, she chimed the bike's shiny bell, and he offered this attractive young cyclist on a cardinal-red bicycle in a cardinal-red helmet a gallant salute of his new fedora. Across Oak Grove a smoky autumnal haze floated. A harvest-time light, a luminous glaze that seemed to have enfolded in its arms all that remained of dusty summer. From beneath the shrubs the scent of vegetative decay rose, Jacob's dried maple leaves chattered as they tumbled across the pavement, and Peter recalled the autumn afternoon he was tracked down in a Roosevelt Avenue bar and informed his father had killed himself.

What your heart denies, your mind substantiates.

The skinny mechanic at Two Wheels and a Dream had carefully measured Jeanette, then adjusted the seat and handlebars and pedals of the bicycle over whose selection she had agonized. An eternity it took the boy to fine-tune the bike to his satisfaction—such high-minded seriousness for such an absurd means of locomotion. Making beneath his mop of carrot hair his own version of an Avis Longstreet face, he consented to attach to the hand grips the red and white tassels Peter had pointed at. They selected a helmet that wouldn't overly squeeze the wearer's brains and rolled the bike out and snugged it into the Cadillac's trunk.

"Now," Peter announced, "my skimmer."

At Sydney's Men's Clothiers Jeanette bounced up and down in her chair giggling as he tried on every hat the store carried, whether they fit or not. Sydney's only customers, they had the showroom to themselves. Peter would pluck a hat from the shelves, concealing it, then spring out from behind the suit display, showcasing his choice. He tried on a big black homburg that must have been sitting on Sydney's shelves since Eisenhower's first inauguration, a little snotty Frank Sinatra number, a straw boater—wrong season!—a Greek fisherman's cap, a beret which brought forth a fizz of abominable French, and finally the lion-colored Borsalino fedora with its grosgrain ribbon, generous brim, and tall crown furrowed with a single deep voluptuous crease. Rabbit fur, goodness—they still make hats out of animals? The zenith of the afternoon, though, was in the T&V, evaluating the orangeness of the oranges and the spottiness of the bananas, weighing the merits of butter lettuce versus Romaine, picking the multicolored bow tie pastas for tonight's dinner. He loved these consultations, the more deadly serious the better. He didn't care what they discussed. He and his daughter could be discussing the butterflies visiting the purple buddleja in the yard or kitchen sponges, it didn't matter. In T&V's bakery Jeanette, acting as his dietitian, agreed reluctantly to add to their buggy a swooningly decadent tiramisu.

"But you're not to eat too much, Papa."

On one of her bicycling cruises past, she pulled up short. Hopped down from her seat and planted her feet firmly bestride the taller bike. Face bathed in sweat, wizard glasses misted at the edges, she pointed at Jacob Weiner's cockeyed house behind its San Quentin fence. "There's a bird in there! It keeps going in and out of the chimney! What's a bird doing in there?"

"I don't know, sweetheart. Maybe he's looking for his wife?"

"Well, I think it's *dumb*—and so are you," his adorable cyclist declared, before remounting her bike and pedaling determinedly—if not quite straight—off.

Turning, Peter studied the trespassing mourning dove as it lighted on the ragged lip of the chimney, its wings making that curious whistling sound, then disappeared below like Kukla going in search of Ollie. Foolish creatures, he was fond of them, their lugubrious cooing that woke him mornings, their necks that woggled as they walked, the way these two mates will perch on his garage roof and frown at each other as if perplexed just why they *had* become mates.

Fay's right, he decided, Jacob should have those pictures.

~ ~ ~

Sunday afternoon brought a delicate moment. As Jeanette was about to run off into her lobby, she hesitated. "Am I supposed to tell Mama about my new bike?"

A question he'd been avoiding. Avis knew there had been a *near-accident*, but she hadn't asked for details and he hadn't volunteered to provide them. It wasn't important, but somehow it was. And Jeanette, wise child, understood that. But the only thing worse than withholding truth is parceling it out in dribs and drabs. Peter tipped his fedora. "Sure, darling, no reason not to."

Jeanette weighed that. "Bikes're probably cheaper in the fall, right?"

"I guess that makes sense. Why?"

"Because we could say we saw it on sale and we bought it for next year? That'd be better, don't you think? And," she added helpfully, "I'll for sure grow more by next year."

Roused at last by all this industrious ten-year-old truth-spinning, Peter gently chided her. "Stop worrying about your mama." Even for him that was hard to credit as he gazed into a pair of chocolate eyes that, uncannily, could be his ex-wife's. "She's going to be thrilled to hear you have a new bike."

Well, it's *possible*, he thought, driving off.

Mending What Is Broken   71

The succession of Schwinns he steered through the leafy streets of Oak Grove had been purchased by his father at a hole-in-the-wall shop in North Ganaego, not far from the cigar factory where Fatty played. The candle-thin stacks of the coke ovens loomed over the shops and houses of North Ganaego; you could sit on your porch at midnight and read the *Citizen Chronicle* by the light of the heavens-filling strobes of the Bessemers. The call came that evening at six-thirty. Peter, steeling himself, waited for the red bike to round the bend in the conversation.

What Avis brought up first, however, wasn't the bike. "So, what did you think of the letter from Bright Ridge?"

"What letter?"

"She didn't show it to you? They sent a letter, the headmaster! You were supposed to talk with her about it. Peter, you weren't even listening to me! I told you she had something to show you!"

"I'm sorry, I must've forgot."

"Ah, this is just unacceptable . . ." Avis's voice trailed off into frustration. "She's falling behind in pretty much everything *and* she got into a shouting match with some girls. She was *supposed* to show you the letter and she was *supposed* to spend extra time studying this weekend—which I'm guessing she *also* didn't do, did she?"

"I thought she was doing fine?"

"As long as she can play 'Jingle Bells,' you think everything's fine. I tell you, Elliott's not going to like this one bit—and neither do I."

Had he even asked Jeanette once—the whole weekend—about her homework? "Well," he vowed, "on her next visit she's studying. I

Robert McKean

want to see her book bag full."

"And why suddenly does she need a new bicycle? What happened to the one she had?"

"Umm . . ."

"You bought a new one because it's *bigger?* They measure kids, you know, before they recommend a size? I can't imagine her needing a bigger bike so soon?"

The sign over the door says *Honesty.* But now he was afraid of what Jeanette might have said, how elaborately their imaginative daughter might have painted her bicycle story. Peter gazed longingly . . . *if only . . .* at the door of truth. "You know, bikes in the fall? We saw a terrific sale and she fell head over heels for it."

"Well, I don't get it."

"Trust me, Avis, on her next visit she's busy studying."

"If there's a next visit."

In the clay works' hundred-and-twenty-five-year history, the summer of 1989 would certainly account for the first sighting of acid-washed jeans shorts and fishnet stockings—*that* girl. The college girl who bent her head to the typewriter keys to see them, who fired up some sort of exotic brown cheroots that made people fear a raid from the narco squad, who had a penchant of lowering her peroxide-blond curls on the requisitions she'd just finished typing to sleep off her hangovers. But it was *that* girl who pushed her way through the works' traumatized employees and climbed into the ambulance that rushed their boss to the emergency room, the last human touch Steve Sanguedolce was to know.

As he was carving away at his third cube of tiramisu, Peter reflected on what he'd heard behind Avis as they talked on the phone: murmur of the television, clink of dinnerware being put out, desultory patter of voices. He could, if he put his lonely soul to it, smell the gourmet dinner on which Avis had lavished her late Sunday afternoon, that after the lingering brunch of bagels and cream cheese, the session on the yoga mat, the brisk autumn walk, the nap: the sounds and smells of an upper-middle class American family comforting themselves on Sunday night, dimming the lights, wintering in. He recalled his mother's soups, the farm-bought chickens roasting in the turquoise Magic Chef until their skins burnished and cracked, weeping fat, the clatter of Nonna's Mahjongg tiles, lamplight falling across the leaves of his illustrated *Treasure Island*.

The phone rang, he jumped. What he dreaded was not Avis, but Elliott, calling to deliver what the darling of a hard-nosed fringe of the county's Republican party like to refer cheerfully to as the *nuclear option*.

But no, not Elliott Fields.

"Hey, neighbor," the voice purred through loop after loop of Ganaego's drooping telephone lines, "guess what color underwear?"

~ ~ ~

She'd hired two goons, one short and bandy-legged, the other tall, with long arms and black Reeboks held together with duct tape. They wore *Harpers Ferry John Brown Wax Museum* tee-shirts and drove an eighteen-foot Penske. While Peter, this Monday morning, stood around trying to stay out of everybody's way, Joe and Ed—or was it Ed and Joe?—carried out on their shoulders the contents of the Halbrunners' twelve-year marriage, wedging furniture and boxes ingeniously into their truck. Randy Halbrunner was manning the register at one of his franchises, or perhaps he was sawing away at a take-out wench in a new crib—Fay was quick to pick up on interesting new terms—it hardly mattered. What mattered would be the look on his face when he came home to a house as empty as the day he bought it.

"Pity to miss that. We should set up a camera or something."

One aspect troubled Peter. "You're taking his *clothes?* What're you going to do with his clothes?"

"Throw them out back for the rabbits to nest in?" She looked at him. "Any ideas?"

"No, no," he demurred.

Teal, he discovered, interesting hue for undergarments. Last night, Sunday night, she'd sat on his chest, then, scrambling off like a Marine abandoning a hilltop, streaked out to check on her brood arranged in sleeping bags throughout the ranch house she'd rented, then returned and sat on his face. Four children, two of each gender. This morning, while the kids drowned their Fruit Loops in chocolate milk and complained about school, he stayed in the bedroom. "Why don't you come out? They keep saying, *Who's in Mommie's room?*"

"I don't know, old-fashioned, I guess."

"You're kind of big to hide?"

"No, really, I'm fine."

"You are so uncool, I love it."

Well, he was—uncool, that is. He knew that because people seemed to take a delight in telling him that. And maybe that was why, as indifferently as he behaved toward his first wife, quiet, bespectacled Vicky, as casually he was used by his second, he never cheated on either of them. Opportunity he had—what commercial traveler doesn't?—he just didn't. And so as the final truckload was packed, rendering the Halbrunner house, as realtors say, broom clean, Peter experienced the guilt of bedding someone else's spouse. At the rented house Fay told her movers to carry what didn't fit into the basement, where she serenely picked through the detritus of her marriage in search of the knives so that the kids wouldn't need to poke their fingers in the peanut butter.

Hours too late, Peter recollected he was supposed to meet Harvey Silverstein this morning. He called, apologized.

"Forget it," Silverstein rasped. "I had with your man Baldwin a fascinating conversation. I believe he may have discovered a whole new species, but, unfortunately, he seems to have blown the poor creature to bits, so we'll never know for certain."

"Just so long as it didn't look like something named Rover."

"Bit of a weird duck, isn't he, your Mr. Feeney? You might think about contracting with a legitimate security outfit, Peter. But we still have these papers—you home tonight?"

Fay Halbrunner surfaced waving a roll of toilet paper she'd also confiscated. "So," she called over, "when're we gonna go visit Jacob?"

He'd been instructed to be discreet. When the custody

Robert McKean

procedures were finalized, Harvey cautioned him that family court looks askance on lapses of judgment—which this could not be anything but. "Ah . . . lemme get back to you, Harv."

That afternoon Peter put the Weiner box in the trunk and drove them to the Sprague Hollow Nursing Home and Retirement Center. A new facility, way out in Rose Township, an unincorporated area of stony pastures and half-finished houses. Maybe it was only him, but it always seemed as if there were too many automotive repair shops in Rose Township, cement-block buildings placarded in Nehi and Quaker State Motor Oil signs, a scattering of cars huddled in front, mouths raised, fenders removed like cancerous cheeks. All of which served to make the modern anodized-aluminum buildings of the nursing home, which was situated in a shallow dell, look even more out of place. Between the buildings, where only recently cows would have nipped placidly at timothy grass, lay a garden, at its center a frog pond, as motionless as a pocket mirror. The garden was charming, although you seldom saw anyone taking advantage of it. The last time Peter was here he noticed but a single person, an old woman sitting on a bench, as if waiting for a bus. She cradled a lapful of black-eyed Susans. He had for Jessica Weiner some sympathy. He'd been faced with the same decision with his mother: Your heart tugs you one direction, your head another. He searched among the autumn-hued trees for the old woman and her flowers. Maybe she was inside, he thought. Or maybe the bus she was waiting for finally came.

Probably the bus. "What's that song?" he mused. " 'This Train Is

Bound for Glory'?"

"I hate trains." Fay scowled at a planter of withered mums. "Should we ask him if he wants his house back?"

Fay, in her teardown-party white toreador pants and blouse, smelled like a basket filled with apple blossoms. He gave her the Kodak envelope of snapshots and asked if she wanted him to carry in the box. Fay looked at the mildewed cardboard and shook her head. He understood that her interest in him was only a passing lark. His amusing girth, his mausoleum of a house whose rooms she wandered through naked, his puzzling lack of attachment to nearly anything, and, today, the hulking 1988 Cadillac Brougham. Gazing out over the transcontinental expanse of the Cadillac's dash, she laughed, *Randy would cream his pants over this! He'd put it on the roof of one of his garages!*

The reception desk in the lobby appeared to be permanently deserted. Fay, impatient, pointed at the bell on the counter. "Smack that again. You'd think everybody in here was dead."

~ ~ ~

"My ass is blistered, all this sitting around. That's what we do, we sit around on our wrinkled butts all day like baboons. Be great to get home, I need a good long soak."

The third time now that Jacob had said something to that effect. The first two times, when he thanked them for coming to get him, they passed the comments off. Pretended they hadn't heard them. Fay inquired about the food. When conversation about nursing home fare proved thin, Peter, reaching, asked Weiner whether he'd heard any good music recently. He knew Jacob liked to listen to his radio. They'd heard it while they waited in the hall for the nurse to get him dressed so they could wheel him to the solarium.

"Rubbish, doctored recordings."

"I was thinking of live broadcasts? The Saturday opera should be starting up soon."

"Wires and tubes." Jacob shifted in his wheelchair from one bony ham to the other. "Bah, they don't have tubes anymore. Probably don't even got wires. What're we doing farting around here for? Let's get going."

It was awkward. Since Fay had taken on the rescued photographs as her project, Peter elected to let her choose when to bring them out. Fay, however, was skittish around the old man. She shielded the Kodak envelope sticking up from her purse and made goggle eyes at him, as if he were something left on a shelf that she didn't quite understand. And Weiner did, in truth, look grim. Once he'd been a formidable man, short and square, a brawler's build one doesn't normally associate with musicians. The director of the music school, who'd seen Jacob play professionally, told Peter that when the conductor asked him to rise and take a bow for his solo in a Brahms piece, Weiner, in his prime, his feet planted as firmly as a Hessian soldier, gazed back at the audience without expression. *Jacob*, the director joked uneasily, *didn't require our applause*. Time had broadened his face and thickened his nose and shot it through with gleaming blood vessels. Age had also taken his wiry black hair and the proper middle-age potbelly he'd acquired.

By now, the old clarinetist's face was slack, haggard. His eyes, hooded beneath more sagging skin and shielded by thick lenses, had a hounded look—not unlike, Peter thought, the look of his blasted house.

"Sure you don't want anything?" The fourth time Fay had asked. "Juice? Pop?"

Weiner stared at the woman in her form-fitting toreador outfit. He twirled his finger at her that included Peter. "You two hitched?"

"Neighbors," Fay said, then quickly rethought that. *"Friends,* we're friends. You must get to know a *ton* of interesting people here? What d'you all talk about?"

"Trust me, lady, people here are potted plants. What's to talk about—who didn't show up for breakfast? They like to dispose of the stiffs at night, when no one's looking. But you can tell. You see them pushing furniture into the hall, you know somebody's bought the farm." He peered at Peter. "Got any of those candy bars, bub?" ,

Jacob loved Heath bars. Peter brought out the five he'd bought. Weiner lunged for them. "Gimme here." He clawed back the wrapper on one and started chewing. Chocolate leaked from the corner of his mouth and bled through his bristled whiskers. There were bitten-off halves and quarters of stale Heath bars strewn across his nightstand. You sometimes saw stumps down in the bedclothes.

He held out the mauled, wet end to Fay. "Wanna bite?"

"No, no." She shivered. "Go ahead."

Peter's mother, before she stopped eating entirely, looked feral in the way she slurped at her bowls of food: You so much do not want

Robert McKean

it to come to this. Peter pretended an interest in the six wan ficus on the window ledge lifting their tropical leaves to the wan northern light. He weighed mentioning something about the beauties of autumn, but thought of Weiner's hacked down arborvitae and decided: *Somebody has to say something meaningful to this old man today.*

"So, Jacob, have you heard from Jessica recently? She's in Boston, right?"

"First thing I'm gonna do when I get home," Weiner confirmed. "Clear the air. I'll probably go up and see her. You want me to ask for a bag? I don't think I got my suitcase here, I can't remember seeing it? They'd steal the coffee outta your cup if you let 'em." He squirmed around in his seat. "Here, lemme call someone."

"Well, speaking of that," Peter said, "we're not really . . ."

It was then that Fay produced the pictures. Her nervous fumbling to pry the yellow envelope loose from where it had gotten snagged on the zipper of her purse and slide out the photographs spared Peter from completing his sentence, but left her with one of her own. "Hey, look, we found these in . . ."

Peter had never been certain what effect these scenes from long ago would have on Weiner, but assumed that Jacob would enjoy seeing them. The old man, puzzled by the wad of snapshots thrust at him, dropped the Heath bar into his lap and pawed through the first few photos without looking at them closely. Maybe he couldn't see them very well. He had to hold each within inches of his thick glasses and squint. But once he'd begun to grasp what he'd been handed, he returned to the front of the pack and started again, lingering over the photos of his young wife in her knitted cap and boxy oxfords. It occurred to Peter that the photos might have been taken the day they passed papers on the house. Wouldn't that be something? There had to be a fourth person—to take the shots that included Jacob and his wife and baby. The realtor? But the pictures could also date from some other significant day, birthday, anniversary? The day they brought Jessica home from the hospital? Or maybe a day of no particular consequence. He was on the verge of asking, to stir the old man into reminiscing, when Weiner pulled the photographs away from his face and glared at Fay.

"Where'd you get these? These are mine."

"They were in your house, in a box."

"You were in my house? What were you doing in my house?" Fay, alarmed, appealed to Peter. *"Answer me!"* Weiner bellowed. "What were you doing in my house?"

"Jacob," Peter broke in, understanding that *this* was what had to be said, "your house was sold. It's being torn down."

"Nobody sold my house, whaddya talking about?"

"Jessica wasn't planning to live there, you know that."

"She sold my house?"

"She's in Boston, Jessica, right? Since nobody was living there, it made sense to—"

"I live there!"

"You live *here,* Jacob. You live here now."

"The hell I do!"

Robert McKean

The old music teacher, struggling to crawl out of the wheelchair, hauled on the armrests and succeeded in lifting himself a few inches before the chair began to roll out from under him. Peter lunged for the handles, as the photos—most of them—along with the Heath bars, scattered across the floor. "Jacob, please . . . "

"Get outta my way, I gotta get home!"

"This is your home," Peter repeated. "You live *here* now, Jacob. The house is being demolished. This is where you live—*here."*

"You can't sell somebody's house out from under them!" Weiner, still a strong man, wrenched his wheelchair free of Peter's restraining hand. He wriggled around in the seat and tried again to lift himself. Spittle ran down his chin. "You can't do that!"

"We didn't do it."

"Who did?"

He did not wish to invoke Jessica's name again. "It just got sold, Jacob, it had to be . . . disposed of."

Weiner shoved his glasses back up his nose, smearing chocolate across his cheek. He tried a third time to lift himself. Exhausted by now, though, he sank back. He clutched at the remaining photographs in his lap. "This is my daughter's doing, isn't it?"

Peter stared at the palsied hands that had been able to produce a run of honeyed Mozart arpeggios, crooked fingers that could negotiate the virtuoso dexterity that Brahms demanded of his instrumentalists. "There was nobody living there, Jacob. The house was empty, the yard wasn't being tended—what else was there to do? It's what's paying for your room here."

The visit soon ended. Weiner, angered, confused, muttering obscenities in outrage and disbelief, went on arguing, but with less and less vehemence. And once he did seem to grasp that he no longer had a home to return to—once that awful truth had soaked in him—he switched tactics. He pleaded with Peter to take him to Boston.

"I'll pay you, whatever you want, let's just go—*now!*"

"Jacob, we can't do that."

"I gotta talk to Jessica. None of this makes sense."

"Jacob, I'm sorry." Peter was irritated with himself for using the tone of voice you would employ with a child. "We have to go now. Would you like me to push you back to your room?" The old man shook his head, and Peter asked again in the same childish voice. "I'd be happy to push you back?"

"We'll come again," Fay promised sweetly.

As Peter and Fay withdrew, stepping softly across the solarium as if they were afraid of waking somebody, Weiner began to sob. Peter turned to look at the old man hunched in his wheelchair, hands cradling his face. In his lap were the photographs and the Heath bars that Fay had hastily scooped up. Peter thought of a hollow-ribbed hound trailing after a lonely man in a trench coat with torn pockets, the smell of foul pipe tobacco lingering in the rainy night air. The world is heartless.

He walked back to the weeping man. "Jacob, let me push you to your room."

~ ~ ~

Robert McKean

Peter tarried at the nurses' station. He wanted to let the staff know that Jacob was upset, maybe in some way to apologize for being the one who upset him. A nurse, interrupted in her study of her computer screen, politely heard him out, then shrugged a shoulder. "He's moody, but that's the way he is. He gets mixed up, he thinks someone's coming to get him, and then he gets agitated when they don't."

"Are there musical events for the residents—concerts, live music, musicians who come here, chamber music, things like that?"

"Wednesdays, sing-along."

"That's it?"

The nurse regarded him as if she hadn't quite made the adjustment from her screen to his face and perhaps didn't wish to. "Wednesdays," she repeated in case he'd failed to take in that simple fact. " 'Home, Home, on the Range' is a popular favorite. When I'm done here, I'll go down and check in on Mr. Weiner. Maybe he'll want a sedative? Is there anything else I can help you with today?"

Fay, orphaned in the huge sedan, did not look at Peter as he climbed in. *"That,"* she announced, "was *not* a lot of fun."

He hadn't managed to apologize to the nurse, so he apologized to Fay. "I'm sorry, I should've given you some advance warning. It's sad, terribly, terribly sad."

"I don't think it's sad—I think it's a crime. How could his daughter do that to him?"

Peter tried to imagine Jacob Weiner singing "Home, Home, on the Range." About as visualizable as Jessica Weiner washing the old man's shorts and pinning them on a line to dry. "What was she supposed to do? He nearly burned down his house, any number of times, wasn't eating, wasn't taking his meds. There were reports he was seen in his yard without any clothes. You know, when you start weeding the garden *au naturel* there aren't many good options left?"

Peter reached out to comfort his new lover, but Fay retreated to her side of the car. "Take me home. I wanna be there when my kids get off the bus."

Turning into his street, he saw Avis's car in his drive, the cobalt-blue fender of the Mercedes convertible and sleepy sloe-eye of its tail lamp. His heart leapt: a rare mid-week babysitting assignment? Not likely. Surprise visits from attorneys—even ones you used to help out of their brassieres—seldom lead to auspicious outcomes. Accordingly, as Peter stepped into his living room he was not surprised to discover but a single person, his former wife, whose face told him everything he needed to know.

"You should change your locks." Avis blew a soft shaft of cigarette smoke to the side. "Didn't your ambulance-chasing lawyer tell you that? I always advise my clients after a divorce to change their locks."

She'd come directly from work. Beside the polished points of her high heels sat the crocodile-leather briefcase, nickel hardware, special padding for her computer. Most importantly, it opened from the top. That had been crucial to the graduate because that was the kind of briefcase that attorneys at the courthouse carried. The mouth yawned

Robert McKean

open: Peter was reminded of Captain Hook and the crocodile who swallowed the clock and ticked.

"You've looked in the garage."

Avis smiled. Her dark eyes behind her glasses shone with pleasure. "You have wonderful intuition, Peter. You've wasted your life selling sewer pipe. But it was very thoughtful of you to keep the smashed bicycle. I thought of taking it home with me, but I have several very clear jpegs of it. They'll do."

"I'm sorry." Whom today had he not apologized to? "But it wasn't her fault. She was doing her kid thing, I was busy yakking to our new neighbors, and—"

"*Your* new neighbors. Listen: I have something to tell you." Avis extinguished her cigarette. She was keyed up about something, something big. He knew his ex-wife, he could sense something coming. She recrossed her legs and leaned forward, hardening herself. "She's not doing well at Bright Ridge, you know that, or you know that now, it's not a—"

"What about intensive tutoring?" He butted into her sentence, broadened his voice and laid it on thickly enough to plaster over whatever she was about to spring on him. "Now, I'm only thinking off the top of my head here, Avis, but I—"

"Peter, shut up. I didn't come all the way over here to talk about tutoring. It's way past tutoring. Bright Ridge is not a good fit for her, even though it's the best school in the valley."

"It should be, given the tuition."

"And don't start in with me about money!" Avis's face, when she was provoked, flooded with blood. "You think that because you—"

"All right, I'm sorry," he said, genuinely sorry this time. "I have an idea: Why don't we let her come back here? I think that's been a major part of the problem all along. She misses her old friends, Mindy and that other girl, you know, Ashley? She's a year or—"

"Would you please shut up and let me finish?" Avis lifted her hair from her eyes with the side of her hand, a gesture dating from the peroxide-blond college girl, even though now the hair was fashion-model styled, spray-hardened, and did not need to be lifted anywhere. Just as she reclaimed the floor, her briefcase began singing. *Bizarre,* Peter thought. If he lived to be a hundred, he was never going to become accustomed to ladies' purses and men's pockets spontaneously launching into song.

Avis lunged into her briefcase to strangle her phone.

"I've been talking with another school, a boarding school." She surfaced with something, a brochure. "It seems perfect. They've got a terrific academic program, you're going to love it. A judge on the Superior Court—someone I've gotten very clubby with—has ties to it. Judge Davis, you don't happen to know him, d'you? His reference is going to be critical, I'm counting on him to put us over. It's in Connecticut. Here, I brought some literature so—"

"No!" He'd been steeling himself for some kind of bombshell. You knew it was coming, it was like hornets buzzing in her. But the enormity of this caught him so flatfooted that he was at a loss. He fended

Robert McKean

off her brochure. "She's not going off to some school in Connecticut! For heavens' sakes—this is completely balmy!"

"Would you please shut up!"

"She's not going anywhere, Avis, and that's that!"

"Listen to me!"

"Is this something Elliott's cooked up?"

"This has nothing to do with Elliott!"

A locomotive bearing down on him. A locomotive a minute ago he didn't even suspect the existence of. "You can't do this, I mean you can't even *legally* do it—not without my approval, and I won't give it, I won't!"

"Either she's going there with it," Attorney Longstreet declared, "or she's going there without it." She tossed the brochure on the coffee table and plunged her hand back into the jaws of her briefcase to dredge up her phone. Jabbed a button and waved the tiny glowing screen at him. "Just how close to being killed was she, by the way?"

A small pink thing swam in his eyes. "I made a careless mistake." Peter pulled back from the memory: the plaster- and lathe-gorged teeth of the bucket, the child lying as still as death in the long grass. "It's not fair to punish Jeanette for my mistakes."

"It *isn't* punishment. Will you get that out of your head?" Avis snapped the phone off. "How can being sent to one of New England's most prestigious schools be called *punishment?* It has nothing to do with punishment."

"Then I don't understand. It must be Elliott."

Avis, annoyed, frustrated, turned away. She assessed the living room, like a prospective buyer might, but with a far different set of eyes than the eyes that took in this room fifteen years ago, older, more sophisticated, less likely to be bewitched by the fussy chattel of the antique upper middle-classes, fringed lampshades, velvet floor-length curtains, Lalique vases. "Peter, what're you doing with yourself? This place is falling down around your ears—it's like some sort of time warp in here."

"I've been thinking about having the couch reupholstered."

Which she took for humor, even if that was not his intent. Avis granted him a rueful laugh. But as much as he'd like to believe that this might signify a break in the tension, he understood that this one-time purchasing department filing clerk was a lawyer now, a real lawyer, and for lawyers there are no breaks in the tension, only pauses to regroup and return to the attack. "Will you at least hear me out? Will you do that much?"

The invoice for her little laugh. "I'm happy to listen—as long as I get to speak, too?"

"Thank you, I'm deeply moved by your kind and generous counteroffer." She made a classic Avis Longstreet face, sour, persecuted. "This is going to take a lot of lifting. We're going to have to go there and spend real time with them. They'll assess Jeanette, they'll want to talk with you and understand something about the divorce, they're going to want detailed financials. It's a very complex, very carefully orchestrated, and very competitive process. And for all that—even with Judge Davis's backing—they may turn us down. Peter, I'm going to need your help on this, Jeanette's going to need your help. Believe me, this is the best thing for her. This will be good for her, and I'm asking for your help—sincerely and politely."

"Ask Elliott's mother. Maybe the Connecticut headmaster is a fellow DAR sister."

"Oh, fuck you." Avis lifted hair out of her eyes that still did not require lifting. "What's the matter with you? We've always been good at parenting!"

"She's ten years old? What is this—David Copperfield?"

"No one"—Attorney Longstreet took possession of her crocodile briefcase and came to her feet—"is saying that but you. But hear me out: If you force me into court, I'll squeeze you out of her life entirely."

"You won't do that—you'll hurt me but you won't hurt her, you *won't*."

A dare deliberately laid. Peter, from the depths of an armchair whose springs long ago gave up the ghost, observed his former spouse weighing his challenge. She was bluffing, he was certain. Avis looked at the room, once fine and elegant, a place of wit and conversation over cocktails and sherry, and scowled. "At least throw a window open!" she cried out, inexplicably on the verge of tears and astonishing him yet again. "This *isn't* Elliott's idea! This has *nothing* to do with him! This is *my* idea, and, damn it, I need your help!"

~ ~ ~

The Plan came to him deep in the Tanqueray.

In the years of his limited drinking the materials science half of him had speculated whether the liquor in the butler's pantry was holding its alcoholic content. The cut-glass decanters with their pear-shaped stoppers, the stubby scotches and gins, the slender cordials lined up like reservists waiting to be summoned back to duty. Well, the eleven-year-old vodka, he was now comfortably able to attest, was fully up to snuff, and the Tanqueray seemed every bit as corking. He took the opportunity of ordering out to Aziz's Pizzas, four large pies, and fishing from the family's antiquated record collection what clarinet pieces he could identify.

A little traveling music, please.

And at some point he did begin ranging through the silent rooms. In the closed-off master bedroom suite he discovered that mice had noodled their way into his parents' things, nesting among his mother's silk camisoles and his father's ironed and folded pajamas. Standing before the deep closet, which blossomed with the scents of Olivia's face powder and cedar from Steve's shoe trees, Peter pondered the lives that were used up and exhausted in the old garments. Why would you kill yourself over a business mistake? His father's investment in the trucking firm was a rash gamble, yes, but it was reversible, fixable. It *was* fixed. Steve's suicide took him and all but took his wife, Peter's poor mother, who never recovered, and became in its senselessness the central mystery in Peter's life: *Why, Papa, why?*

Stockbrokers in 1929 leapt from ledges, didn't they?

Yes, but that was little solace. He'd continued his policy of

Robert McKean

apologizing—since it was working so well—spending time in his daughter's room telling her stuffed creatures how sorry he was to be responsible for their abandonment. And it was here, as he gazed through the wavy old panes at Jacob Weiner's sucker-punched house, that the Plan came to him. Could he do it? Could it be done? Was he the man to do it? In the garage Peter uncovered the block and tackle a previous owner had employed to hoist the monstrous straight-eights from his Packards when they threw a rod. The pulleys were arthritic, but appeared serviceable. Rummaging through eighty years of clutter, he found a hardwood dolly from the clay works, a quilted furniture pad, a coil of thickly plaited rope, and—blessing from Apollo, god of light—a kerosene lantern from his two-week Boy Scout career. Was there kerosene? There was. Was the lamp's mantle still viable?

He pressurized the lamp and struck a match—*smacko!*

Smug with pleasure, he carried his stepladder over to the attractive fence he shared with the Halbrunners. He wiggled the dolly up the fence and over, heaved across block and tackle and rope, then paused: The treacherous northwest passage across the sharp twined ends of the wire promoted thoughtful strategizing. Leaving the lantern, which burned with an intense ball of white light, he jogged back to the house for the gin and an unopened Cutty Sark and a fresh pizza. Spying his hat, he fitted that urbane topper on his head. Back at the fence, he lobbed— somewhat more gently—the two bottles into Jacob Weiner's thick grass, then climbed and delicately let the flat pizza box fall flatly. Paused a final time. *What else?* What else does a man on a stepladder in the middle of the night need?

Courage, he thought, and over the fence he went.

Once inside, he stowed his ladder and collected his campaign matériel. Only foreseeable hitch was his inexperience operating a block and tackle. Threading the double pulleys was not in the Boy Scout manual—or at least in the first ten pages. But the soundness of the Plan seemed unassailable. People winch motors, they winch boats, they've been winching their camels out of the mud since the Pharaohs, haven't they? Holding his lamp aloft like a blazing ball of truth, he wended his way around to the rear and surveyed Jacob's Norway forest. Selecting a good-sized specimen aligned with the back door, he yoked one pulley to it with a spectacular Boy Scout knot, then confronted the house sunk in its doldrums. From the mouths of the windows exhaled a foul odor of wet plaster and decay. He had the wistful notion of hitching his tackle to the house itself, to yank it about and set the woeful thing straight on its foundations. Or maybe bring it into his yard?

"Ah, Jacob," he told a tree, "you're only one step ahead of the rest of us."

Pinning the second pulley and dolly and pad under an arm, taking up his lamp and paying out the rope behind, he slipped into Jacob's doomed kitchen and crept down the hall to the living room. He heard nocturnal things. A bat, bewildered by the brilliance of the light, brushed his hat as it silently flopped its wings and retired upstairs to bed. The Plan rested on a pivotal assumption: that he was strong enough. The piano legs would be no problem. The legs of grand pianos pull out of

Robert McKean

their sockets—they aren't fastened. And Jacob's piano was only a baby grand, a sweet old Ivers & Pond on which Oak Grove Music School's stern, humorless, head clarinet teacher would, if in a sufficiently frisky mood, bang out raunchy burlesque hall tunes.

Most worrisome was the integrity of the floor.

Peter, back to the wall, edged around the perimeter of the room. And for sure, the floorboards complained. He scooted his dolly and pad under the belly of the piano, then rounded the side. He'd watched professional movers—in the plural, never a single man—do this. But with house and belongings destined for the Ganaego landfill, what did he, or the piano, stand to lose? He positioned himself opposite the flat side of the baby grand, bent his knees and embraced the instrument. Summoning his weightlifter's strength, bellowing as weightlifters in the Olympics will do, he hefted the piano an inch and spilled it over onto the dolly.

Sort of.

The frame of the instrument shuddered like an elephant thrown to its side, and a leg—not his—shattered. The soundboard gave forth a chord of such mournful dissonance and dismay as never heard before in Western music. Thrown back, Peter gazed at the baby grand teetering on its dolly: *That thing topples*, he thought wildly, *it's taking both floor and me with it*. He clutched the huge instrument in a mutual death hug and steadied it. There were, in the Plan, a *Part A* and a *Part B*. So obsessed with *A* had he been that he'd not had time to think through *B*. He supposed he might skip *B* and endeavor to maneuver the dolly himself. But that would involve two heavy weights crossing the floor simultaneously, something he'd rather avoid.

No, *ex cathedra*, it was settled: on to *B*.

He excused himself to locate Jacob's first-floor lav. Even if the plumbing no longer functioned and the house stood condemned, you cannot pee in somebody's living room. Then he rebalanced the piano on the dolly, popped off its two sound legs, unwound the rope, and fastened the second pulley by its hook to the dolly. Testing his threading, he tossed the end of the rope through the shattered side window.

A little traveling music, Sammy . . .

Standing outside, sopping in sweat, Peter, keeping a close eye through the window on the piano, planted his feet and tugged on his rope in one direction and, glory be, Jacob Weiner's piano crept forward an inch in the other direction. Pulled again, piano moved again. It was altogether a remarkable sight: In stupefaction, in awe, he watched the harp-shaped fin of the piano gliding across the shadowy living room like a ghost ship. You expected to see skeletons with pails and scrub brushes amidships, tiny red eyes peering from portholes. The house groaned, as if its heart were being wrested from its chest; a chimney brick came stuttering down; and Peter fretted that at any given second Jacob's piano would simply disappear like a magician's assistant. But gingerly, delicately, with a certain lightness of touch Horowitz might appreciate, he winched the piano hand over hand across the room and into the hall and down that short boulevard to the kitchen. From there, with things on sounder flooring, he blundered in and unfastened the block and tackle

Robert McKean

and wobbled the piano on the dolly out the door. He bumped it over the threshold, across the stoop, and into the yard, where a caster sank into the soft earth and the Ivers & Pond flopped over, butter-side up, into Jacob Weiner's unraked leaves.

Peter roared, "Hallelujah! King of kings and lord of lords!"

And it *was* interesting: A piano doesn't really need legs. As he concentrated on his fat, ring-less fingers moving over keys old enough to be real ivory, Peter was put in mind of Beethoven, who sawed the legs off his pianos. He was also, unfortunately, put in mind of Avis's brochure, lying on his coffee table like a warrant from family-court: expensive coated paper, smart, punchy copy, photographs of seriously fulfilled children around impressively broad seminar tables. What was it that those young Connecticut scholars were so trenchantly discussing? Homer? Machiavelli? Schopenhauer? Most likely, he decided, bending into his keys, they were child actors hired for the purposes of making the brochure. He'd always been a big fan of Jack Teagarden's boozy voice—and Billie Holliday's, too—and so it was here then, sometime after Ganaego's lopsided moon had set over the sleeping homes of Oak Grove, his lantern glowing like Liberace's candelabra, Cutty Sark and pizza beside him, that Peter Sanguedolce serenaded the neighborhood with surprisingly decent covers of "In the Still of the Night," "Rockin' Chair," "Stormy Weather," "Summertime," "Stardust Melody," and "Somebody to Watch Over Me." Now, he didn't have the melodies for these lovely standards infallibly beneath his right hand, but he knew his voice and could provide his light baritone solid harmonic chordal support.

~ ~ ~

And there is where he is, sitting cross-legged in his lion-colored Borsalino before Jacob Weiner's rescued piano, his plangent voice rattling through the leafless maples, when the Ganaego PD come swarming across the property like so many fulminating blue devils.

You Gotta Know the Territory

"They're wasting their time, Peter. They can't make any substantive changes in the girl's life without your concurrence. We'll go back to court. More coffee? Get enough to eat?"

Once upon a time Harvey Silverstein's office was on the third floor of the union building. His Palladian windows overlooked Roosevelt Avenue, Ganaego's central commercial street that terminated at the armed guards behind the steelworks' main gates. That bustling street: buses engulfed in diesel smoke chuffing into the curb before the Company Store; slope-shouldered sedans and rust-eaten pickups mired in a thrice-a-day riptide that only added more soot to the scrim of soot that already ladened Ganaego's sulfurous air; sidewalks congested with shoppers and laborers clutching loaf-shaped lunch pails. Harvey held on to his office after mill and union disappeared in Reagan's Morning in America. But with the devastating onset of his second wife's illness, he boxed up books and papers and abandoned town for an unheated three-season porch attached to his house.

"Lawyers don't usually provide breakfast as part of their

services, thank you, Harvey." Peter shifted painfully. A night contorted on a police cot had done nothing for his back. He needed to go home and shower and shave and change his name. He set his cup beside the foot-long stuffed lizard that had been an eternal fixture of the eternal disorder of the attorney's desk. "What do you do for heat? Avis wore fingerless gloves when she worked in Purchasing. We never could get the heat in that wing to work right."

"Sweaters." Harvey cracked a window so he could fire up one of the three cigars he was rationed a day. "Actually fleece — great stuff fleece."

"If we go to court, we know what they're going to say about me — most of which is true."

"Last night ain't gonna help."

"And the bike accident?"

"You know, I hate to see you this way, Peter? You'll pardon me for speaking frankly — this isn't you. This isn't the Peter Sanguedolce I know. Be that as it may, with the offended parties not being overly concerned with your trespassing — I take it you already know your new neighbors pretty well? — I don't think last night is necessarily going to kill us. We can argue that this move is not in the child's best interests and that a couple of indiscretions on your part don't disqualify you from sharing rights. And I have to say that I don't quite get it, to begin with? Why is Avis so hot on packing off her kid to Connecticut? Seems kinda unmotherly? You ask me, this has Elliott Fields' fingerprints on it, but I can't begin to plumb the man."

Robert McKean

"It *was* kind of a strange performance—on Avis's part? It leads me to wonder if something's up with her and Elliott, something not quite right. But it could also be as they say. Jeanette's not thriving where she is—grades, friendships, all that stuff."

"East Stanton Junction? I can imagine how catty that can get. I trust they're assuming the money for this new school is going to come from you?"

To avoid that question, Peter pointed at a painting on the wall. "You know, I believe I recognize that tree?"

Harvey had taken up painting. He and Lloyd Ross, the fellow who owned the art supplies store, would drive out to Biddleford Park and paint landscapes. The attorney appraised his tree. "Lloyd has a conflict of interest in encouraging me. Those little tubes of paint are pricey. But it makes Jenny happy, me and Lloyd traipsing off like Vincent and Paul to smoke our cigars in the woods. Gets me out of her hair."

"How's she doing?"

To avoid *his* question, Harvey fell to carefully rounding the ash of his cigar on the lip of the tray. "D'you know there's different brushes for painting different things? Lloyd sold me a brush for painting clouds."

"Does it work?"

"I can't say I'm seeing much improvement in my clouds, but Lloyd tells me to have patience. Easy for him to say—his clouds always look super. There's no happy ending here, with Jenny? Not in the cards. The good news is that Lloyd and I have discovered that you don't actually have to have a tree in front of you to paint it."

Concerning Harvey's wife, there seemed nothing more to say. "My guess," Peter said, going back to his own problems, "is that Avis sees this as a natural evolution. Lower-middle class, upper-middle class, switch to the tony side of the river and blue-blood husband, now New England boarding school. Horses are next, I suppose. And yes, I'm sure they're assuming I'll cover tuition fees, no matter how astronomical. Which we know I will, somehow or other."

"Why do we know that? I say they should have some skin in this Connecticut plan, too."

"I'm not sure what their finances are. I sometimes wonder if all this social climbing isn't held together with staples and masking tape. But I don't pump Jeanette for family gossip. If we go to court, she's going to have to testify, right?"

"They'll want to hear from her. Courts take an interest in what the kids have to say."

"I can't let her do that."

The attorney relocated his stuffed lizard from one stack of papers to another. "Peter, sometimes even the children have to be sent into battle."

"I can't do it. I mean, I didn't say yes or no to Avis, but if it comes to a dogfight I can't make Jeanette a part of it."

"But she's not going to want to go away to this school, anyway, right? What kid wants to be sent off to boarding school? So it's in her best interests to talk to the court. It's what she'll want, staying here."

"I can't force that sort of Sophie's choice on her: Choose

Robert McKean

between your mother and father. That's not how adults are supposed to act."

At which Harvey Silverstein smiled, his famous—famous in Ganaego—smile: wide, raffish, toothy. "As soon as adults start acting like they're supposed to, I'm out of a job. It happens, son, families hack at each other like Roman gladiators. In that courthouse it happens every day of the week."

Peter scowled at the grass stains on his pants. "Harvey, I need to go home—I'm sore and I stink. Can I use your phone to call a cab?"

Harvey shifted his lizard from the second stack of papers to a third. He pondered this redeployment, then overruled it and returned the lizard to its second stack. "Let me fetch my keys. I can drop you on my way to my daughter's. She's re-found her religion. I promised I'd come by and help her observe *Sukkot*. I confess I don't know beans about it personally, but if it makes her happy, then it makes me happy, too."

"Seems like you're in the business of making women happy these days."

"Good business to be in."

As Peter set himself to heave his sore body out of Silverstein's car before his house, Harvey caught his sleeve. "Peter, whatever these Connecticut fees are going to be, you need to bear in mind that you're not absolutely made of money. It's all the more reason to start talking seriously about selling the industrial property. Jimmy Boswell *is* interested, I know that for a fact."

"I'll think about it, Harvey, how's that?"

"In the meantime I recommend a bare minimum of communication between you and Avis. Maybe I should be the one who calls her? I'll tell her the answer to Connecticut is no—no, for the time being. That'll give us some running room."

This was probably what Harvey considered saying in his office, before the lizard cast a contrary vote against it. "I think Avis and I have to keep the channels open. I dread how all this must be soaking into Jeanette. How can she not feel that she's somehow responsible for our mess?"

"All right, just watch what you say."

That evening Peter stood at the edge of his property staring through the fence into Jacob Weiner's yard. Most of his shenanigans took place on the far side, so from here very little of that was visible, his block and tackle, Jacob's handicapped piano amid the leggy trunks of the maples, even the Sydney's fedora, lost somewhere. He noted his stepladder beneath the shrubs and the Tanqueray resting in the high grass like a lone, last October picnicker. Fay Halbrunner, summoned to the police station, had got to laughing so hard that, hands pressed to her face, tears wetting her fingers, she'd collapsed on a bench and thoroughly annoyed the captain. Despite his scruples about his new neighbor—and who was he to have scruples?—he did like people who know how to laugh, especially women who laughed with their bellies. And for certain, far better it'd been that they reached Fay rather than her husband, who would have had him impressed into indenture as a grease monkey. Tomorrow, he decided, he'd send flowers to Fay and, while he was at it,

Robert McKean

a bouquet to Jenny, too, Harvey's courageous wife.

Have I turned into a buffoon?

That was what Harvey meant. The guy in the clown suit whose nose honks when you squeeze it. He'd been a crackerjack salesman because he was good at reading people. But that same clairvoyance had never extended to himself: He'd never been good at sorting out Peter Sanguedolce. He spotted his other new neighbors, the mourning doves, creatures that for better or for worse stay faithful all their lives. He recalled the bat in Jacob's living room that had brushed his hat: the tiny beast's swoopy wings carrying it up the staircase—on its way to a rendezvous in the Weiners' closet? He loved life, the fecundity of it, the hilarious absurdity of it. Squirrels plucking Jacob's maple samara seeds off his garage roof and gnawing on them, chipmunks rolling rotten apples as big as they beneath his porch, woodpeckers circling the boles of the lilacs tapping out a Morse Code message that only they and the bugs understood. But truth be told, he loved every bit as much going to the T&V or Lowe's and losing himself in the multitude of products produced by man. Over his sales manager's desk he had pinned a quote from Thoreau: *For commerce is really as interesting as nature.* He loved it all, even Dinty Moore stew spooned cold into his mouth. At Harvey's he'd signed more papers, every signature, every scrap of legal *ignis fatus* that disappeared into the attorney's briefcase bringing him a step closer to the final disposition of the clay works. And so, where did that leave him? What was he supposed to do?

Well, there was an answer to that: It's garbage night.

Peter walked back to the house and filled a black plastic bag with empty bottles and stale pizza and rolled their two bins, one after the other, down to the curb. Then he took the broken pink bicycle in his arms, carried it down, and leaned it against one of the bins. Maybe somebody would want it.

~ ~ ~

The earth turns on its belly.

In the lofty oaks of Oak Grove, the final breath of Indian summer rattles the leathery Quercus leaves, the ones most bitterly opposed to falling, and shakes off a season's harvest of acorns to ping the roofs and hoods of Oak Grove's dearly financed vehicles. Color leaches from chemically treated lawns, a neighbor holds a garden hose span by span overhead draining summer water from its coils, the cedar waxwings that rested in the crab apple tree on their journey north in the spring return on their journey south to rest a day in the crab again, full of stories, and Peter wakes to a drizzle falling like hatching in a lithograph and asks himself, *Do I still love Avis?* What are they to do about Jeanette? What kind of monsters ship their babies off to boarding school? How will he bear it? Winter afternoons that close in at four, nights that feather the panes with blue ice, mornings that creep toward a lusterless mid-day that never seems to arrive. Thoughts—hardly questions since they have no answers—that, as he broods on this shivery morning, stand in queue as if they were a gaggle of tax collectors beneath large black umbrellas before his door. But his thinking in these matters has evolved: You must do what is right.

Robert McKean

Even lonely men in pajamas know that.

He ate a heartier breakfast than customary, then shaved meticulously. Of the two suits he owned that still fit him, the double-breasted Brooks Brothers chalk stripe was the finer, the more handsome. He brushed it and knotted and re-knotted a tie hand-stitched in Italy sixty years ago until he achieved with the delicate silk a satisfying Windsor knot. His route took him through Crocker Farms, where Avis and he'd had their first apartment, and then through commercial Ganaego, what remained of it. Idling at a stoplight, he watched a man who had bumped an aging step-side pickup over the curb and parked it in a rubbled lot. He was lifting muddy, fire-twisted piping into the bed of the truck. He wore overalls and a black felt hat and seemed oblivious of the cold rain matting the curly hair on his bare shoulders. Yesterday's *Chronicle* informed its readers that on this same rainy morning Saddam Hussein's trial in Baghdad was to commence, that children in Iraq were being blown to pieces, that the earthquake in Kashmir had likely killed tens of thousands of people, that upwards half of all species existing on earth may well be extinct by 2100. Peter, who'd lived a fortunate life, had come to call what the fellow in the Snuffy Smith hat was doing *urban farming*. The rear gate of his pickup looked to have been fashioned from one side of a baby's crib. Was that true? He strained across the steering wheel to establish this critical fact. But the motorist behind, uninterested in urban husbandry, laid the heel of his hand on his horn.

Piss off, Peter thought.

East Stanton Junction lay across the river, a few miles south of Ganaego. Peter crossed the gray corpse of the Ohio, as dimpled this morning as a perforated sheet of tin, and gazed longingly at a Lebanese bakery he passed. The shop boasted three round tables and smelled of pistachio and honey and yeast dough so tender you could sleep on it. But not today. He pulled his old Cadillac into a narrow parking lot and then a very tight squeeze into one of the berths allocated to the law practice of Fields & Longstreet. Elliott and Avis's offices had once been a frozen food locker, something of which neither partner much cared to be reminded.

He had two purposes for his visit.

One: surely, they could locate a good progressive school somewhere closer than Connecticut? Place the point of your compass on Ganaego, PA, and scribe a circle that encloses eastern Connecticut and you also enclose Washington, Philadelphia, New York, Toronto, and all but Chicago: Had anyone bothered to search for schools in a more immediate vicinity? Also, he wanted to promote his idea of intensive tutoring. The child was intelligent, creative, alert to the world in ways not all children are. What she was not good at was finding her enthusiasms in other people's designs. And that was something she came by honestly: Neither Avis nor he had plotted their lives out in conventional patterns. Well, Avis hadn't until she fell in with Elliott Fields, who appeared to have never even momentarily considered taking a road less traveled. As Peter stepped up to the receptionist's desk, he was thinking of the stuffed creatures on his daughter's bed, their accusing eyes. That was his other purpose: to pry Jeanette free for the evening to talk with her. What did

Robert McKean

she want? You'd think they had visited enough unhappiness on the girl. The last thing she needed was another upheaval in her life. But this was how his thinking had evolved: If going away to a school was something she might want to try, to test her wings, as it were, then, heaven save him, that was what he would help her do.

But first he had to find out.

"Are you sure you have an appointment with Attorney Longstreet? Your name again, please?"

The receptionist was new, new to him. When Peter repeated his name along with his connection to Avis, the young woman, flustered, assumed it must have been her fault for failing to record his appointment with her boss, who was at the courthouse today.

"No, no, not your fault." Peter took a wild guess. "By any chance, is that your bike chained up outside?"

She looked up in mild astonishment. "How did you know?"

"You look like someone who'd pull on her rain gear and pedal her bike through the storm. We have a good bicycle shop over our way, Two Wheels and a Dream?"

"Oh, I know that store—they have really wicked bikes!"

He made it a practice to befriend administrative staff. "I'm sorry, I didn't call ahead. Foolish of me. Of course she's busy, she's a busy person."

"They do recess for lunch? Maybe she'll be free then? I have to tell you, sir—that is *sooooo* pretty, your tie."

Just then Elliott exited his office, nose in a sheaf of papers. To

Peter, his ex-wife's new husband always looked like he'd neglected to comb his hair and shave. Elliott's lantern jaw, ten in the morning, was felted with coarse whiskers, and his short dark hair, curling up from an untamed cowlick, shot out everywhere like an over-fertilized crew cut. Were the man's testosterone levels that high? Glancing up, Elliott switched on his Pepsodent smile. "Pete, hey, what a surprise! Good to see you, pal!"

He pumped Peter's hand and complimented him even more effusively than the receptionist had on his paisley tie, which meant that Elliott—a man not given to spooning over another man's sartorial choices—knew almost certainly that Peter was here before he'd stepped out of his office, the nose-in-the-papers charade notwithstanding. And so, granting all this, since there was no way on earth that he was going to negotiate his daughter's disposition with Elliott, Peter chucked purpose one and concentrated on purpose two.

"I was hoping I'd be able to pick up Jeanette after school? I promise to have her back by eight."

"On a school night?"

"Well, yes, I understand. Make it seven-thirty then."

Elliott scraped his long chin with his papers, cogitating. He was left-handed. As he delivered his verdict, "I guess, I can't see any *immediate* reason to object," he extended that arm with those same papers, corralling Peter. "But look, why don't you come inside so we can talk? What did you have in mind for Jeanie?"

No one called him *Pete* and Jeanette *Jeanie*. Peter detested

Elliott's predilection for renaming people. Especially his snarky way of lifting his leg to re-brand another man's daughter. Peter gave Elliott his phony sewer-salesman's smile and, under duress, entered his office. Where he was left to stew while Elliott went to ask the receptionist to put in an emergency call to Avis. When Elliott returned, Peter attempted to pour oil on perennially troubled waters.

"Elliott, I don't intend to chat Jeanette up one way or another on the Connecticut school—all I want to do is talk with her. I'll be happy to reassure Avis of that."

"Pete, for goodness' sakes, don't work yourself up. I just need to check that she doesn't have something planned for tonight that I don't know jack about."

The younger man practiced high-speed, high-torque workouts, ran 26.2 marathons, possessed a body mass index probably of four, but still had to look up to and around his rival—which he very plainly disliked. Peter observed Elliott agonizing: Should he claim his throne behind his desk or perhaps sit on a corner of it, leg draped over the edge casually, so to demonstrate his ease and gain a height advantage?

"Would you rather I wait outside until she calls? I don't mind?"

"Sit still, Sam'll track her down." Elliott opted for his chair. "Pete, we know how concerned you are with Jeanie's welfare. Again, it's only that if Avis has something going tonight and I screw it up—well, you know how women are?"

No, as a matter of fact, his track record showed he clearly didn't, and, as likely as not, probably Elliott Fields was as fully ignorant of the opposite sex, as well. Peter ransacked his brain for some innocuous male banter. "So, you folks are going gangbusters, I take it?"

"Always going to have bad guys," Elliott confirmed. "You *are* aware that there aren't really that many boarding schools for the lower grades, but, of those, Wilfred Hall is among the top tier? I would know that, of course."

"Of course, I forget your illustrious prep school years."

"But this joint"—Elliott shook the tips of his fingers indulgently, modestly—"is ten times more sniffy than mine. Did Avis run through the admission process with you? Good grief, they're going to want to know everything but the lengths of our male members."

A weird emphatic to choose for an evangelical Christian who didn't drink, smoke, or swear? A weird emphatic to choose, period. Peter replied neutrally, "I gather it's an arduous process."

"But you're also aware that this can put her on track for the ivy league—on the *inside* track, I should say?"

"Well, that would be something, a Sanguedolce at Yale."

Elliott focused on a distant corner of his office, as if, perhaps, there was a grand jury impaneled there invisible to all but future district attorneys. "Pete, just between you and me, I'm not at all convinced there's a big need for this. I'm actually on your side here. She's already at a private school, and a darn good one at that."

Peter thought, *Is that true?* "But we need to know how Jeanette feels."

"These aren't decisions you put in the hands of children. No one

112   *Robert McKean*

asked me as a kid what I wanted to do. But here's the bottom line, if Avis has her mind set on doing this, then we're going to do it. Who knows a daughter better than a mom, right?"

"No doubt about that, moms rule." Peter did his best to lard up Elliott's deep insight and went on to register another point. "The letter Jeanette was supposed to show me and didn't? That's something you can rest assured we'll be discussing tonight. When I pick her up, I thought that I might have a word with her teacher."

A blunder: Elliott pounced. "Peter, we would rather you *not* conference with her teachers. That's part of —"

"I understand, of course." He recognized the seriousness of that *Peter*. "Wasn't thinking, sorry. So, fine, I'll pick her up, we'll have dinner. And again, I'm not going to try to —"

"Gracious, we're not enemies! Or, if we are, it's news to me? All we're trying to do, all *all* of us are trying to do, is ensure that Jeanie gets what she needs—a solid foundation in life. You want that, Avis wants that, I want that. In this game we're all on the same team."

"Absolutely."

"I mean, she couldn't want a more generous dad."

"And you folks, you've been super with her."

"I wouldn't be surprised if she doesn't follow you into business, Pete. She's got your genes—that girl'll bargain you right out of your dessert if you don't watch her."

"Really? You think so? I figured she was destined for the bar, given the examples of her mom and stepdad."

"Fields, Longstreet, and Fields? Maybe you're right. She'd give the law boys something to stare at other than their books, now wouldn't she?"

Another slightly off-kilter remark. If you asked him, Elliott Fields was an odd stick. Yes, he was born of the *beau monde*. But in East Stanton Junction, where money like a deep seam of anthracite ran back to the Pittsburgh robber barons, dynasties like the Mellons and the Fricks, the Fields never played in such rarefied circles. Elliott had, in fact, attended a modest academy. Fortunately, Samantha soon tapped on the door, thus sparing the men further torment of devising ever more extravagant compliments. While Elliott departed to scheme with Avis, Peter, regretting his mentioning of Jeanette's teacher, recalled the grateful poppa who gifted his Uncle Nico with six guinea fowl he'd shot. Nico, who had played a ravishing Pachelbel's "Canon" on St. Ursula's organ for the wedding of the man's daughter, brought Peter with him to East Stanton Junction to have the bloody birds dressed. The butcher, missing the final joint of a finger, led them through a forest of dangling carcasses to an inner room—*this* room—where with a gleaming cleaver he decapitated the six fowl and hung the headless creatures by their feet to drain, just above where Attorney Fields sits to read his email.

~ ~ ~

"I'm in big trouble, Papa."

"You're not in trouble, big or small."

"They're going to send me away."

As witness to his daughter's passage through the shoals of her young life, Peter had imagined—or tried to imagine—his life at those same junctures. But though he could pull back memories of *physically* growing up, he was never convinced that he was able to retrieve with any degree of authenticity his emotional states. A loss, not to be able to re-experience what it *felt* like to be six, to be seven—or ten, his daughter's solemn face tonight in her favorite restaurant.

"No one is sending you anywhere. How's your roll?"

"Fine, Papa."

Jeanette adored the seafood rolls—fake crab, runny mayo—served at this Mom and Pop restaurant in Ridgeport. Four booths, half a dozen tables with sticky vinyl cloths and windows crowded with placards advertising upcoming—or twenty years gone—religious festivals. Beyond the rain-slicked windows, a few streets over, flowed the river, close by the great elbow that begins the Ohio on its journey south, sending it darkening away under its bridges and hills like a departing lover. Because his daughter liked this restaurant, Peter liked it, too, even the seafood rolls, which, if he didn't like quite as much, he ordered out of loyalty. The restaurant's only customers, they were benevolently watched over by Mom and Pop, who peeped out from the kitchen to ensure things were going well.

Which they weren't. He hated this kind of defeatist talk. "That decision has not been made. There are other options we might explore."

Jeanette patted her upper lip and frowned at him. After Peter mopped off his mayonnaise mustache—things like that distressed her—she said, "Elliott told me you got arrested by the police."

Peter looked into the troubled eyes of his daughter. "I was not arrested, I was misbehaving. For which I have apologized."

"Elliott says you're tomcatting with someone."

He wasn't sure she understood that term, but was obliged to presume that in some fundamental, if not technical, sense she did. Peter put down his sopping sandwich. You could wring the bun like a wet sponge. "Well then, I really do need to thank good old Elliott for spreading such abundant and colorful manure about me, don't I? Jeanette, I'm not going to discuss my private adult life with you, and Elliott has no business talking about it, either. The man is insufferable."

Vexed, he listened to the horn of a towboat echoing through the gloomy streets of Ridgeport. Streets whose bricks, fitted into place a century ago by Scottish bricklayers, were now as crooked as an old man's teeth. A stake bed truck, a hand-painted sign attached to its wooden ribs—*We Love Junk!*—wheezed past, and Peter watched his daughter dredging a French fry through her ketchup and licking off the red sauce with the tip of her tongue.

"You know," he said gently, "you were supposed to show me a letter from your school?"

"I hate school."

"That's an answer to a different question, darling. Maybe the question I should have asked is, Are you happy there?"

Jeanette extricated a French fry deep from beneath the jumble of fries and began the tedious process of nibbling it to death—and pointedly ignoring him. "You're *not* happy there," he said, "are you?"

Robert McKean

"They don't like me."

"I didn't know that—and I should know that. Who doesn't like you?"

"Some girls. They make fun of my clothes and my hair."

"Your braids? Whatever in the world could be wrong with your braids?"

"They go around telling everyone I smell bad."

"Good lord—what foul crap." Peter permitted himself a second or two to process that. "You have every right to dress as you please, and I can assure you, you do not *smell*. It's a clique, darling, and cliques cohere around jealousy. They envy you—your beauty, your intelligence, your talent. Maybe it has something to do with your being picked to play the piano for the holiday program?"

Jeanette shoved her plate away. "I'm sorry, Papa, about the letter."

"I need to see things like that—that's important, honey. For both of us. But let it go. At this point, it's water under the bridge, I'm afraid. I have an idea. I have, just this very minute, hatched it. Would you like to hear it?"

Jeanette giggled, the first giggle of the evening. "I'd rather see you hatch it, Papa."

Actually, he was fibbing. The idea began to take form this morning, as he watched the rain slicing across the sodden, knot-weed-free lawns of Oak Grove. Were he to be honest, what he might have said was that he'd just now hatched the courage to voice his suggestion.

A gamble, a risk, but it was the right thing to do, and, if you cannot do the right thing by your own progeny, you should be shot. "Here's my brainstorm, sweetie. What if we go visit this school in Connecticut? You and me? We walk around, we chat people up, we see how it feels, then we come home and talk about it. You know, Jeanette, there's a chance you might actually be happier there?"

"It doesn't matter what I think."

"Stop saying that. You want some dessert? Pie? Ice cream? *Both?"*

"I have a lot of homework. I have to think of an animal I'd like to be and write about it."

Ah, how well Peter knew this girl: It was a straight line she required. "And your animal, darling, would be . . . ?"

"A viper!"

And he laughed, his superabundant flesh quivering as merrily as Old King Cole's. He drove them back through Ridgeport's nighttime streets, crossing paths with the emphysemic *We love junk!* truck that burrowed like an oversized and underfed scavenger rat down an alley just wide enough to admit it. Keeping the car warm for his never-warm-enough daughter—in that way she was a carbon of her mother—Peter turned onto the boulevard that paralleled the river, and they cruised through Western Pennsylvania's derelict river-bottom mill towns: Creighton, Hanover, Ashport, Hurley's Ferry. The public squares lay abandoned, everybody home, snugged in before the telly, feet resting on the coffee table. As they passed Ganaego asleep across the river,

Peter—as all Ganaegoans of a certain age will do—looked over at the slender stretch of land where the nine-mile steelworks once stood. On a rainy, socked-in night such as this, the works within a luminous volcanic cloud of its own making would have throbbed with glittering lights and fiendish flames: Bessemers; garishly lit catwalks of the blast furnaces; open hearths with their lakes of fire; the coke works stacks like a row of slender gravestones over-watching it all. Gone now, vanished like a phantasmagoric mirage. It was only a short way farther to East Stanton Junction, their destination, where the late-Nineteenth Century empire builders, who ordered the brick to be laid for those furnaces and rolling mills and who imported the laborers from Europe to stoke those fires, once built their fortress estates, and who were now no more themselves.

Peter parked a half-block from the condo. Jeanette had hardly spoken a word since they left the restaurant, which was unlike her. His daughter was frightened. And she was holding back. All this loose speculation of a menacing future had come between them. But talk they must, if only to have some sway over that future. "Honey," he said, restating his offer, "we can go look at this school in Connecticut—if that is something you would like to do? But if you definitely don't want to go to school there, then it's off the table—completely."

"Papa, she's going to send me there whether I like it or not."

"Why do you keep saying that? I can stop it, *you* can stop it. If you don't want to go there, darling, you're not going to go there. It's that simple."

"She doesn't want me around anymore."

"Of course, she wants you around. Your mother loves you. You mustn't ever think that. But we do need to find you another school. I can well imagine the viciousness of East Stanton Junction cliques—or maybe I can't. I have half a mind to have a word with your headmaster."

"Papa"—Jeanette, eyes crimped in pain, darted him her impatient-with-Papa look—"Mama's going to have a baby!"

An image, repulsive and insuppressible, blossomed in his mind: the raw, red-knuckled hands of Elliott Fields groping clumsily between Avis's legs. Peter struggled to bring his turbulent emotions into control. He could sense how ghastly his face must look. "I don't know anything about that, Jeanette," he faltered. "I mean, I'm surprised?"

"Something's wrong with the walls, Papa. They're not very thick or something, I can hear them talking. They talk about money a lot. They're going to start a new family and I'm in the way . . ."

Peter leaned across the Cadillac's splitting leather seats and enclosed his daughter in his arms. Jeanette was crying. Peter, fighting back his own tears, tightened his hug. Jeanette pleaded, "Why can't I come live with you?"

How to explain custody laws to a child? How to explain that a fat man prone to binging and melancholia most probably would not serve as a suitable single parent? "The court's not going to let that happen, darling—and maybe it's for the best? But your mother *loves* you, you shouldn't ever worry about that. She's not talking about this new school in Connecticut because she doesn't want you, that's simply not true."

Jeanette pulled away from his embrace. "You're not going to get

Robert McKean

married, *too,* are you?"

And now, at last, he felt what she felt. The Connecticut school was one thing, her troubling relationship at home another, but *this* possibility was also worrying her: losing him. "Darling, I'm not getting married. Frankly, I don't think that's something that's ever going to happen to me again."

He held her until she calmed. There was a box of tissues in the backseat, which he fetched for them. They were both aware that she should not come home looking as if she'd been crying. He started the Cadillac, and they crept up the street to her building, where the lobby doors spilled bright light across the glistening sidewalk.

"Maybe not a viper, darling," he said impishly, or tried to say impishly.

"Papa"—Jeanette looked at him searchingly—"what's going to happen to you if Mama makes me move away?"

~ ~ ~

What's going to happen to you?

He wakes with Avis in his dream. What she will never do again in life, come to him, she will do in sleep. Sometimes they make love— on the undulating waterbed in their Crocker Farms apartment or in his childhood bedroom that became their bedroom. But just as frequently they are engaged not in sex play but in some Hitchcockian plot, creeping out on a ledge to stretch drapes across a wall of windows, trying to stop rainwater from pouring through a roof riddled with holes. He can recollect only wisps of today's dream, but in most of his Avis dreams she's younger, and they don't always get along: dreams of betrayal, of rancor and remorse. Avis Longstreet, a free but determined spirit, knew how the other half lived and craved what her father, a feed and seed clerk who exchanged his job filling farmers' orders for a job shoveling feculent muck in a waste water treatment plant, could not provide. She liked randy sex, greasy barbecue, pungent marijuana, and exotic drinks that glowed in dark lounges like miniature nuclear reactions. Peter, the owner's son, swept into the Purchasing Department flush with tales of a world beyond ledgers and hillbilly roadhouses, and took her where she wanted to go, bought her what she wanted to have, and wakes this morning more or less where he began, in an empty bed with a useless erection.

Last night's proposal earned a swift response.

Lamentably, it was Elliott, not Avis, who interrupted Peter's second cup of coffee. "Pete, old boy, what is this *borscht?* Correct me if I'm wrong, but the understanding we have is that we are in a court-ordered arrangement, which includes all decision-making as to Jeanie's whereabouts. You're not about to go gallivanting off on some sort of cross-country lark with her, I can guarantee you that, fellow. We haven't even applied to this school in Connecticut yet."

Peter kept his voice reasonable. "I'm not talking about a formal visit, Elliott, nothing of the sort. What I'm thinking, if Jeanette would like, is to make a short visit to the campus and have an unpressurized look-around."

"I couldn't care two hoots what you're thinking. We don't

appreciate your going behind our backs and attempting to establish some kind of confidential relation with Jeanie. That we emphatically do not."

"Elliott, I kind of do—have a confidential relationship with Jeanette? I'm her natural father, after all."

"You know darn well what I mean. But if you want it in dumbbell English, we won't have your plotting with her—is that clear enough?"

"All right, I'm sorry, I should've run it by Avis first."

"It doesn't even make sense. If she was in high school—you know, visiting colleges?—then maybe. But a ten-year-old? No. If Jeanie needs to see this school, and I don't see any reason why she should, then we'll take her there when the time comes."

Peter, recalling the shaking girl in his arms, scrapped the conciliatory tone. "Elliott, I don't know why Avis has you making this call, but if she wants to make any substantive changes in the child's life, then she's going to need my consent. She and I are in fact, as you point out, in a legally binding arrangement. Which includes selecting Jeanette's place of schooling. I have an idea for intensive tutoring and would be delighted to research local options for more appropriate schools. But if Avis is determined to exile her daughter to Connecticut, then I am going to be the one who takes Jeanette there for a visit first. Those are my terms."

Satisfying little speech that, he thought, hanging up.

That afternoon, feeling industrious, Peter cleaned out three oak filing cabinets in his father's quiet office, the voluminous paperwork businesses used to generate: proposals, reports, contracts, staff memoranda. But it was the letters he lingered over, letters from an era when people still composed letters—polite, respectful, complex sentences thoughtfully dictated and fastidiously typed on high rag content bond. Letters from Illinois and Kentucky mayors, from state regulators and city engineers, from suppliers and distributors, from an Egyptian vizier who, even though electing to award his lucrative sewer-pipe contract to another firm, took pains to respond to the esteemed general manager of the Ganaego Clay Works in such florid, highly subordinated syntax as to strain the limits of grammar. One letter held him longer than the others: a handwritten letter from a Nebraskan woman whose five-year-old son was swept into a storm conduit in a flash flood and who was so distraught that she could think of nothing but to appeal to the name inscribed on the pipe. Behind her grieving letter lay a carbon on canary paper, his father's reply, also handwritten:

> *My Dear Mrs. Tumm:*
> *There are no words to adequately express my sorrow upon learning of your son's death. It is heartrending, a tragedy beyond the feeble powers of the human mind to comprehend. You and your family have my deepest and most sincere sympathy. I have ordered the plant to cease all operations at noon today to observe a minute of silence and prayer for . . .*

Robert McKean

It was here, while he was arranging stacks of papers across every available surface, that Peter received two additional calls. The first, from Fields & Longstreet's young receptionist. It sounded as if the girl were reading from a script. Samantha informed him that Attorneys Fields and Longstreet had accepted his proposal. They will call ahead to inform Wilfred Hall Academy of the purpose and nature of Mr. Sanguedolce's visit, so they will need to be apprised as to when he wishes to implement his proposal. She actually said that, *implement*. Peter, raising his shoulders in a shrug, suggested this weekend, drive up Saturday, visit Sunday, drive back Monday, then amended his terms, cadging an extra day, Jeanette to be returned on Tuesday after a side visit to Boston to view the old North Church—Paul Revere, you know, one by land, two by sea, or is it the other way around?—then went on to thank the receptionist and ask if she was enjoying her work at the law firm.

"Oh, yes," the young woman gushed, swerving off script. "I'm learning *soooo* much!"

Well, maybe not that much, one hoped. Today's second call began with a helpful inquiry. "Hey, neighbor, you want your hat back? I'm assuming it's yours—I don't know anyone else with a head this big. The thing goes down to my chin!"

Peter, pleased despite all manner of misgivings, plopped in his father's squeaky chair and crossed his feet on the desk. "I imagine it's ruined?"

"Not at all! It was on the stoop. You busy this weekend? Poor Randy's saddled with the kids. I'm going to put name tags on them so he

Mending What Is Broken 125

can tell them apart."

"What's Randal doing for clothes these days?"

"You want me to give him your hat? He could hold it in front?"

While he was taking his own pains to postpone—not turn down—his neighbor's offer, Peter recalled more details from this morning's Avis dream. They were driving. It was summer, a broiling, glary day. The roof of the car was down, which was odd: He'd never owned a convertible. A map sprawled across the dash. He was trying to consult it and drive and was worried that the wind would snatch it away. Meanwhile, Avis was becoming more and more impatient. She was hot, uncomfortable. She wore a short jersey and ugly plaid shorts. Her sweat-shiny belly suddenly swelled hugely out over her shorts, round as a watermelon.

Elliott's child.

~ ~ ~

As agreed, he collected Jeanette Friday afternoon. They stowed her diminutive suitcase, which was as purple as a plum, and her Jet Blue bag in the Cadillac and went shopping. Clearing T&V's registers, they huddled in their habitual indecision before the RedBox cubbyholes, then exited into the cool autumn evening. In the kitchen, whose mahogany cabinetry had darkened to the color of claret, they broiled pork chops and fixed his grandmother's polenta, artichoke hearts, sun-dried tomatoes, onions, basil, oregano, grated Parmigiano Reggiano. They concluded their feast with T&V's version of cassata cake, sponge cake studded with halved strawberries, saturated in syrup. Later, Jeanette, in robe

Robert McKean

and slippers, fell asleep midway through the Disney film over whose selection she'd agonized.

Peter turned off the television. "Time for bed, kiddo."

"I missed the ending."

"It'll be here when we get home."

She'd brought Sock Monkey into the TV room. One of her earliest stuffed friends and one who could have profited from a good laundering. "When are we leaving, Papa?"

That particular piece of information she'd asked for three times now. But very little about the school itself. He found that curious, his daughter's lack of curiosity. But perhaps all it meant was that she was so resigned that curiosity seemed irrelevant—or, that she was so spooked that she was afraid to go near it. The latter, probably. Peter answered his daughter's practical question with a variant he employed each time she asked.

"It's a long drive, honey, pretty much all day. We should be on the road by nine or ten, so that we don't get to the hotel too late. You should shower in the morning, before we leave."

"Do half-sisters ever become friends? I mean, like real sisters?"

"How do you know it's going to be a girl?"

Jeanette gazed, her eyes centered in her glasses, at the pompoms on her slippers. "They don't have a name for her yet. Mama was sick this morning."

"Mothers often get sick at the beginnings of their pregnancies, honey. She was sick a lot with you." As soon as he'd said that, Peter was sorry. "It's a perfectly natural thing. Happens to most moms-to-be."

As he was going to bed, the mom-to-be called. "I'm warning you," Avis put him on notice. "No monkey business, Peter."

"I understand."

"You put a broom handle in the spokes and I will skin you alive."

He'd like to lay an ear to her belly—even now—as he did when she carried Jeanette. "I promise," he promised, then matched her, an old game of theirs, commonplace for commonplace. "I have no dog in this hunt, Avis."

Which made her laugh, just. "I'll let our big-game hunter know, he'll be thrilled. I've told her to speak up and not mumble."

"Sound advice."

The following morning Peter woke to the piano. In all the years of her practicing, he could not recollect Jeanette beginning so early. He lolled in bed on this mist-whitened Saturday, listening with pleasure. His grandfather would play at odd hours. In their narrow duplex on Plan Eight, the baby grand—for which Fatty swapped a Plymouth with a backseat that reeked of cat piss—would be thunderous. Cups rattled, glasses clinked. Nonna, cutting noodles, would sway her wide hips beneath her heavy skirts, and their neighbor, who had to get up early to make his rounds through the county's back roads with his bottled gas truck, would pound on the party wall. This hushed morning Jeanette's notes, produced by that same antique Steinert, traced lightly through the cool, cavernous rooms, as if from another lifetime.

Robert McKean

Peter padded downstairs. Jeanette, two lank braids falling absently across her shoulders, was running through the one- and two-page preludes and sonatinas that she'd learned in the past several years, and Peter understood with a sudden clarity what had drawn her here to play in her pajamas. He longed to assuage her fears that she was being banished into some permanent exile, and that for years to come—for as long as she wished—she would find herself racing through these familiar rooms and seated at this venerable instrument with its alligatored varnish and keys as butter-yellow as her great-grandfather's nicotine-stained teeth.

He waited until she paused between pieces. "Your playing has come a long way this year."

Jeanette swiveled on the bench. "Will they have music and things like that?"

"I suspect they'll have a dynamic music program, sugar. But you can be sure that's something we'll need to find out. And again, we're only window-shopping. Nobody's making any decisions yet."

"Elliott gave me ten dollars."

"Wasn't that jolly of him?"

While they were packing, the landline rang. His instinct was to ignore it, but in this era of cellphones, there was no escaping into the sanctuary of the automobile anyway, so Peter grabbed it.

"Hey, neighbor, if you haven't left yet, I wonder if I can get your help for a few minutes?"

"We've got a long drive, Fay."

"I can appreciate that. But we're in sort of a pickle here? Jacob needs to pee, and I can't very well go in the bathroom with him? You see my problem, of course?"

"Call a nurse. There's a button beside his bed."

"And that would work, I'm sure, if we were at the nursing home. But we're not there, exactly."

"Fay, where *are* you? What have you done?"

"I haven't *done* anything—unless you mean doing something nice for an old man."

"How nice?"

"We're at Bob Evans—you know, by the mall? They have a fantastic breakfast menu. Were you aware of that? But now Jacob has to pee, and I'm feeling a little bit squeamish."

Peter caught sight of Jeanette at the end of the foyer, half in the door, half out. She was chewing on the end of an unraveling braid and eying him anxiously. Perhaps, he reflected, we're all children. "Fay, you need to take Jacob Weiner back to the nursing home—where he belongs. Have you finished eating?"

"Well, yes, as a matter of fact we have, thank you for asking. And it was good! But that brings up the second thing I need your help with. He doesn't seem to . . . ah . . . *want* to go back?"

~ ~ ~

They finished packing in silence. Peter, stalling, washed and buffed four Granny Smith apples and packed them in a T&V shopping bag, along with a bag of pretzels, a loaf of bread, four plastic water

Robert McKean

bottles, a wedge of Jarlsberg, and a jar of peanut butter and paring knife. Finally, he locked the house and made sure his daughter had buckled her seatbelt—unnecessarily, she didn't need his help.

"We have to make a short stop first. Won't take long."

"It's that old man, isn't it? What's the matter with him?"

"There's nothing the matter. When people get old they sometimes can't live by themselves and they need to stay in a nursing home. We're going to take him back there, or maybe persuade him to go back with the lady who—unbelievably—decided to take him out in the first place."

"Is this the person you're tomcatting with?"

"Sugar, when you grow up, you're going to want a private adult life, too."

Peter glanced at his neighbor's partially razed colonial as they drove past. Jacob, outraged one summer at the estimates he was receiving from contractors, had shingled his own roof. Perhaps not very well, but Oak Grove may have never seen a more determined DIY effort: the stocky music teacher, old even then, crouching for dear life on a gable, hemp rope knotted around his waist, hammering away in the dappled shade of the towering maples. This morning, the house's new tenants, Mr. and Mrs. Mourning Dove, were perched on Jacob's chimney, conferring.

Not much heat rising from that chimney today, folks, Peter thought.

"Would you like me to get you a cup of hot chocolate," he asked, "while I'm in the restaurant? One for the road, as it were."

An offer that didn't even yield him eye contact. "I'm fine, Papa."

Fay and Jacob, in the restaurant's lobby area, had been pushed into the corner by the throngs of Ganaegoans who had decided this Saturday to breakfast out, lonely seniors, divorcees, mommies and daddies with their ducklings. The smell of pancake batter and potatoes fried in grease was cloying. Fay sat on the final three inches of a bench she'd managed to defend. She clutched two white take-out bags on her knees. Parked next to her, Jacob, looking sour and aggrieved, slumped in his wheelchair.

Weiner ignored Peter's greeting, and Peter turned to Fay.

"Well," she said brightly to his scowl at Jacob's trousers, "one problem's solved." She held up a bag. "Hungry?"

Peter knelt beside the music teacher. "Jacob? Fay's going to take you back to the nursing home. Did you enjoy your breakfast?"

Weiner brought his head around. The skin piled up slackly along his jowls; in the folds were sharp whiskers, like the steel filings in Jeanette's old Woolly Willy game. The corners of his eyes had collected thick curds of rheum. "No," he said thoughtfully. "I'm not going back."

"You have to go back. Where else can you go?"

"Home, that's where."

"Right—and that's the Sprague Center." For some reason Peter decided to say *Sprague Center,* instead of *nursing home.* "That's where you live now. Your house is being demolished."

"If I can't go home, I want to go to my daughter's then."

"That's impossible, you know that."

"That's what he keeps saying," Fay put in helpfully.

Peter thought of Jeanette in the car: Leaving her alone made him uneasy. "Listen, Jacob"—he layered a warning tone in his voice—"if you don't want to go back, I'm going to have to call the Center? They'll send orderlies?"

"Take me to my daughter's."

"We can't do that, that's impossible."

"Then take me home."

"Oh, for Chrissakes, we're going in circles!"

Jacob surged forward in his wheelchair. "Fuck it," he yelled, "just leave me alone then!"

And at that, Bob's line of waiting customers hushed and seemed to focus on the three of them with more than a modicum of community disapproval. "What *asinine* notion possessed you," Peter ground out between his teeth to Fay, "to do this?"

"I'm sorry! I thought I would do something nice for someone? Pardon me if you think that's so awful!"

Peter seized the handles of the wheelchair and yanked. "Jacob, we're going back—*now.*" He yanked again to turn the chair, jerking Weiner sideways. The old man clawed at the armrests and moaned. "Jacob, *please,* be reasonable." Peter pulled a third time, not quite so hard, but all that resulted in was an even louder, more plaintive moan, and he realized that he wasn't going to be able to do this on his own. "All right, I'm calling the nursing home."

Fay leapt up. "Gotta go pee!"

She foisted her white paper bags on him and scampered past. Peter, clutching both bags, visited his various pockets for his phone, then recalled that he'd left it in the car. Swearing, he steamed toward the payphone by the doors. He had no coins, of course. Who carried change these days? He corralled the take-out bags between his feet, found his wallet, extracted a credit card, and called the eight-hundred number. Squinting at the embossed numerals, he keyed in his sixteen-digit number to reach, at last, information. *Information!* It was at this juncture, as he was requesting the telephone number of the Sprague Hollow Nursing Home and Retirement Center, that Bob Evans erupted in shrieks. Peter gazed over his shoulder to see — in genuine wonderment — Jacob Weiner on his feet, employing chair backs and heads for support, lurching across the restaurant. Amid the pandemonium, the old clarinetist suddenly disappeared and Peter heard what sounded like a generously appointed breakfast table going over, much like the tables do in barroom brawl scenes in cowboy movies.

~ ~ ~

Jacob was surly and uncooperative. But his fall had shaken him up enough that he didn't resist being loaded into Peter's roomy backseat. Fay sat alongside him. She could have followed in her car, but understood that, if the music teacher became disturbed, somebody had to keep him from flinging himself from a moving vehicle. The good news was Bob Evans didn't have them julienned and added to the daily specials. Peter's credit card had been put to immediate use, and the

Robert McKean

wheelchair, folded, fit neatly in the trunk beside the suitcases. The person Peter worried about was his daughter. Jeanette, stonily chewing on a braid, fixed her eyes on the road and never moved her head.

Not an auspicious start.

As Peter turned into the curving drive down to the nursing home's complex, Jacob began to cry. Peter pulled into an upper parking lot and killed the engine. He looked at the shrunken old man in the backseat. Jacob, head between his palms, was sobbing like a child. Jeanette turned to Peter, imploring him to do something.

"Jacob," he said, gently, "why don't I call Jessica? Maybe if you spoke with her that'd bring you some comfort. Do you know her number?"

"I have a better idea." Fay tapped Peter on the shoulder. "Can we talk—outside?"

They convened not so far away that Peter couldn't keep an eye on Jeanette and she on him. The silky morning mist, which had burned off everywhere else, remained in the hollow, rocking like a thinning bowl of dry-ice vapor. Fay laid out her case. "You know as well as I do that calling his daughter is a waste of time. We need to take him there. That's what he wants and that's what we need to do."

"Fay, we can't. We're not his guardians."

"You want to roll him back in there to die?"

"I don't remember rolling him out." One cannot imagine one's children exercising power of attorney over one—or, if one can, Peter reconsidered, you sure as hell don't want to. He pleaded for rationality from someone whom he feared possessed but scant quantities of it. "It's all very sad, I understand, but there's—"

"That old man is *dying*. He wants one last thing in life. I say we help him. No big deal."

"How can you say that? It's called *kidnapping,* and in most legal circles it's regarded as a very big deal."

"You're so melodramatic. I'm going inside and get him released for the weekend, okay?"

"What're you going to tell them? That you're his long-lost second daughter?"

"This is his *last* wish. How can you be such a big meanie?"

"I'm trying to keep my emotions out of it."

"Well, let them back in—hul-*loooo* emotions!"

Peter stared into the hazel eyes of his lover: It was like arguing with a twelve-year-old. A six-year-old? "Then what he needs to do is tell them that he wants to go to Boston. He entered the home voluntarily—I don't think she went through court to have him committed—so I assume he can sign himself out, I guess, I don't know? But regardless, they need to call Jessica and obtain her approval for us to take him up there— for *you* to take him up there. I'm having a special weekend with my daughter. Maybe Jessica'll agree to come here, that would be better."

"That woman's not gonna lift a finger, you know that."

"No, I don't know that, and neither do you. What we do know is what they're going to say when you tell them you want to borrow one of their patients for the weekend."

Robert McKean

Fay wrapped her arms around as much of him as she could. "Peter, you need to get out of that stuffy old house more often. If I can get him released, will you take us? I don't see how I can keep an eye on him and drive at the same time?"

"This is my weekend with my daughter."

"And I respect that. We'll stay out of your hair. She loves her papa, you don't have to worry about that."

"How're we going to travel with him—he's not even completely continent?"

"What's that mean?"

"He leaks."

"Oh," she giggled, "well, that's your department." Fay stood on tiptoe to kiss him on the nose. "I'll ask him one more time if he really wants to go, will that satisfy you?"

Peter looked at the branches of the trees rising through the shredding strands of mist and smelled the scent of apple blossoms lifting from his unwisely chosen lover, then trailed her back to the Cadillac. Jacob's sobs had ceased. Students, cowed by their teacher's mercurial temper, his exacting standards, were known to leave Jacob Weiner's studio in tears of their own. Peter met his daughter's look of consternation with a small, helpless shrug. He started the engine and turned up the heat, while Fay put her questions to Weiner.

"You're sure you're up to it? It's a long drive?"

"I'm not going back in there, lady. I told you that."

"Well, I think you have to—for a few minutes. Peter says you have to tell them you want to be released for the weekend. You can do that, right? They let you come out for breakfast, didn't they?"

"I'm gonna tell them to fuck off."

"No, no," Fay laughed, "that's not a good idea, Jacob. You have to—"

"It isn't going to work," Peter butted into her sentence. "You're building up his hopes for no reason. They're not—"

"Peter," Fay butted into his, "just chauffeur us down the hill, would you?"

As Fay wheeled Jacob up the walk, she stopped to bend over the old music teacher. To clean somebody's spattered hollandaise sauce from his shirt, Peter presumed. Their conference ended in mutual nods and Fay smacked the automatic door button and wheeled him inside. Why she had suddenly taken an interest in a man whose house of fifty years she refused to even walk through before demolishing it—why this reversal?—he had no idea: Fay Halbrunner operated on motivations that would be obscure to the good Dr. Freud. Thirty-five minutes later she emerged with Jacob in his chair. The music teacher, in clean plaid shirt and pants, cradled a T&V shopping bag in his lap. Once he was reinserted in the Cadillac, Fay leaned back and smiled. "So, what's the best route to Boston? Can't say I've ever been there."

"Jessica consented to this?"

"You know, Peter, people can be very nice if you take the time to get to know them? And don't even say it, I know what you're thinking: The ninny forgot his meds. Well, guess again! They're kind of cute,

Robert McKean

actually. Maybe Jacob'll let us have a couple? Anyhow, for the benefit of all the doubting Thomases, the charming Sprague staff is looking forward to seeing Jacob on Tuesday. Tuesday is crafts day, if you didn't know."

~ ~ ~

By noon they were finally and fully on the road. Initially, they'd wound their way back to Bob Evans, then followed Fay to her rented house. Jeanette elected to stay in the car while Peter rolled Jacob inside and helped the old man use the bathroom. Fay came out of her bedroom with her suitcase and said, "Damn, I never thought to grab the pictures in Jacob's room."

"You wanna go back, chew the fat some more with your director friend?"

Fay handed him his fedora. "I hope you don't get head lice—the kids were taking turns wearing it at dinner."

His plan was to tack north the forty miles to catch Route 80 east. Cruising at eighty or eighty-five, the Cadillac's powerful engine would eat up the miles. It was, after all, an automobile designed for comfortable travel. And as Pennsylvania's rumpled silver-brown hills rose and fell in the Brougham's windows, the vehicle's passengers, as travelers will, drifted into their private reveries. Jeanette had never been a fidgety child, and other than shooting him grimaces when someone passed gas or when Fay answered a call from one of her children—*Noooo, honey, don't eat your boogers*—she was content to listen to whatever cassette tapes that appealed to her that had accumulated in the Cadillac's glove compartment. Adopting a guardedly optimistic mood, Peter eased himself into the driving slouch common to traveling salesmen, tipped back his hat, and fondly recalled one of those cassettes Jeanette didn't choose, one he played nearly to death, *The Music Man*, the commercial travelers on the Rock Island: *You gotta know the territory.*

And so you do.

"Can't hold it much longer," Jacob announced.

Inside their third service plaza restroom in less than a hundred miles, Jacob slipped on a pornographic magazine soaking in a puddle of urine. Peter snagged him in mid-air—for some reason Weiner wasn't wearing his glasses—and lowered the old man on the toilet seat, then backed out of the stall to afford him some privacy. While he waited, his phone rang. Peter studied the glowing screen as though it were an indictment—*Harvey Silverstein*—until it blinked off.

"Arrrrrrrrrrrrrag!"

The groan Jacob emitted when the piss, burning as it went, streamed in dribbles from him. His hands were thick-knuckled, tremulous, useless. Peter helped him shrug up his underpants and trousers, tuck in his shirt, buckle his belt. Fitted into his chair, Weiner shifted his creaky bones and said, "Christ, I'll be glad to get home. I'm gonna sit in a hot tub for an hour."

"We're not going there, Jacob. We're going to your daughter's."

He puzzled that. "Jessica didn't practice today. That's two days in a row now. I gotta get on her case."

"Where're your glasses?"

Robert McKean

The old man ran his hand over his naked eyes. "Had 'em, I dunno?"

"I hope they're in the car. We're going to Boston—to visit your daughter? That's what you want to do, right?"

"Sure, sure. Say, who's that little girl?"

Peter rolled the music teacher through the parking lot to the abandoned Cadillac. A few minutes later he watched his lover and his daughter—the little girl who had so piqued the curiosity of Jacob Weiner that he'd inquired twice now who she was—walking back from the concession area, lunch in arms. Fay leaned to the side, curls tousled by the wind, to listen to Jeanette, who was explaining something, her dark eyes serious with intent. What could they be talking about? School? Her new bicycle? Something precious from the quick of her young deep life that she had decided was safe to share with this suspicious stranger. Fay, laughing, threw her head back. Would his daughter become friends with Fay? Someone with whom men *tomcat?* Did he want them to become friends?

Was he going to marry Fay Halbrunner? *Could* he marry her?

Absurdities. For one thing, he was not persuaded that Fay was headed for divorce. It was his considered opinion that despite what she said she was still caught on this philandering motor-oil empire-builder of a husband. And secondly, this was not something he wanted. So no, he was not about to marry Fay Halbrunner—or anyone else. Peter collected the hamburger offered him by his daughter, who reminded her papa that the mustard packets he liked were in the bag, and soon got his party out on America's broad freeways again, increasing by a tad the big Caddy's cruising speed.

Jacob's bladder was setting them back.

~ ~ ~

By ten-thirty p.m., they had checked into a motel. Connecticut's *Quiet Corner,* their innkeeper, a college student in a blazer the color of smoked salmon, enlightened them. Sleeping arrangements? No one had thought about sleeping arrangements. Specifically, who was to be Jacob's roommate? The old man couldn't be left alone and it appeared the only practical solution was men with men and women with women, an agreement Peter accepted but didn't like.

He spoke with Jeanette as he got her settled. "You going to be okay?"

"I'll be fine, Papa."

"I think everybody's so tired that we'll all go to sleep right away, anyway. And tomorrow's going to be just us."

"I'll be fine, Papa. Don't worry."

After hours of driving he had trouble not driving. Talking with Fay in the hall, Peter had the hallucinatory sensation that he was piloting an airplane through a skinny tunnel. The days of massive commutes, back-to-back five-hundred-mile treks to make customer meetings in far-flung cities, were definitely behind him.

"We'll be gone all day," he warned Fay. "Maybe even dinner, I don't know?"

"You take care of your baby, that's your job. Jacob and me will

Robert McKean

go for a roll around the neighborhood. Don't worry."

"I'm hearing that a lot these days. What if he needs to pee?"

Fay leaned into him and slid her fingers across his crotch. "In twelve hours that's bound to happen?"

"What did you tell them at the nursing home?"

"Is that still bothering you?"

"I can't believe Jessica bought into this?"

"Well, I didn't really talk to her, to be frank."

"She doesn't expect us? What did you tell them?"

"What they wanted to hear. I explained that I was an old student of Jacob's and that I was planning a surprise party for him on Monday."

"And they didn't *call* her—to confirm that?"

"Actually, we got a little lucky that way. The director went off to call her, but just then one of the patients took that opportunity to have a seizure. I admit I do feel a little funny about this part, and I'm not sure it *was* a seizure—in a clinical way, if you know what I mean? But whatever it was, it happened in the TV room in front of everybody. In the confusion they were happy to sign us out. I told the director my combo's been working really hard on our Mozart to play for Jacob, since that's his favorite."

"They're not generally called *combos*. And I think you forgot his glasses."

Fay administered another pat below the belt. "Hey, I'm just glad he didn't ask me what instrument it was that I studied with Jacob for fifteen years—I went stone blank. Saxophone?"

"Glockenspiel."

"You worry too much, everything'll be fine."

Sometime in the night he woke with such violence that he knew sleep was not going to return. This had been happening a lot recently. And even when he did manage to sleep through an entire night, he seldom slept well. Because he snored? Sleep apnea, that's what Avis had claimed. But his roommate, who was issuing anguished gasps that sounded like a vacuum trying to suck up a rag, appeared to be sleeping fine. Tomorrow they were to meet with the Director of Admissions and receive a tour of the campus. He didn't expect a stressful day as there wouldn't be any kind of formal assessment. But first impressions matter, and he took Avis's warnings seriously. He respected the thought she'd put into the visit, even on short notice, down to taking the time to provide Jeanette with a special outfit she was expected to wear.

"Dmitri," Jacob muttered.

Peter rolled to his side. "You all right, bub? Need to use the head?"

"Dmitri, stop it!"

He was about to get up, but his roommate, moaning, subsided in his covers. Perhaps Dmitri, whoever he was, had agreed to stop whatever objectionable thing he'd been doing. Peter listened to the blats of the semitrailers' air horns arising from the nearby highway. Reflections from their headlights flitted across the room, the desk and the television whose darkened screen seemed as big as a drive-in theater. As a traveling salesman, he'd had opportunity to note changes in hotel fashion, as the

Robert McKean

roadside cottages with flowered curtains sewn by your innkeeper's wife and pastel toilets whose handles you had to remember to jiggle gave way before the homogenized franchise boxes that now cluttered the interstate exits.

Well, at least the toilets worked better.

From some sonic Lost & Found repository in Peter's sleepless brain a memory surfaced: his grandfather's "Where or When." Fatty's delicate chording would bring a lush orchestration to the piano. He would deconstruct a tune as he explored it, then rebuild it into something other. You had to wonder if the cigar rollers, eyes ringed with tobacco dust, appreciated the artistry, the irony, the surprising urbanity of the courteous, portly pianist in the white shirt and derby perched above. Someone in some faraway room who hadn't heard that this was Connecticut's Quiet Corner whooped, and Jacob thrashed in his blankets again.

"Damn thing's gonna piss all over the rug!"

And Peter remembers: Dmitri was Jacob's hound.

~~~

Their appointment with Wilfred Hall Academy's Director of Admissions, a Janet Considine, was not scheduled until two. But when Jeanette and he rose from the inn's breakfast buffet, Peter suggested that they start their day immediately. His worries remained, and, if anything, had deepened. *Kidnapping* might be melodramatic, but people usually take a dim view of their relatives being spirited away without permission. And Jacob seemed even more confused this morning. He thought he was still at the nursing home. But Jacob would have to wait. Peter committed the clarinetist to Fay's guardianship and steered the Cadillac in a ramble through Connecticut's countryside. Jeanette's special outfit turned out to be a plain cotton jumper, as green as fresh spinach. In the front were two practical patch pockets with oversized buttons. Beneath the jumper she wore a full-body white leotard. The ensemble was attractive, especially the snowy turtleneck contrasting with her dark hair, but its simplicity, its self-conscious plainness, mystified him. Jeanette, being Jeanette, hadn't been able to resist a touch of theater: From his parents' closet she'd brought a small woven-straw purse, a colorful bead-work parrot on its side. The purse, which featured a cross-body strap and swung smartly against her hip, had belonged to Peter's grandaunt, who, the story went, marched in suffragette protests and shot a mean game of snooker. But there was something else about the costume that Avis had assembled for their daughter that worked on Peter: the soberness of the sturdy jumper and white leotard, the seriousness of Jeanette's gleaming dark braids, even in its own way the vintage flappers' purse—somehow it all went together to make his daughter seem suddenly, if not quite grown up, more grown up than he ordinarily thought of her: a maiden about to step forward into her own newly-claimed world.

Call it today's heart breaker.

What they discovered on their drive, a sort of impromptu tour, was that this triangle of Northeast Connecticut did appear to be—disarmingly—stereotypical New England: autumn leaves that had escaped collection lifting from village greens and blowing across the

Robert McKean

Cadillac's faded hood; narrow lanes of dark Emily Dickinson houses like ranks of high-waisted schoolmarms; tall, righteous, congregational churches, communicants ganged on the steps chatting about recycling and God. You would have thought they were motoring through a Robert Frost poem. But honestly, Peter reflected, thinking of the soot-laden skies beneath which he grew up, one could do worse than live out one's adolescence carrying one's schoolbooks across these neatly clipped green swards.

"Are they going to give me a test?"

"No, no, honey, it's not that kind of visit. But I imagine the director will ask you about what you like and so forth."

"Should I tell the truth?"

What a question: He was appalled. "Of course."

They were idling at a stoplight. Along the roadside a single lingering summer rose had bloomed in a witches'-broom tangle of half-dried canes. The rose was a delicate coral. Peter pondered a sign for the Nathan Hale Homestead: Did they have time? Probably not. "Elliott's going to teach me how to shoot a gun," Jeanette said. "We're going to go hunting together."

Which landed, that remark, like a bomb.

An unexploded bomb, but, nevertheless, as Peter weighed this announcement from a discreet distance as an ordinance disposal specialist might, he instantly decided several things, beginning with: This hunting expedition was going to happen over his dead body. But this was not the time to denounce Elliott Fields. He settled on a casual parental demurrer. "Elliott has his own hobbies, and there's nothing wrong with that. But I'm not happy about your going off with him to kill some harmless forest creatures, Jeanette. Maybe there's some other things he can teach you."

That last sentence had not been delivered as a question, but Jeanette seemed to consider it in that light. "Elliott's funny sometimes."

Peter sensed her holding back. But again, this was neither the time nor place to delve into her stepdad's many not-so-charming qualities. "We'll talk about this some other time, sugar, but I'm not thrilled about you being around guns."

~ ~ ~

Shortly before two, they climbed the stairs to the third and top floor of Wilfred Hall Academy's version of Old Main, an imposing columned building that stood at the head of the green that billowed up from town. A winsome old campus: venerable white oaks; fences of cannonball-sized stones fused with a hundred summers' worth of English ivy; impressive stands of rhododendrons, or mountain laurel, he was never sure which was which; sprawling flowerbeds from which the last fainting annuals had only been recently lifted. The academy's gray-block limestone buildings were also spider-webbed with ivy; some windows appeared to be completely stitched over. Indeed, you could easily imagine Robert Frost, or better yet, one of the Nineteenth Century poets with immense beards and three names—John Greenleaf Whittier, Henry Wadsworth Longfellow—strolling these autumn-hued lawns.

"Ready, kiddo?"

"Mama said I'm to look at people in their eyes."

Peter clapped an arm around her shoulder. "Your mama gives good advice."

Inside, they discovered that whatever antique architectural details that might have survived had largely given way to gypsum walls, primary-color paint, fluorescent lighting. No *Middlemarch* doom and gloom here, Peter thought. They peeked in a seminar room. Whiteboards and dry-erase markers, black-mesh Aeron chairs huddled around a conference table. From the ceiling dangled an LCD projector, its diodes blinking humorlessly. He entertained an image of his daughter listening to a PowerPoint lecture being delivered by an instructor wielding a laser pointer with pinpoint accuracy—and sighed deeply. But the building still smelled like a school, and that was heartening: frowzy odors of too many under-washed bodies and under-laundered clothing, along with vague fruit scents, banana, apple, orange. They should pipe in chalk dust, he thought. Sunday afternoon meetings were probably not the norm, he was cognizant of that, and, when Ms. Considine emerged from her office to greet them—there was no secretary—Peter thanked her specifically.

"I had to be here anyway." Janet Considine brushed aside his solicitude. "I have a stack of applications to plow through. So, this is Jeanette? Jeanette, I had a lovely conversation with your mother. She's a friend of Judge Davis. And gosh, that's a pretty pocketbook."

Jeanette bashfully exhibited the purse on its long strap to the director, who ran her fingers over the bead-work parrot. "It belonged to my great-great aunt," Jeanette said, "I think?" She checked with Peter for substantiation.

"Quite a colorful character."

Ms. Considine looked at him inquiringly.

"One of Susan B. Anthony's compatriots," he explained, experiencing a passing qualm: Was his scandalous grandaunt's purse cleaned out before Jeanette uncovered it in the closet? He had a terror of a petrified prophylactic falling out into the director's palm. "As well as other things," he added dismissively.

Ms. Considine shepherded them into a lounge area. Peter and Jeanette sat on a Crate & Barrel sofa whose corduroy wales had been rubbed smooth; the director chose an armchair no less careworn. Peter hadn't known, in terms of the director, what to anticipate, but supposed, had he given it much thought, that they would've been met by, say, a slender woman with silver hair and beaky nose, a native New Englander with scant patience for Western Pennsylvania bumpkins. But Janet Considine, in her mid-thirties, was short, borderline plump, and sounded, given the resonant twang in her vowels, as if she hailed from somewhere south of the Mason-Dixon Line. She didn't so much ignore Peter— although he understood that he was not her focus—as bring to bear her entire concentration on his daughter.

"Your mom tells me that you're a very talented musician, Jeanette. She's very proud of you. I studied the piano, although I haven't played in years. Do you have a favorite composer?"

Jeanette checked with Peter again. Was this the test? "My piano teacher likes folk songs."

"Like what?"

"I have a book with Simon and Garfunkel songs and another one with Peter, Paul, and Mary songs."

"So, are those your favorites?"

Jeanette squirmed. "They're a little too easy," she said, telling the truth. She remembered to make eye contact. "I learned something by Beethoven, I liked that."

" 'Für Elise'?"

"Not that, but I learned that, too. It was a bagatelle. It went real fast. And I'm learning some things by Debussy. I like him, too."

Janet Considine had a scattering of freckles under her eyes and across the bridge of her nose. When she smiled, her freckles seemed to move. "I think if you love the piano, you have to love Claude Debussy. But tell me about yourself. Do you like to read? Who are your favorite writers? Are you a big Harry Potter fan—most of our girls are?"

While the director gently interviewed his daughter, sliding seamlessly between questions, from authors—and yes, of course, Jeanette was mad for Harry—into school subjects, both the good and the bad, then friendship and school life, more bad than good here, Peter steeled himself to face the very real possibility that this might be where his daughter would spend the remaining years of her childhood. *Should* he throw a broomstick in the spokes? Would not be difficult. But he could not make himself do that, and, whenever the conversation turned back to him, he tried not to stir the waters.

"So, what do you do, Mr. Sanguedolce?" the director asked. "I understand your wife, your former wife, is a lawyer."

She stumbled over his name; most people did. He pronounced it—*San-way-doich'-chay*—and delivered the lines he'd rehearsed. "No, no, she's the legal mastermind, I'm a semi-retired businessman. I'm presently occupied with closing down our family business. After that, I'm not sure."

"Closing your family business? Was it a very old business?"

"The company goes back a long way, yes, even before our family's involvement in it."

"That must be difficult—emotionally, I mean?"

Like removing the skin from your palms, he wanted to answer, remembering John Pruce, a Welsh laborer who'd been with the clay works for fifty-four years, the look on that man's face, what had burned in his eyes when Peter handed him his severance letter. Was *he* to tell the truth? John Pruce was seventy-two, an individual of prudence and modesty and, doubtless, adequate savings. What had burned in the crystal-blue eyes of John Pruce was not worry for the future, but naked, undisguised contempt. Instead, Peter gave Director Considine the anodyne answer people wanted to hear. "It's been a draining experience, yes."

"But you do have future plans? Travel perhaps?"

And now the lie, full-throated. "Oh, absolutely, business runs in my blood. I fully intend to get back in the game. I already have feelers out. I'm also interested in the school's emphasis on education by seminar, as you call it? We looked in at some rooms. Do you use the seminar approach even in the primary grades?"

And, to be honest, as the conversation swung back to Jeanette, Peter found that he was, in fact, rather drawn to the school. Its pedagogical principles appeared interesting and innovative, its social life a miniature United Nations—something he would've loved as a boy— and the music program apparently everything one could ask for. After their meeting with the director, they were assigned a tour guide, a girl named Lina, who was Jeanette's height and hardly much older, a Thai girl who wore a man's lumberjack shirt as a jacket and tall riding boots with crisscrossing laces. And as they wended a path through classroom, dormitory, and gymnasium, Peter went out of his way to ask questions and attend to the girl's conscientious, lightly accented answers: to do, in short, what he could to make it as easy as possible for his daughter to face a bigger decision than he'd ever had to face. The two girls seemed to get along well. Lina was especially sweet. It was only later, as they were driving back to the inn after dinner, that Peter realized that beneath her flannel shirt she too was wearing a jumper, not green but midnight blue, with two pockets in front, and that most of the girls they encountered were wearing jumpers, though not all, possibly because it was Sunday. Putting it together, he credited Avis once again for the care she'd put into this visit.

The inn, they blessedly discovered, had not been set afire by Jacob Weiner, nor had Fay Halbrunner been led away in manacles. No helicopters were hovering. With Jacob snoring away like a wheezy vacuum cleaner and Jeanette, within minutes, asleep in front of the television, Peter and Fay had the talk that he'd promised himself they would have.

"Well, he did roll off a couple of times," she confessed. "But I rolled him back. We do, though, seem to have one teeny tiny problem."

Peter lifted an eyebrow.

"He's in and out of it and when he's out of it he thinks I'm his wife and Jeanette's his daughter. He keeps asking me if she's been practicing?"

"So, I can leave you all three here to live happily ever after?"

"D'you know Jessica's address? Jacob's a little unclear on that."

"I don't have a clue. Fay, we need to declare victory and go home. Let's stick him in the car tomorrow and leave. He won't know the difference. We can be back by evening."

"Oh, com' on now, how many Jessie Weiners can there be in Boston?" Fay kissed him. "What color, guess?"

"Actually, it's Jessica, and how would I possibly know the answer to that other question?"

"Guess!"

"Fay, we—"

"They're what I call my *shorties,* you've seen them?" Fay brought her knee up his leg and purred. "Everything's going to be fine. All we're doing is helping the Weiners have a family reunion. We leave them together if that's what they want or we take him back for crafts day—no big deal. Either way, he gets to see her one last time and she gets to say to him whatever she wants."

"I don't like this. It's not going to work."

"That's what they told the guy who invented lipstick."

Awake in the night, Peter put Jacob Weiner and Fay Halbrunner out of his mind and tried to think both coolly and lovingly about his daughter. He'd been aware, as their campus tour wound down—dormitory lights winking on in the old stone buildings, their breaths ghosting before them as the afternoon temperatures dropped—that Jeanette had begun to withdraw. It had been, to be sure, a big day for a ten-year-old. But as they ate dinner and now as he lay sleepless, Peter decided that it wasn't tiredness but reality soaking in: *This could really happen*. Jeanette had declined to take her coat off in the restaurant, even though the room was warm, and picked at her turkey cutlet and fries. He wanted to ask her what she thought of the school, what her impressions were. But no, not tonight.

Tonight she was a very frightened little girl.

~ ~ ~

While his group finished their OJs and chocolate chip muffins the next morning, Peter drove off to gas the Cadillac and check the oil. As a quart of oil gurgled into the engine, he gazed, hands in his pockets, into the grease-caked architecture of the automobile's machinery—pipes, wires, hoses. The big sedan, its V-8 already rebuilt once, had carried him comfortably, like a howdah on an elephant's back, two hundred and ten thousand miles.

"Got a deal going on transmission fluid," the young attendant informed him. "Today only. You want me to check her?"

Peter was dividing two hundred thousand by twenty-five thousand: more than eight voyages around the globe. "You know," he replied, deploring the oil on the boy's hands, "I don't think I want to know what's in the transmission. But thank you anyway."

The young man swiped his nose, adding more petroleum to his skin, and slammed the mammoth hood shut. "Have a good one then, boss."

Not so much a suggestion, as an order.

Sometime today he had to have a difficult conversation with Jeanette, who had awakened moody and irritable. Jacob, surprisingly, seemed this morning to recollect the purpose of their trip. He insisted on being helped into the shower, where there was a low shelf he could sit on, then demanded a razor. As his palsied hands ran Peter's triple-track razor over the grizzle on his cheeks, he shouted through the steam, "I don't wanna be coming home and hearing any more of this half-ass practicing, Jessica! Focus!" He flung the plastic razor into the far reaches of the shower, snapping off its head. *"Focus!"*

Well, maybe not fully recollected the purpose.

Before going back into the hotel, he did something probably ill-advised, certainly something that would not be condoned by his lawyer: He called the offices of Fields & Longstreet and inquired of his receptionist buddy if Attorney Longstreet was available.

"I have precisely one minute," Avis told him when she came on. "So what's wrong?"

This, Peter realized, was the day's first difficult conversation.

Robert McKean

"You sound like my mother. That's what she'd say if you called unexpectedly. We had our visit yesterday."

"And?"

"Went fine, I think. The campus is lovely. It looks like a scene out of Currier & Ives. But they're really picky, Avis? It's not only intelligence they're looking for, but diversity, character, sociability, talent, and leadership. I can't imagine how you evaluate children on their leadership abilities, but it's part of their mix."

"Peter, I know all this. Judge Davis is going to coach us. I'm not worried about Jeanette—I'm worried about you. You better have not screwed things up?"

"I didn't do anything wrong. I was trying to be as helpful as possible. But it's scaring her. Isn't there anything closer—Carnegie, Shadyside, Squirrel Hill? Why does it have to be a boarding school?"

"Peter, they're putting together a jury pool for a clearly guilty client of mine whose only alternative to being flayed alive is to plea-bargain—and who stubbornly *won't*. I gotta go."

"Sorry, of course. We'll be back Tuesday, late probably."

"Well, enjoy Boston." Avis's voice, suddenly falling out from beneath her, sounded tired and bleak. "We had a good time there once, I still remember it."

Boston was where they had honeymooned. "So do I."

A long time ago he'd learned—any traveling salesman will tell you—that you can only ingest so many hotel muffins. Especially the ones as large as a mastiff's head. Perhaps, in view of the shadow his belly cast, he learned that lesson belatedly. But be that as it may, Peter discovered his muffin-fuddled troop strewn phlegmatically across the lobby sofas. He stowed their luggage, returned and rolled Jacob Weiner out, then rolled him back to visit the inn's first-floor lav one last time, and they were, by ten-thirty, steaming toward Paul Revere's hometown.

Jeanette, returned today to regulation jeans and sneaks, awarded him a look of strained forbearance when he asked if she'd slept well. "I'm fine, Papa."

She was rubbing the back of her ear. "Are your glasses bothering you?"

"I'm fine, I'm fine, I'm fine!"

She's fine. Chastened, Peter lowered the brim of his hat and concentrated on driving, which, as they crossed into Massachusetts and entered the crush of the metropolitan area's traffic, he understood what was required of him. Fay, researching on her phone, broadcast from the backseat. "There's a zillion Weiners in Boston—isn't that amazing, who would've thought? But no Jessicas and no listings with *J* as a first initial. But there's one in Hyde Park, wherever that is, and one in Cambridge— that's *Haaar*vard if you didn't know—and a couple in Brookline. Ever heard of Brookline, Peter?"

"What if she's working? Since most normal people—present company excluded—do. What if she's unlisted?"

"Maybe she got married and changed her name?" Jeanette offered dryly.

Fay consulted their other passenger. "Jacob, try again: Where does Jessie live?"

The old man turned to her blankly.

A mistake, bringing Jacob here. Disrespectful of the man, even if it was what he'd begged for, disrespectful of his daughter. How was this any business of theirs whether father and daughter were to be reconciled? But in a restroom outside Boston's city limits, Peter's thinking took another turn. He'd been half-hoping—and more or less counting on— that in the sprawl of Boston they wouldn't be able to track down Jessica and that they'd come away having done no lasting damage. Essentially, as juvenile as it sounded, get Jacob back before anyone noticed he'd gone missing. But as he eased the old music teacher down on the toilet, yanking the man's underpants away from the shrunken penis in its gray fuzz, he recognized that despite moments of clarity Jacob's bewilderment this weekend had steadily deepened.

"Jacob!" he barked, "Jessica works in a clinic, right? Some sort of health clinic? You told me that once, I'm sure you did. Jacob— where's that clinic?"

"Oak Grove."

"No, it's not! Where does Jessica work—in Boston?"

"Oak Grove."

"No! Boston, man—*Boston!"*

"Roxbury."

"Where in Roxbury?"

"Hausman Avenue."

"Thank you." Peter closed the stall door. "Hausman Avenue."

Mending What Is Broken   159

"Just try buzzing for a nurse around here," the old man muttered.

Among the many sunny memories of his honeymoon were the not-quite-so-sunny ones of he and Avis scurrying like terrified mice across Boston's busy streets. But as certifiably mad as its kamikaze drivers were, it was his traveling salesman's opinion that the ineffectiveness of driver education in Massachusetts was fully equaled by the Commonwealth's confusing and inadequate road signage. At eighty-seven miles an hour, barely keeping abreast of the vehicles surrounding him, Peter sliced the lumbering Cadillac across three lanes of turnpike traffic toward a pitch-black exit whose sign was too filth-encrusted to read. Failing to grasp the distinction between Copley and Huntington, once he did fathom the sign's message, he slammed the brakes, steered the car in a claustrophobically tight death spiral, and somehow avoided crashing into a wall to emerge street level headed still further east, toward the retail and business districts, toward the sea.

"Fay, I need help! Where's Hausman?"

Fay quoted from her phone: " 'The Sarah E. Keating Health Center is an independent, community-based outpatient and resource facility for the women and children of Roxbury. Offering compassionate care, our physicians and nursing staff provide a full range of medical and preventative services in seven languages: English, Spanish, Khmer, Cape Verdean Creole, Haitian Creole, Mandarin, and Cantonese.' " She turned to Jacob. "That is a *powerful* amount of tongues. Does Jessie speak all those languages?"

"Hausman, Fay, *Hausman!*"

"Just hold your horses, would you?"

Peter, waiting for direction, conducted them through Boston's Back Bay, past the Public Garden and the Common. At one point they crested a hill and glided under the gold-domed state house, where he was tempted to dash in and introduce a bill on automotive etiquette. Before he was able to formulate his legislative measure, however, they plunged like lemmings over the back of the hill and wobbled down a long street—toward heaven knows where.

"It's off Washington!"

"How do I get to Washington?"

"How would I know? Where are we now?"

"I don't know!"

Jeanette, gazing through both palms pressed to her window, said, "Cambridge."

"We're in Cambridge?" Fay said. "Really?"

"Cambridge *Street*," Jeanette specified, then amended her answer as Peter hauled the Cadillac around a bend. "Now we're on New Sudbury—and that's Bulfinch! The corner of New Sudbury and Bulfinch."

"Fay, hurry!"

"Why don't you pull over? How am I supposed to find out where we're at if you keep moving?"

"I'll be happy to pull over—if I could."

"New Sudbury and Congress," Jeanette reported.

"Fay!"

"Congress and Hanover."

"Fay!"

"D'you think we'll have any time for shopping?"

"Fay!"

"Can't hold it much longer," Jacob announced.

~ ~ ~

Early afternoon, after a meandering tour of Boston's financial district and North End, where they did, as a matter of fact, spot the steeple of the Old North Church—off in the distance, rather as Paul viewed it—and an emergency stop for Jacob at a McDonald's that turned into lunch, they were on Hausman Avenue before the Sarah E. Keating Health Center, a one-story, ramshackle building. The windows of the center, which formerly had been a *Mr. Sweeper*—the silhouette of an upright vac still faintly glimmered above the storefront—were papered with children's crayon drawings on brightly colored construction paper.

Fay had cold feet. "Maybe it'd be better if you took him in? Since you grew up playing with her and everything?"

"I wouldn't recognize Jessica Weiner if I ran into her. I assume you've worked out what you're going to say?"

"Surprise?"

They managed, not without a struggle, to heave the old man out of the Cadillac's low backseat and into his wheelchair. Jacob's patience, along with his energy, was waning. He refused to untangle his feet from the footrests and swatted at their hands. *Sooner we get him into Jessica's care*, Peter thought, *the better*. Fay brushed imaginary crumbs from his shirtfront and assailed Peter. "What're you worried about? She's going to be thrilled—this is her *daddy,* after all. I'm only sorry I forgot to grab the pictures."

"You wanna go back? You might find his glasses while you're at it?"

Raising her eyebrows in exasperation—or in supplication—Fay, trembling, frightened of this reality she'd brought upon herself, took hold of the black handles of Jacob Weiner's wheelchair and briskly rolled him into his daughter's place of business. Peter watched them disappear into the fluorescent haze and climbed back into the car and said to his daughter, who was also frightened, "Jeanette, we need to talk a little— about the school? We don't have to settle anything at the moment but we need to begin. I know you're upset, but I want to help, I'm your papa."

She pressed the tuft end of a braid against her mouth.

He could not have picked a worse time. He understood that. But they *did* have to begin. "Did you like the school? How do you feel about it? Did you like Ms. Considine? I would imagine she's reflective of how the teachers would be. What about Lina? She seemed very nice—maybe she would become a friend?"

"I don't care."

"Of course you care."

"It doesn't matter what I feel."

"Jeanette, what you feel matters more to me than anything else."

"I don't know what I want, Papa," she said quietly. "I'm sorry."

This sounded as if it were coming from a deeper part of her.

"That's not a bad answer, honey. Maybe it means that we have to tell your mama that she needs to put this off for a bit, so you can think about it more? And we can do that, we can stop this right here. Would you like me to tell her that?"

"It doesn't matter."

Back to where they began. Whether the source of such defeatism stemmed from Avis or him or from some grievous alchemized blend— the worst of both her parents who each had so much worse to offer—he didn't know, but he did know that he hated and feared this attitude of hopelessness. "Please stop saying that, honey, you need to be—"

At that moment Fay, minus Jacob, opened the back door and jumped in. She slammed the door and buried her head in her palms. "Peter, you have to go in there!"

"I told you, I'm not—"

"She's going to have us arrested!"

"What did you say?"

"Only that her daddy wanted to see her badly so we drove him up here. Oh, I should've never let myself get talked into this! I should've minded my own business!"

A statement so delusional as to render Peter without a response. Fay stamped her feet. "Go! You hear me, *go!* Calm the bitch down!"

Peter looked at Jeanette, whose speechless reply was in fact the presentation of a face the adult world had with remarkable deftness already taught her. His daughter's expression you might have loosely translated as: *You made your bed, you lie in it.*

Robert McKean

~ ~ ~

He claimed he wouldn't recognize Jessica Weiner, and seeing her—she was on the phone, standing behind the counter—Peter granted the probable truth of that, especially if he hadn't been thinking of her. But he had been thinking of her, and from ragtag bits of memory he identified his neighbor's brittle, intense, volatile daughter: her heavy brows, her wide mouth, her fleshy lips. At Ganaego High she'd had a scandalous reputation. Clearly gifted in a way no one else, student or teacher, could grasp—or deal with—Jessica Weiner had also been one fast girl, someone in constant hot water.

Carmen, Peter had thought, lost in his puppy love, she was his Carmen.

Jessica curtailed her phone call and smacked her palm down on the counter top. "Peter Sanguedolce, what is the meaning of this!"

Not a question. Nor would he have had an answer if it were. Jessica, a woman in a fury, ordered him to follow her. They crossed through a narrow lobby, squeezing between two rows of Black and Hispanic women. The women, infants in arms, toddlers clinging to their dresses, gazed at Peter suspiciously. Of Jacob, Peter saw no evidence. Jessica pointed at an examination room and banged shut the door behind them.

"Sit down!" Her face—older than he remembered, rougher, a series of weathered oblique planes framed by her dark hair—was drawn tight. "The simpering fool who was in here—is that your wife?"

"Not my wife." Which made it worse. "Actually"—only now

Peter recalled this—"she's the person who bought your father's house, she and her husband." Jessica shook her head, even more dumbfounded, and he sympathized: Could it get any weirder? Understanding, though, that confessions, if they are to succeed at all, only succeed when they come unbidden, he waded into his. "They'll be building next to me. I found some pictures, snapshots, of your family when I was helping them clean out the house, old ones, and when I took Fay to visit your father we showed them to him. We thought they might cheer Jacob up, but he got confused. He thought we were there to take him home, and since we couldn't do that, he pleaded with us to bring him here to see you. He was crying, we didn't know what to say. But, still, it was a mistake, we shouldn't have done it. I'm honestly sorry, Jessica."

The room smelled of alcohol. On the counters were glass decanters of tongue depressors and cotton balls, boxes of inhumanly blue latex gloves. Jessica, who had not sat down in the other chair, clenched her fists against her skirt. "And just like that, without giving it a moment's thought, you stash a befuddled old man in your car and drive off with him? Peter, this beggars even the most *feeble* commonsense, I can't believe it."

"I was under the impression that she—Fay, that's her name— had gotten permission from both the nursing home and you for us to bring him here. But I should've checked with you myself."

"At a minimum!"

Jessica gave him an exasperated look, a look not so different from the looks his daughter and lover had just given him and, before

Robert McKean

them, the looks he'd received from former wives, from his mother, even, on occasion, from his father, who had loved him so far out of proportion to what he deserved. "I'm sorry. What would you like me to do? I'll do whatever you want."

"Go to hell would be a good start." Jessica pressed her fists deeper into her skirt. "Listen, you can't stay here—we need every room and we've already lost one to my father. Go sit in your car or something. I have no idea under what pretense you could've obtained my father's release. Why wasn't I consulted? Why didn't they call me? I don't have time for this. We're in crisis here, we're in perpetual crisis, but I need to talk with the nursing home and with my father and then maybe I want to call the police, I don't know."

Outside, Peter found that Fay and Jeanette had locked the car doors. The big burgundy Cadillac had begun to attract attention. Jeanette scrambled across the seat to open his door an inch, then retreated to her corner and returned the end of a braid to her mouth. Peter settled into his bowl of a seat. Fay removed her fingers from her mouth and demanded, "*Well?* Did you talk her down?"

"She's pretty upset. She wants us to wait."

"Are we going to jail?" Jeanette asked.

His daughter was scared—by the threat of arrest, by the neighborhood, by the bizarre way, he supposed, the grownups around her were acting. She was shivering, and not from the cold. "It's okay, honey. We tried to do something nice and it backfired. We made a mistake, but everything'll be fine."

"We didn't make a mistake," Fay corrected him. *"We* didn't do anything wrong." She swiveled her head, looking around nervously. "Why don't we just go? We did our bit for God and country, let's just call it a day."

"She wants us to wait."

"Who gives a shit what she wants? She's a big girl, she can figure out what she wants to do with her leaky old daddy. I say let's go."

"She wants us to stay."

"Well, I don't want to."

"Papa," Jeanette pleaded, "can't we go?"

"See!" Fay exulted. "Let's go, com' on, com' on!"

Jessica Weiner, thankfully not long after, pushed open the lobby door. She stepped around the Cadillac's long prow, eying the antique car with distaste. Peter rolled down the window.

"Come with me!"

Jeanette squealed softly, "Papa!" He tried to bestow on her his salesman's confident smile, but she was staring dead ahead, rigid with terror.

What have I done? Peter thought.

Her heels scraping the sidewalk, Jessica strode to the corner of the building. The day had grown chilly. The sun was lost behind a gray soup of Boston clouds. Jessica, not having bothered to put on a coat, clasped her arms about herself. Beside her, taped to the inside of the window, was a drawing of a scarecrow girl before a house constructed of a square and a triangle. "I talked to the nursing home. I'm no more happy with them than I am with you. They're claiming they called me and that I never returned the call. As far as they're concerned, my father's enjoying a weekend party being hosted by one of his oldest students. I don't believe they exercised even the least due diligence. This is outrageous, you, her, them—*all of it!*"

"I'm very sorry, Jessica."

She jerked her head in the direction of the car. "That ninny wasn't a pupil of my father's, I can't believe that?"

"No, no, she made that story up. I respect your father." His explanation was going to come across as phony and self-exculpatory; nonetheless, he wanted her to hear it. "I admire him. I know something about music, I used to love listening to him practicing on his back stoop, and I've always taken pleasure in our conversations."

He could see her anger lifting, slightly. "Look, I know that you and he were friends, and I know that you're about the only one of his old buddies who do visit him. I know that because the director just told me that." Her anger, which had momentarily eased, came rushing back. "But is this how you express your admiration? I don't get it!"

He suppressed an inappropriate smile. He could see this woman singing fiery, wronged Donna Elvira, having no idea whether that Mozartean role would have been in her range or artistic compass. "Did you have a chance to talk with him? I was worried, he seemed to be getting foggier as we traveled?"

"Talk, you mean did we have a chance to quarrel? Trust me, we never lacked time for that." Jessica, shrugging in total and final frustration, looked at Peter curiously. "So, you're a musician? Is that what you said? I remember you when I was growing up, but not really very well."

As hugely as she had appeared on his radar, he'd always assumed that he'd never appeared on hers. That she recalled him, even slightly, pleased him. "I studied the piano, but I didn't keep it up. So no, I'm not a musician. But my grandfather and uncle were."

"Professional?"

"Small-town. My uncle played the organ at the roller rink."

And at that, Jessica consented to smile. "I remember the organist. So that was your uncle? Mop of fuzzy gray hair, suspenders, fat cigar? He was gay, wasn't he? That's what people said?"

"Uncle Nico, fat cigar, fuzzy hair, gay in a conservative town, yeah, that was him."

"He did a lot of playful things with that honking old Hammond. He was fun to skate to. Anyway"—Jessica's smile disappeared along with, one presumed, any sentimental memories she may have harbored of the Ganaego Roller Rink—"here's what I want you to do. I want you to put my father in your car and drive him back to where he belongs, and I want you to call me when he's there and safe. I've explained all this to him. I've told him he can't stay here. He's not happy about that, but I don't know if he's ever been happy—about anything."

We have a photograph of a happy Jacob, Peter longed to say to this high strung, smoldering woman, *and you're happy in it, too*. "I'll come in and get him and we'll go. I'm sorry, I promise we'll take good care of him heading home."

"I don't want your promises." She hugged herself more tightly. "This is like a bad practical joke, it's a mean and hurtful prank, and I don't like it."

~ ~ ~

He stopped at the first hotel they stumbled upon, the Copley Plaza. No one objected, no one cared. Even the valet, smirking, found something droll about their party. Dutifully, they followed an ancient bellhop to their rooms, where the tiny withered man in his natty livery unloaded their luggage cart and waited for his gratuity. Jeanette curled up in a blanket before the television, and Fay announced that Newbury Street was two blocks away and she was going shopping. She added, "I would've left him there. I still think that would've been best—for both of them."

Peter shifted his shoulders equivocally. "I don't know."

"Well, I do." Fay collected her purse. "Peter, you can be a sweet guy, but you're also a fool. Anyway, as far as I'm concerned, he belongs to you now."

Peter rolled Jacob into the bathroom. He assumed the old man must grasp something of what had occurred, at the very least the rejection by his daughter. But perhaps not. Jacob pawed for the toilet paper. "Call the friggin' nurse, wouldja?"

"Jacob, what d'you need? Are you hungry?"

"You could fill your shoes with piss before someone comes."

"D'you want to take a nap?"

"What?"

"Do you want to take a nap?"

"Oh, sure, sure, why didn't you say so?"

That afternoon Jacob's heavy stertor sounded like someone ripping through a sheet of aluminum siding with a hacksaw. Peter, slumped in an armchair, contemplated the snaggletoothed skyline of Boston's Back Bay. A soaring blue rhomboid dominated the scene. That was the building—he felt pretty confident of this—whose windows came sailing off like enormous playing cards. At the rhomboid's feet, looking as small as a house of worship for Tom Thumb, sat a blocky Nineteenth Century red-stone church. He felt a tinge of guilt for not being able to identify it. Boston's classical library he recognized, and poking up behind the library were the venerable stones of another church campanile. In the center of this hodgepodge urban assemblage lay a plaza from which pigeons rose in a silent rout. When he and Avis had honeymooned here, they stayed at a hotel close to the waterfront and walked or trolleyed to the museums, the Paul Revere House, the aquarium, the symphony, to a used bookstore in Somerville, where he bought for thirty-five cents a cover-less Robert Parker paperback. Lying between his bride's naked legs, making a pillow of her pudenda, Peter read to his new wife Susan and Spenser dialogues. In the North End they had a lobster risotto of which even his persnickety grandmother might have approved.

He lived mostly in the past, yes. A fatal flaw.

At some point Jacob's snores subsided. Perhaps he'd finally

Robert McKean

sawn through the aluminum siding. The old music teacher, bone weary, heart weary, had slipped into a silent, motionless sleep. Peter, a bit apprehensively, checked to ensure it wasn't an even deeper sleep that Jacob Weiner had slipped into, then looked in on his daughter across the hall. Jeanette slumbered dreamlessly. She lay on the floor rolled up in her blanket like a papoose. It appeared that the whole world on this gray, grainy October had elected to abandon consciousness. He considered transferring Jeanette to the bed, but decided not to disturb her. Antsy himself, though, he recalled Jacob's decapitating his razor this morning, and, with that as his excuse, he snatched up his fedora and sailed down the elevator and asked at the front desk if there was a pharmacy nearby.

"What is it you need, sir? I'll be happy to provide you whatever personal items you need."

"Thank you, but I could use a breath of fresh air."

"There's a CVS across the square on Boylston."

He lingered for a moment to enjoy the hotel's lobby and lounge. Veined marble you might find in a Medici palace, magnificent chandeliers whose crystal pendants would probably chime winsomely if you climbed up there to flick them with a fingernail. He watched a young man hand a bouquet of three-foot-tall calla lilies to a young woman— the white trumpets of the flowers were as large as the heads of Siamese cats. But deciding his mood really did call for a walk, he exited the hotel between two gold lions and crossed into the plaza with the pigeons. Filling his big lungs with Boston's not-so-fresh air, Peter glanced back at the hotel, remembered Jeanette and Weiner, and promised to make this short.

A little traveling music . . .

The afternoon was chillier than it had represented itself, as though a tang of winter had arrived on the breast of purpling evening. He hugged himself as he studied the signboard on the church cowering beneath the skyscraper's blue stiletto: *Trinity Episcopal.* An elegant old building, worth investigating. He headed over to the pharmacy. Afterward, he wandered downtown, then uptown and passed another hotel near theirs, this one with a bar that seemed more workaday, closer to his mood. He doffed his hat and ordered from the bartender, a very comely woman of maybe thirty-five in white blouse and black vest, "A Rittenhouse Manhattan, please."

"Thank you, dear," she said when Peter waved off his change.

Her *dear* jollied him no end. His bartender, happy for some company on a slow day, was, as it turned out, a single mom with an eight-year-old boy who was a Lego whiz, but suffered from ADD, and a girl of fourteen who'd been diagnosed with a hearing disorder. The bartender also had a boyfriend vacationing in maximum security for taking a two-by-four to his foreman's forehead. You think you have it bad, Peter ruminated, admiring the woman's wrists exposed within her unbuttoned cuffs—they looked as fine as something Michelangelo might have sculpted—until you've talked to the person who just wiped the bar your hat rests on.

"I knew something was up," she explained. "I asked her to help me, I was standing right behind her with the laundry basket—never heard a word I said. The doctor said she's become a natural lip-reader. As soon as he said it, I knew it was true: When you're talking to her she's always studying you with these big Keane eyes."

"But they're going to be able to help her?"

The bartender straightened her spine: he heard the crack. "We'll see. Refill, dear?"

During his three Rittenhouses Peter came to a decision: Wilfred Hall was not going to do. He'd wound up liking the school, the windows fretted with ivy, the visions of bearded poets with their enormous meerschaum pipes, even the Aeron chairs and their eleven levers and dials. But Jeanette wasn't ready for such a leap. What Jeanette needed was a bedroom under the same roof as her mama and not too distant from her papa and a school that specialized in the performing arts, a school where she could find like-minded friends: young dancers, actors, aspiring eleven-year-old playwrights, moppets with big dreams. Shadyside, surely in bohemian Shadyside—or somewhere in Shadyside's shady shadow—there existed such a school?

So, damn the torpedoes: Wednesday morning first thing, a call to Harvey Silverstein: *No* to Bright Ridge Academy of course, *no* to the Wilfred school, and, for good measure, *no* to any trips into the woods, hunting or otherwise, with Elliott Fields, king of the wild frontier.

No, no, no!

The Rittenhouse Manhattans, having done the job they'd been hired to do, Peter tarried for another minute on the steps of Trinity Church. The stained glass, glowing from within, was as fine as anything he'd ever seen, deep rapturous violets and cobalts and reds and greens. He thought they were having a service, then realized it was choir practice, which was better. The choir was working on something modern, Rutter, he guessed. He drank in the soprano's soaring voice and regretted that he hadn't rolled Jacob Weiner down in his wheelchair to hear this dense and intricate music.

You'd like this, Jacob.

~ ~ ~

Coming back through the lobby, Peter noticed that people were looking at him pointedly. But he'd grown inured to that, people frowning at him: A man with a low center of gravity, a broad gyroscope. He tipped his fedora and nodded cordially to the slightly perplexed, slightly vexed desk clerks. As he ascended in Copley Plaza's humming elevator, he formulated his Henry the Fifth speech to be delivered to his troops: Up by six, shoes in the breakfast room by six-thirty, muffins masticated and washed down by seven-thirty, on the road by eight. Home before dark.

At his feet just inside his room were two folded sheets of paper. From the hotel? They were in hot water? Peter settled in his window chair, and, in the room's fugitive light, read:

> *Peter,*
> *Randy made the kids*
> *pack up all their clothes and*
> *took them back to live with*
> *him!! Plus he's got some chick*
> *on the side!!! We're on our*

Robert McKean

*way to the airport. Sorry things
didn't work out better!!!
F.*

He noted that his lover—well, probably ex-lover—employed a penmanship that featured extensive use of loops and curlicues and little circles for dots. But she had taken Jacob with her—the old man was not in the welter of his bedclothes—and for that Peter gave Fay credit, although he had difficulty imagining how she was going to get him through security or extract him from his window seat when he needed to pee. But be that as it may, though—and it *had* been fun—Fay and Jacob's departure freed Jeanette and him to have a bit of the special weekend he'd envisioned.

He unfolded Fay's second note and recognized the handwriting instantly. Not Fay's, the quick, precise, slashing strokes so unchildlike and so dear to his heart:

*Dear Papa,
I am going back on the
airplane with Fay. I think it is
for the best. I will tell Mama I
liked the school.*

Sincerely,

Jeanette (your daughter)

Something he believed: Your earliest years propose the argument that you spend the rest of your life trying to prove out. If that were so, then he'd flunked—business, marriage, parenting. It was only later, owning up to the fact that his daughter was in some ways more of an adult than her father, that Peter lumbered across the room to peer into the closet to see what all along he would have known—had he used his head—was going to be there. If Fay had taken Jacob, she and Jeanette would not have resorted to slipping notes under the door. And for sure, on the floor of the closet sat Jacob Weiner's wrinkled shopping bag, still stuffed with his clothes.

The desk clerks were no help, or didn't wish to be. Neither were the doormen. It was a valet who possessed the critical information. "Guy in a wheelchair? Sure, I helped him get his chair down the Dartmouth Street steps, then he shot out of here like a house on fire. How long ago? Oh, God, buddy, I dunno, hour maybe?"

And for the second time today Peter Sanguedolce thinks: *What have I done?*

Robert McKean

Lunch at 1200 Feet

Let them scratch where they itch.

On the second-floor foyer he's dragged an armchair over to the windows. The winter's project is Dante. As the lavender silences of the wintertide afternoons descend, he lifts his eyes from condemned souls entombed in flaming chambers to gaze at snow sifting through the branches of the oaks. It is the season of entombment, after all. The snow blankets the disheveled garden and fills the pitted cement urns on the open veranda until they round up in gnomes' caps.

Or dunces' caps.

Why the yearning for a particular taste came upon him—the chewy tang of soured peasant bread—he isn't sure, and shopping didn't help. Good luck finding whole grain sourdough on the T&V's shelves, good luck finding it anywhere. But if you can manufacture clay pipe, you can bake a loaf of bread, right? He tried creating his own sourdough starter, a recipe he discovered online: pineapple juice and flour in a clean mayonnaise jar. That was a bust. He returned to the internet and ordered a starter curated from Poland, and, as January snow laces the kitchen windows and tortured souls crawl around Mount Purgatory's terraces, he watches, fascinated, as his tiny Polish emigrants—not unlike their steelworker brethren of a century ago—take to Western Pennsylvania and flourish, bubbling, foaming, issuing sweet, beery farts.

He has a book, is following directions scrupulously.

Strict temperature control is critical. At Savage's, along with the plastic buckets for his ice dams, he buys a digital thermometer and fusses with the house thermostat so that his Poles won't catch cold. By now the mayonnaise jars have given way to Mason jars—he'd had to buy a dozen, another trip to Savage's—and a rearrangement of counter space. *Pay attention to your dough,* the book instructs. First thing, undertaken several days in advance, he prepares his *pre-ferment* by feeding his starter with the hard red spring wheat he orders from Minnesota. His Polish microbial community likes it warm, but too warm, seventy-five to seventy-nine. Then the mix, more Minnesota flour and an exact measure of temperature-controlled water, allowing the mixed dough to rest for an hour, the *autolyse* period, then the incorporation of the pre-ferment and the mix and series of operations—stretch and folds—to tease out the gluten. He mimics the author's floury hands in the photographs. This period is called the *bulk ferment,* a time of high anxiety, waiting for his Poles at a summery eighty-one to lift high the roof beams. At the end of the day, he turns the developed dough out on the marble slab that his Nonna Sanguedolce had kneaded her focaccia on, shapes his loaves, slips them into their rattan proofing baskets, and tucks them in the refrigerator for a long winter's nap. *Cover them,* the book orders. The following morning, he preheats the oven with the baking vessels inside to five-hundred degrees and carefully, oh so carefully, dumps the refrigerated loaves into the wickedly hot vessels, scores the loaves, smacks his timer, and prays to the god of baking that his Poles will rise to the occasion and make proper parson's hats.

Which they sometimes do, and sometimes perversely do not do.

And so there's trouble, there's always trouble. The temperature in his old kitchen is simply not stable. From Amazon he orders a proofing box, a plastic apparatus that sits on the counter and furnishes a small heated parlor he can peer down into like a diorama in which his finicky Poles might be coddled at any temperature they desire. Good idea, poor design. The proofing box won't maintain a dependable temperature, either. A return to Savage's, where the joke among Mortie Siegel and the hardware boys is that Peter's bread is running him about fifty bucks a loaf, to purchase a roll of aluminum insulation wrap. The quilted wrap creates a circular stockade around the proofing box some two feet in height and three in diameter, the whole affair resembling a kitchen-sized nuclear reactor, and on Sunday mornings, on this Sunday morning, as he fritters away the hours before his supervised visit with his daughter, Peter Sanguedolce, Ganaego's St. Francis of Assisi, shares a loaf of warm sourdough bread with the birds in his backyard.

A plump St. Francis.

~ ~ ~

"Hello, kiddo."

She's setting up when he comes in. Peter throws off hat and coat, gives her a hug, and Jeanette composes herself at an electronic keyboard that has a sonority and touch he deplores. Granted, in Avis and Elliott's tony East Stanton Junction condo an acoustical piano was probably never going to find accommodation. But the sound of the electronic instrument, although sampled from some glorious Steinway, is saccharine, synthetic, sterile—*and* the keys are too light. He mourns the loss of the physicality required by the grappling with the five thousand moving parts of an acoustical piano's action, like Fatty's, whose indurated hammers send arthritic tremors back through the keys. These flyweight keys, he frets, are training his daughter's fingers to slide and skid rather than strike.

"Ready, Papa?"

"Been waiting all week, angel. Let 'er rip."

Jeanette begins with two folk songs, whose arrangements, despite being too simplified for her—or perhaps because they are too simplified—she plays negligently, without commitment, then, at last, a Haydn sonatina, whose intricate dancing runs resist being condescended to and cause her evident effort.

"Let's hear that again," Peter says, hugely pleased, when she finishes.

"Papa, do I have to?"

"And keep your hands cupped. You're flattening them. When you're as good as Horowitz, you can break the rules."

"Yes, Papa."

"Mozart's birthday was this past Friday," he reminds her. "As well as the feast day of St. Gamelbert of Michaelsobuch."

"I *know*."

Robert McKean

"Well, that's right," he laughs, caught out. "You would know that now, wouldn't you?"

The braids are gone. Her idea, after having them yanked on. Gone forever, along with urchin costumes and even some of the droll wit, the goofy flirtation with life that the Sanguedolces always possessed. Are our lives tragedies or comedies? Well, they're a lot like sourdough bread he'd like to answer, for he knows that to lose one's love of the absurd is to lose much. The most stressful visits, such as today's, are the ones monitored by Elliott, who sits on the sofa in his bathrobe over his underwear working his way through his *Wall Street Journal* and *New Hampshire Union Leader*. When the noticeably pregnant Avis oversees Peter's visits, she retreats to her study or the kitchen. Not Elliott. Behind his newsprint Elliott clucks at being so imposed upon as to be forced to sit here for two whole hours. Flaps his pages, clears his throat, inserts his smallest finger into his nose and captures things up there that annoy him. And whatever Elliott doesn't take out on Peter, he'll take out on Jeanette, with whom he has been increasingly strict.

"Trust me, pet," Peter says, reassuring his daughter, who apparently gave as good as she got in a hair-pulling, nail-scratching scuffle in her now ex-school, "you're never going to have a more appreciative audience. Those arpeggios were very smart."

"They're hard."

"And you're negotiating them superbly. Try to relax, try to hear them a beat ahead. You *have* the piece in your hands—you're more than halfway there."

"I hate staccatos—you never know where your fingers are going to come down."

"Ay, that's the rub. But you know, darling, yours're coming down pretty much where you want them to? Just turn them loose and let them play."

Which earns a throat-unclogging from Elliott and a reversal of hairy leg over hairy leg. Does the man never wear pants at home? After music, they review Jeanette's homework from her new school, a parochial school in Ashport, arithmetic, French, and a little paper she's preparing on Gerald Durrell's *My Family and Other Animals*. Which Peter has read, too. He's not allowed to be alone with her, another of the court's many edicts—rulings that drive Harvey Silverstein to a fury. Harvey wants to fight, fight, fight. And so, because they cannot work together at her desk in her bedroom, nor even at the kitchen table, they sit at two dining room chairs brought into the living room, pulled up side by side like two seats in economy. Balancing her books on their laps, they will occasionally lose one overboard. It's awkward, stilted, inhibiting. The artificiality of the situation, especially Elliott's Pink Panther surveillance, has introduced to their interactions a weird, self-conscious formality. They do behave like a pair of well meaning but mismatched seatmates. The Connecticut admission process, which reportedly had been going swimmingly and was all but settled—Jeanette to begin in January—is now on hold. The reason behind the delay is—everyone assumes, since Wilfred has not specified—the fight that resulted in Jeanette's expulsion from Bright Ridge. Everyone save Peter. It seems

184   *Robert McKean*

to him that the process, even before the schoolyard donnybrook, had begun to sputter. But since he's been frozen out of all decision-making, he has no way of knowing what put the kibosh on things. Certainly, it would not be remarkable to discover that the Quiet Corner folks are not so enamored of playground brawlers, either. Whatever the cause, as they review the fussy rules governing the use of other punctuation marks around quotation marks, Peter takes what solace he can in the limited time he's permitted to spend with his daughter.

"Terminal periods and commas go inside the quotes," he recites, recalling the seemingly whimsical punctuation rules learned ages ago. "And colons and semicolons go out."

"That's wrong," Elliott corrects him. "It's just the opposite."

Idiot. He could locate on Avis's shelves his dog-eared *Chicago Manual of Style* and point out the rule, he could lay his hands on eighty grammar books. But is punctuation worth a quarrel? Peter winks at Jeanette, who nods: It's as close to real communication as they're likely to get and allays any concerns he might have about her grasp of punctuation conventions. Indeed, about her schoolwork he has few worries. Perhaps it's due to her anxiety from being thrust into a new school, or her desire to reassure the world that, even if she's had her hair yanked and her glasses knocked off her face, she remains an estimable person—whatever the reason, her grades have gotten much better.

"I'm sure you're right," Peter says to the *Union Leader.*

"Time's up," is his reply.

Peter kisses his daughter. "See you next week, sugar."

"I'll work on the Haydn, I promise."

"He was called *Papa,* too, you know, although apparently he—"

"Time's *up!*"

As Peter shuffles into the foyer, Avis emerges from her study and comes swiftly toward him, or, as swiftly as her condition permits. Lately, every time Peter sees his former wife she looks tired. The pregnancy, of course. But he knows what Avis looks like during pregnancy and this seems like something more. She holds out a sheaf of envelopes enclosed in a rubber band. "Would you mind mailing these?"

"I'm headed to the gym," Elliott snaps, "I told you I'd do it."

Something in Avis's look arrests Peter's attention, a tightening of the little accordion wrinkles between her eyes. Maybe it's nothing, but it prompts him to reach out and snatch up the bundle of envelopes. "Happy to."

Somehow he remains confirmed in his suspicions about the rotten state of Avis and Elliott's matrimonial Denmark: There *is* something foul here. He never had that other conversation with Jeanette, the one about Elliott. But he gathers there has been no further talk of Davy Crockett weekends. In the idling car, Peter stretches off the rubber band and fans the Fields & Longstreet white woven linen envelopes.

Out tumbles a folded note:

> *Can you*
> *meet me at the New*
> *Hope Inn in Ashport,*
> *Tuesday at three? If*
> *you can't, that's fine.*
> *Don't call.*

Robert McKean

~ ~ ~

Snow wreathes the slumping roof of Jacob's capsizing house.
More snow blows in the glassless windows and leaves windrows across
the sodden carpets and an ermine muff about five well-smoked briar
pipes in a rack on the buffet. Discovering a breach in the fencing where
thieves have chewed a hole large enough to accommodate the spiriting
away of Randy Halbrunner's aircraft-carrier-sized grill, Peter debates
chancing one last intrusion into the half-demolished house to rescue the
Weiner menorah. He peers in at the hushed dining room, pondering both
snowbound candelabra and . . . squishy floors.

And declines: You can imagine the headline in the *Chronicle*.

Why the town has not ordered the Halbrunners to complete
the demolition of Jacob's colonial is a mystery. But then again, much
of the Halbrunner universe seems a mystery. On random afternoons
Fay appears at Peter's door in her puffy coat and furry Siberian boots
clutching a bottle of Christian Brothers brandy and they play *Guess
the color of my underwear!* Peter—happy if not thrilled to be Fay's
afternoon man, or one of her afternoon men—gathers that Ed and Joe,
or is it Joe and Ed, have returned the Halbrunner furniture to the original
Halbrunner residence, where the Mrs. dwells on the second floor and
the Mr. in the basement, with the children traveling the stairs between as
emissaries.

"We had three feet of water in the basement once," Fay says.
"I'm hoping that happens again."

With the onset of these early twilights, the heavens-filling washes of salmon and apple-tinged mauve that spill across Western Pennsylvania's hills and flood its wintry hollows with a rueful, enigmatic light, Fay climbs back into her leggings and sweaters and boots that were so much fun to climb out of and motors home to collect her baby chicks when they step down from their yellow bus, model American mom, smelling of cheap brandy and recreational adultery, and Peter lumbers into his cold kitchen to contrive a sort of poor man's *ribollita* from a loaf of stale sourdough and Progresso minestrone. He's reaching the end in his mother's college Longfellow Dante, though his purchase on Paradise feels precarious. In the starry cobalt darkness of these gelid nights, he tries not to overeat and drink too much and is being, on those particular scores, reasonably successful.

Circle Three: gluttony.

Today he rifles through his CD collection. Pauses at a boxed set of Wilhelm Kempff's Beethoven concertos, decides on the first and second concertos, then studies another box, Misuko Uchida's Mozart sonatas, settling on KV 533 and 494, the latter a piece he especially likes. He's not picky. He chooses from the classical or romantic repertoire, if not Beethoven and Mozart, then Schubert or Chopin or Brahms, sonatas, concertos, rarely symphonies. Never voice, never clarinet. The first time he appeared at the Sprague Center in November and asked if he might see Jacob Weiner, the director flatly refused.

"You gotta be kidding me."

One can hardly blame the man. But as any traveling salesman

Robert McKean

who knows the territory will tell you, reasonableness masquerading as humbleness will carry you a lot further than you think. Peter apologized profusely for his part in the fiasco that brought Jessica Weiner rushing from her Brookline apartment and the Boston PD's sirens ululating through the streets. He promised to stay only a few minutes. That visit, reluctantly granted, was monitored, too—is all this close scrutiny going to give him some sort of complex?—as well as the next few visits, and by now his weekly appearances have become reestablished, expected and unsupervised. He brings a handful of Heath bars, a portable CD player and discs he's selected, and either his Pelican Shakespeare or Tolstoy short story collection, both books, board covers showing at the corners, that date from his undergraduate days, and signs himself in.

And braces himself.

Wise beyond understanding, how animals will carry themselves off to die in private. Peter skids an uncomfortable institutional chair up to Jacob's bed and—on good days, days that Jacob recognizes him—asks with a forced cheerfulness how the old man is feeling. On such days Jacob consents to allow himself to be raised by the nurse to a sitting position and to suffer his pillows being plumped. On other visits, on not so good days, he lies moaning and unresponsive. Those days, Peter will play a CD, keeping the volume low, or read Shakespeare or Tolstoy aloud for a while. But before long the CD player will fall silent and the words, though wise themselves and lovely, will seem inadequate in the presence of circling, vulturine death, even pointless, and he will just sit here.

In attendance, in witness.

Today Jacob is already sitting up and seems unusually alert—a very good day. To the proffered Heath bars, he points at his nightstand, and asks gruffly, twirling a finger at Peter's CD player as if it were something he's never seen before, "Whacha got?"

"Beethoven? Mozart?"

"Nah, no music."

Weiner's arms and legs are as crooked as the branches of Peter's crab apple tree. His fingers, grossly misshapen, are blue-veined out to the nails. In his shrunken face his eyes and nose seem enormous, his lips liverish, almost purple. And this, Peter understands, is only death's trivial, incidental plunder before the final prize. "Would you like me to read?"

Jacob waves that off, too. "What's it like, outside?"

"Cold, in the twenties."

He frowns, disapproving. "My dog hated winter. Road salt, burned his pads. Goddamn dog would try hopping on two feet and fall on his ass."

"I remember you carrying him home in your arms."

To which Weiner doesn't respond. At first, these long nursing-home silences, very uncharacteristic of Weiner, made Peter uneasy. Years ago, when he would visit Jacob at home, the retired music teacher would talk compulsively, sentences spilling out without pause. Sometimes they'd talk about music, something Jacob had heard on the radio, but more often he'd go into tedious detail about his everyday life, the dripping faucet he repaired himself, the unbelievable quantity of junk mail he received, the chipmunks he'd routed from his attic, his sciatica. Peter came to understand that the subjects of such monologues were not important. The old man was simply lonely and wanted somebody to hear about his life, the history of the days he traveled his rooms in solitude.

But it's different now: Time for a dying man functions differently.

One day when Peter arrived, Jacob had another visitor. The front-desk receptionist, awestruck, told Peter that it was Walter Zurlo, Jacob's most famous and successful pupil. Peter had never met Zurlo, but knew something about him—everyone in Ganaego knew something about Walter "Buster" Zurlo. Of the hundreds of pupils that Jacob had taught, this short, bristle-headed boy, born to a family who lived in a house clad in tar paper and now in his early thirties, had been one of the fortunate and talented few who'd gone on to professional careers. Zurlo was a member of the Cleveland Symphony and had been featured as a rising young lion on PBS. But he'd come on a bad day.

Peter and he spoke over the sleeping Weiner.

"I kept nagging my parents that I wanted to play the trumpet more than anything. I was too young for the school band, so they brought me to the music school. The trumpet teacher was full, I guess, and I was assigned to Jacob and given a rented clarinet. But Oak Grove was too expensive, my parents fell behind in my tuition and had to take me out. Then some woman—we never knew who she was, other than her name—drove up to the house one day and gave me a cheap clarinet, and the school agreed to let me join the band, even though I was young. Jacob remembered me and went out of his way to hear me play when I was in junior high. He offered to give me private lessons, for free, on Saturdays at his house. If it wasn't for the generosity of those two people, that woman and Jacob, I'd be working alongside my brother in my father's garage now."

"They always talk about how gruff he was as a teacher."

Zurlo stared at the dying man in his sheets. "You have to understand, what Jacob Weiner prized—what he demanded—was that you practice, I mean, really practice. And he could tell in two seconds whether you had or not. And yeah, if you hadn't practiced, he'd come down hard on you. What Jacob taught me was more than music, he taught me discipline and faith."

"Faith in music?"

"Faith in myself."

"Some days he's awake and lucid. You could try again?"

"I'll see, but my schedule's pretty tight."

As today's silence continues, both Jacob's and Peter's eyes drift to the double-paned windows, the garden below: the snow-swept walks and little silvery disk of the frozen pond, its frogs fast asleep in the mud beneath. When he was located in Boston's Back Bay, he and his wheelchair having come to grief in a bank's revolving door, Jacob told the police that he needed to get to Hausman Avenue.

"You can't walk on two legs," he adds twenty minutes later. "Not if you're a dog."

"He liked chasing the squirrels back up into the trees—where they belonged."

"She call you?"

Every visit, every sentient visit, this comes up. "There's no reason for her to call me, Jacob. I'm sorry."

"When I get home, that's the first thing I'm gonna do." Weiner studies his withered fingers. "Straighten all this junk out. Here, gimme a hand, I gotta go to the crapper."

After he helps the old man situate himself on the cold plastic seat, his knees like two fleshless skulls, Peter stands at the window. Even Jacob no longer believes he's going to go home or reconcile with his daughter. Time, on that clock, has run out. Peter notices two ancient souls in the garden below—separate, not together—toiling behind their walkers. One drifts to a halt to gaze at the frozen pond. He thinks of his mother's collapse after his father's death, the event that shattered her life as you might shatter a vase, even as she lived another ten years. He thinks of himself in a silent house hunched over the stove, a forgotten spoon in his hand.

A purulent odor seeps from the bathroom. Jacob groans. "At least the goddamned plumbing still works."

The Sprague pipes? Or his? After he helps Jacob back to bed, but lying now beneath the covers, signifying the conclusion of the visit, Peter notices shit on Jacob's fingers, curled under his yellow nails. He fetches a damp towel, but Jacob brushes it aside. "Beethoven you said—which?"

"Kempff's, the concertos."

He pulls the blanket to his chin, smiles. "Wrote his own cadenzas—what cheek."

"Would you like me to leave them? Along with the player?"

"Nah, I'm done with music." His eyes return to the windows. "They carried someone out last night. Old lady, face up, she lived across the hall. Real quiet, on tiptoes, like they were smuggling diamonds across the border. You think she's gonna call?"

"I'm sure she will."

"Bah, I screwed that up. Gimme one of them candy bars before you go. Take one for yourself if you want, though it don't look like you need one."

~ ~ ~

In the drawer of Weiner's nightstand, pushed back among the boxes of licorice cough lozenges and half-eaten Heath bars are the family photographs. Forgotten and best forgotten. Jessica, perhaps more to keep the director on his toes than for any other reason, speaks regularly to him. But she doesn't ask to be patched through to her father's room, doesn't send cards or notes. Seems wrong, the sort of heartbreaking wrong that once it becomes too late—*Bah, I screwed that up*—will seem even more regrettable. But what can you do?

Nothing, that's what. None of his business. Ask the Boston PD.

Tuesday, he drives to Ashport. It's early, he parks on the main street, saunters north, upriver, then crosses and drifts like flotsam downstream. He had to look up the address of the restaurant and is surprised to discover that the New Hope Inn is not really a restaurant, but mostly a beer and shot joint, beige asphalt shingles sheathing the front and two small windows on either side of the door, both fretted with security wire. A sign, its white Plexiglas stained with rusty tears, presides in glory over it all. Well, he *is* surprised. Not the kind of place you'd expect a chic East Stanton Junction attorney would be seen frequenting.

The mystery deepens.

Since it's still early, he continues on to Kopelman Street, Our Lady of the Sacred Heart, Jeanette's new school. The campus, which he's not supposed to go near—church, rectory, square fortress of the four-story school—is islanded within wrought-iron pickets, a sort of *HO*-scale Vatican. Hollies, sprawling yews, leafless oaks, and the requisite virgin, whose chilly toes dip in the crusty snow that fills a fountain at her feet. Peter walks down to the fountain. Over the decades the valley's corrosive fumes have been hard on Mary: Her limestone fingers and nose look like something's been gnawing on them. Since he has no idea in which classroom Jeanette might be, he imagines her in a first-floor corner room, whose old-fashioned globular lights on this dull afternoon cast a lemony luster across the snow: green sweater, green and tan plaid skirt and knee socks, saddle shoes, wizard glasses. The judge had described his behavior, taking his daughter on a trip with his mistress and an incontinent old man and abandoning everyone to go drinking as being *. . . so outrageous as to constitute abuse . . . faults in judgment severely deleterious to the welfare of the child . . . brings into serious question whether this man should be permitted any contact whatsoever with his* *daughter* . . . .

But the irony is, he's won. By however improbable means, he's ended up with no East Stanton Junction snobs baiting his child and no black-mesh Aeron chairs in a distant boarding school. Instead, he's got decent, local instruction—a program designed for troubled children taught by nuns with real chalk dust on their sleeves and who explicitly disavow corporal punishment—*and* a helluva lot lower tuition fees. What more could you want? You'd think he'd be happy.

He's not.

"We have to stop meeting this way."

He risks this small bon mot with his former spouse who is there ahead of him, waiting in one of New Hope's booths. She appears to be the bar's sole patron, but the room is so funereally dark that it's impossible to tell. Are there really no lights? On opposing sides of the liquor cabinet glowing Budweiser beer-wagons with their teams of glowing Clydesdales appear to be providing what meager illumination there is. Avis, who once found his lame humor funnier, gazes at him without expression. "We need to talk," she says. "I don't know if you can help or not, but we need to talk—about Jeanette."

They have not spoken—about Jeanette or anything else—since the Boston episode. All communication is now channeled between Harvey and Elliott. "I stopped in front of the school, I was trying to guess what room she was in."

"You are not to be conferencing with her teachers! You're not even supposed to be on the same block as that school!"

Oops. Back in the day one met with one's children's teachers, now one conferences. Behind her glasses Avis's eyes look sunken in dark, weary pouches. He longs to ask why she's so listless, and why this secrecy? Clandestine notes are not her modus operandi. But Peter holds back: Better to let Avis come forward in her own good time. "Our Lady wasn't in our division," he says lightly, "but we played exhibition games with them. They have a miniature bandbox gymnasium, wood-paneling, rippling floorboards. You had to adjust your plays, or you'd find yourself running headlong into the wall—or into the cheerleaders. I didn't go inside, Avis, all I was doing was imagining her in some classroom."

"All right, fine. Thank you for not meddling. I know you love her, Peter, but . . . you're not good for her. Even the court said you weren't trustworthy."

"Courts say a lot of things."

"Let's just let it rest, okay?" Avis lifts the hair from her face that does not need lifting and goes on to wave at the dolorous taproom— wired-over windows, adhesive tape on the stools—as if to account for this much. "I represented the owner's son last year—I practically moved in with the family. Not that I was able to do very much for him, Kamal, but I got him placed in a facility that might be able to help him. He was strung out on meth. And actually, Hakim's wife makes a very tasty kibbee, if you're hungry? I can't drink"—she holds up her glass, lime wedge lodged in its ice and sparkling water—"but I don't care if you do."

"From whom would you order?" He cranes around to peer into

the murk. "If you wanted to?"

Which elicits a laugh, half-laugh. "Hakim's around here somewhere, probably in the kitchen. *He's* addicted to online poker. I tell him, one of these days you're going to lose your shirt, Hakim—or your liquor license."

Avis's friendliness—or, minimally, her lack of vitriol—encourages him to risk a personal comment. "Is everything okay?"

"Why shouldn't it be? I'm pregnant, what d'you expect?"

"Sorry, just asking."

Avis puts down her drink, annoyed—with it, with him? "You understand, this school's not permanent? Even if it does have a charming gymnasium?"

It hadn't been he, the Catholic, who suggested the parochial school. It had been, oddly enough, born-again Elliott. "But she seems to be doing well? That last book report she wrote was top-flight."

"It's *provisional,* until we come up with something better."

"Avis"—Peter meets his ex-'s bleary eyes—"I'm not arguing with you. This is Elliott's idea, and certainly the irony doesn't escape me that the non-blood parent seems to be exercising more sway over the child's disposition than the child's blood parents. But we're in agreement: It's temporary. I take it that Wilfred has ruled us out?"

"No, not completely?"

And with that, the rise at the end of her reply, he grasps the purpose of this meeting. "You're thinking there's still something I can do to help?"

Robert McKean

"Rather than fucking things up?"

At which he sits back. You would not want to be cross-examined by Attorney Longstreet. Harvey's theory is that it's Elliott who's been driving this heavy-handed punitiveness toward him and Jeanette. "Why are the Wilfred folks getting their knickers in such a knot? I'm surprised, I must say. I only met the one administrator there, so that's not much to go on, but I got the feeling that they prided themselves on being accommodative—you know, understanding of special family circumstances? I would've thought that you and Elliott would've been able to explain to them the context of Jeanette's fight, the whole bitchy environment at Bright Ridge? She was being *bullied*—surely, they'd grok that?"

"You think we didn't?"

Avis shifts painfully. New Hope Inn's benches, if they ever boasted padding, have long spewed it into the world. Hemorrhoids, Peter guesses and recalls how afflicted she'd been when she carried Jeanette, her prolonged and arduous delivery. A thin-boned, high-voltage woman: not an earth mother type. "Sorry, of course you did."

"It's not an easy thing *to* explain—hair-pulling, biting, spitting?"

"So, why haven't they rejected us then?"

"Peter, I don't *know*. Maybe our connection with Judge Davis, who knows?"

"What would you like me to do to help? Call them? Write?"

"I don't know what'll help—frankly, with anything."

This passivity, this fatalism, is perplexing. Avis never had as much as an irresolute bone in her body: Mistakes were buried in unmarked graves at midnight, and each new morning brought nothing but certainty of further triumph. Peter senses that she wants to talk about something other than their daughter. A conversation about Jeanette would not require this kind of cloak and dagger secrecy. He treads with caution. "So, when're you due?"

"You mean, when can I smoke again?" Avis shakes her shoulders, as if to disown that remark. "April 21, Friday, if you can believe them. Samantha does—she's so literal. She put it in my calendar—like an appointment."

"Stork, two-thirty to three?"

"I guess." Avis lunges for her purse—a motion, coincidentally, reminiscent of a smoker lunging for her cigarettes—and digs out a tissue. She blows her nose and holds the tissue pressed against her mouth, shivering. Then Peter realizes: not shivering. "He's screwing everything up!" Anguish floods her voice. "He's got this goof-brained idea that he's going to run for District Attorney and meanwhile the practice's going to pot!"

"What? I don't understand?" And honestly he doesn't. "I thought you were doing great? I mean, the condo, the convertible, his jungle-ready SUV?"

"It's all financed!" She's speaking through her sobs. "We're living on cash flow—like two immigrants at the corner grocery pawing the coins out of the till every night! Money, what money? Any money we clear we plow right back into the practice. And you have to do that,

Robert McKean

computers, file cabinets, furniture. You have to have all that stuff! Rugs, lamps, magazines for people to read—for Chrissake, you gotta have a coffee table to put the fucking magazines on! And now I'm pregnant and he's off playing Wyatt Earp!"

Although he knows it's clearly verboten, Peter shifts over to Avis's side of the booth and brings his arm down around her shoulders. Avis, surprised, flinches, ready to shake him off, then surrenders. She presses her head against his shirt and lets herself cry. Three years since he's held her, maybe more, three desolate years since he's smelled her hair. He embraces her gently, trying to absorb the cataract of her emotion. Avis, however, being Avis, not satisfied with crying, is determined—as would any good lawyer—to finish her point.

"Who's going to manage the office while I'm out? Who's going to do the title searches, who's going to sort through an intestate succession, who's going to go off and eat jelly donuts with the Rotarians on Thursdays? The money, the money—who's going to make the damn money? And what's so incredible and so obvious is, he's no good at it—the politics! He grates on people, he gets under their skin. He's a terrible public speaker! He puts his head down and mumbles the lectures he spends hours fussing over—he comes across like a sanctimonious old biddy! We're *lawyers,* the goddamned petite bourgeoisie—I don't want to change the world, I just want a toaster oven that works!"

Avis lifts her head. Behind her crooked glasses her eyes are wet, glassy. She kisses him, kisses him full on the lips, astonishing Peter. She pulls back, then presses her lips into his again, astonishing him just as much a second time.

"Get up!" she orders. Not understanding but complying, he scoots out of the booth. Avis, awkward with her belly, rolls out after. She straightens her glasses and snatches up her purse and coat. "Come!"

She plunges into the inky depths, rounding a corner into a hall, where he presumes the restrooms are, if anyone's ever found them. She shoves open a door that spills into a hallway with a stairway. Thankfully, it's not so pitch-black here. A window, panes streaked with bird droppings, furnishes a wan winter light. Up or down? Down, and as he follows her, Peter tries not to stare at her neck and the slope of her shoulders visible into her blouse, changed because of pregnancy and the years gone by, thicker, slacker, the beginnings of lines, yes, but still shapely and statuesque, creamy. In an unlighted hallway in the basement—the Hakim family must have the world's tiniest electric bill— Avis pushes open a door at the end of the hall.

"Kamal's room." She switches on a lamp by the door.

"Most lawyers," Peter, seeing an unmade bed and not much else, quips uneasily, "aren't so familiar with their clients' bedrooms."

"Oh, shut up, d'you ever stop?"

Avis kisses him again, caressing his face with her fingers, smearing his face with her fingers, squeezing them between their joined lips into his mouth—an old trope. Her tongue finds its way along with those fingers into his mouth. Five minutes ago he would have confidently claimed to know everything there was to know about this woman. Now, blood gathering in his loins, he questions whether he knows Avis at all.

But bewilderment be damned, he pulls her toward him, closing her in his embrace, while her hands fall to the buttons of his shirt.

"Gotta go easy," she whispers. "Me on top."

A young man's kip, that little Peter notes—posters over the bed of a model seriously over-topping her bustier, a running back stiff-arming his would-be tackler—before he's taken up with assisting a managing partner out of her blouse, undoing the hooks of her bra, shimmying down the elastic-banded maternity slacks, as she yanks at the buckle of his belt. He finishes her part of the job by unzipping, kicking off his shoes, pulling down his pants and shorts, unfurling his shirt, then, banishing all compunctions—bedbugs, crab lice, the sour miasma that hovers above a mattress soaked too often in an unconscious man's urine—falls fatly onto his back, like a sea lion ready for a romp with his lioness.

Avis, standing by the bed, hangs back.

Second thoughts, he despairs, and feels, all of a sudden, very stupid, wallowing as he is, his male member pointing skyward like a diner attempting futilely to summon a waiter. Of course, she's having second thoughts—how could she *not?* Everybody in this room, including the one who's along only for the ride, is having second thoughts. *No,* not second thoughts, he realizes blissfully, recognizing another Avisism, as she smooths her palms up her thighs over the tumescence of her abdomen, cupping and massaging the pregnant-pendulous breasts, breathing deeply, the body—*her* body—luxuriating in its liberation from belts, buckles, cinches, free to satiate its hunger. She hooks two thumbs in the tiny underpants lost beneath the watermelon belly, steps out one leg at a time, and scrambles into Hakim's son's bed on her hands and knees. She crawls over the flattened mountain of *his* belly, sits athwart and eases herself down. No, not quite wet enough. She rises a few inches and brings herself forward to allow him to moisten her with his tongue.

"Elliott wouldn't do this if you put a gun to his head."

Peter murmurs, "He's a fool."

"He says I'm too old."

Peculiar statement, that. She's thirty-six, four years younger than Elliott? But with her lowering herself, wiggling her hips to absorb him, the incongruous admission is lost in the sexual carnival, the funhouse of fornication. Avis always made love eyes open, which has not changed, and her eyes, devoid of the shimmery bifocals, naked and seemingly oversized, are despite their bruised, pouchy tiredness everything Peter recollects—our eyes age so slowly—nearly round, sable brown within whose depths float black glittering flecks: eyes as fixed with suspicion and disapproval on him as the eyes of a nun, or a hired killer.

"This doesn't mean shit, you understand?" she says.

"Just conferencing."

Closing her eyes at last, Avis concentrates on her rhythm, rocking back and forth over him. "Yeah . . . good to conference."

~ ~ ~

Another time-honored custom: It was always Avis, restless, twitchy, who would be up before indolent he. Ten minutes after she's violently climaxed, letting her voice crescendo to a bitten-off shriek, followed by his climax, not so dramatic, she's up, rooting around for her clothes. Peter watches his former spouse dress, as he loved watching her dress when she was his spouse: glasses first—the Purchasing Department clerk, once furnished with decent specs, claimed she required them to talk on the phone—then all those items which *were* fun to help her climb out of. The Fields-Longstreet marriage is none of his concern. If she and Elliott are struggling to keep their practice afloat, what's it to him? But he'd like to offer sympathy, it's only human.

"I knew about his political ambitions, but I had no idea of the sacrifices. You must be going through hell."

"Screw your pity to the wall." Avis casts around for one of her loafers, stamping her edema-swollen foot into it. "But if you think you can have some influence with Wilfred, go ahead. Try, you have my blessing. It's probably hopeless, but they liked you. I'm not sure they liked Elliott. He'd get himself in a weird stew whenever we met with them, he gets vinegary, tight-assed—I don't know?—*pissy*. But the woman you talked to, Janet Considine, she thought you were very chivalrous."

"She said that, *chivalrous?* I'm flattered. Does Elliott not want Jeanette to go away? I get the feeling that he isn't thrilled about this?"

"What're you talking about? You need to get up—this isn't our room, you know? Why would you say that?"

"Just a thought?"

"Well, I don't get it. It's obviously a prestigious school, why wouldn't he want her to go there?"

Peter hesitates, then backs away. He rescues his shorts lying on his shoes, smothering his shoes. "I'm not sure a call is the way to go. Better in person. This Janet Considine, I could ask for an appointment. D'you think that'd be a good idea?"

"Is it any worse than maundering around your house all day in your bathrobe?"

Ah, the old Avis. Peter invents a nice smile. "Maybe I should go into politics? Some people think I'm chivalrous."

Avis shrugs into her coat. "You know, one of the biggest things that did it for me, Peter, was this—your jokes, your playing at life. As a matter of fact, you *are* maundering around a fifteen-room house stuffing your face—*look at you!*—while you're clinging to a property you could sell or develop or do *something* with. You're farting your life away, and for us who don't happen to have that luxury it wears thin. Do whatever you want."

"I'm sorry."

"You breathe one word of this"—Avis flings a careless arm at the grubby basement room—"and I'll sue you for defamation of character *and* take away your Sunday visits."

Back in his car, Peter recalls the mouse that fetched up this morning in the green bucket in the attic. How did the poor thing get in there? Intrepid explorer? Suicide victim? Just a rotten swimmer? With the Cadillac's tuba-sized heater warming the interior, Peter calls Harvey Silverstein's home office number.

"Harv, let's do it, let's sell it, I'm ready—the whole plant."

Robert McKean

~ ~ ~

"Them broken down trucks, across the road."

Surprised, disturbed, skeptical, Peter has Baldwin Feeney walk
him through the gates over to the strip of ancillary land along the creek
they employ as a staging area. The unpaved area is a splatter field of
hardened mud and aging snow. Except for two abandoned Kenworth
cabs in the back, where scrubby sumacs shield the property from
Cabbage Creek, the lot is empty. Feeney points out the rucked up snow
around the cabs, proof, Peter reluctantly grants, of trespass. But why, you
have to wonder? In the derelict cabs with their flattened tires there can't
be a blessed thing of interest—or profit. Peter warily mounts a sagging
running board and peers in an open window: A piercing smell greets him,
rotting upholstery and deep, elemental rust. But the road, hardly more
at this point than a winding lane, peters out a few hundred yards farther
up in the woods, and so, given the remoteness of the location, the ease
of trespass, and the possibility of someone's injuring himself on the two
decaying hulks, he understands he needs to attend to this.

"Sure it wasn't just kids, not that that'd be any better?"

"Wasn't kids, was junk-metal collectors."

"Good lord, if they come back, they can have them. All they
have to do is ask."

Baldwin, not a big fan of giving things away, casts a narrowed
glance at the out-sized German Luger on his hip and says menacingly
in his best Joe Friday undertones, "Oh, they'll be back. And those kind
don't bother asking."

Peter, alerted to the real threat here, which has nothing to do with junk-metal scavengers, lowers his voice to his best rendition of his father's managerial baritone: It's one piece of theater against another. "Baldwin, *listen* to me: If they come back, you are to call the police. I mean that. You are to call the police and sit tight. Meanwhile, we need to arrange to get these wrecks towed away."

In the hour before Harvey Silverstein is due, Peter conducts an inspection of the clay works. Given Baldwin's news, it will be an hour well spent. He spends most of his time in the manufactory. If there's anything worth stealing, here is where you will find it. The cavernous building, gloomily lit by towering shafts of feathery light falling from grimed skylights, is chilly, raw, damp. Peter zips his jacket to the neck and treads carefully. He lingers at the mixers—the screw blades are flecked with dried clay, residue from their final run—then steps over to the extruders, where the clay, finely ground and moistened, was transformed to a tender-soft, earth-scented pipe that once cured and lowered into the ground might endure a hundred years beneath your feet.

A way lot of shit—yes, he thinks fondly.

He loved this building when he was a boy, walking beside his father, perhaps stopping to have a chat with John Pruce—the laborer he'd kept thinking about—as Pruce lowered a wire cutter to slice as neatly as a bread slicer through wet chimney flue pipe and direct a lettering wheel to slide forward and imprint on the side of each *Sanguedolce: Ganaego Clay Works*. It's as if that taciturn, supercilious man in his clean and pressed chambray shirt were still here—at his post, tending his controls.

The clay works, to a boy, seemed immense, a metropolis unto itself, where men, fitting themselves into a rational, comprehensive design and guided by instructions they never sought to question, operated clicking forklifts and cranes, concentrated over large, dangerous machines, ran alongside boxcars waving flags, lowered green visors over their eyes and applied themselves to tall black ledgers, clattered up two flights of stairs to the office bearing emergency messages and returned with imperious replies. There were sidewalks, garbage cans, bicycles with little carts that trundled along after, a truck that came once a month and sold footwear with metal toecaps, a company post office and cafeteria and a nurse who ordered two-hundred-and-fifty-pound men to lower their drawers for her syringe. It's the silence that has befallen the works that grips him, not only the absence of the industrial chatter, but the loss of sounds as insignificant and ephemeral as the ringing tap of the quality control inspector's silvery hammer against the dried pipe.

But yet in this stillness there's nothing exceptional.

The silence that has engulfed his family's clay works is the same silence that has engulfed most of the Ganaego Valley: fifteen thousand men and women discharged from the steelworks, almost as many from the two sprawling mills in Ashport, sites that are now flat acres of white slag shot through with chicory, thistle, trees of heaven. So many shuttered manufacturing facilities up and down the Ohio and Monongahela that one would have difficulty enumerating them all. It is the same industrial hush that must have overtaken one New England town after another as the great looms were stilled. Pausing, troubled,

Peter stops to identify a shattered pane that has permitted a trickle of rainwater to immobilize and probably ruin the controls of the stress-tester.

Irked, he goes in search of a tarp to pull over the instrument.

Seeing, however, no sign of unlawful entry, other than by the disputatious sparrows that have taken up residence in the rafters, he brings down the garage door and stands contemplating the cafeteria. *Canteen,* they called it, a shed-like structure attached to the office building. There were two cooks, two bosomy Black women, sisters, who every morning stepped down from the town bus with the first shift. Heads wound in patterned turbans, faces bathed in sweat, they moved around each other in the tiny kitchen in an intricate choreography, boiling potatoes and baking meatloaf, frying chicken and chops, dicing more potatoes and simmering carrots and bloody soup bones the size of a small boy's hips. They folded floured crust over fruit pies and made lemonade, iced tea, coffee, washed the dishes by hand, and turned out the lights in time to catch the bus back home at three-thirty, along with the men with whom they'd come to work. When the sisters retired, his father Steve brought in a vendor that delivered meals pre-prepared. Curious whether he might find anything useful to his sourdough enterprise, Peter unlocks these double doors that probably have not been opened since the plant ceased operations.

The dining room, fast asleep in its eternal winter, is cold and clammy and smells of mildew. The wooden folding chairs are lined up smartly beneath the tables; the salt and pepper shakers and sugar

Robert McKean

dispensers grouped at equally spaced locations. The chalkboard above the counter announces the day's specials, and Peter has no difficulty believing he's about to hear the sisters' Mahalia Jackson contraltos booming over the din of their pans as the men, their faces rouged with clay dust, queue up with trays. What would it require to get the plant back on its feet? How much capital to modernize, introduce computers and state-of-the-art process controls, to patch the cracked sidewalks and replace the broken windows, to hire a dynamic plant manager and charge him with putting into place best-practice policies—managerial, accounting, human resources—that an organization requires these days? *Really,* what would it take? This room would need no more than a good scrubbing, some bleach splashed around here and there. What would Harvey Silverstein do, Peter speculates, checking his watch, if I told him I wasn't going to put the works up for sale, after all, but was planning to restart it?

Harvey would fetch Baldwin Feeney's pistol and shoot him.

Unlike the dining area, which, with a little elbow grease could be restored, the kitchen is a complete loss. The rear window, in which an exhaust fan had always been positioned, gapes open. Beneath his feet the floorboards feel spongy. The ever-present sparrows, persistent as tiny CIA spooks, have been in here, too, building nests in the cupboards, along with those rodents cunning enough to escape Baldwin's border patrols. You would not use anything in this kitchen for food preparation. Appalled, saddened, Peter comes away, leaving his brief fantasies of restarting the works abandoned behind.

~ ~ ~

Harvey's late, which is not his MO. And when he finally pads up the stairs in his striped sneakers, Peter knows something is amiss. Harvey's face is iron gray; his eyes behind his black glasses are reddened and distracted. He lugs his briefcase into his lap as if it weighed fifty pounds. "My apologies." He explains that his wife fell on the stairs and that he's spent the night in the emergency room.

"Good God," Peter protests, "go home, man. This can wait."

"Her sister's with her, it's all right. I keep telling her, Jenny, we'll put in one of those stair lifts, but no, no, she won't hear of it. Or we'll move to a one-story apartment, which gets an even ruder reception. But nothing's broken, nothing this time . . ."

The one room Peter had not entered today was the storage area where the Sunday cleaning crew kept its equipment, the room Steve chose because it was a Wednesday, a weekday, to tie a rope to a ceiling joist and loop it about his neck. Peter watches Harvey remove his glasses and rub his eyes, then go on to massage the loose skin of his skull, two gestures—or perhaps a single gesture of two parts—that he has long associated with this man he's known all his life and whom he considers a surrogate uncle. Why didn't his father bring in Harvey when he got in over his head? Harvey, negotiating on Peter's behalf, resolved the debacle, divested them of the ill-fated trucking firm, plead for temporary relief from the banks, went on to reassure their nervous customers.

Why couldn't Steve ask for help?

"I'm sorry, Harvey." Around the subject of Harvey's wife Peter

Robert McKean

is always at a loss. "One doesn't know what to say."

"I lost Caroline to cancer. She raised the kids, kept house and home together, while I huddled in my office nights and through the weekends, doing research, writing briefs. And if I wasn't there, I was hanging out at the Briggs Hotel, drumming up more business. I didn't know what a wonderful thing I had until I lost her. And I figured that was it, you know? I wouldn't find anyone else, I didn't deserve anyone else. But then I did, and why I did, why I should've been so lucky to find Jenny, I'll never know. It's like I was given two miracles in life, not deserving either one. And now, I'm going to lose her, too."

"She's the sweetest, most gentle person I've ever met, Harv. It makes no sense."

The old attorney looks as if he might lose his composure. "That she is," he says softly. He gathers and resets himself. "So, Mr. Sanguedolce: Are you ready to get on with your life?"

"Is that what they told Preston Tucker?"

"Tucker?" Harvey wrinkles his brow. "Oh, him, the car with the headlights that followed you around? Tucker let a lot of people down. You didn't, you didn't let anyone down. You gotta stop telling yourself that, son."

Earlier, Peter had been thinking of John Pruce. Now he thinks of two other men, one, a custodial worker who, rather than bothering to fetch a ladder, climbed a chair he'd stacked on another chair to reach a burned out bulb. The fellow, high on Canadian Club, tumbled along with his chairs into a soapstone spray sink, shattering a patella. He promptly lodged a grievance. Peter recalls the man's family in court—after his complaint, for which he would not accept any reasonable settlement, had wound its way through the grievance process to a lawsuit—his scatterbrained wife, his mother and father, and his six kids. Soon after, the fellow bludgeoned to death that same baffled wife and two of the children unlucky enough to be home at the time. Another worker, a payroll clerk, quiet and self-effacing, who, after experiencing two back-to-back shocks—his wife's desertion and the loss of his savings in an unwise investment—suffered a nervous collapse and had to be sedated and removed from the works. Supporting a payroll, bearing responsibility for hundreds of employees, was never easy, and so, yes, Peter reassures his attorney, "That's an open argument, Harv, my accountability, but yeah, time to do it."

Harvey unsnaps his ancient briefcase. "You do understand that this is going to be a complicated process? I'm going to need to bring in some outside firepower. Surveyors, that's as good as any place to start, then environmental engineers. This was a pottery before it became a pipe works. They no doubt used lead to glaze their wares. God knows if it was anything before that, so we gotta find out whether you have any evil spirits percolating in the ground."

"Let's pray it wasn't a tannery, Harvey, but do what you want to do."

Which elicits a chuckle. "That," Attorney Silverstein says, removing from the breast pocket of his corduroy shirt one of his day's three cigars, "is the worst thing you could ever tell a lawyer."

~ ~ ~

That Sunday Peter comes away from Avis and Elliott's troubled—for various reasons. Even going in, he was uncomfortable. Was the tumble with Avis an easy-in, easy-out Halbrunner oil-change, an unhappy woman needing servicing by a lonely mechanic? Or did there exist the possibility of a deeper re-entanglement? Was that something she wished? Was that something he wished? Whatever, being around her was bound to be awkward, so, as Peter rose in the building's cherry-wood elevator he told himself to keep it light. *Bouncy:* a nice air-head sort of word. Before he got two steps in the door, Elliott detained him in the foyer. Elliott demanded to know what he intended to discuss with the Wilfred people.

"Just a little powwow, Pete. You know, to get an inkling of your game plan?"

He disliked being interrogated. But seeing that his hush-hush meeting with Avis was public knowledge, or some greatly sanitized form of it, and since this concerned Jeanette, Peter kept his voice polite, businesslike. "I haven't thought much about it, Elliott. To be honest, I haven't even called to make an appointment yet."

"What d'you think your game plan is going to be then?"

"First of all, it's not a sporting event, is it, Jeanette's education? And the honest truth is, I don't know what I'm going to say, okay? *Now,* may I go in and visit with my daughter?"

"A wise guy." Elliott maneuvered into a more centrally placed blockade. "So, if you don't have a game plan, then we need to be thinking of furnishing you with such. We're at a delicate inflection point in these school negotiations, and I don't appreciate the idea of you bopping in and just winging it."

Peter understood that his height unnerved the smaller man. They would have had a happier conversation had they been seated. But it hadn't been he who picked the venue for this charming little *powwow.* Peter opened his big round eyes in his big round face and trained them down on the bandy rooster who'd cuckolded him and to whom he'd now returned the favor. "As far as I know, Elliott, I was a bigger smash hit at the Connecticut box office than you were. But since you did ask so *tactfully,* I imagine I'll talk to them about how the Wilfred staff might constructively contribute to my child's developmental needs and how, in turn, she might contribute to the diversity of their community— intellectually, culturally, emotionally, whatever."

"You think something that pig-simple is going to work?"

Pig-simple: Peter was offended. Impromptu as it was, that had been a very tidy speech. "Short of a bribe, I think it's about all we can do. It's called dialogue, reasoning, a civil meeting of like minds."

"Spare me the civics lesson. These are heavy-money toffs—you wouldn't know squat about them." Elliott was in his Puma sweatshirt and pants. All that stood in the path of his high-intensity cardio routine was Peter's visit. "I don't know if you noticed, but there's been a huge influx of foreign nationals in these highbrow schools. Lots of little Arab faces. You ask me, I think Jeanette's doing fine where she is. You want discipline, you can't beat a nun with a ruler. But all right, if you blow it,

Robert McKean

it's on you." He cupped a palm under an armpit and rotated his shoulder and headed for the living room. "No whispering, no conspiring—or you will find how quickly these visits can be curtailed. That clear?"

"Perfectly."

"And when I say *time's up,* that's *exactly* what I mean."

Vexed as he'd been with Elliott, that wasn't the most troubling part of his visit. When he came into the living room, Jeanette was at the piano, about to start on something. So as not to interrupt her, he said softly, "Hi, darling," and let her begin. She'd chosen a contemporary piece, another Simon and Garfunkel or Joan Baez composition, something he didn't recognize, but it was not the what, but the *how.* She was playing without interest, without concentration, without *focus,* as Jacob Weiner would say. Her fingers slid carelessly across the plastic keys, now ahead of the pulse, now behind, frequently failing to sound at all, and the finished article which emerged was slapdash and uneven. Worse, it was *indifferent.* Perhaps you might generously dismiss it as a quick reading, a run-through, but no, no, no: He did not like what he was hearing.

"I think," he said dryly when she finished, "you might want to essay that piece again."

Jeanette jumped. "Papa, I didn't know you were there!"

Was this how she practiced? He hugged her, kissed her on the forehead, then said seriously, because about her music he never lied, "I would like to hear that piece again, darling. Graystone's not going to check it off in that condition."

Jeanette swayed her shoulders, as if to disagree, and Peter realized, yes, bubbly young Graystone Tanner probably *would* check it off, since it'd been he most likely who taught her to play it that way in the first place. But not him—*he* was not checking it off. "It's a pretty tune, darling, let's hear it played as it should be."

Let's hear it played the way Uncle Nico would play it, he longed to say, the way Nico would play it to skaters shrieking as their legs shot up into the air, the way he would play it in a Knights of Columbus lounge at one in the morning for three plastered businessmen and their yawning wives; the way Fatty would play it for women so busy gossiping over their monotonous labor that they were no longer listening. But Peter could not say that to his daughter.

Music either comes from inside—or it doesn't.

Still, her playing, with him here, picked up. That didn't totally relieve him of his concerns, to be sure, but by then he'd gone on to stewing over something else. And today, Tuesday, *this* is what troubles him the most: When he told Elliott that he didn't have a plan for his conversation with the Wilfred people, he'd been telling the truth. At first, he was more taken up with why Elliott had come on so strong, leaping out at him like a troll, then, puzzlingly, seemed to shrug it off—and answers his own question. Elliott was probably relieved to discover that he doesn't have a plan and thus more likely to do more damage at Wilfred than good, which seems clear—clear to Peter, at least—is what Elliott desires. But it also means that, if he doesn't want to bear out Elliott's low opinion of his talents as a deal closer, he does need to think

Robert McKean

about what he's going to say to the Wilfred folks. He needs to make the call setting up an appointment and he needs to work out his script: Traveling salesmen who know the territory don't wing it.

So, why hasn't he?

~ ~ ~

He intended to call the Wilfred school yesterday. But then, worried that Baldwin Feeney would gun down the surveyors Harvey had engaged, he spent the day at the clay works putting his father's office in order. He sorted through files he'd pulled in October and left marooned around the room. Coming home last night, he glanced over at Jacob Weiner's shipwrecked house—and Jacob Weiner's shipwrecked house was no longer there.

Had to happen sooner or later.

But he'd grown fond of the little askew colonial peeking out from behind its two redoubtable yews and would miss it. Peter entered the property via the thieves' portal in the fence to stand on the front stoop like a messenger come too late. He gazed into the muddy cavity that had once been the Weiners' basement. Even though it had been a small structure, he was disconcerted to see just how modest a hole it had left. Fifty years of washing dishes, of carrying groceries in and garbage out, of plunging stopped-up toilets, changing pillowcases, and stooping to collect the mail beneath the slot, five decades of singing, practicing, making love, making war, making dinner, celebrating nuptials and births and mourning separation and death, and all that time misunderstanding the good intentions as well as the bad: one insignificant hole in the ground. In this house, Jacob Weiner's wife perished, his daughter abandoned him and fled with his money, his hands stiffened into appendages as useless as the bound claws of a lobster in a tank.

Of all that, here's what remained: stray lengths of lathe with tufts of plaster clinging to them, contorted piping, shards of a shattered mirror, fragments of bricks, a chunk of mint-green porcelain from Jacob's toilet, a sleeve from a shirt, a rag that perhaps once had been a prom dress. Likewise gone was the legless Ivers & Pond, toppling through the air, one visualizes, from the mouth of a front-end loader, along with Jacob Weiner's pipe stand, his dog's collar, his menorah.

We love junk!

He's remorseful: *Should've rescued the menorah and the collar.* And that's what Peter is thinking about this afternoon, Jacob's vanished house, as he sits in the nursing home beside the all-but vanished Jacob. When he stated at the front desk that he'd come to see Jacob Weiner, the receptionist looked perplexed, then pained and defensive, as if it were she personally being charged with responsibility for mislaying one of their patients.

The woman excused herself to investigate.

"He's been moved," she said when she returned, relieved. "SNF."

Peter waited the polite few seconds anyone would wait to have an unfamiliar piece of jargon graciously explained, then, when forced, asked.

"SNF," she snapped. "Skilled Nursing Facility."

Robert McKean

She pointed to a building across the quad. And so here it is where Peter sits, in a small, antiseptic hospital room much like Jacob's former antiseptic hospital room, identical institutional bed, nightstand, chair with ill-positioned chrome arms. But this new room has a different view, which makes it, in that regard at least, different. Instead of overlooking the interior garden, the windows here face away from the complex, providing an infinite-seeming panorama of the hilly, subsistence-level farms that constitute the greater portion of Rose Township. And perhaps that's on purpose: If you've reached the SNF, you may as well set your sights on some faraway horizon. When he stepped off the elevator, the nurse at the central station, a woman whose snow-white hair provided a brilliant frame to her dark face, a more sympathetic individual, told him that Jacob, since his transfer, had been awake but only sporadically.

"He took some water and juice this morning."

"He's failing then?"

The nurse, Southern Indian Peter guessed, nodded. "Are you his son?"

"A friend." He held up his CD player and bag of CDs. "We were neighbors. I was thinking of him this morning."

He's brought a recording of the Vaughn Williams Fantasies, "On a Theme of Thomas Tallis," "Greensleeves," "The Lark Ascending." The pieces are played by the Academy of St. Martin-in-the-Fields under the baton—as the FM announcers like to unctuously mouth it—of Neville Marriner, a compact disc, if you could wear out a compact disc, he would have worn out ages ago. He keeps the music low and sits in witness beside the wasted man beneath his scratchy sheets: bloodless face, emaciated cheeks, eyes closed but restlessly sliding to and fro beneath the webby wrinkles they're buried within. Weiner's limbs quiver, his breath rasps labored and uneven, and Peter has no reason to second-guess the nurse.

He gets up and stands at the window. Directly before him across a plunging ravine, a young girl, maybe a year or two older than Jeanette, is urging three wholly uninterested cows to move along. The girl, in dungarees and pea coat, swats the lethargic animals on their bony rumps, waves her arms and points indignantly at the heavens. Peter imagines the words emerging from her energetically moving lips, the wonderful imprecations she's heaping upon her apathetic beasts. "Greensleeves" always puts him in mind of Elizabethan England. The hopping mad girl and her stolid cows with their swaying bellies and shrunken teats might have walked out of a pasture in Stratford-upon-Avon, and Peter knows perfectly well why he has not called the Connecticut school. Since his conversation with Avis, he has arrived at the conviction that whether he keeps his daughter or loses her to the boarding school has come to rest in his hands. And to the weight of that reckoning he feels unequal.

How can the world ask this of him?

They are not, despite Elliott's inflation of their status, in negotiations with Wilfred Hall Academy. The admission process has definitely stalled. Whether that's due to what everyone believes, that Jeanette's expulsion for brawling spooked the gentle Wilfred folks, or

Robert McKean

whether there's something else gumming things up, isn't clear. What is clear is that the recommendation coming from the judge whom Avis has befriended might be serving to keep Wilfred from rejecting Jeanette outright but is not enough to persuade them to admit her. And, as every traveling salesman knows in his blood, the longer a sale remains stalled, the less chance of its consummation. So why is he so sure he can have any more influence than anybody else?

Well, he's not.

But a salesman's hubris leads him to believe that he still possesses the talent to close the deal, to wake the process from its slumber—and he cannot bring himself to do that. It's that pig-simple, to borrow from eloquent Elliott. As long as Wilfred Hall has not delivered an irrevocable no, it's not likely that Avis, who is overburdened with distractions, will look for another school, and so Jeanette is likely to stay at Sacred Heart. And as bad as the winter has been—bitterly cold mornings when he's read every line in the *Chronicle,* including *Neighborhood Notes* detailing the Cullenes' family reunion and the Rafanelli twins' acceptance into Duquesne, evenings he roams his shadowy rooms in pajamas and robe—at least he's had his Sundays to look forward to, the goofball absurdities he stores up to drop sotto voce to make Jeanette giggle or groan, the reading he faithfully undertakes in parallel with her assignments, the luminous principles of arithmetic and the somewhat more opaque principles of punctuation and grammar that unite them in intellectual pursuit, her music which he treasures, and the few brief seconds when he's permitted to clasp her in his arms: How can he live without that? And why should he have to? The world can only ask of us what we are capable of giving. Peter looks over at the semi-comatose Jacob Weiner. Upon coming in today, he'd deposited his six Heath bars on the nightstand, then touched Jacob's left shin where it lay outside the sheet.

The flesh was cool, gray, dense, insensate.

Packing up his CD player and books, Peter allows his eyes to rest on the nightstand. Curious, he passes around the foot of the bed and slides open the drawer. Inside are Jacob's stale, slobbered Heath bars, scrupulously moved over to his new room, his cough drops and tissues, and the yellow Kodak envelope. Peter slips the envelope in his coat pocket. He'll mail the photographs to Jessica: He'll meddle just that much more. Declining health and impending death have robbed Jacob Weiner of what dignity he once possessed. But he had *had* dignity, he'd had presence and purpose, he'd brought beauty and integrity into the world and helped children bring those things into the world, too. He'd believed in discipline and in keeping faith in oneself and instilled those character traits in his pupils. He was, as people will say, a man. Before he leaves, Peter kisses Jacob on the forehead, feeling a trifle peculiar doing that, but doing it all the same.

~ ~ ~

Little Boy Blue, come blow your horn.

His inclination is to leave the Cadillac running. And although he doesn't go that far, he lingers at home for under an hour. Doesn't even remove his hat. A more intelligent plan would be to call ahead: He could find himself in Connecticut without an invitation, could drive all night to be told Janet Considine's gone snorkeling in Bermuda. Yes, yes, yes, but there are sound reasons to get himself on the road without delay and to place the Connecticut call in Connecticut, which will make his request more difficult to decline. He rolls a tie—navy with pink polka dots— around his hand, so it won't wrinkle in his duffel, folds in the Brooks suit, adds a pocket square that mates with the tie, underwear, shirts, socks, shaving kit, and his Pelican Shakespeare. In the kitchen he scarfs up a loaf of sourdough and wedge of fontina and is underway, steaming eastbound, by four-thirty. Behind him the twilight oranges, sends streaks of iodine across his mirror, burns down to cinnamon, and is overtaken by lowering black clouds approaching from his front.

The sheep's in the meadow, the cow's in the corn.

The Rose Township cows have reminded him of the rhymes someone read to Avis's mother who read them to Avis who read them to Jeanette. An image of Avis and Jeanette in lamplight glows in his mind, a snippet of lost tenderness from memory's vast, melancholic, and melodious storehouse. He's been trying to think of traditional names for cows. It's a traveling salesman's way to while away the hours. He's got *Clarabelle* and *Henrietta* and *Buttercup* and *Daisy* and *Esmeralda* and a dozen more. But there's one more common than those. Well, even if he doesn't know what you're supposed to name your most beloved ungulate, this much he does know: If he is to lose his daughter, it's because of three wobbly cows with their rubbery dugs and a young girl smacking them smartly on their rumps.

Cows.

One sweet, lost memory will only lead to another and another,
so, to ward off further crippling nostalgia, Peter turns his attention
to the road ahead. An even *better* plan would've been to check the
weather forecast. The dense brow of clouds he's slipped beneath turns
out to be—a state trooper in a mid-state service plaza informs him—
an immense serpent of a Nor'easter coiling up the Atlantic seaboard.
The trooper recommends that Peter find a hotel and points at a line of
towering lollipop signs whose neon blurs in the thickening air. Peter
thanks the man for his advice, but retakes the highway, preferring
to press on. The storm, as storms will, begins in innocence, flakes
scattering randomly in the cones of his headlights like the tiny particles
physicists track on their photographic plates, then intensifies rapidly.
His windshield turns into two half-moons. Gusts grab at the car. Still,
as a sales rep who once covered his territory in weathers fair or foul,
he refuses to worry. Despite its old-fashioned rear-wheel drive, the
Cadillac—two tons of chassis and four-point-five-liter V-8, plus his
larboard—is like a great passenger steamship confidently plowing the
churning, wine-dark seas.

God, he reminisces, *I did a lot of all-night driving.*

When the management of the clay works fell to him, it was the
freedom of the outside salesman he most rued surrendering. An executive
is a man beset, a poor devil imprisoned within four walls. Clutching
his spreadsheets, he scurries like a dung beetle from one meeting to the
next. Not so the outside salesman. Peter loved his solitude, the hours-

Robert McKean

long meditative silences under a paper lantern moon—his tapes, his audio books, his mind at play. As an outside salesman, you operate your own business within the larger business, and your job description is not, as commonly parodied, to be the shyster, the flimflam man soft soaping the buyer with your razzle-dazzle patter. No, no. How far from successful salesmanship that parody is. He was a sewer-pipe salesman from Pennsylvania, but he regularly outsold the big boys because he understood the essential nature of sales, the fundamental task of the salesman: to unravel within the buyer's soul the knot of uncertainty and fear that abides there. And to do that, a salesman befriends his buyers, he woos them, he shuts up. He listens!

Peter, his father clapped him on the back, *you could sell carpets to the Persians.*

Because he *could* quell his ego, *could* shut up, *could* listen. And now his assignment is to sell—terrible word, given the context—his daughter to a boarding school. A school he hopes she won't ever attend. Thinking not of Shakespeare and Homer, but of Elliott Fields, Peter farts, then, for good measure, lifts a flabby cheek and vents again. At the northeast corner of Pennsylvania, sailing down the long plunge into Wilkes-Barre's Wyoming Valley, his attention strays for a moment, and the Cadillac slides out from under him—a sensation the hands recognize before the mind does. The car's trajectory alters, the steering softens, and the big chassis, creaking in its arthritic joints, yaws like a wallowing tanker. His concentration suddenly engaged, his heart pumping, Peter hunches his shoulders over the wheel and plays the skid. One second he's headed sideways this way, the next he's sideways another way, yet he compels himself to countermand the instinct to slam the brakes and steer away from the skid. It's more bobsled than car, or that bizarre sport in which men shoot down icy chutes flat on their backs a hundred miles an hour. The good news, the *only* good news, is that he has the road to himself: Whichever way he wishes, or not wishes, to go, he's got the room to go. Hovering high over Wilkes-Barre and heading toward the abyss, he finally regains control of his vehicle and brings it to order.

A momentary lapse, but chastening.

That night, humbled, he finds a motel outside Scranton. Before going to bed, lingering in his pajamas before yet another metal-framed institutional window, he looks out on a field that slopes up to the interstate. Beneath the unnatural light of the hotel's mercury lamps, the snow, filling the heavens with squalls and blanketing the ground, resembles an exotic yellow yeast. A semitrailer, negligent of danger, takes a deep turn on the freeway and barrels on through, amber lights gleaming like jewels through the murk. *Where is that boy who looks after the sheep? Under the haystack fast asleep.* And he wonders: Did the Rose Township girl ever get her cows into the barn before the storm?

Bess, ah, it comes to him, Bess of course, Bessie.

~ ~ ~

Once in the clay works, the key to a heavy duty padlock securing a tool cage went missing. Saturday, a day the works locksmith did not come in. Roused by phone at home, the grumpy smith identified the lock in question and instructed the caller to take a small ball-peen hammer and tap the padlock very lightly at a particular place on its side—and the massive lock sprang open.

Sales can be that way.

In the morning, Peter removes a tablet from his duffel and eases his generous self behind the flimsy desk the motel provides. A public school has to take all comers and make of their ingredients what gumbo they may. Not so a private school. And his worry is that, if Wilfred has pegged his daughter as a child not worth the bother to integrate into its ideal community, it is going to be nigh on impossible to overcome such a fixed impression. But try you must. On the left side he lists Wilfred's possible misgivings, what salesmen call *objections*. Most prominent among these, one has to assume, is the worry that the girl's a troublemaker, a disruptive element. Perhaps, related to that, she's thought to be too much of a loner? Her introspection was flagged by their tests, and we know that people have a tendency to mistrust the quiet ones: *What is going on inside that head?* And while he grants that self-absorption may pass over into an unhealthy morbidity—good heavens, he's a walking example of that—Jeanette is not that self-engrossed. She's alert to others and engaged when drawn to them. Perhaps she's being perceived as far too self-possessed, too stiff and unshapeable, a child already old beyond her years and too rigid to change? This apprehension he grants, too. Heartbreaking to see a child forced like a hothouse flower to forfeit parts of her childhood. And given the socioeconomic bracket that Wilfred Hall Academy exists within, you would have to assume that this is something they see all too often. But this isn't true of his daughter.

Despite the immaturity of her guardians, big children masquerading as adults, she's not been required to bypass her fledgling years.

She's not become a child-woman, not yet at least.

So, what does Jeanette Sanguedolce—pianist, bicyclist, lover of small animals and keen selector of ripe fruit and melon—have to offer Wilfred Hall Academy? On the right side of the page, after noting that the hair-pulling fracas was the result of relentless goading and bullying, Peter spells out what Jeanette might bring the school community. She's a serious child, a child of intuition and discernment. She grasped the import of the wrecked pink bike before he did. She knew her parents' marriage was in jeopardy before they did—well, before her papa did. She understands that her separation from him probably costs him more than it costs her and that he is too emotionally dependent on her. He can't cite these examples, of course, but he recalls two homework assignments, one, in which she, on her own initiative, compared Durrell's family chronicle with *The Wind in the Willows* and another in which she analyzed a theme in a C.E.P. Bach piece she was learning and contrasted *that* to a song by Paul Simon. She does delight in comparing things, whether it's characters in short stories or images on cans of soup, and isn't the fondness and facility for objective comparison—weighing *worth*—an indicator of intelligence? The test of a first-rate intelligence is the ability to hold two opposed ideas in mind at the same time—F. Scott Fitzgerald said that. As well as the test of civility and civilization—Peter Sanguedolce said that. Furthermore, beneath her poise the child possesses an active wit, a ready and sometimes kooky (wrong word, scratches that out) *quirky* perspective. This sounds, he understands, like every parent speaking, but Peter sincerely believes that his daughter is an authentically interesting and interested person, someone smart and canny enough to bring credit to and perform effectively in a new environment—to thrive in it.

If that environment will give her a chance.

But that's only part of it. What he'd like to say to Janet Considine is that what he finds unappealing in most educational institutions is the preoccupation with teaching narrow skill sets—no doubt because specific skills can be clearly described in curricula and success quantitatively measured. But what a focus on such limited objectives doesn't recognize is the broader spectrum in which those skills comprise but slender bands. And it's that broader spectrum, what he calls imagination—and to him little distinction exists between *imagination* and *mind*—that he is most desirous in exposing his daughter to. Yes, Einstein and Picasso and Shakespeare and Jane Austen possessed the requisite technical skills required to bring their gifts to civilization. But if anyone thinks what defined the genius of Albert Einstein was his math skills, or Pablo Picasso his paint-mixing skills, or William Shakespeare and Jane Austen their grammar skills, he has the brains of a cantaloupe. What those individuals possessed was *imagination*, and he believes that Wilfred Academy might be better at cultivating that aspect of a child. *Why?* Janet Considine might ask. *What makes you so sure we'd give a plugged nickel about your daughter's imagination?* Well, he isn't sure. But what he *is* sure of is that Bright Ridge Academy doesn't, nor the parochial school. But of course he can't run on about this stuff. What he can talk about is his respect for a school in which one's chums are from Asia and Europe and Latin America and where fossilized thought seems not to be absolutely worshiped.

But there he goes again—like every parent. And if the Wilfred folks have already classified Jeanette as a stormy petrel, it's probably futile, anyway. But what Peter keeps harking back to is this: If that *is* their assessment, why not simply wash their hands of the Sanguedolces' girl and decline her admission? Or is there *another* objection lurking beneath? This happens in sales. That what you are being told is the problem is not the problem, and the exercise falls to you to probe even more sensitively the tangled forebodings in the buyer's heart and unwind that knot—thread by thread.

And that he's not going to discover sitting at a desk in Scranton.

Just before checkout, with the storm having passed through leaving snow plastered to the windows and buildings like the work of a mad celestial cake decorator, Peter makes his call. He's surprised, gratified, to discover that Janet Considine, despite the storm, is at her post and willing to answer her own phone.

Although she's cool. "What is it you think we can do for you, Mr. Sanguedolce?"

Peter looks down at his notes and does not find, to this most obvious of questions, a succinct answer. He's out of practice, and answers from the heart. "I love my daughter, and I think your school can help us find the ways we're failing her."

~ ~ ~

While he waits outside Janet Considine's office, he listens to sparrows flitting about the eaves. Spooked by the heavy counterpane of snow that has softened beneath the sun and is sliding from Old Main's slate roof in great landslides, the birds sound like indignant tenants in a building gone to wrack and ruin. Snow cascades from his slate roof the same way, thundering avalanches that used to make his mother jump. A small boy, wound as tightly as a Bedouin in scarves, enters the Admissions Office. He delivers a single Number 10 envelope and in his Admiral Byrd boots marches stoutly back out. As Peter is called into the director's office, he contemplates what success at this meeting would mean.

I can throw this fight and nobody will be the wiser.

"You'll have to forgive us." Janet Considine emerges from her side of the desk to shake his hand. Gestures at her woolly sweater and jeans. "We're all in our blizzard gear." She settles him and returns to her chair. "We kind of lost sight of you, Mr. Sanguedolce. I thought we might see you again. I hope you don't think we weren't interested in your input?"

Janet Considine knows: There's no reason to skirt the truth. "There've been some changes. My former wife and her husband have reduced my interactions with Jeanette. I chose not to contest those changes."

"I know these custody things can get complicated."

"But they're fully behind this visit," Peter adds.

"Well, that's good." The director rests her hands on their edges, fingers knitted, on what he presumes is Jeanette's folder—which, if it is, is impressively thick. "So then, what exactly is it that you think we can do for—or with—Jeanette that you're not doing? I don't often hear a parent talking about failure, to be honest."

Since he's known that this is going to be where the conversation begins, the only place in light of what he blurted out it can begin, he's thought about his answer. "We have our differences, my wife and I. But one thing we've been good at is parenting. We've always worked together with Jeanette. We never fought over her or through her or used her as a pawn in our divorce. But with the separation, the changed circumstances, the stress, we aren't doing very well. And I don't mean that we're fighting over her, no one's trying to manipulate her, I don't mean that at all. But it's as if we're rolling over her concerns—and that isn't quite right, either—we're rolling *past* her concerns, that's better, she's getting lost in the noise, and I don't like that."

"I appreciate your candor." Peter remembers the constellation of freckles under her eyes. "I don't hear that kind of thing very often, either. I don't know how much you want to share with me, I don't know that it's even necessary or will make a difference. But if you want to talk a little about Jeanette, and your . . . difficult . . . circumstances, that would be okay. I'm not sure what role a school can play in a situation as you're describing, but I'll leave that up to you."

He guesses that she is well acquainted with the impact of broken marriages and is far from unknowledgeable of the role a school, especially a boarding school, will sometimes play in family dynamics, but is professional enough to consider it part of her job to hear him out. "I don't know whether Avis would agree with me on all this," he clarifies. "It's just my opinion?"

"I'll keep that in mind."

And really, how much *does* he want to share? Jeanette's growing estrangement? Avis's pregnancy that Jeanette feels is squeezing her out of her own family? Elliott's ugly punitiveness? His own melancholia, his food binges? Beneath his desire for candor, he has to think that Janet Considine might well subscribe to the world's most common opinion: that in a dysfunctional and estranged family, the source of all problems *is* that failed marriage. And so, isn't he obliged to wade into the marital unhappiness, too, all the things between Avis and him that went off track? Perhaps, but that seems too much of a swamp. He limits it to Jeanette's schooling. "We have her at a good parochial school. It's solid, but very traditional. Her grades are improving, and so there's nothing to complain about there. But it's only a temporary solution. We need something more permanent."

"Why? Why move her again, especially if it's, as you say, a good school?"

"Because it's not the educational and cultural environment we want her in. And that's true for both Avis and me. Meanwhile, we aren't making up for what Jeanette is missing on our own—we can't. We're not her teachers, not her schoolmates, we're her parents, and I'm worried that we're losing precious time."

"Well, yes, it can seem like that, I'm sure . . . "

She's unimpressed. Even though she's nodding in agreement, her fingers—impatiently knitting and re-knitting on the folder—tell him different. His arguments are weak ones, these are the arguments of every concerned parent. She's heard all this a thousand times. He puts a little more into his voice. "Kids live at a different speed than we do. Things can turn around for them before we're aware of it, and then it's too late."

"Well, that's true, but there's lots of good schools? What makes you think that we're the right one for Jeanette? Why *Wilfred*, Mr. Sanguedolce?"

If you exit a sales meeting with the uneasy feeling that you did most of the talking, you probably have lost the sale. He's talking too much, he needs to get her talking, otherwise he's just fishing. But first he has to state his brief, as Harvey Silverstein would say. He senses that Janet Considine's question—and her restless fingers—are seeking two answers, with the *us* part being the less important. But he takes that first. "Because the Wilfred Academy offers an environment we're looking for. She's a bright child—your tests show that, she has talent and insight, she's curious and inventive. She works hard, she goes about things thoughtfully, analytically, but she also has an active imagination. She loves comparison. A paper she wrote this year—the topic was entirely of her own choosing—was a comparison of a theme in a C.E.P. Bach piece with a theme in a Paul Simon song. These are qualities your literature says you're looking for, and from what I've seen I think that must be true. The school is multicultural, which we particularly value,

Robert McKean

it's supportive of independent thinking and liberal in the old-fashioned sense. I can see Jeanette, maybe not in fifth grade, but soon, at one of your seminar tables, being part of a discussion on human rights in Uzbekistan or on Matisse's role in Fauvism. I think she'd thrive here."

Janet Considine lifts a shoulder—a judicial lift. She's recognizing his points, better than he's gotten so far, but miles from any kind of commitment. "Your wife shared Jeanette's paper on Bach and Paul Simon with me, so I've seen it."

"I didn't know that. I'm glad she did."

"And I am, too. It was very good, I mean, more than good, it was work you wouldn't expect from a ten-year-old. We're not discounting your daughter's intelligence and her creativity, Mr. Sanguedolce, not for a minute, please don't think that."

No, he didn't think that. Mostly, he wanted to put those points on record, but, now that he has, he has no choice but to go on to the second answer her question seeks, the more problematic one. And with this one he sees no alternative but to confront it directly. "And I think she'd bring valuable things to Wilfred. She's not a troublemaker, not a truculent child. Her dismissal was the result of bullying. I know that's not Bright Ridge's story and I know, when it comes to kids, minor slights can get blown out of proportion, but, in terms of what happened at Bright Ridge, Jeanette was more sinned against than sinner."

"How do you know that? How can you be so sure?" For the first time, the director leans forward over her hands. She's skeptical, combative, her freckles on the move. "You weren't there, and the Bright

Ridge people were—the teachers, the monitors, the headmaster. They say your daughter *was* the instigator. Their letter, I have it right here." Janet Considine stabs the folder with a finger. "How do you know she was the one more sinned against? Please understand me, Mr. Sanguedolce, I'm not trying to slander anyone, I'm not trying to criticize your daughter, that's not my purpose, but I do think this is a crucial point: How do you know?"

This he's prepared for. He leans into her. "Because they were baiting her—the kids she had the fight with. And they had been, for some time—it was not a one time event. They were ridiculing her clothes and her hair. Jeanette will sometimes choose something unusual to wear or something to complement her outfit—she was carrying that antique purse of my aunt's when we were here last time, if you remember? And this particular group of girls didn't like her style, her independence and flair. I assume it threatened them."

"Is that all? I don't mean to imply that's a good thing, but is that all they were doing—making fun of her clothes? And her hair?"

"They also didn't like that she was smarter than they were. They didn't like that she was asked to play the piano for a school production. They didn't even like her name."

"And you know all this to be true?"

Peter nods. "Plus they were spreading a rumor that she smelled bad."

"Ooo." Janet Considine sits back in her chair. "That's pretty icky, even for kids."

Robert McKean

He pulls back in his chair, too. "Jeanette's no angel, but she's not someone who's going to stoop to that level of petty ugliness. She's not spiteful, not vindictive, she's not mean. She didn't start the creepy stuff, she walked into it, and once it began she didn't throw that kind of fuel on the fire to feed it."

All of which, with a pregnant pause, brings them to an inflection point. But it seems too soon, too precarious of a plateau to push toward closure, and so, before the director answers or is forced to answer, Peter tries to back off a little. "Do you do any of the mentoring? You're probably too busy for that?"

She looks at him oddly. "Why do you ask?"

"I remember something Lina, the girl who gave us our tour, said. We had a very thoughtful conversation. She told us that every student has a mentor they meet with. I thought that was very interesting. I can't tell you how many times as a kid I would've loved to have someone grown up to talk to, other than my parents."

"Actually, I do some mentoring." The director smiles. "And it's nice you remember Lina, she's a sweetheart. We all mentor, that's an essential component of the school's philosophy. I have five advisees, including a new one, this little duckling who wants to be a forest ranger—don't ask me, he's from Dubai and I'm sure has never set foot in a forest—and four others. My oldest graduates this year, she's captain of three teams."

"You've known her twelve years? Or did she come later?"

"No, no, all twelve. She was my very first."

"You're going to miss her?"

"Oh, will I!" The director's freckles jump. "I'm so proud of her. Let me tell you, you don't want to get checked on the lacrosse field—accidentally or otherwise—by Astrid Storgaard. Astrid will lay you out flat as a buttermilk pancake!"

Janet Considine laughs, a good throaty laugh in which Peter joins, and he ponders: *Have I done it?* You can never ask until you're sure and hardly need to. He watches her hands relax and flatten, her fingers spreading across his daughter's folder. He believes he's turned it, made the case for his brief, or is convinced he has—until suddenly he knows he hasn't.

The director reknits her hands.

Peter watches Janet Considine's face drain of light, stranding its yoke of inert freckles against the pale skin, as she returns, a complete person, to a pleasant, businesslike impersonality. "I'm very happy you've come in to see us again, Mr. Sanguedolce. And we owe you an answer. It's clear that as a family you have a genuine urgency, and we shouldn't be holding you up. We'll think about what you've said and we'll get back to you." She adds, chippering up her voice, "The last time you were going on to Boston—is that your itinerary this time, too?"

He has but a second or two before she rises. Ignoring her question, clutching at straws, he asks a question of his own. "Is it all right if I bring up one more thing?"

It isn't. Janet Considine's expression and the off-balance shift of her body—she was, indeed, about to stand—tell him it isn't. But civility,

Robert McKean

the common everyday courteousness that she, as he, is enslaved to, drags her back. Helpless, she resettles in her chair. "Yes, of course, but it *is* a busy day, I'm sure you understand? The storm has compounded what was already a complicated week."

"I understand. I'll be brief. Is it not Jeanette, or not wholly Jeanette?"

"I don't understand, what do you mean?"

"Is it Elliott Fields who's the problem?"

Whatever run of popularity he might have had in Connecticut's Quiet Corner is rapidly evaporating. "Mr. Sanguedolce"—the director's voice, as she grasps his point, is scolding—"we've really swerved off course here?"

"But is it Elliott ? Is he the impediment?"

Peter's pretty sure he's about to be chucked out on his beam. But a part of him watches, fascinated, as Wilfred Hall Academy's Director of Admissions works out the lines of an argument inside her. "I'm not comfortable with this," she says after a pause whose duration is clearly meant to be discerned. "But I'm going to answer you candidly—under one condition: Everything from now on is off-record?"

Peter nods.

"*Strictly* off-record—I want that agreement upfront."

"I agree. You have my word."

She reknits her fingers, swallows. "Mr. Fields said and did some things during our meetings that raised questions—that raised eyebrows, to be frank. He seems to be a very unusual man. And that's all I'm prepared to say."

"May I add one more small thing?"

Her hands positively clench, whitening.

And he smiles. Probably not wise, but he likes this woman and her mentees in knee-socks who would send you sprawling on a playing field. But what he's begged permission to additionally contribute to the conversation is not humorous. "I can't do much for my daughter. What legal recourse I have is very limited. But I have reason to believe that her present home environment is not entirely suitable."

"You're worried about her? Her safety?"

"Some things aren't adding up. Worrisome things."

"All right then." And with that the admissions director does rise. She holds out her hand, which trembles ever so slightly: an official handshake, not strong, not warm, not clubby, not even close to a *Hey, you've-got-our-business!* shake. "I promise, we will get back to you— soon."

"Thank you."

That evening, finding a restaurant dim enough to match his mood, Peter eats without appetite and decides not to stay the night. He'll go back to the hotel, pack and leave for home. The sale has been lost. You don't sell from weakness, from desperation. What buyer wants distressed goods—a daughter expelled for brawling, a divorced set of parents at loggerheads, a weird-ass stepfather who sends chills up your spine? So, if he's lost, paradoxically, he's actually won then, right? Wilfred's rejection means Jeanette will remain in the Ganaego Valley

Robert McKean

and give him the time and leverage to advocate for a local solution. He'll keep his precious Sundays, their books and music and eye-rolling drolleries. Even having his divination confirmed that the sticking place was not Jeanette should be cause for minor celebration, should it not? So, hello, Joe, he's got a beautiful daughter and he's one hell of a cunning salesman: He should be happy.

He's not happy.

Peter thinks longingly of his house candied in snow—roof fanged with icicles, windows rounded to portholes—and is reminded once again of his mother. One of her many tiny anguishes in life was that no one they visited should ever think they overstayed their welcome. *Now, let's not stay too long,* she'd caution his father, who liked nothing better than staying too long. And then the supreme irony: His father dying far too young, his mother living far too long.

I've stayed too long here, he thinks.

But when he lets himself into his hotel room, the king-sized bed and its six plump pillows call to him like goose-feather sirens, and he's asleep in seconds after changing into pajamas.

~~~

He wasn't sure why. Perhaps it had something to do with the clumsy way he sat down in the Cadillac. He'd been loitering by the raised hood as the same young man who had serviced the car last fall fed the Cadillac another quart of oil and promoted his transmission fluid special. "Today only, never gonna be this cheap again. So boss, should I deal you in or out?" Peter declined a second time, then tripped over his big feet and tumbled into his seat, trapping the panel of his coat beneath him. And so perhaps it was that, identifying as he came up the ramp what it was making his coat catch: the Kodak envelope. Or perhaps it was the dazzling morning, the pristine snow and a crescent day moon sharp as a scimitar in the cloudless sky, too glorious of a day to die alone in a hospital room. Whatever, something operatic swelled in his chest and Peter Sanguedolce at the top of the ramp changed his mind and his plan and possibly his life and turned, not south and west toward home, but north and east.

Madness!

The trip seems faster. Probably his imagination, but the drive *is* easier. And some of the credit for that has to go to the Cadillac. You can hardly claim that a wallowing five-thousand-pound sedan is adept at threading traffic, true, but what you can confidently claim is that, if driven with a certain aplomb, the faded old Brougham parts traffic with remarkable efficacy. It also helps that he knows the territory, and so he finds himself parked—a little too soon—on a busy street in Roxbury. He dallies, indecisive. All he promised himself when he slipped the envelope in his pocket was that he'd mail the photographs to Jessica. And there's no reason why he can't just do that. Find a stationery store, buy a larger envelope, ask about a nearby post office.

And for a while that is what Peter decides he will do.

In the meantime he watches a young man drift by, a college student he supposes, but costumed as Abraham Lincoln in black beard and pasteboard top hat. The boy, walking backwards, is presenting advertising fliers to people. After him comes a young mother in hijab pushing a stroller. She's trying to conceal her exasperation with a tyke tugging at her hand and the stroller whose bent axle resists being steered in a straight line. Beneath her white headdress her dark eyebrows sizzle. Across the way is a neighborhood package store, and he goes on to note the wrinkle-faced pug waiting patiently outside and parade of people exiting with one-bottle bags. All this Peter takes in—a world going on with its business oblivious of the prematurely retired man dawdling at the curb in an aging sedan—and puts it to himself directly.

So boss, should I deal you in—or out?

Out. Peter kicks over the engine and draws into traffic. Lunch is on the Common, a decent, if not memorable, Polish sausage, and, afterward, two hours prowling the towering shelves of the Brattle Book Shop. He discovers a bargain-basement *Webster's Second Unabridged*, the classic American dictionary, dirt cheap because some bored child long ago scribbled on its prefatory pages with a crayon. He carries the huge volume in his arms to the desk for safekeeping, then goes on to find a Frank Kermode Shakespeare he doesn't have and a scholarly exploration of Shakespeare's morphology, and then, small miracle, Erich Auerbach's *Mimesis*—books he pictures himself reading in his armchair in the upstairs foyer as a straw-hued Elizabethan light refracts through the bull's eyes indentations in the old glass.

But as pretty as that scene is—monastic, safe, cozy—it won't do.

At two-forty-five he's parked a block from the Sarah E. Keating Health Center, before a corner luncheonette that Edward Hopper might have painted. Slamming the car door behind him, Peter admits the truth that has been nagging him: He's not here entirely for Jacob Weiner's benefit. Well, all right, motives are usually mixed. He removes his hat and smooths his hair, squares his suit coat, and walks to the health center to inquire for Ms. Weiner, half-hoping to be informed that she's embarked on an around-the-world cruise.

He's answered from behind.

"Peter, what're you doing here?" Jessica is dressed in dark, navy-blue blouse, shiny, satiny, and black pleated skirt, probably the same skirt she was wearing on his first visit. He's a full head taller, possibly three of her in width, yet finds himself nervous, as Jacob Weiner's daughter rests on him her dark scolding eyes. "This had better not be about my father again?"

He wangles for a small perch from which to state this, his second brief, in two days. "I mentioned something when I was here before—some photographs we found in the house? And since I was going to be nearby, visiting my daughter's school, I figured I'd bring them over. D'you have a few minutes?"

Trapped by the same civility that had trapped Janet Considine, Jessica looks around helplessly. "I suppose."

"There's a luncheonette up the street?"

"What is it you have? Pictures? Can't you just give them to me?"

Robert McKean

Traveling salesmen know their territory. They also know what's in their trunk. "Well, there's a big box of stuff? I left it all in the car."

"Good grief, how many photos *are* there?" Jessica turns to the receptionist. "Cindy, I'll be back in ten minutes. If Dr. Rosen calls, get a specific time I can call him back."

"The temperature's dropping," Peter cautions when it looks as if she's just going to step out the door. "You may need a coat."

"It's always dropping. Welcome to New England."

She consents to fetch her coat, although not button it, and, clutching the panels with an ungloved hand, strides out into the wind. As they pick their way along the snow-narrowed sidewalk, Jessica determinately stays a half-step ahead of him. At his car, which earns the same disapproving scowl it earned before, Peter says, "Let me get the pictures." He snatches up the yellow envelope on the seat. He would have liked, before presenting the photographs, to create a dramatic structure to showcase them, build a little proscenium so they receive a proper sendoff. But this he's known all along: Jacob Weiner's daughter, like Jacob, is not the patient type. As they settle into a sun-lit booth in the empty luncheonette, they're instantly set upon by a waitress who looks to be desperately in need of some tipping business.

Given the circumstances, he does the best he can.

"There was a box in a cupboard—the cupboard beside the stairs going into the basement?" He traces a descending staircase with his fingers, self-conscious about describing to someone the inside of that person's house. "It was pushed way back. There were papers in it, in the box—which I promise I haven't been nosy about—and these old family snapshots."

Sorry, Jacob. He hands over the Kodak envelope as if it contained nothing more than a wad of receipts from 1953. He has an image of Jessica Weiner's cold-bloodedly ripping each photograph in half and presenting the halves back to him. But no, she begins flipping through the photos, eyes narrowed as she scans and assesses each, and, as she does, he tries—and mostly fails—to locate in this middle-aged woman the Ganaego High School vixen who rode off on a Manx Norton with a married man. How do you locate the younger self in any of us? Who was that naïve neighbor boy who was mortified by the angel he was secretly in love with having sex with the grown man who taught him shop? Saws, hammers, varnish—and sex? Her dark hair, he notices, is graying at the temples. Her complexion is sallow, the skin roughened. Over her mouth are the same *A* lines, only shallower, that tent her father's mouth. And something else that's familiar: a concentration that her father had, an interior life that shuts out the world. He's especially gratified to watch her linger over the shot of the triumphant Weiner holding her an infant just above eye level.

It is, whatever else one may say, a magnificent moment.

When she's finished, Jessica taps the black and white photographs into alignment like a deck of cards, a record of but a single day out of the thousands lived in that house in Oak Grove, a house now demolished and carted away. She slides the photos back into the time-softened envelope in which they have slept for decades. Peter goes on

Robert McKean

discreetly observing her, as he did Janet Considine, lost for a moment as she pieces out something inside her. The waitress, waving her scratched pot and tut-tutting at the unconscionable neglect of their coffees, comes by. Jessica absently slides her hand over her cup: She needn't, she's hardly touched it. Peter lets the woman top off his—bringing her to a minor rapture, she smiles brilliantly—and waits for the resolution of whatever Jessica is thinking. Finally, she looks at him.

"You're still going in to see him, aren't you? That's what they tell me."

"Easy enough to stop in."

"You're about the only one who does."

"That's not surprising." He deflects her comment. "Not many people came to see my mother when she was in a nursing home. If you live long enough, you outlive everybody in your time capsule. I saw him Tuesday, in his new room. He's got a prettier view."

"I don't think he cares much about the view."

"No, not this week. But the time before that he had a good day. We were able to talk, a little." Peter doesn't say about what, not yet. "About as good a day as he's likely to have."

"You aren't busy? Doesn't your family own a business of some kind?"

"Once upon a time."

Jessica's eyes play over his face, troubled. He senses she's picking up his mixed motives. "Your daughter's in college here, is that what you said?"

"Not college. We're trying to get her into a boarding school in Connecticut, my wife, my former wife, and I. I was there meeting with the admissions director."

"Connecticut? You're calling that nearby?"

"Ahh"—reaches for his traveling salesman's chuckle—"Just over the border." The photographs may have gotten him a hearing, but in their austere silence they have not made his case. They can't, that's his task, and Peter realizes he can't either—or rather, cannot do both. He's come with two briefs, his and a dying man's, and you can't plead two cases simultaneously. It *was* madness to think he could. Forsaking his own petition, his shy longings, he searches for a way to plead for Jacob. He'd like to tell Jessica of a sobbing Jacob Weiner, abandoned in a solarium, snapshots and candy bars heaped in his lap, or a moaning Jacob Weiner, determined to get to Boston, lurching across a restaurant using people's heads for support. But that seems guilt-laden, ham-handed. "The Tuesday before last—when we *were* able to talk—Jacob spoke about wanting to get in touch with you. To talk. That seemed important to him. I hope I can say so without offending you?"

Well, no, he can't. Jessica's face clouds: so much for his perch. But she keeps her voice cordial. "I need to get back. I have a call I'm expecting. Where're you staying? Are you at the Copley again?"

"I haven't checked in anywhere yet. There's a hotel up the street from the Copley? I don't remember the name of it—maybe a tad less fancy?"

"There's a lot of hotels in Boston anymore. You can find pretty

Robert McKean

much anything you want." Jessica slides to the edge of the bench and stands. She holds up the Kodak envelope. "Thank you, this was very thoughtful of you, to bring these. And I appreciate your visiting him. He's . . . well . . . thanks again."

"I'll get the box and carry it back for you."

"Let's see how heavy it is, maybe I can handle it. The Lenox—that's the one you're probably thinking of."

~ ~ ~

He's . . . a very lonely man.

That's what Jessica meant to say. Has no proof of that, of course; nonetheless, he's convinced that is what she meant to say. He's thinking of Jessica Weiner and her unfinished sentence while he's seated at a small semicircular bar eating oysters. A sign informs him that Daniel Webster supped here daily, consuming no less than a half dozen platters of oysters and washing them down with flagons of brandy. An impressive intake, something to set a solitary diner's thoughts turning: The thrashing seas from whose shores Daniel Webster's oysters were harvested would have been both more bountiful and more dangerous than a modern traveling salesman's seas; Daniel Webster's oysters would have been carried to market, not in plastic tubs stacked in the back of diesel trucks, but in woven baskets lifted into the beds of horse-drawn carts; and this public room in which Daniel Webster slid his oysters down his eloquent throat, while possessing probably the same low ceilings, would have been lit by tallow candles or lamps aglow with oil rendered from the whales that once swam in the nightmares of Herman Melville.

But really, when it comes down to it, an oyster's an oyster. Peter catches the bartender's eye. "Do we know which stool he sat at?"

"One you're having no trouble filling, mac."

Sorry he'd asked. Another difference, apart from the tobacco smoke and dripping spittoons that would have been fixtures of Daniel Webster's world but have now, blessedly, been banished, is that Daniel Webster would not have had occasion to withdraw from his pocket an illuminated device and receive a note that, in seconds, had traveled many hundreds, if not thousands, of miles: *Hey, neighbor, what color?* The note, finding him a stranger in a strange city, cheers him, albeit in a bleak way. The ladies and gentlemen of Daniel Webster's era wore, one presumes, linen of a uniform nondescript color, but were no doubt, once out of their plain shifts, every bit as frisky. Adultery's but adultery, after all. But the affair with his neighbor-to-be has about worn itself out, and it worries Peter that some afternoon in a moment of *in flagrante delicto* Randy Halbrunner is going to show up with a tire iron.

Well, he'll just have to wait in line behind Elliott Fields.

About the afternoon he feels bad. If his instincts are correct, Jessica's unfinished sentence means this: Because Jacob Weiner had not been a man who bothered with friends, because he'd been a man who hadn't needed friends, who beyond his wife hadn't needed much of anybody, possibly including his own daughter, he's lying in a room whose windows look out on a world that carries on indifferent to his death. After dinner Peter wanders through the North End, stopping for espresso and cannoli and an opportunity to employ what little Italian he

Robert McKean

retains. Returning to the hotel, he peeks in the lounge, hoping to spot the bartender with the pretty wrists. He'd like to ask how her daughter is doing. But she doesn't appear to be on duty, and he takes the elevator to the tiny room that the Lenox has consented to rent him, a room not much bigger than a closet.

Where a light on the telephone blinks in the darkness: a message.

Peter, I understand why you went out of your way to bring me the pictures—and you're right, I need to say goodbye to him. Are you going back tomorrow? Can I bum a ride from you? I can't fly, it's a phobia. If you aren't leaving tomorrow, that's fine. You're welcome to call me, if you get in before eleven tonight or in the morning before eight. I'll be happy to pay for gas. If this is any inconvenience, just ignore this.

It's eleven-forty-five. He calls and gets a sleepy, borderline grumpy answerer. "Sorry," he races to apologize, "but sure, I'd love to have the company."

"I can't go before ten. I have to go into the clinic—I usually work Saturdays—and make arrangements. Is that going to hold you up?"

"No, that's fine, I'm in no hurry."

"I'm not much for small talk, I should warn you of that?"

"I'm not someone who has to talk all the time."

He showers and lies in bed. He's not sleepy, but in such a small room there's hardly any other place to be. He's keyed up, excited. He frets how he came across, then rounds on himself: What is he, a high school kid the night before his first date? Listening to the Back Bay going about its Friday night, shouts, cries, and the honks and blats from the long green plastic horns somebody should be garroted for inventing, he worries about that last remark of his. Did that sound too much like a personals ad?

SWM, mid-forties, love sunsets, quiet drives and small animals with oversized eyes.

~ ~ ~

Shortly after ten, Jessica is waiting before her apartment building in a chasm that appears to have been hewn from a block of ice. The weather has warmed, and this morning a fine rain falls, hardly more than a cold mist. She's wearing jeans and loafers, no hat, no gloves. The shoulders of her coat and the backpack at her feet are wet; her hands are red and chapped, as is her nose. She might have waited in the lobby. He's seen college kids plodding through the slush in Bermuda shorts: Maybe people in Boston can't be bothered with winter?

"You're sure this is all right?" Jessica's suspicious eyes gauge his expression: She's mistrustful of a situation that she herself has engineered. "You were going back today—no other plans?"

"Absolutely. Busy time of year, things to do, people to see."

"I'm sorry I couldn't leave any earlier."

"No, no, I've got all the time in the world."

He realizes, a second after this leaves his mouth, that, taken together, his last two sentences make no sense. Peter stows her backpack in the trunk, and Jessica squeezes between the hardened wall of dirty snow and the car and slides in. Minus her weekday makeup, her face appears even more washed out, more sallow. She has a slight mustache, he notes, and chides himself for his appraisal. Her own eyes dart around the Cadillac's messy interior, then are circumspectly pulled back.

She pushes—discreetly, daintily—a single, lost mitten out of the way with the toe of her shoe. "Did you have a good evening?"

He's worked out his route, spread his maps across the Lenox bed, knows he needs to wend his way through Brookline and reach something called Route 9 and from there Route 128 and the Mass Pike. People in Massachusetts seldom say *Massachusetts*. Too many syllables? It's nice that she's asked. "I had dinner at the Union Oyster House."

"It's sort of a tourist trap."

"No, no, it was an honor to sit on the same stool that Daniel Webster sat on."

"Did they sit at bars back then—or stand?"

"That's a good question, actually. I guess you don't see cowboys slumped at the bar watching the game on TV? I had a good fish dinner. Did you get everything done you needed to this morning?"

"We never get everything done."

And that's about the extent of their conversation for the next hour. As she warned, she's not a talker. Traffic, Saturday morning, is sparse, and they clear the city and find the open road sooner than he expects. He listens to the efficient swish of the Cadillac's long wipers across the broad windshield and the crush and splash of the tires below. And when the mist thins and the clouds begin to scud off, they do not have even that for a soundscape. Peter notices Jessica shiver and realizes he has the heat set to where he ordinarily keeps it, low. A big person, he serves as his own furnace.

"I'll turn up the heat."

"No, don't, I like it cool."

"Healthier," he concurs.

"People who visit me always know to bring an extra sweater."

A little while later, in a minute when she's distracted by something outside, he surreptitiously ticks up the heater and notices, soon after, that she's slipped off her coat and is sitting back in her seat, more relaxed. Better: It's going to be a long trip. A cheerful sign welcomes them to Connecticut, a state scrupulous about pronouncing all its syllables. *We're full of surprises,* the governor promises. Peter scans the governor's name, M. Jodi Rell, curious about that *M,* and several follow-up signs, warnings not quite so jolly, and goes on, his mind woolgathering, to think of the girl Lina at Wilfred Hall. Weekends at a boarding school: *What is that like?* What is Jeanette up to this morning? Practicing, he hopes, before she dons a sweatshirt and goes off to kick the Catholic stuffing out of the Catholic soccer ball. He's looking forward to Sunday, her new math chapter, beginning statistics—means and averages and medians. He's got a silver dollar that he intends to use for flipping.

"How old is your daughter?"

Did she guess he'd been thinking of Jeanette? "Ten." Then, because it pleases him, Peter amends his answer. "Or, as she would say, ten and a half."

Robert McKean

"Halves can be important at that age."

"True." And before she can voice what he fears she's thinking, he adds, "I know that's a little young to be going away to boarding school. But there are extenuating circumstances."

"Sounds good to me. I wish somebody had sent me away."

Which shocks him, a little. As they enter Hartford's city limits, Peter puts aside conversation. Hartford's freeways, he's come to believe, were designed by someone who'd taken to sniffing airplane glue. For the harrowing minutes they plunge through the vehicular morass of Connecticut's capital, Peter concentrates on not only his driving but on the cognitive limitations of his fellow motorists, too. *We're full of surprises:* poorly lit underpasses, crumbling pavement, middle lanes that mysteriously become left-lane exit-only lanes. Left exits, oh really? Only on the far side of the city, once they pass beneath the sign for Asylum Street, where no doubt resides that particular highway engineer, does Peter breathe a theatrical sigh of relief.

"Like a Mobius strip, or a worm hole in space."

"Try it on a motorcycle at ninety."

He recalls a shop teacher explaining to a group of half-asleep boys—boys who would consider it fortunate to escape the class without having their thumbs pounded flat—what *kerf* was. What *is* kerf? A few months later Mr. Finlay chucked his miter boxes and crosscut saws, his wife and children, for a girl eighteen and a day. When did the young woman with a voice of a diva get down from that hot Norton? Did she go on singing? Still sing? And whatever became of Mr. "Measure Twice and

Cut Once" Finlay?

"What do you do," he asks, "at the health center?"

"Right now, I'm helping them turn out the lights."

"You're closing?"

"We don't have much choice. The days of independent clinics are over. What I *did* do was development, raise funds—write grants, hobnob with bluenoses, go begging on my knees—and serve as community liaison. I also managed the office, rationed the scotch tape and emptied the buckets when it rained. I still ration the tape and empty the buckets."

"I know something about buckets. There's no hope?"

"We can't compete, not with the big hospitals."

Peter thinks of the Black and Latino women he squeezed between, the suckling babes in their mothers' meaty arms. "So, what're you going to do next?"

She's a fidgety traveler. Jessica shifts in her seat, twists, flexes her legs, rolls her shoulders like a prizefighter. "I've been too busy to think about it. We're still in mourning, all those years of effort going down the tubes. I looked at a cabinet drawer the other day, at a label I pasted on fifteen years ago—*Pap smear stuff*—and laughed. *Stuff*. But I'll do something, I have to work, or I'll go crazy."

"Can't sit around doing nothing all your life," he agrees.

At a service plaza in New York Jessica offers him money for gas. She takes two twenties from her wallet and holds them out. He refuses, and she insists on buying them lunch. As they start across the

Robert McKean

parking lot, a bus rolls past with teenagers chanting, *Hit 'em, knock 'em, sock 'em! Slam them, wham them, and cram them! We're Racine West, and we're the best!* Behind that chug in two more rollicking buses, and Peter suggests that they buy something here but press on to a rest stop he remembers. *Twelve hundred seventy-five feet,* the sign informs them when, a half-hour later, he pulls out of traffic, *highest elevation on this highway in New York.*

"Picnic?" Jessica asks, then answers her own question. "Too cold."

"Indoor picnic."

They spread their late lunch between them on the Cadillac's wide bench seat, hamburgers the texture of thatched roofs, salads a rabbit wouldn't recognize, soggy fries his daughter would cross her eyes at. He wishes he knew Jessica well enough to talk more Jeanette. Nothing heavy, just the idle chitchat every parent likes to indulge in. He has no one to do that with. Instead, Peter asks whether she has other family in Ganaego. It's a subtle—and non-prying—way of asking where she's planning to stay.

"I thought I'd have you drop me at one of the hotels by the airport—if it's not too much trouble?"

Perhaps it wasn't so subtle? "No trouble."

"D'you want to walk a bit when we're done? Stretch our legs?"

Even though the sky has been whisk-broomed of clouds, leaving a bright, bonny sun, this high up on the shoulder of the mountain you can hear the wind moaning and feel the car quivering as ragged gusts snatch at it. Jessica scoffs at bothering with a coat, and he, alpha male, renounces his, too. They pace—Peter keeping a finger on the brim of his hat—the length of the turnoff, passing two trailers unhooked from their cabs. The trailers, tires immobilized in snow, look like something forsaken by the Soviet army. Reaching the end of the small turnoff, they turn and march back. Not much of a walk.

Jessica points at the eastbound turnoff above. "You think they have a better view?"

She likes mischief, that's clear. They cross their two highway lanes and climb to the eastbound lanes, stumbling and staggering up the embankment through deeply creviced snow. Waiting for a break in traffic, they dart—well, she darts, he lumbers—across those lanes and hike along the road a short distance to the opposite rest area. As a fat man, slow and clumsy, and as a nominal law-abider, Peter has more than a few reservations about this, the primary one being he doubts the view will be better from this side.

"Trees," Jessica concedes. Long-legging it through the snow down to their side again, she points along the road west of their rest area. "There!"

Trying to ignore the eighty-thousand-pound rigs roaring past a few feet away, he follows her single file along the shoulder of the highway, then hauls himself over the retaining rail. Stumbling down the hill a bit, she finds a fallen tree trunk for them to sit on. And now, for sure, with the wind, a low sonorous wail, flouncing their clothes and ruffling their hair—his hat's long off, clutched in his fist—the world

Robert McKean

sprawls at their feet in all its splendor, thirty miles of patchwork farms and Sleepy Hollow villages nestled in mauve-gray and evergreen woods: clapboard houses, smoke curling from their chimneys, gambrel-roofed barns and their silos like stubby sentries, cows clustered beneath naked trees.

"I remember reading somewhere," Peter says, "you only have to go a short distance into the air—much less than a mile, I think—to lose all the noise and racket of mankind."

"Plan Five," she says.

He smiles. "You could stand there and hardly hear the mill. Sundays, when we came to dinner at my grandparents, we'd make the trek up to Clayborne Field. It was like looking down on a giant Lionel train set."

"Except the pipe mills. You could hear them even in Oak Grove."

"Hard to get away from the pipe mills," he agrees, although he questions the authenticity of that particular memory. "You could certainly hear the whistle in Oak Grove."

"Remember the Bessemers—that sound?"

"Ah, a little." The Bessemers were pretty much gone by the time he was growing up, but he can more or less recall the hoarse bellows from those enormous throats, the blood-red throbs across the night sky. "Hurley's Ferry."

"We used to neck there."

"Also at the dump."

"I was always a little frightened of the dump."

"The girl raped and murdered there? I never knew if that story was true?"

"True enough for me."

The day has been pleasant, oh, more than that, but only now does he feel that they are connecting. Nothing special, only a relaxing of the cordial formality. Meanwhile, though, Jessica's jeans are wet to the shins. Her lips look like blue ice. Peter puts his foot down. "We need to go back—you're freezing, *I'm* freezing."

Jessica hugs herself. "Just a little longer. I'm so glad you thought of this."

"Hold on then, I'll get our coats."

It's a compromise, to buy some more time. The slog up the hill, as it turns out, is more of a challenge than getting down was. By the time Peter makes his way back, having collected their coats and unfinished coffees, most of that coffee has sloshed over his hands and his shoes are soaked through. As he wallows down through the snow behind Jessica, he stares at her openly, frankly. A traveling salesman is at home in the world because, ironically, he has no home. Only with his coming to spend his days in an office and starting a family did Peter dare to believe he had found a home of his own. Well, okay, he's not the world's first betrayed spouse, nor the first to discover that betrayal is nine-tenths self-deception. But he understands himself well enough to know that he's been thinking of this woman with more than a casual interest, a woman who once filled his adolescent fantasies and who seems to be—and on

Robert McKean

this he may be dead wrong—as unattached as he. He drops her coat across her shoulders from behind and is happy to see her snuggle into it.

"You're right," she says breathlessly, leaning back against his legs, "my toes are numb!"

"You might try banging on your knees to see if they have any feeling."

He delivers her coffee, then comes to sit beside her. Points at a pickup far below toiling along a snowy road. "I got waylaid by a blizzard once in a tiny town in the Rockies. Couldn't have been more than twenty benighted souls in the whole hamlet. A family volunteered to put me up, mostly because they were dying for someone new to play scrabble with."

"New words?"

"I taught them *fossa*, an animal in Madagascar, and they taught me *transhumance*, moving your sheep from low to high pastures and back."

"Someone got *that* in Scrabble?"

"Well, I'd just put *human* down—it killed me."

Jessica hugs her knees. "So you travel a lot?"

"Past tense. And it was mostly business travel—hotels, rental cars, conference rooms, dinner alone in an Olive Garden. They bring you crayons."

"Not very romantic."

"Oh, I don't know, Ashtabula, Oklahoma City, Skokie? You've not lived until you've spent a night on the town in Killdeer, North Dakota. I learned a few things: carry a good book, you don't want a trashy dinner companion, and bring your pajamas."

"What happened to your family's company, it's closed?"

"We lost it. I lost it."

"I always thought your father was this rich ty—*oh, my God!*" Jessica, mouth open, claps her hands to her cheeks. "I just remembered! I'm so sorry, I don't know what to say!"

How many times has this happened? We have conventionalized, agreed-on forms for acknowledging conventional death, but no ritualized condolences for the family of someone who has taken his own life. "That's all right."

She lays her hand on his arm. "I heard about it—from somebody, I don't remember who told me—but I completely forgot. It must've been awful for you—and for your mother?"

"It pretty much destroyed her."

"Have you gotten over it—or is that something one never gets over?"

"You don't want to hear about all this."

"No, I do. Tell me, please."

Peter watches her hand withdraw. He seldom talks about these things and feels slightly embarrassed. But for some reason he wants to tell her this: It is who he is. "What happened for me was, it—his death—got tied up in the loss of the business a decade later. I mean, I was devastated at the time, but the real impact came later, a kind of delayed reaction. Maybe I was too busy trying to save the works—that's why he killed himself, because he made a stupid mistake—taking on a role I was unprepared for, I guess, I don't know. But we *did* save it, and it became for me—and this was true for the workers, too—a memorial to him, a ratification that he'd been right to leap into buying the works in the first place. Not only was it a gutsy thing to do, it was the *right* thing to do. It was a good solid business. We had three hundred employees, we celebrated engagements, weddings, births, and mourned the deaths among us. We had company picnics with horseshoes and potato salad, we had Christmas parties, softball teams, a *bowling* team . . . . And then I lost it."

"So, what happened—*after* you saved it? I don't understand?"

"You mean, what did I do wrong?"

"That's not what I said."

"Fair enough." He retracts his self-pity. "My attorney maintains that we couldn't compete, we were too antiquated. We were Nineteenth Century in a world moving into the Twenty-First, and we were too under-capitalized to modernize. This all happened really fast. It was like musical chairs: The music stopped and we were caught out."

"Sounds like the clinic. So, it's like you lost him twice, is that it?"

"And somewhere in that mess I lost my marriage, too."

"Which brings me back to my question: Have you gotten over it? Doesn't sound like it?"

"You're turning blue!" He throws an arm around her shoulders. "We should go—you're going to catch pneumonia."

Jessica leans against him. "I won't, and if I do, I have access to some of the most potent drugs in medical use. You're avoiding my question. You're very good at that, you know? Steering conversations where you want them to go—or not go. *Have* you gotten over it?"

"You're awfully insistent."

"You should see me go after a socialite with coins jingling in her pockets. You haven't gotten over it, have you?"

"No."

~ ~ ~

If automobiles had souls, the 1988 Cadillac Brougham, a sedan that has carried Peter coast to coast through downpour and fog, would have desired nothing more than to carry him home one last time and expire in its stall like a loyal old potbellied mule. In a service station in Snow Shoe, Pennsylvania, center of the state, Jessica returns from the restroom, Peter slides the shifter into *Drive*—and nothing happens. Beneath the enormous hood, the four cavernous chambers of the carburetor deliver a swooningly sweet mixture of oxygenated petroleum to the cylinders and the V-8 throbs with impatience to get on with the next hundred thousand miles—all for naught: The wheels do not turn. Peter rocks the shifter back and forth, then shuts down the engine and restarts it, as if the Cadillac were a computer that needs rebooting.

Reverse works, he discovers.

He persuades the car behind to give him some breathing room, and he tools the Cadillac like a plump ballerina in a very pretty reverse circle and parks beside the office. Inside, a young clerk draws her jet-black bangs away from her slitted eyes to ensure that Peter receives her most scorching gaze. She's got four islands to keep tabs on and people crowding her counter to pay for their Marlboros and neon energy drinks. Nevertheless, she consents to report Peter's transmission troubles to someone named Fred, a young man with bangs that match hers, who agrees to abandon a huge truck tire he's spread-eagled over and slouch into the office. When he draws his straggly black bangs away from his eyes, Peter's convinced that he and the desk clerk are twins.

"Saturday night? We got no mechanic on duty tonight, mister. Besides, if it's your tranny, ain't no one here gonna be able to help you anyways. There's an AAMCO down the road, but they ain't gonna be there 'til Monday morning."

"Can I leave it here?"

The young man's lips are fringed in fever blisters. "Never turn away dinero, I always say."

Peter brings out his wallet. "How much?"

"Two sawbucks should do it."

Fred and his sister don't own this gas station, but he doesn't care who gets his money. "Is there a place around here where I can rent a car?"

"Best bet's State College, twenty-five miles."

"Place to eat?"

"Pizza?"

"Other than pizza."

"Ditto."

"Ditto?"

"State College."

"Can I get a taxi?"

"You can try."

Peter takes that in. "Can *you* drive us to State College?"

"I'm pretty busy . . ."

"How much?"

Fred's fever blisters glow like tiny stoplights. "Two sawbucks."

In the car Peter finds Jessica asleep. She's wrapped in her coat, feet on the seat, snuggled against the door. He feels rotten waking her. Embarrassed, apologetic, he quickly fetches their bags and organizes everything under the overhang, beyond reach of the minute pellets of snow that land dancing on their jackets. He's anxious to get back on the road. The Cadillac is next week's problem. Unfortunately, Fred has to finish his truck tire, either repairing it or mating with it, before gassing up his car, a primer-gray Camaro. Then the young man elects to take not the most direct route, surely, but a winding mountain road that at last brings them, backfiring and gasping, into the snowy town where Peter once went to college and which he no longer recognizes.

Well, he concedes, that's probably mutual.

Fred deposits them at a rental car office and collects his money. He holds each bill up to the dome light of his Camaro to ensure it's not counterfeit. When Peter finishes his business at the counter, Jessica points at a hotel across the street. "There's me. You can go on, I don't mind. I'll catch a bus tomorrow."

Of course he's not going to abandon her here. After she checks in and he checks in, he suggests dinner. It's eight o'clock. She's tired, frazzled. He forgets how draining it can be to be a passenger all day. "As long as it's someplace where they know how to pour scotch into a glass"—she shrugs—"and don't have forty-seven televisions tuned to some basketball game."

A college town on Saturday night? But the desk clerk directs them to a tavern they can walk to that pours a generous Johnny Walker Black, which pleases Jessica, and that boasts but a single flat screen. Since their lunch at twelve hundred feet, she's withdrawn. That disappoints him, but might be in some ways his preference, too. He feels strange about the twist their lunch took, his going on about himself. Typically, he's more confessor than penitent. And given the awkwardness of the situation, he's not sure where he and Jessica stand, if they have anywhere at all to stand. But his instincts tell him that he's piqued her interest, or, at a minimum, persuaded her to modify whatever opinion she may have formed of him when Fay Halbrunner rolled her father into the clinic.

And so, perhaps of unspoken mutual accord, they choose to talk of things other than themselves. They discover they both like movies, screwball comedies, Jean Arthur and Rosalind Russell and Cary Grant, as well as art films, Bergman and Truffaut and Fellini and Bertolucci and Terry Gilliam's *Brazil*.

"You saw those things in Ganaego?"

She's skeptical, he loves it. "You're casting aspersions on the Egypt?"

"If you saw Ingmar Berman in the Egypt, I'll eat my hat. It burned to the ground twenty years ago, didn't it?"

"Actually, it moldered to death, along with its ushers. When I traveled, I'd stay over an extra day and look for something to do, especially if I was in a big city or college town."

"You sold pipe to big cities?"

"People in cities have the same needs as people in the country."

It takes her a beat to get that. "Okay . . . what d'you like to read, you do have a good library in Ganaego, I'll grant you that."

As it turns out, she's an adventuresome reader, fully his equal. They like German literature, Thomas Mann and Günter Grass and Heinrich Böll *(Heinrich Böll!)*, and Austrian, Kafka and Joseph Roth and Robert Musil—"Well, come on," he challenges her, "how much of Robert Musil *can* one read?"—and, in no order and for no reason other than the conversation like a firefly alights here and there, Anthony Powell, James Agee, Flannery O'Connor, Virginia Woolf, and, surprise, Mikhail Bulgakov. But not all such passions do they share. He loves Henry James; Jessica loathes Henry James. She loves Henry Green.

"I confess," Peter confesses, "I find Henry Green tedious."

"Hersey, I'll hear no more of it."

They also disagree on contemporary painting: Jackson Pollock, Mark Rothko, Cy Twombly. But that doesn't matter, it's better that they do disagree. Peter's delighted. He never gets a chance to talk about these things. In Ganaego? With Baldwin Feeney? When he checks an armful of books or DVDs out of the library, Darlene Paczkowski, Ganaego's longstanding assistant librarian, thanks him for justifying her most controversial purchasing decisions. But for all this, all this lively talk, it doesn't feel lively. Puzzlingly, the conversation feels desultory. Lots of names cited, lots of ground covered, but Jessica seems distracted. Her weariness, he decides, or maybe she's worrying about what awaits her? He hopes it's not his company she's tiring of. Her first scotch led to a second before dinner and another during dinner and a fourth after dinner, and Peter, who followed his single Manhattan with a glass of wine, realizes at some point that his companion, face reddened and blowzy, has become quite drunk.

Very strange that, very unexpected.

He pretends not to notice her slurring speech, the infantilization of pronunciation that happens to people when they've drunk too much. Stalwartly, he carries more of the freight of the conversation, finding ever new artists to raise from the dead. One thing, conspicuously, they have not talked about is music. That subject he's leery about. Endeavoring to keep her from drifting away, he brings up theater. They haven't talked about theater, the work of the absurdists, which he particularly likes.

Jessica interrupts him mid-sentence.

"I know what you're thinking." Before Peter can protest—frankly, at that moment he has no idea what she's thinking—she goes on. "It's what everybody at the clinic is thinking—why aren't I there, emptying his bedpans, sponging his bedsores?"

"That's not for me to judge."

"Peter, don't be an ass—everybody judges." Jessica's voice

rises, loud and hollow. "I couldn't do anything to please him. I'd practice the piano until I fucking hated the pieces I was learning, I'd get them so they were so picture-perfect they weren't even good music anymore. Precious little things, stillborn babies I'd bring to him so he could pick them apart—gleefully, note by note. The only good lesson, as far as Jacob Weiner was concerned, was one where I ended up in tears."

People are pausing in their own conversations to look over. All day Jacob has been the elephant in the room. Peter certainly has felt no compunction to bring him up. He's meddled in the Weiner family quite enough. But for Jessica, he understands, it's different, and her complicated relationship with her father *is* worrying her, after all. Telling himself to be patient, Peter lets her get this off her chest. "I know he had a reputation for being rough on his pupils," he says. "I didn't know that extended to you."

Jessica swallows off her scotch. "I switched to voice in junior high—something you don't use your hands for, thinking, you know, he might back off? Stupid, *stuuuuu*pid Jessica, he just came on stronger— and *now*, since it *was* voice, it was like he was *inside* me! I could not please him, could not, could not."

"I sometimes wonder if I—"

"And you know why? Because music was *his*. Music *belonged* to Jacob Weiner, and, honestly, truthfully, at bottom, he didn't want me there."

"Where?"

"In music, *music*. He'd demand that I excel and then would be more upset—in a way—when I did. It was a rigged game, you couldn't win. I'd get a note right and he'd grunt, like so what's the big deal? I'd get a passage wrong and he'd wring me out. But then when I'd get one better than right—you know, lovely, just knockout?—he'd find *something* wrong with it, he'd make it sound like it was the worst thing that ever happened. Bad note, good note, great note"—Jessica waves her arm extravagantly—"it didn't matter, he had the waterfront covered. And you know why, of course? Why he was like that?"

She looks around, dissatisfied. Peter hopes she doesn't want more to drink. She does. Waves her empty glass over her head and unfortunately it's refilled. Jessica takes a deep swallow, coughs on the scotch, and falls silent. What is he supposed to know? He's not sure it matters. "No, I don't know why?"

She looks at him in bafflement. "You don't know why what?"

"Why Jacob came on so strong, why he was like that?"

She looks peeved. "Because he was disappointed in himself. I only realized all this later, too late to make a difference. First-year Freud. You never performed professionally, right? You said you didn't?"

"My grandfather and uncle did."

"Then you don't know what it's like, you can't. My father wanted to be famous—oh, more than that—he wanted to be revered! Jacob Weiner wanted presidents and prime ministers and popes and the wives of millionaires to throw themselves at his feet. He was so convinced he was better than anyone else that he just expected that the world's adulation would come to him—it had to, how could it not?"

Jessica hunches up her shoulders and spreads open her upright palms. "But it didn't. That never happened, and he turned all that bitterness on me. You have to understand: He didn't *want* me to succeed. That I might become famous when he hadn't? That people might throw themselves at *my* feet?"

"I'm sorry."

"And *God,* was I an easy target, so convenient, available twenty-four-seven."

"I'm sorry, Jessica, I—"

"He had a chance to join a woodwind quartet once. Did you know that? They were out of Chicago, or San Francisco, somewhere, I don't remember, they were just beginning to attract recognition, get a recording contract—all that. But it wasn't a full-time gig. There wasn't much money in it, and then a baby came along and that screwed everything up. New baby, mom at home, Dad schlepping his clarinet across the country? He decided it was too irregular, too risky, so he took the job at Oak Grove. But he was always sure that something else was going to turn up, something even better than the quartet, and, you know, the *weirdest* thing is"—Jessica laughs piercingly, her wet lips parting against her teeth—"he *was* good! He was a superb musician! The world picks winners and losers and merit often has little to do with it." She brings her glass down on the table hard, nearly losing control of it beneath her hand. "Put that on his tombstone: Great clarinetist, lousy dad. Com' on, let's go back to the hotel and screw."

As a young man, he often fretted how these moments leading

Robert McKean

up to lovemaking should be handled. As an adult, he came to realize they come naturally or not at all. But experienced or not, this cut-to-the-chase leaves Peter reeling. Avis Longstreet's pulling him into a grungy basement bedroom was one thing, he'd been married to the woman, but this takes him aback. He settles their bill, helps Jessica into her coat, and supports her with an arm as they walk the few blocks to the hotel. In the hotel lobby she lurches toward the wrong wing, and he pulls her arm to steady her and steer her in the right direction. When the elevator doors close behind them, she leans into him, kissing him wetly, sloppily.

And that, for him, nearly kills it.

This isn't what he wants. Maybe there's a way he can slow things down, salvage the moment? But at her door, as he helps her locate her plastic key-card in her purse, inserts it for her, and holds the door open, Peter understands that this is no more than a drunken, trashy fuck, take it or leave it. He holds her in his arms and brushes his lips against hers.

Does she even register his kiss?

"Go to bed," he orders. "We'll talk more tomorrow, I want to spend the whole day talking to you. I want you to tell me what I'm missing in Mark Rothko and Jackson Pollock. Go to bed, Jessica, sweet dreams."

~ ~ ~

And later, of course, he regrets his gallantry.

The next morning Peter comes down to the lounge for breakfast early, before eight. He stretches the meal past nine, reading the paper, sipping coffee. He wants to be here when she comes in so that they can get the day started on a solid footing. He's no teetotaler—ask the Ganaego PD—and he carries a lot of unhappiness around with him, too. During the night he's thought of Malcolm Lowry and the early trilogy of Beckett. Also, he remembers he *does* like the sculptor Giacometti—what fat person wouldn't like Giacometti?—and, ironically, Botero's roly-poly nudes. Grok that. At some point, as time passes, he decides to go up and slip a note under her door. The best cure for a hangover is sleep, and he doesn't mind when they start today.

Heaven knows, he's got nowhere to go.

But when Peter steps off the elevator and sees the maid's cart parked before her open door, he knows again what he's known since last night. A traveling salesman's most constant companion is, after all, remorse. Later this morning, after leaving a message on Avis and Elliott's line that he's going to miss his Sunday visit with Jeanette, he inquires of the desk clerk if his friend Jessica Weiner got off well this morning.

"Yes, sirree, she did." The clerk—a woman with Alfred Einstein hair and a pin that says, *Hi, I'm Efrieda!*—points a wizened finger at him. "She asked for a taxi—well, shoot, you aren't going to find a taxi at that hour on a Sunday, but Mel—he's our custodian—he drove her to the station."

"Good," Peter says, "she wanted to get an early start."

Next he calls the Snow Shoe service station. The manager won't be in until later. With a day to kill, he wanders over to the campus. In twenty-five years he's never been back. The university, he discovers,

Robert McKean

which was always changing, has continued to change. Beneath the new, though, Peter identifies the old campus, *his* Penn State: the lecture halls in which he encountered the professors under whom it had been an honor to study, the student union where the more clamorous it was the better he concentrated, the library whose open stacks he loved roaming. Early afternoon finds him in town, west side, before a clapboard house. On an elevated side porch is a door; above it are two windows on the third floor, the tiny apartment where he waited for Victoria Kostas—Vicky, owl-eyed library science major he'd met, appropriately, in those Pattee Library stacks—to come to him through the leafy streets of State College, smelling of library paste and dust. They were children, they had no business marrying. He, teetering in indecision between returning home and working for his father or staying at the university and pursuing a doctorate in literature, and she, his waif-like lover who boiled pots of spaghetti that would stuff the bellies of a battalion of soldiers, and then, in the dimness of the apartment's only room, would remove her tiny round spectacles, fold back the stems and lay them on the dresser, and bashfully slip out of her blouse and jeans. He could have been kinder to her—he should have.

"You ain't gonna try to get that pig *fixed,* com'on, man."

The voice, brusque, irritated, issues from beneath a car dripping with filthy slush. The Snow Shoe manager, pelvis swiveling with agitation back and forth on a skid, smacks something down there, smacks it again resoundingly. Presumably satisfied, he rolls himself into view. His face is streaked with grease and cinders. "Transmission's fried.

It's not worth fixing. Basically, it's a pile of shit."

A man not delighted to be under a dirty car on a Sunday evening. "No, I guess not."

"In Maine it's what we called a *beater*. Gimme a hundred bucks, plus ten for last night, and I'll get her squashed to a five-foot cube. Don't suppose you're traveling with the title?"

"No, I'm afraid not."

"Car that old, you should." The manager shoots himself back under his dripping chassis. "I'll need it this week, or your Caddy's gonna start racking up storage fees."

Finding an empty T&V shopping bag in the backseat of the Cadillac, Peter collects his maps that are separating at their seams, the small attaché case of screwdrivers and socket wrenches he's never used, the Swiss Army knife whose corkscrew he has used, his tapes, his much thumbed-through *Peterson Field Guide to Birds of North America*, as well as whatever stray paraphernalia that has in nearly two decades gathered—accreted?—in the crannies of the old car. None of it, except penknife and field guide, is worth saving, he'll throw it all out once he's home. But he can't bear the thought of someone's pawing through these things. He transfers his Brattle Book Shop finds to the rental car, then climbs back in the Brougham to pat around under the seats. Objects don't have souls; once he reached maturity he ceased to believe that even men have souls. Car, man, dog—we're all molecules and atoms and too much bad gas. But still, he's spent a significant portion of his life in this luxury motorcar he inherited, and he'll miss it. He remembers the first

Robert McKean

time he climbed in and turned the key, the day after his father had been buried. Lives pass, so they must. Maybe the Cadillac's a camel, a ship of the desert, he'll entertain that, but it's not a pig, not a pile of shit, it never was, not even now as it awaits decommissioning and dissolution. The last thing Peter does is pry open the attaché case, remove a corroded screwdriver, and unscrew his license plate.

    SANGUE.

Pastel Townhouses
with Rooster Weather Vanes

You would have thought a meteor had plowed into Oak Grove.

With a rising sun and blast from an air horn as if to announce the start of a fox hunt, the excavation for the Halbrunners' long-delayed house commenced. A yawning crater that would spread nearly to the boundaries of the property, swallowing as it went Jacob Weiner's forest and remaining shrubbery. Oak and linden, wild chokecherry, ailanthus, Norway Maple—the good with the bad, even the redoubtable yews, whose tenacious roots had clawed their way into Jacob's foundation and whose bushy balls had smothered his front windows and hung on even after the windows themselves were gone.

Well, it was spring, the vernal equinox, time to start building your nest.

The cairn of earth and stones that the excavation created, heaped on the sole corner of the lot not excavated—the stuff had to go somewhere—was topped by the upended trunk and complicated root system of one of those waylaid maples, perhaps the one beneath which had lain the withered haunches of Weiner's old mutt, Dmitri. After removing the foundation forms last week, the contractors erected a small wooden structure reminiscent of a bulletin board in front of the property. A temporary electrical fixture, wires loop to it from the street. On Friday a semitrailer arrived with a load of two-by-fours and two-by-twelves. No sooner had the deliveryman driven away than the blue tarps he'd carelessly flung over the blond stacks flapped noisily in the fretful March winds and slid off.

So much for wild turkeys and Big Foot.

So much for chipmunks and squirrels and woodchucks, so much for robins and jays and starlings and grackles and cardinals and, now that they could use them, the lugubrious mourning doves. Yesterday the *Chronicle* obituaries included a modest thirty-line article reporting the death of Jacob Weiner, chairman emeritus of the Oak Grove Music School Woodwinds Department. The burial service was to be private, followed in April by a memorial service at which Jacob's most celebrated pupil, Walter Zurlo, has agreed to perform. Surviving Weiner was listed his daughter, Jessica, of Brookline, Massachusetts.

Death doesn't dignify, it only takes. The old man died inch by inch. In his final agony Jacob's face, rendered to bone sheathed in crinkled parchment, became haunted and wolfish. Flesh shrank from his skull, his eyes seemed to grow larger. They roved sightlessly, like yellow marbles rolling around in a box. His skin mottled and blued, pulmonary edema required his lungs to labor harder and harder. He had seizures.

The Indian nurse, whom Peter had befriended, said it was what doctors sometimes call a *difficult death*. It had been, God knows, a difficult life, one could hardly be surprised if death would choose to absorb Jacob Weiner beneath its cloak any more easily. Jessica stayed this past month, saw it through. That's all Peter knows for certain. The nurse said that she visited in the morning, so Peter, respecting her privacy, visited in the afternoon. As he sat beside the dying man, he found himself thinking about what Buster Zurlo had said about Jacob, that the old man taught more than music. What had that meant to a boy who showed up for his first lesson with a plastic clarinet? And how did Buster's Jacob Weiner fit with Jessica's Jacob Weiner? They didn't—that is, not in a way Peter could see. The contradictions our lives present to others, the even more puzzling contradictions our lives present to ourselves: Does anyone add up?

He'd hoped he might run into Jessica in passing, but hadn't.

Meanwhile, it appears that the Halbrunner hacienda will be every bit as frightful as Peter fears. A plastic-sleeved pastel of the estate-to-be has been thumbtacked to the electrical board, along with building permits and a sign admonishing all that *This is a Hardhat Area! If you don't want to wear a hardhat, don't enter!* The new structure, which will be disproportionately large for the lot, promises every piece of architectural gimcrackery one might click on in an online catalog: gables and dormers and shutters and polyurethane corbels and ox-eye windows, a cupola on the garage, even what look like several *diamond jobbies*. What Peter dreads, however, is not so much an outré house as a cackling

Fay Halbrunner running between the adjoining lots clad in nothing but a towel. A morning recently he glanced out an upstairs window and noticed what appeared to be two workmen in white hardhats at the rear of the construction site talking. Suddenly, one of the men fell to his knees before the other, and, as Fay's curls spilled from beneath her hardhat in a blond aureole, her face disappeared into the other's crotch.

Oh well, there you go.

And he's restless, uncomfortably so. Perhaps it's the construction activity: the trade vans and pickups lining the street; the incessant beeping the vehicles make when they back up; the men who play their talk-radios too loud. Does each man have his own Rush Limbaugh? Or perhaps it's only the weather. Something's pitched him into a fitful state. He's as unsettled as March, scratchy, prickly, nettled. The weather, to be sure, is a trial: one day languorous spring, the next jaws of winter. But you can't blame Mother Nature. Spring may be a fickle companion, but it was coming, it's here. Snow has receded from even the most shadowed corners, leaving in its wake downed twigs and a scum of some gray, indeterminate vegetable or animal schmutz, and the shy warmth and high fine light of these early months have begun their return engagement. Crocuses have emerged beneath the shrubs and the lovely, diminutive wild violets, which the new people loathe, speckle the greening grass. And it isn't that he couldn't go out and rake the yard—to tidy things up and dissipate his restlessness. But that's just it: The thought of finding his gloves and bamboo rake, of winding the leather laces around the hooks of his stiff clodhoppers, doing something only for the sake of doing

Mending What Is Broken 283

something is precisely what he doesn't want to do.

He reads, he eats, he reads some more. Hamlet's Ghost: *I am thy father's spirit,/Doomed for a certain term to walk the night,/And for the day confined to fast in fires,/Till the foul crimes done in my days of nature/Are burnt and purged away.*

And it's not only him: Everybody's at sixes and sevens. The Wilfred school, despite Janet Considine's assurances to render an expeditious decision, continues its policy of silence, and all parties involved seem to have finally conceded that hope. Avis, when Peter catches sight of her, suffers with her near-term pregnancy. She bears her swollen belly from room to room like another burden she can't put down, as well she can't, while Jeanette grows more distant—from her mother, from her father, from her playing. *It is a wise father,* another line from his Pelican Shakespeare, *that knows his own child.* Peter despairs of a disaffected breeziness he's seeing in his daughter and worries about the troubled children she may be befriending in a parochial school that, after all, specializes in troubled children.

Well, that's not quite all true. Not everybody's on edge.

Elliott Fields seems indefatigably chipper. He is, Peter gathers, approaching his big announcement, the birth of his ascendant political career. On Sundays Elliott still assiduously monitors Peter's visits with Jeanette, but apart from that appears to be away from home much of the time, closeted, one presumes, in dark, smoke-filled rooms. Do politicos still huddle in smoky rooms? But Harvey was right. Staged around the condo, resting on chairs, are mock-ups of Elliott's potential campaign

Robert McKean

posters, images that will, hopefully next year, sing of the various Jeffersonian qualities of Elliott Fields, Esq.: the law-and-order District Attorney Fields, striding across dawn-lit, stubbled fields in tall brown boots, shotgun lying aslant his forearm; the devout DA Fields, standing before a Sunday school class of preteens and pointing at cutouts of Christ and his disciples; and the family-devoted DA Fields, preggers wife to his right, his arm looping her waist—that's his bun in the oven, you know?—other arm draped lovingly across his stepdaughter's shoulders; and flags, flags, flags, blowing, billowing, rippling in the wind.

Land of the free, home of the brave.

But it's Harvey Silverstein about whom Peter worries the most. Harvey's wife has taken a second, very serious fall. While Harvey was off painting his imaginary trees—the first time since last fall that he and Lloyd Ross had been back to Lake Biddleford—she slipped in the shower and lay helpless there for hours, her forehead gashed, her pelvis fractured in two places. Jenny, whom Peter visited in the rehab center, remains in good spirits by sheer force of will, but Peter's never seen the old attorney—who held his own with trade unionists and corporate bullies, with mobsters and testy judges—looking so entirely overwhelmed. It's as though Harvey Silverstein is being swept out to Jacob Weiner's sea, as well. And what Peter is about to tell Harvey is going to make him no sunnier. Or thinks he is about to tell him. A dozen times Peter has set himself to make the call, vowed to make it right after breakfast, right after lunch, first thing tomorrow—and lost his nerve. It's completely lunatic, just more evidence of this unsettled, plasmatic state he's in. For even to entertain the possibility of resurrecting the clay works is folly.

"But *is* it?"

From his father's dusty office windows he can see the surveyors' fluorescent-pink stakes and the obscure collection devices installed by the environmental engineers: The re-purposing of the site has started, it's already well underway. To call it off would be crazy. But it nags at him, it nags, it nags. It's Hamlet's Ghost come for him, yes, but he has his reasons, too, he has a brief. *One,* the recession that sounded the death knell for the works has passed. Capitalism's scythe has harvested the weak and spared her darlings. And there's no point in kvetching about that. Business is business, it's how things work. *Two,* money, as the financial pages report, is flowing in the pipelines like Saudi crude again—or like waste in a sewerage pipe. *Three,* he still has, or believes he has, his connections, the telephone numbers of a few powerful men who will return his calls. He's reviewed his address book, brought his Rolodex up to date. Perhaps he's suffering delusions of grandeur, perhaps those men will simply ignore him, but you only know if you try, right? And *four,* people, of whom one can confidently wager had never stopped needing sanitation pipes, surely, by now, need them even more.

But the reasons are only a part of it. The reasons came later.

What seized Peter's imagination was something he discovered in the maintenance foreman's desk during one of his inspections: an invitation from 1968, carefully preserved in its envelope, to the company Christmas party. Sliding the invitation from its envelope was like

Robert McKean

opening a box of memories. His mother spent months planning those galas, conferring with Tommasco and Virgil Ferrara: with Virgil over the antipasto and *primo* courses, cold cuts and cheeses, olives and pickles and green salads and other hors d'oeuvres, and the pastas, soups, and polenta; with Tommy over the *secondo,* beef, lamb, poultry, sausage, and fish dishes; and with the T&V's bakery manager over the spectacular *dolce* display. Wielding a three-ring binder of notes, she oversaw the preparation of the house, the noble firs that kissed the twelve-foot ceiling and required three men to erect and a week to decorate, the garland swags across the valances and up the banisters, the teardrop crystals that sparkled in every window. She met with the wait staff, the beer distributor, the sourpusses from the state liquor store, the small orchestra conducted by Uncle Nico, and the peculiar man from Tonnesdatter's who, crossing his eyes and twitching his nose like a rabbit, would supply her with as many folding chairs as she required. The night of the party—to which every employee had received an invitation—the house, redolent of balsam and spice, blazed with light that spilled out over the frosted lawn and the heated tent, where the crowd overflowed. Loud, buzzy, boisterous parties, hundreds of employees dressed in their finest party duds, whatever that meant to a crane man and his wife and to the Director of Personnel and his wife, all of them tramping up the porch steps, squeezing through to reach the buffet tables, eating too much, drinking too much, but never forgetting to collect from the company's owner their envelopes with their bonus checks inside. The invitation Peter found, holding a place in a ledger whose fountain-pen ink had faded, was the first year he was allowed to stay up the entire evening, to wear a clip-on bow tie with his madras jacket and be clapped on the manly shoulders and told again and again that his father was a jolly good fellow.

Confined to fast in fires, till the foul crimes are burnt and purged away . . .

The house has become dark and shabby. His daughter, before she was forbidden to visit him, had told him as much. And it's through her eyes that he sees the bulbs so long ago perished in their fixtures that their bases have become corroded one with their sockets; the paint blistered on the calcified ceilings making some of the rooms look like they'd contracted the mumps; the drapes that make you sneeze. *It's spring:* The windows need to be washed with vinegar and rubbed dry with balled-up newspapers; the pantry needs to be swept of moth husks and cobwebs; the rugs need to be rolled up, taken out back, and thrashed within an inch of their lives. Peter, stepping up his inspection tours of the clay works, stood one afternoon in the silent cathedral of the manufactory: to have this much, to own and control this much, and allow it to fall into ruin— that was unforgivable.

As there are sins of commission, there are sins of omission.

The clay works calls out to be recapitalized and repopulated with men like that Scottish maintenance foreman who came to those yearly Christmas parties in a brown tweed blazer that smelled of mothballs and who gazed open-mouthed at tables of carved roasts and stuffed fishes and wedges of taleggio and English Stilton and Gorgonzola Dolce warm to the point of melting. And thus Peter, son of the man who stood, cheerful and confident, at the throbbing center of all those parties, wakes, this fresh-scented morning in March, some thirty-seven years later, with no milk in the refrigerator for his coffee and with nothing to do with the remainder of his life.

He finds one clean sock.

On his way out to the store he stares at the phone. Harvey, as expected, is aghast. "Peter, we've been through this. You have to let it go, son."

"Maybe I caved too soon, Harvey."

"You did no such thing. You did everything you were supposed to do. You captained your ship as well as anybody could, but it went down—that *happens!* You gotta get over this, it's poisoning your life."

In Harvey's frustrated voice he hears his weariness. God knows what kind of a night the old man has had, and Peter realizes that, if he carries through with his audacious—deranged?—plans, he's likely going to have to without Harvey Silverstein's blessing. He holds back on the emotions: Harvey doesn't want to hear about Christmas parties in 1968, even if he and his first wife had danced a rumba there. "Think of the work that's been put off—municipal projects, housing, business development? If I can get ten million dollars in backing, I think I can make this work."

"The whole town's not worth ten million dollars. D'you have any kind of business plan, have you talked to anybody? Have you done any research?"

The phone rasps across Harvey's whiskers: Not to be shaved by this time in the morning only confirms what kind of a night he's had. "Harv, I wanna take a run at it. We'll convert the kiln from coal to gas—we should've done that decades ago. We'll modernize, update, computerize, and automate. I can only find out if I try?"

"Well, I dunno what to tell you. I think it's wacko."

"How is Jenny?"

To which Harvey Silverstein responds with more of a groan than a recognizable word.

~ ~ ~

He's driving a Toyota now, and, despite his loyalty to his fallen Brougham, he likes this new Avalon. Over the years he mashed the Cadillac's bench seat into his customized bucket that left his lower back and legs very sore. The Avalon supports and balances his oversized frame. The instrumentation is practical, the fit and finish are superb, and the engine, two-thirds the size of the Cadillac's, packs more wallop and gets far better mileage. The Avalon is also, as Peter discovered after driving it off Jimmy Boswell's lot, an automobile that yearns to travel. And so, before stopping today to buy milk for his coffee, he takes the Toyota on a tour of the valley, passing through one by one Western Pennsylvania's ramshackle mill towns asleep in the morning sun like a company of scruffy hounds, then heads back to the 7-Eleven in Ganaego.

"That it?"

Peter contemplates his single carton of two-percent milk. "I guess?"

Robert McKean

"No Powerball?" The clerk, a young Black woman in a uniform stained with what appears to be baby food, scans his face in disbelief. "It's up to a hundred-seventeen million?"

"Well, that would do it." Peter, allowing the clerk her point, fishes out a dollar bill. "If I win, how much do you get?"

"I get to come to work the next day."

When his garage door lifts, he finds Avis's blue Mercedes parked inside. Dead center, blocking both berths. He supposes you should change the code on your garage opener, too, but why Avis is here, why her car is in the garage, and why she has felt it necessary to hog both berths—all constitute this morning's mysteries. He's perplexed, a trifle worried and a trifle amused—will they have another roll in the sheets? But Avis turns her back to him as he steps into the living room as if she's hiding something. And indeed she is: a towel pressed against her face. "Accident," she mumbles. "Hit my head on the steering wheel."

He can hear the ice cubes in the towel clacking. She's having difficulty keeping them from falling out. Her blouse is rucked up; the elastic of her underpants shows above her slacks. Her hair is mussed. "I can take you to the hospital. Are you having contractions?"

"I'm fine."

It hurts her to talk. "Let me see," he says.

Avis presses the towel closer to her cheek. "Nothing broken."

"Where're your glasses?"

She shrugs.

"You *drove* here without your glasses? Avis, you're not thinking clearly. We really need to go visit the nice folks at the emergency room."

"I'm fine!"

Last fall he had this same argument with his daughter: Like mother, like daughter. "I'm going to call 911."

"No, don't! I just need to hang out here for a while."

Something smells fishy. "Most divorced women," he points out, "don't *hang out* in their former husbands' living rooms." Avis flinches; two ice cubes escape her towel and slither across the rug. "I'm sorry. Here, maybe I can help—remember, I was a Boy Scout?"

"You're still a Boy Scout," Avis says but surrenders her towel. The bruise, fire-red and already beginning to purple, encompasses her right cheek, from chin to eye socket. It will, before it's done, no doubt greatly enlarge its borders. The side of her nose is nicked, probably from the nose pads of her missing glasses. He's afraid of bone fractures and concussions, or, God forbid, a miscarriage. In the kitchen Peter refolds the towel, creating a kangaroo pouch, and replenishes the ice. The terrycloth smells of her cologne and has lipstick stains and rouge smudges, but there's little blood. When he returns, he pleads, "It would help—help me—if you told me what's going on. Where was your accident, Avis? Was there another car involved? You aren't fleeing a hit-and-run, I hope?"

Shifting awkwardly in the chair—as her medicine ball of a belly barely permits her to sit normally—Avis cups her face in the towel. "It wasn't an accident."

"I didn't think so."

Robert McKean

Shakes her head, wincing. And instantly, he knows. "What kind of a man would strike his pregnant wife?"

"Someone," Avis mumbles, "who hates women—or grown women."

Which lands like the bomb that landed in the car in Connecticut. Except this one explodes. "Where's Jeanette?"

Peter's on his feet, but Avis waves him off. "Jeanette's fine, she's at school."

"That's not good enough."

"She's at *school*."

Peter consents to sit, but only on the edge of the chair. "I know it hurts, but I need to know, Avis: What's going on?" She clenches, unwilling to speak—not so differently, probably, from any number of hostile witnesses she's prodded. "Tell me," he demands, and Avis falls into herself, probably as those same witnesses will do, surrendering.

"We heard from Wilfred. They accepted her for September."

"And no one," Peter snaps, "told me?"

"Because it has nothing to do with you."

"Maybe you want your loving husband to come and pick you up? So he can show you how effective his right cross is, too?" Avis shakes with silent sobs. "Sorry," he says, not particularly sorry. "So, you had a fight and Testosterone Sam socked you—outstanding way for a district attorney to settle a dispute—but what's that got to do with Wilfred and this someone-who-doesn't-love-grown-women stuff?"

"Not going to be district attorney." Her voice is small, muffled.

She's trying to employ as few face muscles as possible. Peter has to lean in to hear her. "He found out last night. The party passed him over. They're going with someone else."

"What a crying shame, gee whiz."

Avis, shifting the towel, pulls back, withdrawing from him again.

"You still haven't answered me," Peter presses. "I don't give a tinker's damn about Elliott's political aspirations. What's this about Jeanette?"

Avis pushes the towel up over her eyes, blotting them or perhaps withdrawing from him, then lowers it. "This morning, I saw him coming out of the bathroom. Not ours, hers. He had two rolls of toilet paper. I didn't think anything about it. Then I heard the water running—she was showering. When I was taking her to school, I asked her. I guess this isn't the first time he's invaded her privacy by barging in on her like that. When I got to work, I mentioned it to him, before Samantha came in. All I did was *mention* it, I wasn't *accusing* him or anything, I just didn't think he should be doing that—and he blew up. I don't know what triggered it, the political stuff, I don't know?" Avis shakes herself, then winces for having done it. "He slapped me, then hit me, he hit me really hard. I mean, he really hit me! No one's ever *hit* me before, and I ran out . . ."

Peter's on his feet again. "Okay, we need to go. I'll drop you at the hospital."

"I can't go to the hospital! It'd kill our legal practice! This is a

Robert McKean

small town, word would get around . . ."

"All right then, we won't go to the hospital." He waves his arm in exasperation. "But you can't stay here by yourself, either, you might have a concussion or something, I don't know, and I need to go."

"Go where?"

"Where d'you think? I'm going to get Jeanette!"

"I told you—she's in school!"

"And Mr. Goofy Pants? Is he in school, too?"

"He's got a deposition to videotape! He's going to be tied up all day."

"I still don't like it. I'll drop you somewhere safe. Bring the towel with you."

In the car Avis huddles against the door. Peter keeps pushing her. "And you had no idea he was getting weird around Jeanette? *None?*" When she doesn't answer, he raises his voice. "Avis, talk to me!"

"All I know . . . is that he stopped being interested in me. I thought it was the pregnancy, or maybe he was seeing someone else, I didn't know . . ."

"So what he wanted then was an attractive wife for his campaign posters—is that it?"

"I guess."

"And for that he busted up our marriage?"

"That wasn't the only thing that busted up our marriage."

"Avis, you're lying. People like that don't just jump out of the bushes full grown. You knew this about him, didn't you, you knew it last

fall? That's why you wanted to send her away to school, right? *Right?*"
She presses her face deeper into the towel, and Peter has his own answer.
"So, what you've done, essentially, is put our daughter in jeopardy to
save a goddamned law practice."

"Fuck you." For this she lifts her bruised face free of the towel.
"Where're we going? I told you I don't want to go to the hospital."

"You require the services of an honest lawyer."

Who needs, Peter thinks, an abused, pregnant visitor thrust on
him as much as he needs a hole in the head. But what choice does he
have? And if Harvey isn't home, he has no backup plan. Harvey lives in
South Ganaego, in the little hodgepodge of houses and shops that lie in
the lee of the dike by the river. South Ganaego is, in fact, only slightly
out of his way and will cost him only a little extra time. Avis waits in the
car while Peter gallops up onto the Silversteins' porch and jabs the bell,
once, twice, three times.

When Harvey answers, Peter blurts out, "I can't stop to explain,
I—"

"They got a hold of you, too, huh? Good, come in, we got big
trouble."

"How do you know?"

Harvey is still unshaven, and his L.L. Bean wilderness shirt is
untucked. Never in seven decades has Attorney Harvey Silverstein been
seen in an untucked shirt. "I told you that guy was making me nervous,
the rats and everything? We need to do some deep thinking, son, this is
not good."

"Rats?"

"Whatever they are that he's been blasting to kingdom come." When Peter continues to stare at him agog, Harvey figures it out. "You don't know yet, do you?" Harvey's big black lawyer glasses have always magnified his eyes. Today, the sacks beneath his eyes resemble enormous pools of tar. "This time your man Feeney's gone and shot one with two legs. What makes it worse is that the guy he shot was off your property."

"Baldwin *shot* somebody?"

"When the cops called, they said he asked for me. I assumed they called you, too—why else would you be here? He saw someone fooling around near some old trucks, I guess, and he let go with that pistol of his. I don't have the whole story yet."

"That *is* our property," Peter corrects him. "That's where we always parked our trucks. But no, no one called me, I have no idea what's going on."

"Not your property," Harvey insists. "I have the survey maps in my office. The cops don't know that yet and presumably the wounded man's lawyer, when he gets one, isn't going to know that yet, either. But it won't be long until everybody does: Baldwin Feeney, a man in your employ, shot somebody in the leg with an unregistered gun on publicly owned land, where your trucks've been rusting away illegally for eighty years."

~ ~ ~

This is why you need good legal representation, Peter is thinking as he speeds off, leaving behind in Harvey Silverstein's lap his assaulted former wife and the disposition of his trigger-happy security guard. Now to be fair, Ashport is only across the river, a short zoom down the boulevard to the bridge, across, then a zigzag through the brick streets of Ashport to Kopelman. Avis, before he left, protested again that all this haste wasn't necessary.

"He's going to be tied up all day."

They were in Harvey's kitchen. Silverstein, twisting a tray to free ice cubes to refresh Avis's cold pack, also tried to deter him. "Peter, we need to focus on this Feeney stuff. This could ruin you. Why don't you call the school?"

"I need to get my daughter."

He parks in front of the parochial campus and hurries down the walk past Sacred Heart's eroded Virgin, up the scalloped steps into the school. The hall smells exactly as a school ought to: sweat, chalk, bananas, bologna, and that red compound janitors sprinkle about to attract the dust before they sweep. A wooden sign in the shape of a hand points to the principal's office. Peter strides down a hallway whose glossy old wooden floors groan beneath his weight.

Since he's not the parent of record, he has his story prepared. "We've had a family emergency." He's addressing a secretary seated at a desk behind the counter. Pulls out his wallet to show her his driver's license. "I need to pick up my daughter, Jeanette Sanguedolce."

"Oh, you'll be so relieved." The woman removes her glasses and lets them dangle in their harness against her breast. "Her step-daddy already came for her."

Robert McKean

"When?"

"I'm not sure, around eight-thirty? Let me ask Peggy, I didn't talk to him. Oh dear, I hope everything's going to be okay?"

Peter doesn't wait for Peggy's input. In the car he calls the condo, reaching their voice mail, Elliott's nasal greeting. He could call the doorman's stand, he supposes, but there's no reason to think Elliott has taken Jeanette home. From Ashport, it's twenty minutes or so, depending on traffic, south along the river to East Stanton Junction. In the parking lot beside the law offices of Fields & Longstreet Peter looks around in vain for Elliott's Land Rover. He calls Avis, castigating himself for failing to ask for some critical information. But all he reaches on her line, as well as on Harvey's land and cell lines, is another inbox with a voicemail message. Pocketing his phone, he pauses a minute to collect himself.

"Uh-oh, why no fancy tie today?" Samantha asks.

A good sign—she doesn't have a clue. But she's only the receptionist. "A complete disgrace," he says, fussing with his open collar. "But I left in such a hurry that I didn't have time to put one on. But next time, you just wait! Has Elliott left with Jeanette for the lodge already? I hope I didn't miss him? I nearly killed myself trying to get here."

"Long gone."

"Darn it!"

"They weren't here any time at all. Blew in and blew out. Mr. Fields had me reschedule a deposition for him and away they went. Is it important? Do I have you in his datebook? I don't remember that I do?"

The girl falls to her computer screen, distressed. Peter stops her. "No, no, this has nothing to do with business, but it would've meant a heckuva lot to Elliott. It's my way of paying him back for being so good with Jeanette. I bet he was excited about spending the weekend with her?"

"What is it, if I can ask, that would've meant so much to him?"

He considers that, her trusting, inquisitive eyes on him while he weighs divulging the real purpose of his mission, what has brought him crashing into her life this morning, then he lies expansively. "Sure, it's no big secret. Actually, I'd be surprised if he didn't mention it. I promised Elliott he could borrow a fancy shotgun of mine. I have it outside—in the car." Peter makes a broad entreaty for the young woman's sympathy. "I was supposed to drop it off earlier, but I got tied up in a meeting and then the *traffic!* Are they fixing every road in East Stanton Junction?"

Samantha smiles conspiratorially. "I've had to devise a whole new route to get to work."

"How many miles a day do you bike?"

"Five miles each way, well, five and a *half* now."

"Good for you, you're an inspiration! He did mention that I was bringing the shotgun over, right?"

"He didn't say anything."

"What a scamp. What I have, Sam, is a very rare and unusual shotgun. It's inscribed *1824,* and it's been in our family for generations. I promised Elliott he could borrow it—you know, to show off to the big mucky-mucks he's got coming this weekend? He told you who's all

Robert McKean

coming, didn't he?"

The receptionist, pulling back, receives this with skepticism. Which is fine. Skepticism is the first sip. "I'm not sure what you mean?"

"Judge Davis," Peter clarifies, "for one. He's one of the key politicos who's coming, fantastic guy, but even he's not the biggest cheese. Elliott's got the party chairman lined up along with the top state hierarchy. This weekend at the lodge is going to launch his candidacy with a bang. Oh, God, it's going to be an incredible sendoff."

"But it's not that large of a place, the lodge? I mean, I don't know, but he always describes it as a wee little cabin? How will they all fit in?"

"Tents, tents like the generals have, Sam, not the kind the Boy Scouts crawl under at night. You camp, of course?"

"I *do*—with my boyfriend."

"Then trust me, these tents have wet bars that would put the Ritz to shame. So anyway, here I am with the weekend's show-stopper a day late and a dollar short. You know, I could run the shotgun up there, I don't mind?"

"I'm sure he'd love it if you did."

"Well, I will, I'll do it. But first I'll need some directions. I know his private compound is way up in God's country, Warren County, but that's all I know."

The poisoned cup: The young woman looks at him in deep suspicion and flees toward the nearest moral exit. "I can't, I don't really know where it is."

She's protecting her boss, and Peter wonders if Elliott's definition of nymphets is elastic enough to encompass *jeune filles*. "Well, all right, I'm sure he'll do fine. He's got people from the White House coming, you know that, of course?"

"He didn't say *anything* about this?"

He debates a gamble: Decides to risk it. "You could call him on his cell, what a nitwit." Peter bops himself on his forehead. "He can give me the directions himself."

"But there's no service up there?"

"None?"

"It's in the middle of the woods! Oh, I don't know what to *do?*"

Now Peter commiserates with her, this problem of his that has somehow become her problem. "White House," he confirms. "You can imagine the pleasure Dick Cheney would get out of firing a weapon that once belonged to Andrew Jackson? Cheney's left-handed, too, you know?"

"Can you shoot a gun that old?"

"Oh God, no, not if it's been neglected—it'd explode in your face!" Peter, horrified at such a thought, holds up his palms. "But we're not about to blow up our beloved VP. This gun's been pampered like a prize bambino. I mean, good heavens, this is a left-handed shotgun from the 1800s! You can imagine how significant a piece it is—it's worth a small fortune."

Samantha's agony takes place in the public square. She's too young to know how to conceal these moral brawls. She wrings her hands

Robert McKean

and produces a low bleating sound deep in her throat, such as the lamb might make before the butcher strikes. *"I'm* left-handed! I didn't even *know* there were right- and left-handed guns!"

"Exceedingly rare. Most lefties have to reconcile themselves to shooting right-handed."

"But Mr. Fields told me never tell anyone where his lodge is?"

The customer's private crucifixion: Peter showers the young woman with his most compassionate salesman's smile: no teeth, only lips and more lips.

"Oh, all right!" Samantha the receptionist swallows the poisoned draft. "It's been a crazy day—I can't reach Avis, either! Oh, I just *knooooow* he's going to kill me!"

~ ~ ~

Well, he might.

Peter allows that he could have asked the girl directly for her help, appealing to her conscience. It wouldn't spare her Elliott's wrath, but Samantha would at least know that she had been dealt with honestly. But bursting in and informing her that her revered boss was a pedophile could have easily backfired, traumatized her to such an extent that she would have clammed up. But be that as it may, what retribution comes of Samantha's betrayal are her worries, not his. *His,* which have two-and-a-half hours to simmer, are that, because he's been a second-rate father— self-absorbed, melancholic, debauched—he'll arrive too late.

And your animal, darling, would be . . .

Jeanette's troubled eyes that rainy evening in Ridgeport: *They're going to start a new family and I'm in the way!* She was holding back, he'd felt that. Did she know about Elliott? Even then? In Connecticut: *He's funny sometimes.* How could *he*—Mr. Deeply Intuitive Salesman— have missed this? Exiting East Stanton Junction, Peter takes 79 North, climbing toward 80. But this trip is brief, for the almost immediate turn north, straight as an arrow into the heart of the Alleghenies. Years it's been since he's been up this way, passing through remote villages loomed over by their solemn mountains: asphalt-shingled houses whose yards have only surfaced from thigh-deep snow; mounds of damp earth in whitewashed truck tires awaiting bachelor's buttons and pansies; the ubiquitous garish Fisher-Price toys. He drives past a hardware store with a brace of green Lawn-Boys in front, then an evangelical Baptist church notched into the side of a hill and the crumbling cement steps beside it, up which an old woman hobbles painfully.

    . . . *a viper!*

    Peter, heavy-hearted, turns away from a never-ending procession of village yards awakening to their longed-for spring and increases the pressure of his fat foot on the accelerator. Deep into the trip, he swerves into a small stucco gas station, jams the nozzle in the tank, races inside as it fills to ask for the restroom key.

    "You think someone's gonna steal the soap?" The attendant's occupied with probing an open sore on the back of his hand with a toothpick. "Around here, we don't need to be locking up the terlet."

    The *terlet* in question, filthy beyond description, is stopped up with God only knows what sorrow—into which he pees regardless. Peter charges back out, giving cash to the attendant—still contentedly self-doctoring—to hasten the transaction, and peels out, thinking, Might not be such a bad idea to lock the terlet up after all.

He makes great time, until the end, the last leg of the trip.

When Samantha gave him directions, she did so from memory, getting things jumbled more than once. Like a cat worrying a patch of baseboard behind which lurks a mouse, Peter repeatedly reverses the car, passing back and forth over a narrow bridge where the road constricts to a single lane. *Just past that,* Samantha told him, *there's an itty-bitty cutoff into the woods. You can hardly see it, it looks like an animal path.* Number nailed to a tree? Mailbox? Sign? *Jesus Loves You,* she said, but that's a good mile before you get there. Well, he finds Christ, as it were, and the wasp-waist bridge barely wide enough for the passage of the Mennonite buggy with its orange triangle he's had to stew behind for three miles. But no cutoff, itty-bitty or otherwise. He makes half a dozen three-way turns, traveling and re-traveling this same stretch of road, scrutinizing an unbroken wall of brush and trees. On his fourth pass he finally spots the cutoff—on the other side of the road. And scolds himself: When the left-handed girl said *on the right,* she pointed with her left hand, index finger aloft.

Always believe the hands.

Envying, for the first time, Elliott's Land Rover, he noses his Avalon into the thick underbrush and creeps forward, praying that the sedan's clearance will suffice. At this elevation and this far north, the trees have only begun to bud. He's able to peer deeply into the woods.

He sees bedraggled nets of vines and half-downed trunks leaning against their neighbors, beer bottles, little outposts of trash, a sodden pizza box, and what appears to be the orange and white stripes of a road construction sign. The sign has been flung—by an irate libertarian, one assumes—high into the crotch of a tree. The woods are damp and gloomy. Honestly, he can't imagine Vice President Cheney taking much pleasure in his weekend here. But no clearing, no lodge. The receptionist, who likes adding extra *o*'s, cautioned him, *It's a looooong way back.* The baying of a hound unnerves him. The ominous ululation echoing through the desolate woods raises the hair on his arms. Peter frets he's going to discover that the real cutoff was somewhere on the right-hand side, after all, and that he'll lose an axle here or drive smack into a mountain family's gunsights. As his car labors up what seems an endless hill, the muddy ruts he's been wallowing in become stonier, more sharply eroded. The Avalon's underside takes an agonizing scrape. Peter, squeezing the steering wheel, visualizes oil from a ruptured oil pan spilling out.

"Just stay with me a little bit longer," he pleads.

As he crests the hill and minces forward, the scent of wood smoke seeps into the car. At that, he comes to a halt. Surely, this far in there can be but a single human habitation. Whether it's Elliott's hideaway or a mountain family's A-frame replete with hot tub and humidity controlled wine cellar, he decides that this is as far as he can go. And he'll certainly not be able to negotiate this charming lane in reverse. So, as quietly as he can—and it requires a good twenty niggling back and forths—he manages to get the Avalon turned around and pointed downhill. It's risky, but he decides to leave the keys in the ignition and closes the car door softly.

Within a quarter of a mile, he comes upon a clearing in the woods, a small wood-frame structure at its center and a white Land Rover parked alongside. It looks tidy enough, no stumps, no brush, no rubbish or beer bottles. But to call this a lodge or a *compound* is blatantly dishonest. Peter pictures the posters on chairs around the condo: Elliott Fields' noble Faulknerian stride across the early-morning meadows, Wellington boots, herringbone sporting jacket with elbow patches, his narrowed eyes fixed on wild game. Elliott's hunting lodge is maybe ten by twelve and looks to be hardly more substantial than a storage shed from the Home Depot garden center, a place to store your rake and riding mower.

The smoke he's been smelling eddies up from a fire pit. Peter hangs back in the woods, wishing to plead with any Supreme Being available for a small favor: That Jeanette will come outside for a bit of fresh air and they can steal off together. That isn't likely to happen. Taking his requisite deep breath, he marches into the clearing past the fire. As he reaches the door, it's opened from within by his daughter. Still in her green and tan plaid uniform and knee-socks.

"Papa!"

Just reach in and grab her, he thinks, but formulates that thought not swiftly enough. Elliott, hidden behind, pulls the door all the way open. "What the fuck?"

Peter ignores him. "Come with me," he orders Jeanette. "We're going."

Elliott yanks the girl inside by the arm. "She's not going anywhere."

Peter thrusts himself across the threshold before Elliott can shut the door, essentially, with his size, crowding all three into a dim, dreary structure you indeed might stack bags of mulch in. There are, exactly, three small square windows. The thought of his daughter trapped in this enclosed space with Elliott Fields chills him. "Let go of her," he says as calmly as he can. "She's going home with me."

"You have no legal rights here."

Odd answer that? "Elliott, we're not having a legal discussion."

"You're trespassing."

"I imagine I am, I don't really care."

They cannot have been here terribly long, with Jeanette still in her school uniform and Elliott in his lawyer's suit, white shirt and silk tie, which, to accommodate his wilderness chores, he's consented to loosen. "I *repeat*," Elliott doesn't say as much as intone in what sounds like an imitation of an English barrister he may have heard on Masterpiece Theatre, "you are here without my permission and are infringing on my legal right to privacy. Do you understand that?"

"I do, as a matter of fact. Com' on, darling, we've been asked to leave."

"Alone."

"Elliott, she's com—"

"I will advise you one last time." Attorney Fields hauls himself erect. "You are to quit these premises immediately. Otherwise, I can't be held responsible for your welfare."

By now, Peter gathers—senses—that Elliott has entered into some sort of weird fugue state. He's in over his head, or, perhaps better phrased, out of his head. Peter worries that this might actually come to blows. A fistfight, really? Releasing Jeanette's arm, Elliott turns in the ruddy dimness, scrabbling for something, and swings back with a rifle, a shotgun.

Not a fistfight, Peter thinks, how stupid of me.

"You've been warned," Elliott announces in his Old Bailey voice. "You have *precisely* one minute to vacate these premises."

"We won't need a minute, trust me."

"Alone!"

Something Peter taught himself as a kid: When people drop something, they reach to catch it where it was when it left their hand. By then, it's long gone. Better to reach *below* where you dropped it, where it's going. The lesson's never failed him: Think one step ahead. When Elliott snaps the barrels of the over-under shotgun closed and levels the weapon at him, Jeanette screams and Elliott's eyes dart toward her. In this second of distraction Peter flings out his arm and smashes the broad side of it down into Elliott's face.

The gun goes off.

In the small structure the blast of the shotgun is shattering. The explosion momentarily stuns everyone. Thankfully, the weapon discharged toward the ceiling as Elliott toppled backward, clutching his face, and Peter realizes now—*only* now—that shooters will shoot in the direction of their eyes. He scoops Jeanette under the arms as if she's a bundle hanging on a hook and he's on a train plowing through. As he lumbers with them out the door and past the smoky fire, his daughter's legs dangling on either side, he speculates whether he's going to have a heart attack or be shot in the back—or both.

"Papa, we can go faster if I run, too!"

Which turns out to be true. She reaches the car long in advance of him—fat men are lousy runners. She's looking out the window as he staggers up. Behind her glasses her eyes are wide with terror. At the point of throwing up, Peter bellows, "Get down, *down!* On the floor!"

He squirms his way, gasping, into his seat, kicks over the engine and floors it, sending the Avalon crashing down the narrow passage between the trees with him bouncing behind the wheel and Jeanette being knocked about in the passenger well. He's worried he'll rip a brake line off or lose control and plunge into the woods—and, for sure, at one bend in their slipping and sliding descent, the sedan lurches sideways, slamming broadside into the trees. Branches slap the windows and rake the doors, producing a metallic screech, but Peter muscles the Avalon back onto the path.

"Papa," Jeanette shouts, frightened, "can I get up?"

"No! Stay down!"

As they come slaloming down through the woods, he keeps expecting to see in his mirror the glint of white fender. Spotting, after what has seemed an eternity, patches of blue sky in the brown sketchy

Robert McKean

branches, he guns the Toyota. Crossing the drainage ditch to gain access to the macadam, he bangs the bottom of the car hard and nearly loses control again. But he hand-over-hands the wheel, gets them righted, rocking on all four tires, and heads south—toward home. Next his worries shift to getting stuck behind a logging rig or, heaven help them, another Mennonite family trotting home for a large starchy supper. But they shoot through the tiny aperture of the bridge, reverse the numerous turns he made getting here, and find the open road, or at least a road with two lanes. Only then does he pull out of traffic and creep the car behind a country store. Jeanette's crying. She's gotten tumbled about and banged her head.

He pulls her—she looks like a crumpled flower—up into the seat and hugs her.

He's still worried that Elliott will dash around the corner, that he'll call the state police and somehow use his political connections to have them stopped. Improbable, yes: The bright red syrup of blood seeping through Elliott's fingers almost guarantees that he's got other matters to attend to. Nonetheless, Peter worries. He holds his shaking daughter until the tension in her begins to release, then fetches out his handkerchief for her to blow her nose. She hasn't said anything, and he decides that's okay: There will be time to talk. Her cheeks are smudged, a knee is scratched. She smells of wood smoke. But more than smoke, she smells of fear—and he supposes he does, too. Understanding that they cannot linger here, she pulls away from him and settles herself in her seat. Peter, risking another five seconds, watches his daughter—

having survived something that he as a child her age could not have even envisioned—snap in her seat belt buckle and jiggle her shoulders to get comfortable, as if they were about to undertake nothing more than a trip to the T&V.

~ ~ ~

Coming up through Ganaego, reaching the intersection at Wendy's, where a right would take them to Oak Grove, Peter continues on through. He follows the curving road to the valley floor, where Cabbage Creek, polluted with sulfurous mine waste and dead fish, meanders in indolent elbows toward the Ohio. He's leery of returning home: Elliott is still very much a threat. He wonders if it wouldn't be better to check them into a hotel, but he doesn't much like that idea, either. He needs to stop at the clay works anyway, so it's a convenient way of procrastinating.

"A few minutes, honey."

The works are quiet. No detectives scribbling things on pads, no reporters, no yellow tape. Peter scowls at the two Kenworth wrecks squatting in the mud: his fault. He'll need to do what he can for the man his guard wounded and for Feeney and his misbegotten clan. Peter unlocks the padlock on the gate and draws in his badly gashed car, then, rattling the lock in its chains, fastens it behind them, something he never bothers with. They had only one other stop on their flight, for gas, and, though he used the restroom, fretting the whole tedious time his hot stream hissed into the urinal, Jeanette refused to leave the car. Near his office is a bathroom she's familiar with, and he waits for her outside.

Robert McKean

It's cold and clammy in the unheated building. In his office he lifts one of his old suit jackets off a hook and hands it to her. She swims in it, the thing drapes to her knees, and this vision of his daughter matter-of-factly folding back the cuffs, exposing her delicate wrists, breaks his heart.

"I'm all right, Papa. He didn't do anything."

"Did he try?"

"He kept talking to himself. Like he was making a speech or something?"

"But he didn't do anything?"

"No, Papa, I knew he wanted to, but he didn't."

"*Has* he ever done anything—other than barge in on you in the shower?"

As soon as Peter asks that, he regrets it: A therapist he is not. But Jeanette, marooned within the huge coat, looks at him clearly through her wizard glasses. "Papa, I'm not doing so good, but I'm all right."

And with this exchange he knows, once he's done here, where they're going: This girl needs to be home in her own bedroom with her stuffed creatures.

Home today, home tomorrow, home forever.

This part, stopping at the works, is a fool's errand. He doesn't know if the documents he recalls seeing long ago even survive. Has no clear idea where to look for them. All he knows is that they're not in his father's office. Peter leads Jeanette down the hall to the office of the Chief Engineer. When Perry Newhart died suddenly, his assistant who became his replacement, elected to remain in his own warmer office, fetching files as needed from the chief's, and Perry's office was never actually cleared out. Peter supposes, if he's to make this a proper scavenger hunt, he'll need to check the assistant's office, too. With Jeanette revolving herself in thoughtful circles in the chief's swivel chair, he paws through the filing cabinets, then decides it's unlikely the site plans would be here, they wouldn't fit. Probably not in Perry's desk either, for that same reason, and he stands, hands on hips, scanning the room.

His eyes light on the coat closet. How old-fashioned: When did coat closets disappear from office buildings? On the upper shelf, behind Perry's scuffed hardhat and a hotplate with dried macaroni glued to its coils, Peter discovers what he remembers: a four-foot tube of many sheets rolled inside each other. As he brings the roll forward, he sweeps a small red cardboard box before it out onto the floor. A Stahrenberger's chocolate box—anyone born in Ganaego would instantly recognize it. Ignoring the tiny box, he gingerly peels back the roll's outer sheets. The paper is dry and fragile, mottled like the hands of an old man: the original architectural and site plans. Or, as original as an industrial facility this old might have. He has no reason to doubt Harvey Silverstein's surveyors, but he'll study these at home, just to make sure.

Jeanette stoops to pick up the chocolate box. "What's this?"

"Goodness." He entertains images of decades-old, wormy truffles. "Throw it away—in the waste basket over there."

Jeanette shakes the box. She frowns at the thumping noise

Robert McKean

inside, something sliding back and forth. She pries off the lid and holds out what she's found: a locket, or, rather, a locket which has been broken, shorn raggedly in half, like a jagged half-moon. But no, not a locket, Peter sees, taking it and turning it about in the light. The gold piece, about the size of a quarter, is solid. More like a large bracelet charm, a bracelet charm with a complicated zigzag edge, no engraving, its top loop also halved.

"What is it, Papa?"

"A charm, I guess? Looks like it's been hand-cut." He holds the half-disk out to her. "Finders keepers. But be careful—it's been sanded and polished, but it's still kind of pointy on the edges."

Jeanette slips the charm into one of the suit pockets, pats it.

So, a scavenger hunt, after all. "Let's go, sweetheart, dinner awaits."

~ ~ ~

As they come past the darkened kiln, Jeanette stops and points at the building. Specifically, at the stubby, three-story tower on the near end. "Is that where your papa took you?"

Perhaps he's told that story once too often? "Yes, I suppose, I guess."

"I want to go up there, too."

"Maybe someday, darling."

"Papa, I want to go up there now."

Peter switches his architectural plans from one armpit to the other. "If you want"—he offers a compromise—"we can go out on the second floor roof, though I don't know why we can't do this some other time? There's steps to the second floor."

Jeanette points at the tower. "But how do you get up *there?*"

"You have to climb a metal rung ladder from the second-floor roof up a very tall wall, something you've probably never done and I'm no longer rated for."

"I want to go up there."

"Second floor only."

Why she's suddenly gotten this into her head—why she wants to do it at all, let alone today, after the trauma she's been through—baffles him. But *because* she's had such a day, Peter unlocks the door to the kiln office and lets them in. When he conducts his inspections, he spends little time in the kiln. It's essentially a windowless tunnel through which the wet extruded pipe moved, curing. Feeney stages enormous rat traps here, out-sized mousetraps whose tension is so great you have to worry that, if he slips while arming them, the hammer will come over and crush his wrist. Or amputate a toe, if he forgets where he's planted them. *Feeney and his rats:* The man should've stuck with saving souls. Snatching up the flashlight on the expediter's desk, Peter tracks a pool of light for them to make safe passage across the soft fire brick to an enclosed stairwell. Chicken-wire windows here admit just enough light to see. He leads his daughter up the metal stairs and out onto a flat, gravel roof. He walks over to the low ledge, turns, smiles.

Jeanette is unimpressed. "So where's the ladder?"

"You're as stubborn as your mother, you know that?"

Robert McKean

"Back there?"

Indeed, the ladder is around the back behind them. Peter, hoping perchance that the old rusty ladder has been taken down or come rattling down of its own, escorts them around the corner. Vain hope. And though the ladder bolted to the bricks isn't, in actuality, quite as tall as it stands in his child's memory and though there are safety railings up the sides that enclose the climber, which he has forgotten—*still,* it's a good fifteen feet straight up. He yanks on it, aspiring to pull the whole affair down or set a bolt chattering. That failing—the ladder's tight to the bricks—he has no choice but to play mean parent.

"Jeanette, no, we can't go up there. I'm sorry, maybe some other day."

"But your papa took you up there?"

"And he shouldn't have. My mother was furious with him."

"So why did he?"

"How should I know, darling, I was only four years old."

A mistake, a colossal mistake. Jeanette huffs up an eloquent Avis Longstreet shoulder. "Well, I'm ten—*almost* eleven!"

"Could I offer you a bribe?" When a parent's reduced to offering bribes, that parent has already lost. Peter, against all better judgment, states his conditions. "All right then, listen to me. First, you have to take the jacket off and you have to go ahead of me. You have to hold each rung as tight as you possibly can, and you have to make sure your feet are absolutely secure on a rung before you go on to the next one. And we need to go one step at a time, not hand-over-hand. Is that clear?"

It isn't.

"One step at a time," he repeats. "That means you lift your left arm"—he takes hold of the ladder and demonstrates—"and then your left leg. Then you bring your right arm and your right leg up. Then you stop and take a breath. Then you repeat, left arm, left leg, right arm, right leg, stop, pause, breathe. One step, one breath—not continuous, not hand-over-hand. We're not firemen, we're not racing up the ladder to rescue a damsel from the flames."

Will this complicated explanation discourage her? No, unfortunately. Jeanette slips off his jacket and conscientiously folds it before resting it on the gravel. Peter tucks his architectural tube beneath the folded jacket and restates his conditions. "Very, very slowly, you need to be paying attention the whole time. No sightseeing as you climb. You take one step, you pause, you breathe, then you take another, pause, rest, and breathe."

"I understand. I won't do anything stupid."

He looks at her, her composed face, her dark intelligent eyes, the same worry lines between her eyes that her mother possesses beginning this year to express themselves: Peter looks at his daughter perhaps in a way that he hasn't in some time, maybe not since he hovered over her in Jacob Weiner's autumnal grass when she *had* done something stupid.

"I believe you. When we get to the top, keep in mind that the roof will have a slight pitch. Keep your weight ahead of you, the top of you from your waist up, keep that *ahead* of you, and walk upstream a little. You're going to be careful now?"

Robert McKean

"I promise."

"This is not a joke, Jeanette."

"I promise, Papa."

Yes, it's nuts. But Peter senses that this climb means something to his daughter, and he decides to honor that unknown something. He also senses something else, something inside him, a feeling concerning himself that he also cannot quite pin down. He knows the source, the ancient memory—half-real, half-re-imagined—of the ascent of this ladder in his father's arms. But what he is *feeling* is more elusive. Putting that aside, heeding his own advice to concentrate, Peter watches Jeanette step up on the first rung, pause, then grip the rung above her head with her left hand and at the same time lift her left leg, set it and pull herself up, bringing right arm and leg up to their mates. She's climbed ladders to monkey bars, after all, and, thank goodness, kids' saddle shoes nowadays come with rubber soles.

"Like this, Papa?"

"Precisely, that's very good."

When her feet are at his shoulder height, Peter starts up. He cranes his neck and shoulders outside the safety bars to keep an eye on her progress, ready to scold if she gets careless. But she's been sufficiently warned: They both proceed one step at a time, pausing between steps to certify all feet are secure before continuing. The top of the ladder brings—as he knew it would, despite his coaching—its own challenge. Stepping from a ladder, even from a ladder with safety railings, onto a pitched roof requires an act of faith. He still remembers the first time he did that.

And when Jeanette does hesitate, he says, "Darling, you don't have to go any farther. What you've done, going this far, is very brave. We can head back down one step at a time, the same way we came up?" When she shakes her obstinate head, he speaks to this moment of authentic danger. "All right, then: Pull yourself up and lean forward from the waist and step firmly out onto the metal. Don't hurry—and remember, the roof will have a pitch."

When Peter comes over the roof, Jeanette has moved back from the edge. She's at the peak that the corrugated panels incline four triangles up to. She's crouched down, gripping the raised lip of a seam. Peter sits, happy not to be walking up a slope himself. He loops an arm around her and feels the tension in her release—the second time today—as she unfolds her legs, slithering them across the warm metal to lean into him. Over the edge they can see the sun-splashed works below, the quad with its marooned flagpole, the main office and manufactory, the rust-red arteries of the tracks.

How eerily silent it is.

"You'll be staying with me now." He's not sure it's necessary to state this explicitly, but wants her to hear it. As Peter delivers this formal declaration, Jeanette's face grows thoughtful. "You're moving back home—where you belong—and we'll find you a new school right around here."

She bites her upper lip, troubled.

"It's all right. Your mother's going to be very agreeable. I don't anticipate any trouble in that way. We'll find a good school close by."

"Papa, I want to go to the school we went and saw together."

Peter labors to conceal his surprise, his immediate and immense disappointment. "Are you sure, honey? It's a long way off and you'd be living by yourself?"

"We could still have our summers together?"

She meets his eyes. She's so grown up, so wise, that it frightens him: She has not answered his question. She's bypassed it to answer the fear in him. He pulls her closer. "Absolutely," he says, ratifying in a second a decision he would've thought, if they ever had to face it, could only be reached by days of agonized discussion. Peter firms up his voice: She must never know how much this separation will hurt him. "We'll have our summers, you bet, red bikes and trips to the zoo to see the zebras—this summer and the next summer and the summer after that."

"D'you think I could write to Lina, the girl we met?"

"I think that would be a terrific idea."

"She might not write back?"

"We'll just have to give her the benefit of the doubt."

Jeanette pulls back to look at him again. "And Papa?"

"God forbid, what is it now, darling?"

"I want to quit the piano."

Her first desire, given time, he might have suspected. But this one, never. But hasn't he rehearsed this conversation, rehearsed it over and over? Understood that when it came—and it comes to almost all parents with children involved in music—that he needed to be prepared to insist on the difficult thing, even if it meant risking his daughter's love? His mother and father didn't. They couldn't bring themselves to risk his love. They argued with him, especially his mother and Uncle Nico. But ultimately they gave in and let him follow his adolescent follies, wherever those follies were to lead him—until it was too late, until he had drifted too far from shore to be able to turn back again in a serious way to music.

"Here's what I'm thinking." Peter squeezes his daughter's shoulder. "I'm thinking we need to get you hooked up with your old teacher, Mrs. Cleveland? For the summer, I mean, until you get a new teacher at the new school? Graystone's nice enough, but he's a lightweight. Mrs. Cleveland can steer you back in the right direction."

"Papa, I really want to quit."

"Darling, please, listen to me." Behind Jeanette, over her shoulder, the old clay works decays in the sun. The exposed iron burns, the wood rots, the rows of brick in the walls shift and sag like the teeth of old men. Peter digs in his heels. "Lots of kids start and quit. And for most of them, it really doesn't matter. They don't have a passion for music, it's only something they take up for a while and then put aside. But you're different, Jeanette. You have music inside you, and that's rare. You've been given something infinitely precious."

"Papa, I'm tired of it, it's hard."

"I know, darling. Things in life that are meaningful *are* hard."

"It's no fun anymore."

Not fun anymore: The same complaint he made to his mother,

Robert McKean

who begged him not to abandon his lessons. And it is his mother's voice that Peter hears as he pleads with his daughter. "I understand what you're saying. But there's something you need to understand, too, honey. What seems like it's hard for you is actually coming much easier than it would come to someone older. And if you give up now, you may never have another chance at becoming a musician. *No*, let me say this without sugarcoating it: You will *not* have another chance. And that's real, Jeanette: That's what happened to me."

"I'm tired of sitting there all by myself."

What he wants to tell her is that when one is truly playing music one is never alone: one is surrounded by, sheltered beneath, the joy of Mozart, the passion of Beethoven, the beauty of Chopin. But he can't, of course. "It's not for fun, or for fun alone, that we study music, honey. Music is a door into a very special world, and it's only available to certain people—and you're one of them. It's called a *gift* for good reason. I have an idea. Why don't you take this summer off? Lots of musicians take breaks. You can play for fun this summer if you want—or not—then pick it up in the fall in a new school with a new teacher. How's that?"

"Papa, I still want to quit."

Beethoven's alcoholic father beat him if the boy missed his lessons; Mozart's father exercised tyrannical control of his son into the boy's adulthood. Peter thinks of what Jessica said about Jacob and knows that he is the son of Steve and Olivia Sanguedolce: He will do what they did. Music might lose a contributor and his daughter a vocation, but he'll not risk losing her love. He's a good man, but not that good.

"I'm sorry, Papa. I don't want to disappoint you."

"Don't be sorry, Jeanette. Don't ever be sorry."

He promises himself that this isn't the end of it. He'll circle around to this again. But not today. Peter kisses his daughter's forehead so she can't see in his face the emotion he knows is playing there. His mother, who wept at his quitting, wept alone in her bedroom. He manufactures a smile. "And now, I think it's time to get going—before someone spots us and calls the fire department."

"Are you and Mama ever going to make up?"

He hadn't expected this line of inquiry, either, even though the thought of reconciling had crossed his mind today. "No, honey. Your mother and I will go on being friends, but she and I aren't going to go back to the way we were. That's not going to happen."

"You could give her the benefit of the doubt?"

He hugs her again. "You're going to make a great lawyer someday. But before we go, I need to tell you something."

"Is it something about going back down?"

"It's harder going down a ladder than it is going up."

"Maybe we shouldn't tell Mama about this?"

"Just my thinking, darling. We'll keep this a secret between ourselves."

The last thing Peter Sanguedolce does before stepping backwards out into empty space and onto the ladder is to scan the silent quadrangle below. And in doing so, the sensation that has been hovering in the back of his mind makes itself manifest. He lets himself *feel* the works, the whole of it as it was: the wobbling, creaking freight cars; buzzing tractors; frantic flagmen; coal gas fumes and falling fly ash; and always the pungent, earthen smell of drying clay. He breathes it in, as his father breathed it in a June morning long ago, brings it stirring up again so that he can let it go: All this soon will be pastel townhouses with rooster weather vanes.

I'm sorry, Papa.

Memorial for Jacob Weiner

On an unusually warm Saturday in April, Peter, downstairs first, discovers in the *Chronicle* that today is *Draw a Bird Day*. While the bacon he has peeled from the slab fries, he makes a small stack of sourdough pancakes and draws two misshapen but endearing mourning doves and props his drawing beside the plate and silverware he's set out. The sourdough pancakes, he concedes, are probably better than his sourdough bread, which his daughter refuses to touch. He stands her white bread preferences, which he deplores, in the two toaster slots, puts out her strawberry jam, and opens the door to admit today's wanton visitor: simple, joyous sunshine. And while he waits for the appearance of his sleepyhead daughter, he has his own breakfast: one half of an unsugared grapefruit and coffee with skim milk.

How yummy.

Jeanette arrives in the kitchen with a single shoe in hand, a diminutive red velvet evening pump with mother-of-pearl accents. "One of them is missing," she informs him.

"Well, your grandmother had two feet, darling, that much I can vouch for."

After breakfast, in his parents' bedroom Peter draws back the curtains that have not been opened in a decade, and he pulls everything from the upper closet shelf. Boxes of shoes and hats, belts, sweaters, blankets, books, a stack of Montgomery Ward catalogs, and an antediluvian hairdryer that looks like something John Glenn might have worn as a helmet on the moon. But no left to the red pump's right. Jeanette, on hands and knees, mouses into the farthest reaches of the deep closet, sweeping out as she goes her grandfather's wingtips and cordovan cap shoes in their cedar trees, his fawn and white golf shoes, what appear to be bowling moccasins—when did Steve have time to bowl?—a half-dozen wrinkled ties that fell and perished in the jumble, more belts, more books, business cards, and a plaid suitcase with a lone pack of Chesterfields inside it.

But no left pump.

It is, however, as if the exercise has given him incentive, and Peter begins removing the clothes from the closet in armfuls. From one side: high-waisted summer day dresses and sherbet-colored evening gowns, blouses, robes. The other side: white dress shirts with collars that have yellowed, patterned shirts, somber winter suits and seersucker summer suits. He strews them all across the bed. When the closet is empty, father and daughter ransack the bureau and the dressing table, his mother's low vanity that has always reminded him of *The Thin Man*,

Myrna in her slip before her mirror, William pouring martinis. By late morning there are, across the room, disorderly piles of reindeer sweaters and Argyle socks, woolen golf knickers, brassieres and boxer shorts and Stanley Kowalski undershirts, camisoles, slips, menstrual belts, garters. When a snowfall of summer flies comes tumbling from a valance, Peter traipses downstairs and returns with a box of Glad trash bags. He finds Jeanette holding a dress with Swiss Dots up to her chin. She has, since moving back with him, lost some of the precocious adolescent snarkiness she'd previously been exhibiting. But she's also turning inward, becoming increasingly serious as she internalizes these tectonic upheavals that have rocked her world. Coming upon his daughter now, as she ponders salvaging the elegant summer dress, Peter sees her as a young woman in a café at twilight, tea lights being lit by a waiter, across from her a companion, a man—boyfriend, lover, husband.

"Take whatever you want," he says gruffly to disguise his emotion. "The rest is going to the Mission."

He's promised her, if the day's warmth holds, that they will have dinner outside on the veranda beneath the fattening moon. A sight the old house hasn't seen in many a year: candle flame in the darkness, white tablecloth, linen napkins, crystal water goblets. After emptying the bedroom without ever discovering the pump's AWOL mate, they extend their spring cleaning campaign to the attic, or anyway, he does. Somewhere along the way, his assistant abandons ship, and Peter begins hearing the *briiiiiiiiiing! briiiiiiiiiing!* of a bicycle bell. On a trip through the first floor he pauses to regard—with deep suspicion—the

Robert McKean

furniture. Two weeks ago all he thought the place needed was some attention, whack the rugs, wash the windows. Today, as he eyes the punch-drunk sofa, the lampshades whose delicate silk has become as brittle as paper-thin ice, and the dining room table that serves primarily as a repository for unsorted mail, all of it seems as if it were longing to make that final journey along with the old clothes to the Mission.

"I'm moving," he says to himself in surprise. "Who would've known?"

Elliott Fields, still wrapped safely—but securely—in an enfolding gauze of political connection and influence, has relocated his solo law practice, Peter is told, to his former childhood bedroom in his parents' neoclassical colonial revival. Elliott no longer possesses a promising political career, a poster-ready *Father Knows Best* family, nor even the fine straight patrician nose his Mayflower ancestors bequeathed him. But with his having only ogled the goods and with, especially, his having the good fortune to be born into a social coterie that keeps a handy stack of *Get-Out-of-Jail-Free* cards near by, he appears beyond the legal system's punitive reach. It has been Harvey Silverstein—poor Harvey, the Sanguedolces are never going to permit the man to retire— who's been diligent in keeping Peter apprised of these matters. *The Man with a Mouth* has also informed him that he believes he has persuaded the Feeney-wounded party to settle with Peter out of court, although any such settlement Harvey cautions is likely to absorb a significant portion of anything yet to be realized by the sale of the clay works property. Peter hauls his trash bags downstairs. Bags with Mission-destined goods piled alongside the car in the garage, ones with real garbage outside by the drive in a pile that metastasizes like a giant blackberry.

We love junk!

Up in the attic, he's collected his ice-dam buckets and muscled down an old crib. The crib would not be considered safe these days, and so it and its soiled mattress and the one-arm crucifix go out by the drive. Behind the black and white television and its shipwrecked brigantine, he discovers another box of his mother's things—holiday cards, restaurant matchbooks, her high school graduation program, tinted albumen portraits of her parents, and yet more costume jewelry, a cache that includes a three-inch pin in the shape of a tarantula that he *knows* is going to make Jeanette's eyes go as round as her glasses. The box also contains a small velvet bag inside of which he finds a red Stahrenberger's box. The box thumps when he shakes it. Inside is a charm, a golden half-moon with a deeply serrated, hand-cut edge.

Oh.

You don't want to park your memories on the curb with the trash. But sometimes you would like to send them on an extended vacation. Peter carries the half-charm down to his daughter's room. On Jeanette's desk the charm's golden mate lies in a saucer. He brings the two pieces together into a whole. So, *Perry Newhart:* thin, sandy-haired, soft-spoken Perry Newhart, a trim, tidy package of a man, by far the brightest, most competent plant engineer the works ever had. Percival Newhart, who monastically ate his lunch at his desk, casseroles he brought from home and warmed on his hotplate, who nursed the aging

Robert McKean

infrastructure of the works and patiently coaxed back into operation
machines that had stuttered or went lame, a confirmed bachelor,
reserved, taciturn, who came to their Christmas parties and drank nothing
beyond a ceremonial glass of champagne, who before he left made
certain to shake the hand of his boss and best friend, who then walked
quietly away from those wild parties, hands in his pockets, disappearing
into Ganaego's cold winter nights . . .

Is this true? Can it be?

Not something the mind, the soul, the heart wants to believe of
one's mother. Surely, he's leaping to such an accusation unjustly? One
piece of highly interpretable evidence? Maybe Olivia Sanguedolce and
Perry Newhart were only friends? Maybe the hand-cut charm was some
foolish adventure they once shared, a harmless keepsake? Peter considers
adding the half-charm to its mate, leaving them there to surprise Jeanette,
then hesitates. The clay works clerk who suffered the double-blow—the
loss of his wife and his savings—and went to pieces at his desk: What
would it have taken to drive his father to suicide? Someone as brash, as
confident as Stephano Sanguedolce? A bad business decision? Would
that have been enough?

And his mother's inability to overcome her sorrow? The
crushing silence and depression into which she descended? Peter slips
his mother's half of the charm back inside its chocolate box, closes the
box, and stuffs it in a trash bag. And with that, he's finished—fini, finito,
terminado. Done. He washes his hands and his face and puts on his
hat and carries a dining room chair to the curb. And when his daughter

pedals in to report interesting happenings on adjoining streets, he grants himself leave to bask in the grace of this rare, warm, April day.

Dolce far niente, sweet idleness.

He had been hoping that Jeanette might reconsider Wilfred Hall. But after she received a reply to the letter she'd sent Lina—a missive on gossamer-thin blue paper with which Jeanette had sequestered herself in her bedroom, reading and re-reading—he's come to accept that she's crossed that particular Rubicon. Fatty's piano rests asleep and untouched. She still has, he wants to believe, a couple of years before it's too late. Perhaps the yearning for music will return? Perhaps being thrust into an environment with what will certainly be the smartest people with whom she's ever had to compete, she will rediscover music as a way of distinguishing herself? Janet Considine has volunteered to mentor her. Perhaps Janet will urge Jeanette back to the piano bench? Perhaps, perhaps. Honestly though, the lunches he prepares in the morning, dots of cold butter that tear at the soft bread, and the commute through old Ganaego and across the rusting bridge to Kopelman Street bring their own music, their own sweet consolation.

She's knocked the cover off every one of her last math quizzes.

The Halbrunner contractors—Peter turns to note—seem to be employing a new insulating panel board that he doesn't know much about. Some sort of extruded polystyrene: large, green, 4 x 8 sheets. But the blond framing struts that outline spacious rooms that might well swallow Jacob Weiner's colonial whole have a resiny scent that he likes. And *because* it's Saturday and the tradesmen are receiving their political instruction from a source other than their work radios, the neighborhood is blessedly quiet, lost to its drowsy afternoon. But then a noisy ruckus erupts on the deserted construction site. Peter watches a squirrel chasing a second through the unfinished rooms in madcap zigzags. Well, you have to allow, it is that time of year and it will probably be, after all, that kind of house. When he turns back, his eyes follow a car he doesn't recognize draw up and stop.

Jessica Weiner steps out.

Black hair fringed in gray, large, almost-coarse, features in an angular face, eyes that always seem to be seeing something behind as well as forward. She's in jeans and a spring jacket and steps briskly around the car and over his way. She's here, he decides, to see what has become of her family homestead, and he stands to greet her, saying as much.

"No, I came to see you." She does, in an obligatory fashion, glance over and acknowledge the construction, shielding her eyes with a palm, then shrugs. "I want to apologize. It was a nice day, our drive back, until I messed things up."

"You didn't mess anything up."

"I got drunk, I got vulgar. I've been known to do that."

"No apology is needed," Peter says. "And actually, what you said, about your father got me thinking about my father." Why he feels a need to share things from his life with Jessica Weiner baffles him. "He was a good man, my father, a good guy, but he had a way of stealing the show. And as you know, there's a certain tyranny that perfection invites?

That's what you were saying about Jacob, isn't it? My father had to take over every event, he had to be the star of every performance, and that had a tendency to crowd the rest of us off the stage. I'm pretty sure that it crowded my mother off, and to some extent I think it crowded me off, too. Maybe the world's a heartless place, or maybe we only make it that way, but no, please don't think you spoiled anything. I had a good time with you."

Jessica—not agreeing, not disagreeing, and perhaps wishing to prolong the conversation a little—contemplates his impressive pile of trash bags. "Are you moving?"

He likes her intuition. "I've got a salesman's itch, and I thought I'd scratch it. *If* I can find a company willing to pay me to do their traveling for them, that is."

"You're looking for a job—you, too?"

Peter hears Jeanette's bicycle bell coming from far off. On every sortie she goes farther and farther. He knows what she's doing: building herself up for the leap that awaits her. And for that he's proud of her. Within days she's to have a new half-sister—a sister who might well call West Virginia home—and all too soon she'll have a new dorm room in Connecticut and new things to see through those new windows.

"I will be soon," Peter owns up. "This fall."

"I've been living off his clarinet, and that's about gone."

"Seems fair—he lived off it, too."

"Well"—Jessica laughs lightly, looking again at a house under construction in which she has no interest—"I gave some of his money to the clinic, too. We're closing this summer, but we still need supplies. I'm not sure what the chairman of the woodwinds department would have made of his clarinet's paying for cervical caps and condoms. But thank you," she continues, turning back to Peter, "for visiting him. I think you were his only friend."

"I miss hearing his clarinet through the trees."

"Are you coming to the memorial tonight? It's a short program, an hour or so?"

The memorial, he's forgotten all about it. "Would you like me there?"

"Yes, I would. I would like that very much, Peter."

"Then it's settled, we'll be there. And I'd like to make you a counteroffer: Would you like to come back here after for some dinner?" He gestures at the veranda, the ancient stones that have risen unevenly beneath the snowy blankets of countless Western Pennsylvania winters and are, in the shadowed summers that follow those winters, carpeted with silvery-green moss. "My daughter and I are planning to dine— weather permitting—under the gibbous moon."

"I'm not imposing? Is it a special occasion?"

"Not unless you consider Draw a Bird Day a special occasion. No, you won't be imposing." Peter Sanguedolce reassures the troubled daughter of Jacob Weiner, as he used to assure the troubled Jacob Weiner about his runaway Norway maples. "We were just about to choose our menu."

Acknowledgments

Peter Sanguedolce's story dates back more than a dozen years, a party at a construction site, an accident, the ensuing aftermath. In the writing and rewriting of the novel's numerous revisions, I have had the invaluable assistance of the criticism and advice of several readers. Always my first—and frequently, toughest—reader is my wife, Sloan Nota. Very little gets past her critical eye. I am fortunate to have three long-term writer friends without whose insights and editing suggestions I would be lost, Paul Bellerive, Michael Colonnese, and Kevin McIntosh. I also wish to thank Christy Hallberg and Cheryl J. Fish, new writer friends who have generously offered me their wise counsel, and Pauline Kao Hilborn, artist extraordinaire who designed the cover and my website. As a special note, I would like to acknowledge the background help of my oldest brother, James McKean. Jim has been all his career a master salesman, and, while Peter's story is not my brother's story, some of Jim's salesman's wisdom and lore have sunk into me and thence into Peter. Lastly, I am indebted to Caitlin Hamilton-Summie, publicist, and Joe Taylor, Director of Livingston Press, for accepting the novel into his fold and ushering Peter's story through the publishing process.

Populating Robert McKean's novels and stories are some five hundred characters, steelworkers and bankers, doctors and jewelers, teachers and librarians, lawyers and yardage clerks, salesmen and ballet instructors—all residents of Ganaego, a small mill town in Western Pennsylvania. McKean's short story collection *I'll Be Here for You: Diary of a Town* was awarded first-prize in the Tartt First Fiction competition (Livingston Press). His novel *The Catalog of Crooked Thoughts* was awarded first-prize in the Methodist University Longleaf Press Novel Contest. The novel was also named a Finalist for the 2018 Eric Hoffer Award. Recipient of a Massachusetts Artist's Grant for his fiction, McKean has had six stories nominated for Pushcart Prizes and one story for Best of the Net. He has published extensively in journals such as *The Kenyon Review, The Chicago Review, Armchair/ Shotgun, Kestrel, Crack the Spine*, and *Border Crossing*. For additional information about McKean and his Ganaego Project, please see his author's website: www.robmckean.com

Robert McKean